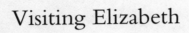

Visiting Elizabeth

Visiting Elizabeth

a novel by

Gisèle Villeneuve

Series Editor
Rhonda Bailey

National Library of Canada cataloguing in publication

Villeneuve, Gisèle, 1950–

Visiting Elizabeth

(Tidelines)

ISBN 1-894852-08-7

I. Title. II. Series: Tidelines (Montréal, Québec).

PS8593.1415V57 2004   C843'.54   C2004-940119-X
PS9593.1415V57 2004

Legal Deposit: First quarter 2004
National Library of Canada
Bibliothèque nationale du Québec

XYZ Publishing acknowledges the financial support our publishing program receives from the Canada Council for the Arts, the Book Publishing Industry Development Program (BPIDP) of the Department of Canadian Heritage, the ministère de la Culture et des Communications du Québec, and the Société de développement des entreprises culturelles.

Layout: Édiscript enr.
Cover design: Zirval Design

Set in Bembo 12 on 14.
Printed and bound in Canada by Marc Veilleux imprimeur
(Boucherville, Québec, Canada) in March 2004.

XYZ Publishing
1781 Saint Hubert Street
Montreal, Quebec H2L 3Z1
Tel: (514) 525-2170
Fax: (514) 525-7537
E-mail: info@xyzedit.qc.ca
Web site: www.xyzedit.qc.ca

Distributed by: Fitzhenry & Whiteside
195 Allstate Parkway
Markham, ON L3R 4T8
Customer Service, tel: (905) 477-9700
Toll free ordering, tel: 1-800-387-9776
Fax: 1-800-260-9777
E-mail: bookinfo@fitzhenry.ca

To Tom Back

yet women have always survived
dans une autre langue
— Nicole Brossard

Contents

Parc Lafontaine   1
Corona   17
Carnaval   29
Tripper   57
Café de l'horloge   79
Streets of Desire   107
Surviving Sunday   135
Montage   161
Bed & Breakfast   189
Bouillabaisse   219
Rush   257
La Cité l'Underground   285
Tea Ceremony   315
Passage   341
New Flight Plan   351
Cracking the Gold   369

Parc Lafontaine

His sudden shadow on my sewing startles me, the needle pricks my finger, a drop of blood appears, I look up, je pense, is he the law, or just a man on the prowl, seven eh-em, c'est tôt pour cruiser, will he ask the usual questions, do you come here often? why do you sew in this patch of grass when the park is a stone's throw from here and much quieter? après les questions, the dropouts talk about the places they will visit when they have money, the students with their lumberjack shirts de la révolution talk about big changes, the books they read, the films they saw, they say, as-tu vu le dernier Brault, le dernier Godard, not the honkers the flashers the catcallers, non, the honkers the flashers the catcallers have a tongue, oui, but they have no words, they just honk flash feut-fiou, they are gone, this one with his shadow on my white gypsy skirt n'a pas encore dit son mot, what does he want, peut-être, he stopped by on his way to work, will offer me a cup of coffee, like the workman who delivers the hot dogs to the restaurant by the pond, peut-être, he finished his night shift, wants a quickie, like the businessman from Ottawa who said he was staying at a swanky hotel, a quickie at the Swanky, I said, non, merci, monsieur, je suis en deuil, he understood non, merci, he thought je suis en deuil meant I have VeeDee, I will never finish mending that hem with him standing over me, what is this, l'Inquisition first thing in the morning, oh, that man, with his black boots in the grass and no smile on his face, that man is a motorcycle cop in full regalia.

Le parc Lafontaine, mademoiselle, the cop says. C'est pas un parc à gypsy.

I cannot speak. His arrival gave me un gros point au cœur, how to tell him I must not move not talk, just breathe shallow 'til the pain in my chest unstitches, this one is lasting a long time, he will think I keep my mouth shut to hide something, cops have a nose for secrets, I suck my finger, so the blood will not stain my skirt again, peut-être, he smells blood, not mine, Elizabeth's, Gérard made me javex her blood off, the silk taffeta shimmered white aux funérailles, between the cop's booted legs, the pavement of rue Sherbrooke, now clean and dry, I breathe a little deeper to test, enfin, I can inhale all the way to the bottom of my lungs, you have no idea, monsieur l'agent, how good that feels. Now, I can speak. I articulate clearly so he does not think je suis une fille vulgaire du bas de la ville.

Je ne suis pas une gypsy, monsieur.

He does not believe me. I can tell, by the way his boots shift, what else could he think. A nineteen-year-old girl, barefoot, repairs her skirt, surrounded by a backpack, a tote bag, une valise de fin de semaine, is she arriving, is she leaving. I tell him I live across the street with maman, in that three-storey stone house, third floor. He does not believe me.

Ton nom? he asks.

Such familiarity makes my skin shiver.

Ariane Claude, I say.

Papiers d'identité, he demands, like un gendarme in a French movie.

I don't trust him, too cocky for his high boots. If I show him my passport, he will say in his cocky cop's voice, people who sit across the street from home don't carry a passport, I will have to tell him, Friday, le 6 juin, I was leaving for a six-month trip around the world with my friend Elizabeth Gold, that is why I have a passport, I could show him our plane tickets as proof of departure, cops want proof, I don't have our tickets, why not? Elizabeth carried both tickets in her clutch bag, what bag? the bag is lost, he will narrow his eyes, will want to know about Elizabeth, there was an accident, accident? I show him my driver's licence. He studies it, his long legs an inverted vee planted on the ground right in front of my face, I study his crotch, he hands me back the permit, points at my luggage.

J'ai passé quelques jours chez un ami, I say.

He looks at my house, wants to know which flat on the third floor.

I put on my cat's eyes, tell him the third floor has only one flat. C'est la vérité. He is confused impressed, only two persons living in that enormous place, people are always impressed, but maman is not rich, elle est secrétaire dans un bureau, people are always confused. We examine the stone balcony, covered like a loggia, the battlements lining the edge of the roof and the turrets rising at the corners.

Ah, maman, I say, drawing attention to her glasses, not unlike mine. Je vous assure, monsieur l'agent. C'est ma mère.

Parfois, she comes out on the balcony, not for a breath of fresh air, even with the balcony facing north, what fresh air on rue Sherbrooke, and now, in mid-June, it will soon get sticky hot, the cop wants me to wave.

Elle est myope, I say, not waving.

He studies my cat's eyes, nods satisfied that I may be maman's daughter. She leans over the stone parapet like I did that Friday to see if Elizabeth was coming, he stares at my luggage, I have been staying at Pierre's place since les funérailles, the cop wants to know if there is trouble at home.

Non, monsieur. Tout va bien.

The cop leaves. What will I do today and all the other days of this summer and autumn of travels now ruined? Tout va bien, things we say. I need to walk, haul my luggage to le parc Lafontaine, wash my feet in the pond, the water feels good around my ankles, an early kid like an early bird watches me, his mother pulls him away, what did that cop want, did he notice my fingers full of needle holes, moi, la narcomane de la couture, that is no crime, the crime is that killer traffic on rue Sherbrooke, cette artère infernale, maman calls it. I wash my hands in the pond. The cop straddled his motor-cycle, where were you le 6 juin, monsieur l'agent, why are you never there to give tickets to the speeders the tailgaters, he started his engine, moved into traffic, can you jail the drivers of killer cars, will you jail le gros monsieur dans sa Chrysler chromée, that Friday you were nowhere near, he opened the throttle, you saw the papers, she was plastered all over the front pages, Montreal Photographer, the large title screamed in fat black letters above a bad photo of the wet pavement, Accident mortel sur Sherbrooke, La Presse wrote, Carnage, the yellow press called Elizabeth's body, the cop revved speeded away, he was gone. I let my feet dry in the sun. Even deep in parc Lafontaine, I can hear sirens screaming rushing to carnage somewhere.

I could not stay at Pierre's apartment any longer, Pierre invited me to stay as long as I wanted, non, I gathered my backpack and maman's former valise de fin de semaine and Elizabeth's tote bag that cleverly transforms into a rocksack.

Un rocksack? Pierre said. Es-tu sûre, ma puce?

Oui, I said, no longer sure.

I told him Elizabeth called it a rocksack, probablement, because the canvas is so sturdy it can carry rocks without tearing. He did not believe that, but kissed me, at sun-up, I walked from his apartment on rue de la Montagne back here to my patch of grass at the edge of the park. I take off my sandals, my feet still tingle from pond water, wiggle my toes, lean against the rough bark of the maple tree, should get on with that mending the cop interrupted, why does the hem keep coming undone, better shorten the skirt by two inches so it will no longer snag, that means redoing the entire hem.

I measure carefully, push the pins against the resistance of silk taffeta, twist the skirt and measure, twist and pin, when all the pinning is done, I stand up, the skirt swings back into place, I sit down again, fanning out the hem so as not to sit on a pincushion. I cut a length of white thread, hold the eye of the needle close to my eyes, make a knot at one end of the thread, take a deep breath, start sewing. This is like suturing, Elizabeth took photos of corpses for teaching anatomy to medical students, she took photos of surgical procedures, close-ups of rubbergloved hands stitching flaps of skin with silk, wire, catgut, I did not believe her, she said, it's all true, she knew about sutures. Malheureusement, her body could not be mended, all the silk wire catgut in the world would not have been enough to sew her back together.

Why are people late, faire attendre les gens n'est pas poli, parfois, I try to be late to see if it makes me feel important, c'est inutile, j'arrive toujours à l'heure. That Friday Elizabeth was late. The late Elizabeth. Say the words out loud, louder than traffic.

Elizabeth is dead, I cry out.

Don't be afraid of words, she said. Le 6 juin, I wish I had no words. It sounds silly saying I learned to speak with Elizabeth when I have been speaking since I was one year old, c'est ce que maman dit, but there is speaking and there is speaking. That day, Elizabeth died, such is the power of speak. Le 6 juin, c'est le grand départ, cannot stop talking, excitement fizzes on my tongue, I am wearing my spotless gypsy skirt, white, not good travel clothes, but I am wearing it in honour of Elizabeth's famous picture.

I pace up and down the flat, keep looking at my watch, my backpack has been leaning by the front door for a week, I drink a glass of water, careful not to choke, check my eye makeup in the bathroom mirror, have a pee, go stand on the gallery, will not see la ruelle for six months, will discover other kinds of ruelles, ancient winding streets with goats tap-tapping on paving stones, go to my bedroom, everything I leave is in its place, maman reads dans son boudoir, in the dining room, she set an afternoon table for tea and petits fours, I rearrange the spoons and cups, Gérard offered to drive us to Dorval, I wanted us to ride in his red and black Mercury with the top down, like queens of the road, Elizabeth said she would have tea with us, but after, we would hail a cab downstairs, the trip starts with the taxi ride, what if the plane leaves early, I pace up and down the flat.

Quelle heure est-il? I ask, in case my watch is slow.

Maman laughs, I know she is a little anxious, my first trip, and it has to be around the world, quand même, she is happy for me, last night at supper, mon oncle Joseph was happy for me.

Crisse, Claudette, he said. Les voyages forment la jeunesse.

Mon oncle always talks about l'expérience la vie. Last night, his eyes sparkled, but I could tell, l'expérience la vie is not always enough. Ma tante Rita worried, all those countries full of foreigners, they are not like us, ma tante sipping tea and saying, leurs maladies ne sont pas comme nos maladies, ah, seigneur, ah, seigneur de la vie. Maman assured her older sister I got all my shots, mon oncle reassured his wife I would be travelling with a woman who knew l'expérience la vie.

Crisse, Rita, mon oncle said. C'est une femme du monde, madame Gold.

Ah, never mind, là, ma tante patted my wrist, not wanting to ruin my trip.

On the balcony, I lean way out, enfin! Elizabeth est là, I shout to maman to pour the boiling water dans la théière, she hates shouting, on n'est pas des sauvages, but what can she do, her daughter is going on a world tour.

Elizabeth pays le chauffeur de taxi, she looks great in the raw silk pantsuit I made for her, the tunic side panels I had to add to accommodate her orange-crate hips give her ease of movement, but all that waiting made me crazy anxious, words of anger spill out.

Maudit, Elizabeth, le temps n'attend pas, I yell, tapping my watch. On va rater l'avion.

She cups her ear, takes too long to translate, steps backward into the middle of Sherbrooke, look out! this is not Saint-Polycarpe, she looks up, her face, a happy grin. My hand clenches the hem. What did she say? Je ne me souviens pas. Her last words. Gone. A fistful of pins. Nothing to feel. I sew.

On the street the cops, with their job to do, later that afternoon Gérard, wide-eyed and pale, that evening Pierre, holding me tight, aux funérailles my best friends Nicole et Diane, flanking me like I needed protection, surrounding Elizabeth's closed coffin her friends, Virginia, Mike and Nancy, Moffat and Pauline, Raymond, and Gérard, bien sûr, they all wanted to know quoi comment pourquoi. Last night, Pierre insisted I talk.

Parle, Ariane. Tu dois parler. Parle-moi.

Okay, I speak. Elizabeth is dead, it is his fault, if he were not always late, Elizabeth would be alive today, the last day of Expo he was late, Pierre pulls on his beard, puzzled, that was two years ago, he tells me, not understanding, I say, tu me donnes rendez-vous au Pavillon de la Jeunesse, the party is over, it is October, he is late, all summer, he kept saying, les gens à l'heure n'ont pas de vie. I pace up and down, catch the heel of my clog in the hem, ah, misère, a rip in maman's wedding gown I unstitched to make this skirt, erasing her wedding day stitch by stitch, must sew the hem back before Pierre gets here, sit on the low cement wall, left ankle resting on right knee for balance, Pierre has so many projects, he may be too busy to bother with me, probablement, it is over between us, I don't know much about the dating game, I hear a series of clicks, loud and persistent, slip my glasses off, they fall into my gypsyskirted lap.

Don't take them off, a woman's voice commands.

The needle grazes my finger, I squint at the woman with a telescopic black trunk in the middle of her face, the elephant woman shoots non-stop like a movie fashion photographer. She is out of focus.

Keep sewing, she says. Pretend I'm not here. You look great.

I slip my cat's eyes back on, don't know why I obey une madame touriste.

I look like I am scraping dog shit off my shoe, I say.

I have a nose for those things, the woman laughs. Trust me. You're not like the others.

Je pense, what is she, a fortune teller with a camera.

What will you do with me? I ask.

Photo show. The youth of Expo. Why don't you come to the opening? Openings are a hoot.

What is a hoot, I do not ask, she moves closer, gives me un carton d'invitation, her metal trunk still glued to her face. All I see on the card is the name of the place, Corona Gallery, and a date and time, Friday, November 17, 1967, 5 p.m.

Vous invitez tous les jeunes que vous photographiez? I ask.

She does not answer right away but stops shooting, I can hear her brain translating.

Just you, she says.

My skin tingles, I concentrate on my sewing, will my hands to remain calm, careful that the needle catches only one thread of fabric per stitch, that the sewing thread remains invisible on the right side of the hem, pull on the needle, tighten the stitch, smooth the fabric with my thumb, look up, she is gone. A drop of dried blood hides at the lip of the hem on the wrong side of the fabric, I scrape it off with my nail, check my finger, no more bleeding but the hole the needle punctured appears bigger deeper as I peer into it over my cat's eyes. Time to leave. Halfway to métro Île-Sainte-Hélène I remember Pierre. No strings attached he always says, d'accord. I slip the métro ticket in the slot, the turnstile unlocks, en tout cas, I tell him last night, if he had been on time Elizabeth would never have seen me waiting for him, we would not have become friends and I would not have had to yell at her for being late. I stop. He mutters it is normal to feel bad, I had been a little testy with Elizabeth and, then, that car hit her. Horrible, oui, mais ce n'est pas un crime. After last night, I could no longer stay at Pierre's.

We did not know where to bury her. Elizabeth never talked about family, none of us could imagine her dans une réunion de famille, she came from no place, had no shitty childhood like normal people, she was Botticelli's Venus, woman born right out of a shell. Does not matter now she lies under the ground, elle mange les pissenlits par la racine, mon oncle Joseph likes to say about the dead, Gérard put her au cimetière Notre-Dame-des-Neiges. What did I do with her clutch bag, a vintage bag Gérard gave her years ago, oyster grey leather with a mother-of-pearl clasp, sans doute, when the Chrysler hit, the bag flew from under her arm, landed deep in the wilds of parc Lafontaine, what if un robineux found it, would he know how to transform her traveller's cheques into hundreds of bottles of booze, what if un rôdeur found it, would he sniff the mother-of-pearl clasp, like he sniffs little girls from behind bushes, what would either of them do with two tickets to London, England, the departure date expired, they could sell her passport, a terrorist or a smuggler would call herself Elizabeth Gold, changing one's name is easy as paille. No matter how often I go through Elizabeth's tote, that cleverly transforms into a rocksack, I cannot find her clutch bag, it is lost forever, unlike the one ma tante Rita gave me when she no longer wanted it, that one I lose and find again that Good Friday when I am twelve.

Standing in line for hours with the neighbourhood kids to see that movie, Les Dix Commandements, clutching the purse under my left arm as hard as I can, like ma tante showed me, holding in my right hand a paper bag with a cheese sandwich and four giant Gattuso olives wrapped in wax paper, the olives a rare treat, maman buys them at Christmas never at Easter, she told me I will have to eat during the movie, it runs for four hours, olives are better in a theatre than celery sticks. Waiting in line, what if they close the doors before I can get in, no more seats, come back next year, waiting in the flat, what if the plane is full, when will Elizabeth get here, the queue snaking toward the ticket booth, better take my ticket money out, my purse! lost my purse! must have stopped clutching, panicking dropping the sandwich bag, searching between legs, the kids resisting protesting, finding the purse in the dust, Elizabeth looking up, grinning speaking, saying what? the woman in the ticket booth telling me to hurry, the silver screen lighting up, no olives for me today, must watch Les Dix Commandements on an empty stomach, Dieu zapping down his law to Moïse, Ariane! the angels play their trumpets, no killing allowed, zap! there will be hell to pay, Ariane! the trumpets fill the heavens.

For Christ's sex! Silence! I holler.

Hé! Ariane! a man calls my name and leans on the horn.

I look up from my sewing, squint, Gérard appears in his black convertible, the tail sticking out into traffic. I cut the thread, hang on to the needle so as not to lose it in the grass, when I get up, my skirt swings back into place, the warm taffeta strokes my thighs, the sidewalk burns my feet. Gérard slides over the red seat to the passenger side, I kiss him on both cheeks, he has not shaved, the roughness burns my lips breaks my heart, tears roll down my face, drivers swerve, blow their horns blow their tops.

Maudit cave, they shout at Gérard.

Maudit épais, they shout at one another.

Gérard does not notice care, his lips move, I lean against the door to catch his words, his white shirt has a ring around the collar, Gérard, habituellement tiré à quatre épingles, today looks like he has not changed not washed for days, he strokes my arm, I am the one who should be consoling.

Ariane, he says. As-tu une idée pour une inscription sur la pierre tombale d'Elizabeth?

Blood rushes to my ears, Elizabeth's body bubbles underground, Gérard waits for words, what words, his hand burns my arm, je pense, do the words carved on stone have to be the last words of the dead, après les funérailles, he wanted to know Elizabeth's last words, we sat in his boutique of antiques, the afternoon so sunny, un sacrilège de lumière, I shake my head, non, he looks at me, his eyes steady, his hand on my arm trembles, a tremor before the earthquake, my tears unstoppable fall ploc-ploc on his hand burning my arm, why ask me, the words he needs he will find inside their history together, a driver shouts something like, quel tyran for making the pretty girl cry. We manage a little smile, he asks that I phone him if something comes to mind, he moves the Mercury into traffic with one hand on the steering wheel, not looking over his shoulder.

I jolt myself out of that crying by jabbing the sewing needle exactly in the middle of my left palm, grab my luggage, rush downhill, need to move, I know now that the intensity stored in the point of a needle can stop tears, I walk fast, stumbling on the unfinished hem, fish a dime out of my pocket, it clinks down the slot.

Allô, maman? C'est Ariane. Dis-moi. Are we responsible for the dead?

Claudette? Parle donc français, seigneur de la vie.

Ma tante Rita? Mon nom est Ariane. Ariane Claude.

Never mind, là, she thinks changing my name is betrayal.

Ta mère est malade d'inquiétude, she whispers.

Bien sûr, ma tante exaggerates. Maman knows I was staying at Pierre's, en plus, she trained herself not to worry during my trip with Elizabeth, what difference does it make, travelling the world or travelling the streets of Montréal, ma tante insists I have been missing for days, not sleeping at home means missing, trust her to smell a drama, cook it in a vat or serve it raw, how can I be disappeared if I am talking to her on the phone.

Où es-tu, là, Claudette?

Au Café de l'horloge.

To prove it, I hold the phone up, so she can hear the music, so she can hear people parler de la vie, argue disagree without throwing cups of coffee at each other, by the way she woofs in my ear, I know she cannot decide whether le Café de l'horloge is the bus terminal or the airport, she is convinced maman will die if I take off on my own.

Salut, ma puce, Pierre says, as ma tante tries to drum sense into me.

He trails his lips along my neck, I can tell, he wants me to come back to his place, my head says, non, his beard tickles, I push him away with my ass, he presses harder against me, he loves it when I struggle, I left so suddenly this morning, am I angry with him? my head says, non, Elizabeth was his friend too, my head says, oui, I wiggle away from him, he goes back to his table with his friends, ma tante says something about girls and women should not be friends, it is not natural, I squint at Pierre's girl du jour, this one wears granny glasses and un béret noir, she looks at me comme si j'étais sa rivale, Pierre tells all his girls du jour I am his special good friend, they feel threatened, they don't understand no strings attached, things are that simple between Pierre and me.

S'il te plaît, ma tante, je veux parler à maman, I say, singing the line in my best mezzo voice.

Ah, seigneur, she giggles.

Claudette?

Mon oncle Joseph? I say, laughing at the family lineup, but concerned something may be wrong at home.

Crisse, ma Claudette, he says. C'est rough, la vie, eh? Years ago at the Works, a fellow fell off the rafters, crisse. He broke his back. Splat crack, fini kaput.

In the background, ma tante yells something at her husband about French not being a Dead Sea language, maman laughs.

We waited for the ambulance, mon oncle says. I gave the fellow a cigarette. Crisse, nothing nobody could do. The poor bugger knew it too. But, crisse, flat on his back as he was, he was standing taller than all of us. Said he didn't feel a thing.

Elizabeth felt everything, I whisper.

You don't know that.

Elizabeth stepping back into traffic, such a small step, the day hot, people wanting shade a cold beer, the Chrysler all over her in a flash. If only I smoked I could have given her a cigarette, she loved her cigarettes, we could have shared that final moment, how stoic we would have looked, Elizabeth blowing smoke, moi holding the cigarette, les badauds gawking, I had no cigarette, Elizabeth hurting everywhere, the driver of the silver car blabbering, madame était un mirage, his dangling hands wanting to mend what his car had crushed.

Mon oncle, je veux parler à maman, I say, deadpan.

Ma pauvre Claudette, he sighs, choking a little.

Ariane, mon oncle. My name is Ariane, now.

Pauvre petite fille, he says, as he drops the receiver.

Maman? Dis-moi. Are we responsible for the dead?

So important a question, just this once, will she answer me, I hold my breath, she sighs, puis, dead air. The air trapped inside a coffin, does it turn into antiquity, as in the tombs of the Egyptians, what is the scent of dead air, does it sit intact, does it decompose? Maman inhales, I exhale.

Absolument, she says softly, like a secret shared.

We are?

You mustn't blame yourself, Ariane. Tu comprends ce que je te dis? But the dead leave things behind. We must pick up after them.

Qu'est-ce que tu veux dire?

C'est difficile, she says. Très difficile. We mustn't hate them.

What is there to hate, the phone went dead, the setting sun paints a splash of red across my grassy place, the new hem of my gypsy skirt finished at last, sewn with tiny stitches it will not come undone again, peut-être, she could say no more. The end of the day in parc Lafontaine, they come out en gang, les filles et les gars on the prowl, I will go home, not to bed, non, have not been in my bed since departure aborted, will sleep on the balcony, dormir à la belle étoile au cœur de Montréal, like camping, will not go back to Pierre's apartment, don't want him to think I cling to him because I don't know where to go. I know what to do. Walking back to the park from le Café de l'horloge, I had an epiphany, as les Anglais say.

D'abord, I will stop dragging all those bags, trop encombrants, tous ces bagages, Elizabeth said we would travel light, I will travel so light, will only wear my gypsy skirt, let it take on the grey green sheen of the streets. Ensuite, I will knock around this city comme si j'étais en voyage, 'til December, like we were supposed to, and will carry Elizabeth everywhere I go as I work on my project en son honneur, and when it is finished, Virginia will exhibit it at her Corona Gallery, it is fitting, I smile at that, fitting, Virginia cannot say no. After the exhibit, I will deal with my lips. Elizabeth died, I spoke. Non. I spoke, Elizabeth died. Ce n'est pas la même chose. Maman will insist I not blame myself, not a question of blame, Pierre will tell me I should not feel guilty, not a question of guilt, people will whisper, does not matter what people think. Like les Anglais say about their stiff upper lip, what I will do, I must, that, the last thing to share with Elizabeth. Exactement what that thing is, I don't know, pas encore, it is only a notion, as in sewing notions. A sensation, like punctuation, heavy on the skin, deep in the flesh, triggered my notion. But skin and flesh are silent, secret. I have 'til December to think things through, to discover the nature of that sensation, to know the meaning behind the punctuation. When the time comes, I will know what to do. No fear.

Maman said we are responsible for the dead, they leave things behind, I do not understand. One day, peut-être. L'expérience la vie. She said we must not hate the dead. What if the dead hate us? Does she keep a picture of Dead Man in her bedroom to remind herself she must not hate him, but it is hard, because what if she loved him and he left her sans dire un mot never to come back.

Elizabeth is not coming back, underground, son corps se décompose, aboveground, tombstone, blank, waiting for words to be carved on black granite, oh, what perfect words Gérard wants pour sa chère Elizabeth. I will not wait for perfect, will work on my project and remember her bons mots. Peut-être, that is what maman means when she says we are responsible. I must pick up after the dead.

Corona

I am only seventeen have no money must sew all my clothes by hand but that Friday le 17 novembre I walk into that galerie d'art dans le Vieux-Montréal wearing my ankle-length maroon velvet coat and that causes a small stir.

Gorgeous, a woman says, fondling my velvet.

She is dressed in a silk caftan the size of a sheik's tent in midnight blue with silver thread, I'd kill, like they say in movies, to lay my hands on fabric like that.

Très beau, I say, fingering her silk.

Je pense, this woman is ugly.

I spot the photographer Elizabeth Gold, she is out of focus, but, définitivement, it is her, she looks taller and thinner in black cigarette pants and a long jacket, well-tailored clothes do that to bodies, must escape the silk woman to thank her, oh, non, misère, I forgot le carton d'invitation, the ugly woman slides her arm around my waist, all the beautiful people with their glasses of white wine kissing and saying, mon cher ma chère, they all stare, I did not want to come.

Nicole et Diane want me to go, après tout, they say, I am beginning to study l'histoire de l'art au collège, I need gallery experience, puis, everybody knows, artists are much more interesting and good-looking than ordinary guys, quelle chance.

Imagine, Nicole says.

We imagine. The three of us sprawled on my bed. It will not work, why not? Claudette Lalancette, that is no name to bring to an art gallery, artists have names like Cézanne and Rembrandt and Vermeer and Renoir and none of their friends are called Claudette Lalancette, ever.

On est à Montréal, Nicole says, rolling her eyes. Pas à Paris.

I hate that silly name, d'ailleurs, what do I know about openings, Diane implies if I am too shy, she will take the invitation.

Oui, Nicole says. Diane et moi, on va y aller.

Non, I say. Je vais y aller.

So glad you came, the blue silk woman says.

I smile non-stop to stare better at the ugly woman's potato nose, pale moustache, thin lips, perfect white teeth, receding chin, blond hair in a French twist, cheeks pock-marked like the pit of a peach, eyes more blue than her silk, and short legs, tiny titties, large hips the magnificent textile cannot hide, how can I go, have nothing to wear, only normal school clothes and my white gypsy skirt, I am not wearing that à un vernissage in the middle of November, Nicole suggests I sew something new, no time, make long stitches is Diane's idea, long stitches save time, oui, mais, I have no money to buy material, wool fabrics are more expensive than cottons, sheep live far away.

You have wine? a man with a pipe and un collier de barbe asks me.

I left it home, I say.

He raises his eyebrows, I can tell, he does not believe me.

The artist really invited me, I say, pointing with my chin at Elizabeth Gold, now surrounded by a thick layer of gallery people. Ask her, she will tell you.

Is that right? the ugly woman says, pinning me tighter against her.

Ah, the man with the pipe and beard says. Tu es Ariane.

They both laugh, I feel like un imposteur, will have to tell them I am not Ariane who ever she is, my name is Claudette Lalancette, should have gone out with Nicole et Diane, c'était décidé, I was not coming here, but six days before le vernissage, the same Saturday in November maman always bakes her Christmas fruitcake at ma tante Rita's, stays for supper, plays cards well past midnight before mon oncle Joseph drives her and her fruitcake home, that day the old maroon velvet drapes dans le grand salon catch my eye, c'est ma destinée, that little idea grows, I cannot stop thinking about it, more than enough fabric to make the Butterick long coat with narrow cuffed sleeves and the Peter Pan collar, it won't cost me a cent, nine pieces to sew together plus twenty-five buttonholes to construct and twenty-five five-eighths-of-an-inch buttons to cover with velvet plus the lining, no lining, that will save time. But the living room drapes? They have lived with us forever, at ten I play, the Queen of Spain Queen of Olives commands her army of kitchen chairs, cookie sheet breastplates shining under her maroon train, careful not to pull on the rod, cannot stop myself, let the velvet panels slip off the rod crumple to the floor, daylight floods le grand salon, that stale birthday cake of plaster mouldings and wave crests, swirls and curlicues Dead Man never had time to eat, time to shake antique dust away, this is 1967, les temps modernes, we just had Expo.

The ugly woman and the pipe man are still laughing.

There's someone I want you to meet, she says, tugging at my waist.

Enfin, Elizabeth Gold will explain everything, the gallery people follow, I don't mind, je suis chic dans mon grand manteau, stood on a chair in front of my bureau mirror to make sure the light reflected in the right direction on all the panels, it did, because I remembered to pin the pattern pieces correctly, velvet has a nap, peut-être, they know I have nothing underneath but black tights black boots, the coat worn like a dress next to the skin, how daring, we reach the photographer, I smile, ready to thank to congratulate her, she greets me by bending at the waist, Elizabeth Gold is a man.

Ah, I see, chère, the man says to the ugly woman, you found your muse. Gérard L'Heureux, he says to me. Enchanté.

Moi, une muse? I say, as we shake hands.

The sophisticated people laugh like movie characters at a cocktail party.

Elle est charmante, one of them says.

So, you're the model? a woman says, like this is a sin. Hi. I'm Virginia, the owner of this little parcel, she adds, looking around the gallery.

Everybody laughs, Virginia the owner smirks and drains her glass.

Show her, chère, Gérard L'Heureux says to Elizabeth Gold. She's probably dying to see what you did with her. C'est très réussi, vous savez.

The way he looks at me I am not sure if he means the portrait or the coat. He too fingers my velvet, I feel like merchandise, what if he is un couturier and his nose tells him I have no lining, couturiers can be devastatingly critical, I saw that in a movie once, they speak with razor blades between their lips.

I don't have a sewing machine, I say, so he may forgive the shortcut.

Elizabeth Gold hugs me.

I told you, Gérard. The girl's a genius.

Maman would be proud of my success, même si, she lost her drapes, en plus, nobody thinks I am a window, velvet touches my skin, everything is délicieusement out of focus, how to be admired invisible in a room full of people, I am beginning to enjoy myself.

Ah, Raymond, Elizabeth Gold says. Join us.

The pipe man Raymond looks me up and down, what does he want, better not trick me with art questions, j'étudie l'histoire de l'art seulement depuis septembre, I keep an eye on him, he on me.

Elizabeth Gold transformed her black and white photos of the yoot of Expo into tableaux by adding splashes of paint, bits of mirrors, metallic threads, feathers, by cutting the boards into asymmetrical shapes, that must be avant-garde, in my course, we are into la Renaissance, l'avant-garde, ça viendra plus tard. She gathers the beautiful people with their glasses of white wine in her sweep, like maman's vadrouille catches dustballs under the beds, l'entourage d'Elizabeth Gold, dustballs under her silk, j'ai le fou rire, must not spoil cette soirée, Nicole et Diane will want to know everything.

We tour the exhibit, I am right back at Expo, jésus guys and bike guys, girls galore in bright clothes, Indian shirts and leather jackets, grass joints and mean sexy eyes, miniskirts and long legs, guitars and love-ins, mouths kissing under floppy felt hats and crotches bulging in tight striped pants, bare feet in sandals and white socks in black shoes, beards and handlebar moustaches and sideburns, long hair, short hair, they are all there, la jeunesse qui dirigera, my Expo passport said, the yoot Elizabeth Gold captured in her photos, black guys from New York, white girls from Vancouver, red guys from Australia, brown girls from India, yellow guys from Hong Kong, ebony girls from Sénégal, the new rainbow, la jeunesse de l'Expo who will shape the destiny of the world, my Expo passport said. Et puis, I see me.

I see me hanging on the wall, bigger than big, elongated in a tall narrow tableau, like this is un Greco, scraping the dog shit off my shoe, holding a gold needle, sewing with gold thread winding and disappearing into shadows, my long hair darkening the sky, my skirt, a sheet of plastic ice over my thighs, and, recognize, don't recognize, my cat's eyes, their frame feathered and mirrored comme pour un carnaval, I don't want to look, cannot stop looking, that printed face that is me that is not me.

Take wine, madame la muse, time to amuse la muse, Raymond says loud enough for the gallery people to hear his bon mot, but so close to me I can smell his pipe tobacco.

He brushes against my velvet, his eyes enjoy themselves, Elizabeth Gold's eyes warn him, she blows cigarette smoke out of her nostrils, je pense, I can take care of myself, une chance, she did not ask me to critique my portrait, better bite my tongue. The crowd moves away, refills glasses, in a recess of the gallery, Virginia sits on the corner of her desk talking on the phone, watching me, what does she think, I will walk away with my portrait under my coat, I read the description on the wall next to the picture, in the fuzz of my myopia appears Aviune 1967, Aviune? I get closer, smell the white paint on the wall.

Ariane 1967, b&w photograph on board with gold thread, 24 x 60 in., by Elizabeth Gold, $800.00

Ariane 1967. Cannot keep my eyes off that title. Ariane, c'est moi. Puis, that red dot glued to the description cardboard.

Elizabeth Gold's hand tightens around my waist again, what does she want, the hand strong and steady, so sure of herself. Her cigarette smoke fogs Ariane 1967 and that red dot. Vendu, the word of slavery, the word of betrayal. Elizabeth Gold m'a vendue pour quelques écus, she did not ask my permission, peut-être, there is a loo-pole, like they say in movies about composers who have their music stolen by bad guys in top hats, am I her property now to sell, un deux trois, vendu, I will hang in a stranger's house, a bored hand will dust me leave me crooked on the wall, rich unruly children will draw a moustache donkey's ears, I will adorn some office, important men in suits will make jokes to my cat's-eyed face, such exposure, why didn't I tell her, no photo, please, I will mildew in a lakeside chalet, raccoons will shit on my white gypsy skirt.

I am happy for you, madame, I say, pointing at the red dot. Félicitations.

Call me Elizabeth, Ariane, dear.

Je pense, should I say Elizabeth, vous, or should I say Elizabeth, tu, tutoyer Elizabeth Gold does not feel right, she is as old as maman, bien sûr, je tutoie maman, c'est normal, I have known her all my life, but Elizabeth Gold is a stranger, quand même, I am her muse, I know nothing about this artist-muse thing.

Gérard L'Heureux takes Elizabeth Gold away, they say words to each other, this weekend we will, my love, tu te souviens, chère, words that connect them depuis longtemps. Elizabeth et Gérard, the ugly woman in midnight silk and the tall elegant man in black, did she marry him like maman married Dead Man? non, les bohèmes ne croient pas au mariage, quand même, they are in love, I can tell, are they happy? being in love does not mean being happy, Gérard L'Heureux est-il heureux avec Elizabeth Gold, sa femme en or, that I cannot tell, there is love and there is love, d'ailleurs, les artistes vivent toujours des amours tumultueuses, that is why they are exciting people.

Claudette Lalancette stares at Ariane 1967, Ariane punches inside my head, what is she telling me, I am Claudette Lalancette, plain and silly, when Elizabeth Gold finds out, quelle déception, she cannot have a muse called Claudette Lalancette, kids in school making jokes all the time, Claudette Lalancette, l'agace-pissette, at the kitchen tap every morning, maman wetting braiding la petite Claudette's hair that shone like two chocolate slabs all day, qu'est-ce que c'est une agace-pissette?

Dis donc, tu t'appelles comment? Raymond asks, handing me a glass of white wine.

I take the wine, become a mon cher ma chère person.

Claude… Ariane Claude.

He smiles with his eyes, tells me he writes songs, ah, un chansonnier, he nods, il chante dans les boîtes à chansons et les cafés, will I come and see him? I tell him I hang out au Café de l'horloge, he will check that out, I tell him j'étudie l'histoire de l'art et la littérature au cégep, quel cégep? le Collège du Vieux-Montréal, he tells me he used to study in that building when it was called le Mont Saint-Louis before les cégeps existed, oui, les cégeps started only this September, he would like to show me his latest songs, would I give him my opinion? is he tricking me, his voice sounds plain enough, c'est un beau gars, ce Raymond à pipe with smoke in his eyes, waves run through my belly, he is about Pierre's age, mid-twenties, I could go out with him, is Raymond dreaming of becoming un grand chansonnier like Pierre dreams of becoming un écrivain engagé, do I want to go out with un chansonnier, something behind me catches his eyes, he rests his hand on my shoulder, I want his hand to stay there.

Excuse-moi, he says.

I stand alone, hold the wine, how to join the hoot, I am seventeen, sew all my clothes by hand, without the heavy drapes, le grand salon looks moderne, un vrai facelift, maman standing in the doorway of my bedroom with her cup of Salada tea, watching me sew her drapes into my coat, wait 'til I tell her about my gallery success, elle me fait les gros yeux, elle n'est pas contente, we said nothing, just stared at each other, we still have not talked about the drapes, mais je suis une muse, have been sold for 800 dollars, looks like I am in the hoot. Oh, mais non, Claudette Lalancette will ruin everything with her cartoon name, velvet coat will crumble to antique dust, gold needle will puncture write Claudette Lalancette across her body, what a cheat what a fake, pranc-ing about, naked between deux identités, I sip the wine, it burns a thin line down the wrong pipe, cough and cough, eyes full of tears, false lashes come unglued, through tears and myopia, I push open the metal door, heavy for a washroom door, find myself outside at the back of the gallery, the cold air feels like lake water.

Elizabeth and Raymond kiss, ils s'embrassent à pleine bouche, passionnément, I am so close to them in that tiny enclosure, they will see me, ça, c'est certain. Raymond's hand hidden in the silk tent, his finger deep inside Elizabeth, Elizabeth's hand, sure and knowing, at Raymond's fly, they rub against each other, moan, mean it, know how to, I too want to. Ariane would use her finger on herself watching them, Claudette just gets weak in the knees, wet and confused and a little frightened, I glance at the door, this could turn ugly, wait for Gérard to burst outside, aha! like le mari cocu in a French movie, Gérard, a sophisticated black-haired black-dressed man, sailing through the bright gallery, knowing the rules, does he know what goes on in the dark, and now Claudette opening the wrong door, something rattles. Elizabeth s'apprête à jouir, she grunts, annoyed, Raymond's finger must have slipped off the button, the sound in Elizabeth's throat changes, more relaxed, Raymond's finger found the button again, she is climbing climbing, my heart pounds with hers, she lets herself go, I go back inside before they come back to earth, what will she do after Raymond, wipe him off inside her caftan, les bohèmes don't mind body fluids.

When I come out of the washroom, my false lashes safe in one velvet pocket, le vernissage is over. The last mon cher ma chère people linger in the doorway, half hanging inside Corona, half spilling into rue Saint-Paul. I linger too, not because I am an intimate of the artist, non, vous-tu, tu-vous, même si maintenant, I know a thing or two about Elizabeth Gold, I linger, la muse confuse, because I don't know how to leave.

You like the country? Elizabeth asks, pushing smoke out of her mouth. Raymond tells me you're an art student. Saint-Polycarpe's an artsy little village.

Where's Gérard? I ask, practising my gallery person's casual voice.

He went home. Why?

Will they have a fight, est-ce qu'ils vont faire l'amour, what if the three of them do it together, those things happen now, more often since Expo, hope they don't ask me, can a muse say, non, merci?

Come for a visit, Elizabeth says.

Why?

Why what?

Pourquoi l'invitation?

Fuck me gently, she says softly, must there be a reason? Goodnight, Ariane, dear.

She kisses me on the mouth, I taste Raymond's pipe tobacco, she walks away, sweeping the floor with her shimmering silk.

When? I ask.

I don't want to go, but am conducting a little experiment, because there is invitation and there is invitation.

I can come Saturday.

Saturday's no good.

Je pense, aha!

I don't mean Saturday tomorrow. I mean any Saturday.

Why am I insisting, d'ailleurs, where is Saint-Polycarpe, what if I cannot afford the bus fare? Peut-être, I want to go, a little.

I'm afraid Saturdays are no good for me, Ariane, dear. Saturdays, I shoot weddings. Friday afternoons are good.

Fridays are good days for me too.

I have morning classes, but next semester and all of second-year cégep I will keep my Fridays classfree, what is the matter with me, this hoot is going to my head, déjà, I see myself visiting Elizabeth every week. I want to kiss her back like a gallery pro, she moves away, the raw edges fraying inside my coat itch and scratch. Time to leave.

I close the door, through the window, watch Elizabeth and Virginia gesticulate in front of Ariane 1967, l'artiste et la marchande de tableaux, comme Van Gogh et son frère Théo, deep shivers twist through me from head to toe, good thing I had no time to line, skin against satin lining on cold night gives the chill of death, I smile at that, watch Elizabeth flick her wrist as if to say, who cares, watch Virginia throw her arms up in the air as if to say, you'll be the ruin of me, they laugh, drink the last of the wine, hold on to each other, do a comical little dance, the lights go out.

Ariane 1967, alone in the dark empty gallery, Claudette Lalancette, alone in the dark empty street.

I walk.

Carnaval

My leather sandals crunch wet sand, the crowd on the cobblestone streets, thick and loud, le peuple est dans le mood de la fête, I would not have come down to le Vieux-Montréal, not on a day like this, celebrating, too soon after Elizabeth's death, but today, le 24 juin, Virginia will close her Corona Gallery for the summer, donc, this is my last chance to talk to her about my project.

We're closed.

Allô, Virginia.

Oh. It's you.

I walk toward her desk, past a stepladder and a toolbox, she appears fuzzy to my myopia and out of reach, the afternoon drizzle darkens the white walls, the empty gallery, a desert in mourning, would I be in the Desert of Death with Elizabeth, the Dasht-i-Margo, she called it, J'te-dis-Margot, I said out loud, using maman's name to remember the desert's exotic appellation, non, in June, we would be on a Greek island drowning in light, Virginia shuffles papers, I swing ma valise de fin de semaine flat on her desk, she has her summer plans, I have mine, sésame, ouvre-toi, ta-dah, ma valise, full of Elizabeth's photos. I lean over the desk, force Virginia to listen.

I will design a huge dress and will call it Gold Rush 1969.

Oh, brother, she says, rolling her eyes.

Okay, you choose the title, call it Composition 33½, I don't care.

Ariane, I don't have time for this, she says, pulling on a piece of paper sticking out from under ma valise.

This won't take long. Listen. I will articulate the bell-shaped sleeves at the wrists and elbows with brass eyelets, so the arms can be raised with invisible wires, as if the dress caught the last dance of life at the exact moment the body left. The dress will be constructed of cut-outs, details I will choose from these photos, do you follow? Each fragment I will cut into a rectangle three inches long by two inches wide, will glue two rectangles back to back, so both sides will show something photographed, like a nose a branch, recto verso, like a dead fish on a rock a chair in semi-darkness, recto verso, you see what I mean? When the rectangles are all cut and glued in pairs, I will punch tiny eyelets at each corner and will construct the whole structure, sleeves and bodice, by tying the rectangles together with lengths of fishing line, fishing line being nearly invisible, the viewer will have the impression each rectangle floats in mid-air, separate but together, you know? Gold Rush 1969 made of hundreds of fragments of Elizabeth's photos, what she saw or felt or thought when she pressed the shutter release, the cut-outs, the residues of her eyes and heart and mind. What do you think?

Virginia stares in shock at the black and white snapshots lying pêle-mêle dans ma valise, as if I had opened Elizabeth's coffin to reveal her corpse.

You can't use those, she says.

Elizabeth gave them to me. Yes, she did. Last summer. When I worked for her, sorting out thousands of photos just like these. She had so many, she did not mind I took a few.

You call that a few, she says, pointing at the overflowing valise. Besides, they're her intellectual property. You can't just cut them up. It's mutilation. I can't allow this.

What mutilation? Non non, you are wrong, this is inter-
pretation, Virginia, Elizabeth interpreted everything, regarde
ses tableaux, she would approve, you know she would.

The phone keeps ringing, like it has the hiccups, I can
tell, Virginia thinks my idea is a silly nineteen-year-old-girl
idea, she needs more convincing, the phone stops ringing,
she tries to move ma valise off her desk to go back to her
papers, I hold it down, we are not finished.

Gold Rush will be in the shape of a caftan, I say. Like the
one Elizabeth wore the night of Ariane 1967.

That bloody composition, she says, lighting une Du
Maurier-la-cigarette-de-bon-goût.

But much bigger, I say, climbing up the stepladder to
demonstrate. Un caftan énorme, ten feet tall, it will hang
from the gallery ceiling by invisible wires, will float fly never
land.

I had promised it to a regular client. Holy shit. That's no
way to build a clientele.

And you will build a ramp. Like a spiral staircase surrounding the dress.

I will, will I?

Oui. So viewers can walk up and down to see each and
every photo fragment, a smile a breast, the wing of a bird a
salt shaker, so many images, in the front of the bodice, in the
back, along the sleeves, from floor to ceiling.

How can I keep this gallery running if the artists refuse
to sell.

You set the price. The photodress, a symbol of Elizabeth's
life. That will sell.

Get down, she says, jumping up, like a bug on her chair
bit her. I don't have time for this.

Elizabeth was your friend too, I say. We are doing this to
remember her.

Virginia on the ground, moi at the top of l'escabeau, I
reach, arms fully extended over the parapet of the balcony,

lose my balance, dégringole, she breaks my fall, I could not break Elizabeth's, the thud of my feet landing on the oak floor, I show her my hands.

These hands have sewing experience. Six years. Since I was thirteen.

She backs away from me, I walk toward her, we do the tango of not touching, I show her my fingers with pinpricks and needle holes.

Parfois, Virginia, I sew thread of different colours to my fingertips, no big deal, this is not mutilation, non non, don't be silly, non, just a game. These hands can pull thread through cloth, leather, anything, they can build a giant dress with photo cut-outs and fishing line. Elizabeth said my imagination was growing. You cannot let that die.

The phone rings again, she swims toward it, like it is une bouée de sauvetage.

Elizabeth always encouraged me to be creative, I say, following her.

C'est inutile, her mind is elsewhere, she will go away for the summer, where, she does not confide in me, she puts her hand over the receiver.

Be creative elsewhere, Ariane. This is long distance.

Ah. Who can compete with that. Okay, I leave Corona, leave Virginia. When she comes back in September, Gold Rush 1969 will be completed.

I swing ma valise into the thick of la fête, bodies smell of hop and patchouli, church bells and car horns compete with rock and folk songs seeping out of windows, I walk toward la place Jacques-Cartier, men stare at me, I don't mind, Elizabeth taught me not to be shy about my body, my gypsy skirt beats against my thighs, silver hoops dangle in my pierced ears, a red kerchief covers my head, my long dark hair hanging down my back, my white tank top does not hide my braless nipples, I don't mind the damp cool clinging to my arms, brass bangles ring around my wrists, the setting sun dries the rain out of the clouds, tints orange the stone walls of the ancient houses.

Loud crash. People start to run, what is going on, peut-être une émeute, like the one last year dans le parc Lafontaine, the Saint-Jean parade at night made people go banana split, this year, la Ville scheduled the parade in the afternoon, daylight keeps trouble away, quand même, this morning, maman jumped in mon oncle Joseph's car and, with ma tante Rita, they drove to le chalet, she asked I not come home 'til everything was over, night has arrived dans le Vieux-Montréal, la voix du peuple, will it shout angry, will it shout happy, will there be night trouble. A wolf with a plastic nose pursues a girl in a red cape, what will it be this year, cop cars on fire or fireworks, blue-and-white silk spilling over balconies or red-and-white silk burning, I bump into les fêtards, il y a bousculade, the crowd tightens like a fist, where is Pierre tonight, a hand slides along my ass, I spot the face to which the hand belongs, the eyes pretend they don't see what the hand is doing, I jab the side of ma valise into the innocent shin attached to the lying eyes attached to the guilty hand, the revellers shift, a line of fiddlers snakes through, people lock arms, spin dance, the sudden smell of pot, I take a puff, pass the joint, someone grabs my shoulder.

Hé! la gitane, veux-tu me lire la bonne aventure? Quand est-ce qu'on se fait libérer?

The shoulder grabber, maintenant, his hand opened, palm up to show me his lines, wears a blue tee-shirt with a large white fleur de lys on his chest, I squint, the tee-shirt is painted directly on his hairless torso. I study the line on his arm where a real short sleeve would end, examine the back, his skin painted below the waistband of his jeans, as if the fake top were tucked in, look at the front again, under the royal blue paint every pore visible, touch la fleur de lys, c'est comme toucher à fleur de peau.

Magnifique, I say.

Le Québécois fleurdelisé flashes a proud smile, I put ma valise down, pretend to read his hand, tell him the lines are blurred, he tells me it must be because he has been drinking all afternoon.

Je suis paqueté, à soir, he says. À soir, c'est un bon soir pour prendre une brosse, à soir.

He brings news, the parade was quiet, but a huge demonstration followed all along Sherbrooke, in the west end devant le Ritz, ils ont décapité le Saint-Jean-Baptiste, bien sûr, not the real curly-haired boy holding a live curly-wool lamb on his lap, like when we were little, non, we demanded a man to represent us, they gave us a statue, I want to know if the head was stolen, après tout, Jean Baptiste always loses his head, le Québécois fleurdelisé laughs and laughs. Were people fighting in the streets with the police like last year? He says, non, mais des contestataires threw bottles and broke windows.

Ce soir, smelly horses pull des calèches, l'année dernière, horses tumbled into the crowd, much panic, mon oncle Joseph says horses are doomed, they carry the terror of ancient wars, firecrackers make them battle-crazy, ce soir, the horses clip-clop tranquillement on cobblestones, un rien could turn them into killer beasts, we let them pass.

A shadow passes between us, out of the corner of my eye, I see ma valise lift, walk away.

Hé, là! le Québécois fleurdelisé yells, as he dashes into the crowd. Lâche sa valise, tabarnac! Stop, voleur!

I run after him, le voleur lets go, worms away, ma valise hits the pavement hard, the clasps spring open, all the photos spill on place Jacques-Cartier, everything happens in slow motion, the crowd heaves like the sea, I throw myself over the bundle, many photos scatter, I spread arms and legs, a fallen snow angel pinned down, how to start gathering what is not lost, feet shuffle close to my face, hands pick up stray photos, I get up carefully, people dans un mouvement de solidarité step on the bundle, a clown with purple hair plucks photos out of the grime, le Québécois fleurdelisé shovels handfuls back into ma valise, I close the lid, snap the clasps shut, what a mess, I could scratch that vandal's eyes out.

Maudit salaud! le Québécois fleurdelisé shouts, as if le voleur had not made tracks.

Il a filé à l'anglaise, I say, sure we will never find him.

Maudit Anglais! he shouts.

Then he took French leave, I say, brushing dirt off my skirt, laughing alone at the strangeness of languages.

Le Québécois smells of beer and garlic, I stare at his hard blue nipples, show him my hand with the needle hole piercing my lifeline, our heads touch, I tap the needle mark in the middle of my palm.

C'est petit, he says.

But runs deep, I don't say that. I tell him, a couple of weeks ago a friend of mine was struck by a Chrysler on rue Sherbrooke right in front of my eyes, he whispers sympathy, Elizabeth Gold, peut-être, he heard about her, une artiste anglophone, peut-être, he read about the accident, he shrugs.

Ce n'est pas important, I say.

He wants to know how the hole appeared, peut-être, he thinks I am having une extase religieuse, I tell him I stabbed myself with a sewing needle, but that is not the point, the point is, with Elizabeth I could speak, même si c'était en anglais, all of us, Québécois, we never learned to speak, we don't know the names of things, ever since we were little it was forbidden to think, in school questions were not allowed, he nods, I tell him, notre devise is not Je me souviens, non, notre devise is Motus et bouche cousue, I put my finger across my lips, he nods and nods, I tell him it does not matter how we learn to speak, as long as we speak.

En anglais ou en mandarin, I say, les mots sont les mots. Tu comprends? Peux-tu comprendre ça, toi?

Oui, je comprends, he says. Il faut que ça change. On doit parler à tout prix.

He gets speak-excited, tells me I can talk all I want now, dans ma langue, le Québec aux Québécois, he shouts, people who cannot hear our conversation shout back the slogan, I tell him, parler is good, parler pour parler is dangerous, how so, he wants to know, I tell him, learning to speak is not enough, parfois, we must choose our silences, not imposed silence like when we were little, non, we must learn about silence the same as we must learn to speak, but I don't think he understands, he goes on speaking abstract words comme la solidarité, la revendication, I watch him, he stops, word-exhausted.

C'est ça, demain, tout le monde va se découdre la bouche, I say, pretending to unzip lips, imitating huge cacophony, the misunderstanding coming out of newly open mouths.

He stares at my lips, I can tell, he wants to, I let him, c'est soir de fête, everything impromptu, he French kisses me, c'est un bon soir to French kiss, I kiss him back, will the blue of his torso rub off on my white top, will la fleur de lys transfer, this afternoon thousands of feet stamping over molecules of Elizabeth's body transferred into the pavement of rue Sherbrooke, bien sûr, they could not remove every single bit of her, she will not rest complètement 'til la Ville paves over her and when will that be, his kiss tastes sweet and sour, Elizabeth's thin lips kissing tasted like cool air, never of stale cigarette, as if her body never produced bad odours even in the morning, I cannot ask Gérard or Raymond, Pierre, oui, I will ask Pierre si Elizabeth avait mauvaise haleine le matin, Elizabeth, a kisser, a rare thing, surtout pour une Anglaise, kissing like a mother like a friend like a sister like a lover like a man like a woman, Elizabeth is kissing dirt.

Ah, c'est beau l'amour, a man shouts, while his friends do the catcallers' chorus.

Soudain, le Québécois fleurdelisé becomes belligerent, je pense, never disturb a kissing man, the catcallers welcome

une bagarre impromptue, last year, Pierre shouting, il y a du
sang dans les rues, rushing to our balcony, his tee-shirt
ripped, like un aventurier in a movie who just escaped the
red ants, below us, everything normal, the parade moving
along rue Sherbrooke, le peuple enjoying la fête, even all
those cops watching from the rooftops, street fights breaking
out in parc Lafontaine, chairs, bottles, paint raining on,
horses panicking, cops at street level matraquing heads and
kneecaps, Pierre leaning over the stone parapet, maman
holding him by the belt so he would not splatter himself on
the crowded sidewalk, Pierre gesticulating, so many wounded,
même des spectateurs innocents, maman saying, pour
l'amour, imagining the sacking of Montréal, down the street
the bands marching on, in the park flames cutting through
the darkness, cars on fire, débris now pelting the parade,
maman calling us inside, Pierre wanting to go back down to
fight, le Québécois fleurdelisé and the catcallers throw their
sharpest words at each other, demonstrators shouting,
Trudeau au poteau, in slow motion a bottle flying toward
l'estrade d'honneur on the steps of la Bibliothèque municipale, mon oncle Joseph phoning, things are ugly on rue
Cherrier, he and ma tante reporting from their own balcony,
mon oncle involved in something at his shop, le syndicat ou
un comité de travailleurs, he does not tell me, not even en
anglais, does not want to worry ma tante, their two daughters live in Toronto, each married to un Anglais, mon oncle,
split down the bloodline, I want to split, leave le Québécois
fleurdelisé to fight his drunken fight, Pierre raising his fist,
stumbling on abstract words, les travailleurs au pouvoir,
démolir, rebâtir, bristling with desire for action, pacing up
and down, our balcony too small to contain his rage frustration, moi pouring him a drink of maman's sangria, Pierre
calling la sangria, le sang des taureaux, downing several
glasses, not quenching his thirst, le mood est à la parole, our
fingers dipping into le sang des taureaux to get at the orange

and lemon slices, our mouths munching on their flesh, like Pierre's words, tinted red.

Allons prendre une bière, I invite.

Le Québécois fleurdelisé s'est volatilisé, what is the matter with him, taking French leave like snatchers of valises, peut-être, my kiss only rated four on his Richter scale, pas de tremblement de terre, ce soir, look at me, filthy skirt, toes black with mud, no wonder il a filé à l'anglaise after French kissing, I chuckle at that, what is Pierre doing tonight, will he come down, he said he might. I walk.

On rue Saint-Jean-Baptiste I keep my eyes open for Jean Baptiste, he may have come down to enjoy la fête, his head tucked under his arm. The wall surrounding une porte cochère is covered with tiny white lights like a dress studded with sequins, dance music reaches the street, I peek inside the courtyard, bûcherons dance with cowgirls, princesses drink with bikers, what! no gorilla, we have to have a gorilla, I squint at a long table set against the back wall also studded with lights, the white tablecloth covered with pyramids of sandwiches, baskets of strawberries, rounds of cheeses, les fêtards costumés drink fizzy drinks in tall narrow glasses, sans doute, du champagne, gorillas come out in winter, summer is not gorilla season.

I go in, nobody seems to mind, have been walking all evening, no food no drink, pop a finger sandwich into my mouth, a strawberry, pop pop, ni vu ni connu, sit on a folding chair, open ma valise to assess the damage, pour bubbly wine in a cup, clean the dirt off the photos with napkins dipped in wine, horse shit, puke, ah, cochonnerie, maman would say. How many did I lose, may have to go to Saint-Pol to get more, could I have this one, Elizabeth? and that one? do as you please, Ariane, dear, as long as you're creative, she will not mind, that is not stealing from the dead like the women in that Greek film, follow your instinct, she said, all those photos she would use later dans des tableaux d'avant-garde, she will never, now. What will happen to her collection, will Gérard sell it at that hawktion place he knows? A good word that, hawktion, people like birds of prey snatching. Gérard vendra aux enchères les photos de sa chère Elizabeth.

Une Colombine watches me work, not for long, the crinolined batiste skirt with the yellow and blue diamond pattern disappears from my field of vision, son Arlequin carries her to dance a rock around a clock.

Editing the family album? a man's voice says.

I look up at a tall thin asperge blanche, the man dressed in a white tuxedo, white shirt, white bow tie, white shoes, his face a darker shade of white, his short hair so pale he appears bald, his sparse beard so fine his face seems to have caught a shower of pollen.

I'm Duane Svenson, he says. What's up around the French Quarter? I just got here.

French Quarter, hein? I say, with a mocking grin. This is le Vieux-Montréal.

I know, he says. I did my homework.

Don't tell me. You are from the Yew-Ess, right?

Why would I be from the U.S.?

Les Étasuniens have a French Quarter à la Nouvelle-Orléans. They come here and think this is the French Quarter à Montréal. They know nothing about us. Par exemple, during Expo, they did not understand what la place d'Accueil was. They kept asking for the Plastic Eye.

The Plastic Eye, he repeats, laughing. What is place d'Accueil? he asks, chewing the words like caramel.

Where are you from?

Distraction, Manitoba.

His hand, long and fine, avec la dextérité du prestidigitateur, makes a half-dozen fancy sandwiches disappear into his mouth.

Ever been to Distraction? he asks without mockery.

Gabrielle Roy is from Saint-Boniface, I say. Je m'appelle Ariane Claude.

Très Montréalais, he articulates slowly. I was on Mount Royal a while ago, he says. Beautiful up there with the city lights spread out below the belvedere. Packed with people too. Quebeckers know how to have a good time.

I shake my head, see broken windows, cracked skulls, Colombine et Arlequin rock wildly, I clean dirt off the corner of a boat tilting to one side at low tide, je pense, that man, Sven, how would he take on film, would light pass through him or would he burn la pellicule, so tall and pale, presque transparent.

Were they hostile to you up on the mountain?

No, no, he says. I sang Alouette and a song about a quail with a broken wing. People explained the words, I sang with them.

Everybody's chummy tonight, I say. We have our troubles, mais ce soir, we drink la bière de la fraternité universelle, everybody dances with everybody, mother's tongue and queen's tongue, we French kiss tonight, look at that mud, a thief spilled my photos on place Jacques-Cartier, next fall, an art gallery will exhibit my work, you should come if you are still here, openings are a hoot.

He carefully closes the lid of ma valise, offers his pale hand.

Let's dance.

Je ne sais pas valser, moi.

Just let yourself go.

The white-clad man takes me in his arms, I become a diaphanous dancer, my feet follow his feet, my waist bends under his guidance, we spin around the old stone walls strung with white lights like cotton wool, a guitar and a violin lift me off my feet, I see people's faces, don't see them, see the lights, don't see them, we spin and spin, my gypsy skirt wedges between Sven's long legs, the soprano's voice soars, I catch a few words, south wind and gentle rain, the song, an ancient tongue in her mouth, the costumed dancers sway like exotic trees in a south sea wind, people in black capes and blue satin dresses, hunters and buccaneers, Colombine danse avec Arlequin, nous valsons de plus en plus vite, we do not bump into the others, we float fly, white lights, painted faces, violin and guitar, happy-sad song, someone lost at sea, my mind cannot make out the story, my skin shivers, emotions only, the singer's voice, an invisible thread holding us in suspense, stitching her song, nous sommes suspendus à ses lèvres, we spin, lights, we turn, voice, we spin and turn, violin and guitar, spin turn, dancers in costumes, je suis légère comme une plume je suis dans un état second, I can catch you, Elizabeth, climb a little higher, a singer's voice will hold you, suspended, catch her thread, Elizabeth begins her descent, I am flying with the sweet Swede, where would I be this night, en Grèce en Turquie, à Venise, somewhere where a warm wind blows and soft rain falls, flying in my usual city, en costumes bigarrés people celebrate their blue-and-white night, leur nuit, ma nuit, notre nuit, I am waltzing with pollen-plated Sven, night flying sun rising plane descending, Elizabeth landing, alone, the pale of her clothes reddening, people crowding, the driver repeating, c'était un mirage c'était un mirage, the spinning stops, my body lands, heavy.

The song's over, Sven, son of Duane, whispers, his lips brushing against my red scarf. Are you okay?

Hold me a minute, I say. My knees turned to jujubes.

His hand on the nape of my neck, my head cradled in the crook of his shoulder, he smells of honey.

That was no waltz, I say.

Celtic. Ariane Claude? Do you want to spend this night with me?

After just one dance? Even a Celtic waltz?

Je pense, les Manitobains are quick on their feet, and how do you refer to the residents of a place called Distraction. He picks up ma valise.

No, no, he says. I'm taking the train home in a few hours. You know, you're a better dancer than you think.

Merci.

We leave the courtyard as fiddlers break into an explosive song, une gigue québécoise, the crowd goes wild, jumps on its collective feet, sings in its collective tongue, we run out into the street, my sandal catches on the uneven stones, sweet Sven holds me steady, he bumps into le Québécois fleur-delisé.

Ostie, regarde où tu mets les pieds, maudit cave, le Québécois shouts, his own feet knitted together.

Sorry, man, Sven says bites his mother tongue.

Hé! c'est encore toi, la gitane! le Québécois shouts, friendly. Peux-tu me la lire, la bonne aventure? Quand est-ce qu'on se fait libérer, là?

He laughs and reels, his eyes the size of pinheads, he sizes up l'Anglais in the white tuxedo, looks at him up and down, is getting le mal de mer, will collapse either in a deluge of expletives or vomit.

Il est Suédois, I say. Du Manitoba.

Pas de problème, bonhomme, le Québécois fleurdelisé says, slapping Sven on the back like men do. Je suis plein comme un œuf, à soir. Je voulais pas faire mal à ta blonde, he burps, brushing dirt off my skirt. I want not to do fear to the tourists, he says to Sven with a happy grin.

He sets out toward rue Notre-Dame, changes his mind.

Hé! Le Manitoba, là, c'est-tu avant ou après la Saskat, la Katsach?

He breaks into a song of his own invention, as he weaves down the street, in wider and wider arcs. I check that Sven still carries ma valise.

Look, he says, pointing toward le fleuve.

Ah, oui! I say, squinting hard. C'est magique!

The sky is alive with white moths. A man wrapped in a baby blue blanket squeaks like a bird in a hurry.

As-tu vu les papillons de nuit? he calls out, flying toward the water, mouth wide open.

Let's go see un show québécois, I say, taking Sven's hand. Viens.

Ce soir, Raymond chante au Vieux Fanal. I have not seen him since les funérailles, the place is crowded and smoky, I sit on ma valise, Sven finds a stool, asks me to guard it with my life, goes beer hunting, a thin girl in a black pirate outfit with a yellow patch over one eye and a green plastic parrot sewn to her shoulder sinks to the floor next to me.

Mon chum vient de me lâcher, she says.

I touch her parroted shoulder, she mistakes my interest in the rough stitching for sympathy, tells me love things never work out for her, a curse, but she always bounces back, I ask her if the figure-eight stitch is strong enough to hold a six-inch parrot, she shrugs and the parrot wobbles dangereusement, ready to drop off its perch, I have thread and needle dans ma valise.

Au diable, she says. Mon chum vient de me lâcher, je me fous des perroquets.

Sven comes back with bottles of Molson. I give one to the girl pour qu'elle puisse noyer son chagrin, je pense, if I were a guy, I would get her on the rebound, surtout ce soir, everybody is on the rebound, would le Québécois fleurdelisé take advantage, Pierre would, I glance at Sven.

Lui, c'est Sven, I say to the girl.

Duane, he says.

Sven Duane, de Distraction, au Manitoba, I add. This is the pirate girl, I say to Sven. Moi, c'est Ariane.

Whatever, she says, guzzling half her beer. On va se raconter nos vies, là, j'imagine, she says with a laugh that sounds like a snort. Ton Anglais, là.

Il est Suédois, I say.

Ton Anglais suédois. Hé! Chez vous, when you fall in love, do you stay in love?

Why do you ask?

Maybe it's more healthy là-bas, she says, les champs de blé et tout ça. Maybe people's hearts are not so fucked up.

Son chum vient de casser avec elle, I say to Sven.

What's a cassay-ave-kelle? he asks.

That sends the girl roaring, I tell Sven we are not laughing at him, she tells him her boyfriend's a fucking fink, Sven drinks his beer, she announces she works dans un hôpital pour les incurables.

In that place, she says to Sven. People stay alive just to wait for death. Rien d'autre. Une vraie danse macabre. Cha-cha-cha down the black hole, she taps him on the knee.

She guzzles her beer to the last drop, he gives her another one, she drains half of that, l'alcool qui délie la langue.

Les gars, toute une gang de pricks, she says, licking beer off her lips, resting her hand on Sven's knee. Maybe not where you come from, she says, squeezing his knee, clinking her bottle with his. À soir, mon ostie de chum me dit qu'on n'est pas compatibles and out the door he scuttles. Pas compatibles! How was I to know? Each time I asked him what was the matter, he said, rien. Rien! Maudit cave.

I ask Sven if he understands what she is saying.

She's unhappy.

She finishes her beer, we give her another, she tells us she should admit herself to her own hospital.

Mon cœur, tu comprends. Incurable, mon cœur.

She looks at Sven, rests her fist over her left breast and makes it beat like a fish dying in the sun, the parrot's feet shift on her shoulder, I want to check the stitches, but she goes on talking about her hospital work, emptying bedpans, preparing pap in the basement kitchen, washing sheets in industrial machines, dealing with humans with one foot in the grave.

The classy woman, she says, rubbing Sven's thigh. I clean up her mess ten times a day, each time she says, I'm so embarrassed, Miss, that never happened to me before. And the burly man, his spine collapsing, he can't look at the sky anymore. I fixed little mirrors on the tip of his shoes. Fuck. Puis à soir, mon chum. You don't suspect a thing, that's how it starts. A tiny crack in your lifeline. Okay, fine. Just a small one. But watch out. The beginning of the end, fuck de fuck.

Une ballade québécoise starts playing, Sven takes her by the arm.

Let's dance.

Une valse? Je sais pas danser ça, moi, la valse.

Vas-y, I say. L'homme est un sorcier.

People move chairs and tables to make room for them. They waltz in the cramped space surrounded by une palissade de chaises, but their arena seems to expand as if seen through a gallery of mirrors, in the false mirrors the elegant woman dances, no longer fearing her incontinence, the giant man uncoils his spine, immense python climbing the sky, the pirate girl, as light on her feet as if she were dancing with the devil, what can she give him in exchange for such lightness, but her incurable heart.

The green parrot lies on the floor, his feet tangled in a mess of thread, I set the plastic bird on my lap, weave the purple thread around my fingers, the music stops, people applaud whistle, the girl steadying herself against Sven so tiny she disappears into his whiteness.

J'ai besoin d'air, she yells.

People open a path to the door, Sven supports her, they rush outside, Raymond comes on stage with his guitar, he spots me, I have to stay, will Sven come back. Raymond annonce sa nouvelle composition, Chanson pour Elizabeth.

My heart knots into un point au cœur, oh non, pas encore! must not move, must breathe shallow, Raymond strums his guitar, the thread tightens around my fingers, I need air, Raymond sings about the desert and the sea, water on sand never stays long, Elizabeth était l'amante l'amie, things people say in songs, tears release my breath, fall ploc-ploc on the parrot, we are responsible for the dead, non, responsible for a single death, oui, the parrot slides off my taffeta skirt, I catch him before he falls to the floor, my finger-tips, as purple as my heart, I loosen the thread, the door opens, is Gérard here, bien sûr, he is not, not on a night like this, Sven stands in the doorway, catches my eye, the pirate girl will not dance sa danse macabre ce soir, a moth came in with Sven, searches for the candles, I cradle the green plastic parrot, will dress him up in red and blue and yellow oripeaux, plain parrot, Quetzalcóatl réincarné, forgot to show the pieces of fabric to Virginia, forgot to tell her I will sew them on Gold Rush to break symmetry of precise black and white rectangles, Raymond sings higher notes a cappella, like Elizabeth calling from the other side, at home, emptying her travel bag, ripping her clothes, edges fraying, shapes uneven, Raymond makes music with his mouth, sounds like Elizabeth laughing not angry, just poetry, the moth flutters, takes too long to translate that this light on its wings is fire, ripping strips of blue from jeans, yellow from camisoles, green from pants, Elizabeth packed no red, sacrificing my percale shirt, a fantasy of fibres at my feet, sneezing de la poussière de tissu, hands throbbing from the resistance of cloth, Raymond looks soul-ful, the exhaustion elation of ripping, he finishes the voice soul-oh, sings words again, strums cords, au temps des vrais beaux jours, don't worry there will be plenty more, a chair grates against the wooden floor, I smell a freshly lit cigarette, feel her hand on the nape of my neck, we are responsible for the dead but the dead must rest, I look back, Sven seems to understand the lyrics, she is unhappy, he said about the girl with the broken heart, the last notes get lost under applause, we are searching the streets for the pirate girl.

I left her in a doorway, Sven says. I didn't want you to think I walked out on you, but I must make sure she's all right. You can go back, if you want. I didn't know the singer was your friend.

Where is she?

He looks lost, turns west, walks à grandes enjambées, long legs made for wheat fields, we follow rue de la Commune as it veers off to the south, he does not recognize anything.

All those stones right in your face, he says. That fore-shortened view is very disorienting.

Stop, I say, out of breath. Look, this is already rue d'Youville and up there is rue Saint-Pierre.

Is that significant?

Too far west, Sven. A few more streets and you are home.

He smiles sees himself free of those walls like free of jail, walking into vast distances drowned in vast light.

Let's go back via rue Saint-Paul, I say. This time, I lead, okay?

It's your city.

I call out the main streets we cross, Saint-Pierre, Saint-Nicolas, Saint-François-Xavier, Saint-Sulpice, Saint-Dizier, Saint-Laurent, Saint-Jean-Baptiste.

We danced here, I say. Did you come back with her? Does it ring a bell?

Those streets all look alike to me, he says, waving his arms. How do you make head or tail of all those saint this and saint that?

The bells of Notre-Dame chime.

One o'clock, I say.

Is that significant? he asks again, his tongue in his cheek.

I take his long bony hand, we end up on place Jacques-Cartier, almost deserted now. A drunken voice breaks the silence.

Le p'tit tabarnac! j'vas casser qu'que chose à soir, moi.

That's her, he says. I'm sure I didn't leave her in that dark alley.

She is free to wander, Sven. This is rue Saint-Amable. Another appellation saint contrôlée for your collection. Viens.

The pirate girl is reeling in the middle of that narrowest of narrow streets, her eye patch still in place. She is lining up beer bottles at the base of a brick wall.

J'ai ton perroquet, I say.

Whatever. Salut, le Beau Grand Blanc, she greets Sven, cuddling up to him. Thought I lost you. Sooner or later, sacrament, they all disappear into the white blue yeah wonder.

She picks up the first bottle, offers a toast, guys are all shits, drinks le fond de bouteille, like biting into a half-eaten apple found in a garbage can, throws the bottle against the old bricks, green glass shatters in slow motion, she picks up the next bottle, guys are all pricks, drinks, smashes vitrified sand against fired clay, we wait 'til the jilted girl has thrown all seven bottles, all those guys now out of her system, she lets out a joyous holler, tries to dance with Sven, stops dead, balanced on one foot, completely sober.

C'est-tu ton chum, lui? she whispers in my ear.

I tell her I only danced with him once.

Puis-je? she asks, lady-like.

Je t'en prie, I reply on the same tone.

She brushes against Sven's thigh, asks him if he is busy tonight, if he wants to have a wild time, she raises herself on the tip of her toes to lick his ear, he looks at me, none of my business, if you want her on the rebound, she is all yours. First, she needs a drink, she is parched, second, food, she is ravenous.

On va se raconter nos vies, okay, she says, cuddling. No point rushing into things. The Big Bang only takes two minutes flat. Anticipation, mon Beau Grand Blanc. Tout est dans l'anticipation.

Frightening shouts warn us we have toppled over the other side of the night, les fêtards have turned nasty. A human wave fills la rue Saint-Amable, the voices rumble as one, hands armed with sticks beat on pots and pans, a deafening racket, the kind of noise that terrified battle horses, faces slashed with smears from blackened corks close in on us, I grab ma valise, we retreat toward the other end of the short street our only exit, the compact mass engulfs us, the rhythmic beating splits my eardrums, the pirate girl laughs slaps shoulders, elle encourage l'anarchie, la cacophonie, hands press on my breasts, slide down my belly, my heart beats so fast my throat throbs, I use ma valise to shield myself, but must pretend, such fun, fun so wild it is menacing, a girl bites my lower lip, I tweak her nose, she giggles, a guy lifts one stick to make me chevalière de la nuit, taps one shoulder, taps the other, hope he does not crack my skull, he hollers, beats his pot, guerrier féroce, I am pinned against stone steps leading to a door set in a recess, one step two steps to that small refuge, this is no dance, the pirate girl, so tiny, bobs up and down, sinking and resurfacing, caught in human frenzy, madness and desire, quel désir? celui d'être entendus, bang on pots bang on pans, le fracas est terrifiant, Sven, tall tall, a white rock rising above turbulent water, the air reeks of the crowd's collective stink, beer cigarette sweat puke semen, I tighten the grip on ma valise, press against the locked door, ma valise gets trapped in legs like in seaweed, my refuge not protecting, I will be crushed, the fleshy current moves on, I stay anchored to my door, like a mussel to her rock weathering a ferocious storm, Sven and the girl, swept away, spin and tumble dans une valse out of control, the wild ones reach the other end of the street, enfin, they will release my friends, mais non, they beat faster and louder, I squint watch as the wider rue Saint-Vincent gives les fêtards space to break into une folle farandole.

Viens avec nous, the pirate girl shouts, appearing and disappearing, waving her arms. Viens-t'en, la gypsy. Viens-t'en, sacrament.

Ariane, you're not going to see me off? Sven calls out.

Four o'clock, Sven, I shout. Four o'clock in front of Notre-Dame.

Soudain, le silence. One could drown in so much silence. I check that both clasps of ma valise have not sprung half-open, resume my walk, feels like le Vieux-Montréal two centuries ago, in Jeune-Montréal did pirates with yellow eye patches attack la ville fortifiée, in the distance, in my century, sirens, la police les pompiers les ambulances, all rushing to a carnage, we have reached le cul de la fête, le Saint-Jean-Baptiste décapité sur Sherbrooke, cette urgence d'être entendus, on a night like this, débris everywhere, I walk, thirsty, so thirsty.

With my nails, I tap on shop windows, sounds like raindrops hitting the glass, thirsty, so thirsty, my lips stick together, a glass of water, tap, a drop of orange juice, tap tap, pitié pour l'assoiffée, tap tap, tap tap. Un fêtard titube past me, his arm extended, puts a bottle of cold beer in my hand.

J'ai assez bu à soir, he says, walking away, his legs like jujubes.

La manne québécoise. Merci.

I drink, wonder what happened to le Québécois fleur-delisé, the bells of Notre-Dame ring twice, je fais cul sec, set the empty beer bottle in front of a shop door, take off my red scarf, shake my hair loose, tie the scarf around my neck, let both ends of man-made-not-worm-made silk trail down my back, the tail of a quetzal, my legs bring me to Gérard's boutique of antiques, the darkness inside so palpable it would spill into the street if the door opened, bien sûr, the door remains locked.

I peer in. Elizabeth's silk caftan hangs on the black mannequin with the ostrich feather in her black nylon hair, my maroon velvet coat keeps it company, draped open over a Chinese screen, its saffron lampas lining catching a bit of street light, I am pleased I lined that coat after all. Peut-être, Gérard drinks alone among his dead things, on that bright afternoon après les funérailles, Gérard drinks cognac, his hand, distracted, squeezing my thigh, Gérard et moi sitting on the Mediterranean blue plush sofa called une méridienne de la Restauration, Gérard wanting to know what Elizabeth said, my mouth against the window says, come out of the dark, the night is almost over, Gérard drinking and telling me when someone dies in someone's arms, la mourante says something, always, Gérard squeezing my thigh, my mouth saying, dans les films, oui, pas dans la vraie vie, tap tap on the window, quelles étaient ses dernières paroles? he was asking, drinking cognac, tap tap, the night slowly pales, I can't bear Gérard to be sad, I said Elizabeth said, his hand squeezing so hard, oh, why did I tell him that, tap tap.

Gérard, c'est Ariane. Ouvre-moi.

Hope he opens, hope he does not, knock again, something stirs, coat and caftan moving in a draft, I slide down into the recess of the doorway, épuisée, all that night walking, a little foggy, that miraculous beer, take the strips of fabric and my sewing kit out of ma valise.

Ce soir, tout le monde se déguise, I say to the parrot.

In the distance, scattered voices let out the last call of les fêtards, the shadow of a car slides past on its rubber shoes, a siren far far away screams briefly, silence falls back, like that gentle rain in the Celtic waltz, what if I took that train, ah, to arrive in the full of summer, pollen-plated Sven sans son habit blanc standing tall in his field of wheat, his whiteness burnt in the noon sun, I smell grass toasted in that sun, can taste les graminées croquantes, hungry, so hungry, with long stitches I sew swatches of brightly coloured cloth, transform the fifty-cent parrot into a bird of paradise with vibrant plumage, si votre ramage, sire corbeau, est aussi beau que votre plumage, imagine a ball where everybody dresses up as the animals dans les fables de monsieur de La Fontaine, what a hoot, will Sven come to my exhibit, l'automne, c'est la saison des récoltes, Virginia cannot say no, my head spins a little, sleepy, so sleepy.

Un lion et une souris waltz together, the green parrot holds a wedge of cheddar in its beak, la fourmi does the jitterbug with the turtle, Raymond sings a Celtic song in a soprano voice, the words, clear as a brook, soft rain falls in the desert, I hear the sea, waves crash and people dance une farandole on top of a white cliff, maman says, un accident est si vite arrivé, Elizabeth smokes with le Québécois fleurdelisé, Gérard prances about in the silk caftan, an ostrich feather in his hair, Sven, son of Duane, does abracadabra over Elizabeth's glass coffin, she laughs, saying, fuck me gently, I can't just get up, I'm dead, remember.

I jump out of my skin, the spit in my mouth thick as cement, the bells of Notre-Dame ring once, I wait for the other rings, no more, le temps n'attend pas, did I miss Sven, would he bother with me, he has the pirate girl, he wanted me to see him off, faire attendre les gens n'est pas poli, I stuff my things back into ma valise, Sven will be gone by now, my legs are asleep, debout, les jambes paresseuses, en avant, marche, I turn the corner of rue Notre-Dame, empty at this hour, must see if Sven, oui, ils sont là, the wolverine in the black pirate outfit clawing the sweet Swede, did he already get her on the rebound, I approach la basilique, la place d'Armes in front of the church, deserted, the sky opens up a crack, I smell a mauve perfume, peut-être du lilas.

Dawn catches Sven whiter than white, the girl clings to l'homme diaphane, I put on my cat's eyes, hide behind one of the portico columns, spy. Sven strokes the girl's hair, red and cropped, she lost her black scarf, still wears her yellow eye patch, stronger daylight pushes the shadows into corners toward the door of the basilica, shadows protect me behind my column, the girl melts, soft as candle wax, la nuit a con-sumé sa rage.

Baise-moi, l'Anglais, she says.

Anticipation, remember? he says.

Assez, là. Time to act, l'Anglais. Baise-moi sur le parvis de Notre-Dame.

He kisses her, long and slow. She climbs him, a wolver-ine climbing a tree. Après la farandole, sans doute, they spent the rest of the night talking, teasing their desire, maintenant, she knows more about him than I will ever know.

Let's go to your place, he says. Ariane's not coming. We have plenty of time before my train leaves.

Es-tu fou! My house needs fumigating. A louse used to live there, remember? Don't worry. When you do things in plain sight nobody sees you. Baise-moi, le Suédois, before I break something.

He hesitates, baiser devant les églises is not done in Distraction, Manitoba, or he is afraid to catch the Montréal plague, he made me waltz in an ancient courtyard, he made her dance on a dime, maintenant, she shows him how to baiser in sacred places.

She pulls down his white pants, pushes his back against the column next to mine, I shrink deeper into the shadows, hold my breath, he is stiff stiff, so close to me I could touch his penis, she kisses his dick, Elizabeth said, dick, she slides down her black pirate pants, lentement, comme une courtisane, she plays avec sa vulve, stares at Sven who stares at her fingers, she offers him her wet fingers, he sucks them, the hem of her flowing black pirate shirt grazes her white buttocks as she climbs the sweet Swede who stands with his back against the column, his feet wide apart to steady himself, she squeezes her small but powerful thighs around his hips, what is she, a medieval acrobat entertaining townfolks in front of churches, she lifts herself and sits on the Swede's cocky member pointing straight at the sky, both sigh grunt as she penetrates herself with him. They press against the stone column, their bodies, jet and alabaster gargoyles fused together in that deadliest of deadly sins, la luxure, their faces, like the faces of saints, turned to the sky, waiting for ecstasy. They find their rhythm, move à l'unisson si lentement they appear motionless, their pelvic plates grind into each other, she presses hands and feet flat against the column to support her weight, she has experience, that girl, his long hands cup

her hips to guide her as he guided us in waltzes, for two people so motionless, they move well together, he the magician,
she the acrobat. I take off my cat's eyes, pick up ma valise.

On the church steps, I leave the green plastic parrot with
wings of blue and a tail of yellow and feathers of scarlet, her
newly baptized bird from paradise, I veer north.

On boulevard Saint-Laurent, I watch the light in the
eastern sky spread like flood water over a dark plain, turn east
on rue Sherbrooke, walk into parc Lafontaine, the sky fully
light-flooded.

Ariane! Hé! ma puce, salut. Quel bon vent t'amène?

Pierre wonders about ma valise, I tell him about the photos, Virginia, my project, we kiss, he tastes as if il a passé la nuit
à parler, no dancing no necking for him and his friends last
night, non, just lots of beer and an all-you-can-eat buffet of
all the words needed to fix the world, he looks happy, they
may have found the solution, does he have the patience to
mend that old old fabric, I tell him Raymond sang au Vieux
Fanal, a new song about Elizabeth, Pierre thinks Raymond
should write des chansons engagées, mais l'amour, c'est un
engagement, I want to tell him, I don't, his tongue may be
too chafed the morning after to engage in a fresh debate.

Guys are shits, I say.

I laugh, tell him about the pirate girl et ses peines
d'amour, am glad Pierre is not my boyfriend, lui et moi
sommes des amis, plain and simple.

Loving friends, he says, en anglais, quoting Simone
Signoret dans un vieux film we saw together once.

Fuck buddies, I say, stray words picked up near McGill.

Nos bons mots send us into a dawn-after-the-carnival fit
of gaieté, what luck we ran into each other at dawn, we step
on cigarettes smoldering in the grass usé jusqu'à la racine by
too many feet dancing, too many bodies fucking, the morning air stale, too many mouths drinking puking the good
time, singing hollering la liberté, such happiness hope,

aujourd'hui, c'est la gueule de bois, demain, on se découdra la bouche, and then what.

We walk smack into les excréments du party impromptu, in my head spin jilted pirate girls' parrots of paradise abandoned at the doors of basilicas, sweet Swedes from far far away, a long summer of no travels without Elizabeth, I slide my arm around Pierre's waist, he wraps his arm around my shoulder, his chest still vibrates with the left-over words de sa nuit idéologique, les mots do not matter this morning, only vibrations and body contact, we are fuck buddies, not fucking at this hour, we both rumble, hungry stomachs stop words.

Viens déjeuner à la maison, I invite.

Holding hands, we run across parc Lafontaine, across rue Sherbrooke, this night ends with an offer of strong Salada tea, as maman nous accueille en robe de chambre. I have never seen her wear anything but her day clothes before.

Tripper

Maman dans la ruelle wears her Playtex dishwashing gloves to pick up trash scattered all over, last night we thought les matous mités were fighting among themselves, in and out of garbage cans, such mauling and mewing on a hot July night made us shiver, this morning, we discovered yoots in heat made the mess, even from our third-floor gallery I can hear her letting escape a discreet, ah, cochonnerie, mais elle s'arme de courage, gathers lengths of toilet paper and steak bones with charred meat still attached, I must help, not barefoot, put on my sandals, open the door to le hangar at the end of the gallery, switch on the naked bulb, le hangar smells of old dust and trapped heat, unlock the other door to the wooden interior staircase, two children's heads poke out of their second-storey hangar, they see me, retreat inside like turtles into their shells, Ana comes out on her landing, carrying an empty garbage can, no gloves, bonjour bonjour, she speaks to the kids in her language, something in her tone stops me from going down, instead I push open the wooden panel, study the rusty iron hook anchored into the masonry that movers use to lift black pianos and white washing machines like puzzled mammouths énormes, when I was little I played dans mon donjon, with the sea breaking at the foot of the tower, les chats de ruelle, great sharks waiting for me to dive off, how often I wanted to throw a rope over that hook and escape like le comte de Monte-Cristo, Ana comes out, she says, ve vere avaken, there is no double you in her language, I can tell, maman is ashamed of those Québécois yoots from last night, what will our downstairs neighbour think, a foreign femme raffinée as versed dans la discrétion as maman, unlike the type of women ready to ring our door-bell at all hours, wanting to borrow a cup of sugar as an excuse to look at our furniture, after the sugar, they complain about their no-good husbands, whine about the scars on their stretched bellies, a tiny step before les calomnies et les médisances start flying d'une fenêtre à l'autre comme des ordures, maman disapproves of le voisinage, her motto for urban living, be polite, but no chatting, this morning, her pinkrubbergloved hands full of garbage, she is chatting with the woman from Bohemia.

I could not bring myself to visit Elizabeth 'til the new year, what does a woman like her want with a girl like me, bien sûr, I was curious to see how she lived, sans doute, in a rambling country house filled with things and people I would not understand, foreign newspapers and garden tools in the living room, jazz playing jour et nuit, unmade beds and dirty wine glasses, cigarette smoke as thick as the London fog in spy movies, I could not bring myself, de toute façon, je n'avais pas d'argent.

The bus fare costs two-fifty return, c'est-à-dire, ten cof-fees au Café de l'horloge. The bus arrives in Saint-Polycarpe at noon and returns to Montréal at five, no need to reserve a seat, just jump on the bus like busy characters in old French movies jump on trains pulling out of stations, kissing madly waving desperately, to be such a character on an ordinary green country bus I need a trench coat, like Françoise Arnoul pursued by Nazis through the rainy streets of Paris, like Jean Gabin catching fatalism in a dive bistro. That Friday in January 1968, eighteen months ago, a movie lifetime ago, I am in bed, no class on Fridays during the winter semester, why don't you

go, whispers the ten-year-old Queen of Spain Queen of
Olives, nothing frightens that warrior queen in her cookie
sheet breastplate, waving her broomstick sword, at the head of
her army of kitchen chairs she assaults the fortress of the
chest-her-field, conquers la flotte anglaise, I can conquer the
strangers in Elizabeth's house, après tout, je suis charmante,
the gallery people said so, Elizabeth invited me, why not make
her world my world, maman chatting with Ana dans la ruelle,
Ana's world now Montréal, en terre d'Amérique, that was no
game when she decided to stay après l'Expo, I dove in, that
January Friday, je pensais, si l'aventure finit en queue de poisson, it will only cost me ten coffees, it cost maman thirty dollars pour m'envoyer à l'Expo, how much did it cost Ana, I
know how much it cost Elizabeth.

   That Friday in January, sunny cold, I slip knee-high black
leather boots over my jeans, must hurry, the bus will not
wait, Elizabeth did not give me her phone number, ce n'est
pas poli d'arriver chez les gens à l'improviste, what if she is
not home, what if she forgot she invited me, I button up the
long rust tweed coat I made out of an old coat from the
fifties ma tante Rita gave me and wind around my neck the
burnt orange scarf I knitted over the Christmas holiday, tear
down the stairs, give the front door a good tug to keep the
wind from pushing it open and anybody from walking in,
take le métro all the way to the end of the line, never been
farther north than la station Laurier, enter terra incognita,
like in a Jules Verne story the train bores through the belly of
Montréal, no monsters to rock us, we emerge in new lands
of light and terrazzo, Rosemont Beaubien Jean-Talon Jarry
Crémazie Sauvé, at Henri-Bourassa, the man on the loudspeaker says, terminus, tout le monde descend, Saint-
Polycarpe, c'est la vraie aventure qui commence.

   To reach le Terminus du Nord faster, I cross two streets
at once along the diagonal, a tug at my hair, un accident est
si vite arrivé, un robineux runs after me across the same

diagonal, brays about flying saucers, waves his arms at the green country buses parked along the curb, water trickling from the kitchen faucet, the ritual before school of morning braiding and lessons in city survival, maman telling la petite Claudette to be prudente, traverse toujours la rue à la lumière verte, le robineux grabs my scarf, his breath smells like the bottom of a garbage can in July, he runs back across the street away from the green aliens, spit dribbles down his chin, water trickling, regarde à droite regarde à gauche, he does not, a truck that is no soucoupe volante misses him by a hair, maudit câlice de fou, the driver mouths nervous angry words not spilling into the street, his window rolled up against the January cold.

In the bus depot, I buy my first ticket, aller-retour, careful not to flaunt my money, the one dollar bill folded on top of the two, the two on top of the five, so as not to draw la convoitise from thieves, the first day of Expo, maman sending me into the world with plenty of advice, watch out for purse snatchers, keep your eyes open but don't stare, don't give your address to anyone, amuse-toi bien, Claudette, I speak clearly but not loudly to the ticket man, sit and wait. A girl my age wearing a knee-length beige shirt of rough linen over faded jeans and with eyes the size of soucoupes volantes talks to me.

Hé! je peux-tu te bummer une cigarette? J'ai pas mangé depuis deux jours.

I wish I smoked. I buy a pack of Export, mon oncle Joseph's brand when he does not feel like rolling his own, when I am little he lets me, la petite Claudette removing the cellophane wrapper, pushing open the pack, pulling off the foil, I get to keep that silver, offering him une cigarette like a vamp in a movie, I push open the pack, offer the girl a cigarette, maman forbidding me to touch mon oncle's lighter, I tell the girl I'm out of matches, she asks a guy, as-tu du feu? I close my eyes, inhaling mon oncle's first draw, the girl's first draw is deep, I get up to wait outside, leave the pack on the seat, through the window reflection, watch the girl eye the pack, pocket it, the cold air plasters itself on my face, like a snowball thrown by bratty boys.

I choose a window seat on the left-hand side toward the back, only les jeunes filles idéales sit in the front, twist the handle of my bag around my wrist, watch people fill the bus, the driver starts the motor, no one sits beside me, the motor sputters, black smoke comes out of the exhaust pipe, the driver's hand grabs the handle that connects to the pipe that connects to the door, as he closes it, the passengers crane their necks to watch une grosse madame run toward us, she hoists herself up the two steps, grabs the pipe that connects to the door, puffs and rolls down the narrow aisle, hits people with her parcels.

S'cusez-moé, s'cusez-moé, she laughs.

She jams herself next to me, nearly rips my shoulder off with her hippopotamus hip, I huddle by the window, she needs two seats only has one ticket, the bus is still in first gear she wants to know where I am from.

La rue Sherbrooke? she says. Ohhh, c'est chic, ça, la rue Sherbrooke. Ma sœur vit à Longueuil. C'est au diable vert mais, la chanceuse, elle a un beau bon-gallows.

Where I am going.

Saint-Polycarpe? Je connais pas ça, Saint-Polycarpe.

If I am still in school.

C'est nouveau ça, le cégep, hein?

La madame quit school after starting grade seven four times, ces maudites longues divisions, but in her days it was different, girls weren't supposed to get a 'ducation, what you need alzebra for to raise children, what you need to know where Mount Vishnou is, sainte viarge, at sixteen she went to work dans une manufacture de culottes d'hommes stitching elastic bands on men's underwear, for fifteen years stitching and stretching and getting knocked up six times, not with the same man twice, she laughs, her jellyfish neck shakes, they didn't have the anticonstitutional pill in those days but she should have known better, en tout cas, c'est la vie. She shifts her hippo hips.

Moé, l'experte en culottes d'hommes, she continues. J'aurais dû leur dire, baissez pas vos culottes! Oups, too late, sainte viarge, she says, miming being pregnant.

I smile see a chorus line of men at her door dropping their underwear one after the other. La madame aux culottes d'hommes with her fat face polished smooth like a stone in a stream is younger than Elizabeth, but looks older in her baggy brown coat she unbuttoned for the trip and her brown fake fur hat. Her busy print polyester dress clings to her nylons, je pense, what kind of underwear does an underwear seamstress wear, probablement, a panty girdle, but she likes to laugh and screw, peut-être, she slipped on pink bikini briefs, I try to imagine that.

My lips are in the mood for stories, maman did not raise me to be a blabberblubber mouth, mais cette madame is easy to speak to, told me right away about ses six amants de passage and her six pregnancies, she wants to know if I have brothers and sisters, non, I tell her my father died when I was little, I don't remember him, maman once let words escape, il est parti pour la gloire, after that she said no more, just drank her Salada tea, for a long time I saw Dead Man dying pour la gloire in the mud under a red sky and played the game, mon père est mort à la guerre, bien sûr, later, counting the years between war conception birth, that made no sense, I should ask maman how Dead Man died, I am old enough to know, la madame agrees, we try to get confortable for the trip.

S'cusez-moé, she says, failing to keep her flesh confined to her seat. Ces bancs-là, c'est pour les enfants d'école. Vous, mademoiselle, c'est pas pareil, vous êtes slim comme un mannequin. Mon rêve, savez-vous c'est quoi, mon rêve? Vous parlez-vous anglais, vous? Good. Parce que je vas switcher en anglais pour pratiquer. One day, I'll take a trip on a train with plenty of room for my legs and seats wide enough for both my hips. Me and my sister, the one who lives in the bon-gallows in Longueuil, one day, we'll go down dans les États and travel luxury-like on the transincontinental train.

I tell la madame my only trip ever was at Expo, around the world in one hundred and eighty-three days, I even had a passport, un passeport de saison, it was called, maman bought it for thirty dollars.

Trente piastres! la madame shouts. Sainte viarge, c'est pas donné.

That is why I spent most of my time at Expo, pour que maman en ait pour son argent, la madame approves, I went every weekend from opening day in April 'til high school graduation in late June, après, I went almost every day 'til closing time at the end of October, parfois, with my best friends, Nicole et Diane, souvent, alone, because last summer Nicole et Diane were nineteen and a half, not seventeen like me, and they were genuine bona fide Expo hostesses, did I have a good time, oui, but I also visited everything systéma-tiquement, I had to learn all about those countries, there were so many, did I get lost, I did, waited in line everywhere too, but had to learn, it was my duty as a yoot, why? sainte viarge, because mon passeport was a special passport only pour la Jeunesse/Youth. In it, an important message said that one day la jeunesse du monde dirigera la Terre des Hommes, we, the yoots, will shape the destiny, ces mots prétentieux written twice, en français and in English, to make sure we understood, la madame shakes her head, she does not want to be a killer of joy, but words sometimes are too big for our britches, I know I know, mon oncle Joseph thought les poli-ticiens, comme d'habitude, got in over their heads, crisse, cette Terre des Hommes will cost us the earth.

La madame gets a box of Petit Beurre cookies out of her immense handbag, she offers me one, I tell her ma tante Rita likes to dunk her Petit Beurre in her tea, la madame too, we eat, crumbs fall on our coats, we don't care, ma tante telling us Montréal will be invaded by tourists, des étrangers partout, and garbage and drugs and pickpockets, ma tante dunking and wondering, the sheer number of visitors will sink those Expo islands, mon oncle Joseph saying, crisse, il va y avoir un quota, figuring controllers at the gates will count the number of feet and divide by two, la madame laughs and laughs, cher mon oncle, crazy as a broom, quand même, ma tante had visions of Expo as a circus cataclysm, with frogs raining into un fleuve Saint-Laurent of blood and grasshoppers devouring Montréal, la madame bites her cookie, she did not set one foot at Expo, let alone two feet, she was never counted, la madame swallows, a lot of people made a lot of money avec cette folie-là, including her boss, à la manufacture, they made tons of special underwear with the Expo logo of the stick people in a circle printed smack on the front panel of each pair, they sold comme des petits pains chauds.

Ma tante Rita heard all the hotel rooms were booked solid for the next six months, she heard people rented rooms in their homes for a lot of money, they would get rich, retire to Florida, did la madame's sister rent rooms in her bungalow, Longueuil was not far from Expo, she didn't, dommage, mon oncle Joseph told ma tante people with walk-in closets turned those into sleeping quarters, la madame says, sainte viarge, if she had known, she could have rented her bathtub, her ad would have read, bath with room, ma tante wanted maman to rent rooms, we have lots of space in our flat.

C'est grand comme une gare, I say.

Big enough for my transincontinental train? she asks.

We laugh à gorge déployée, passengers turn around to stare, we don't care.

Maman suggested ma tante rent her daughters' bedrooms, I tell la madame my two cousins are long gone, married to des Anglais in Toronto, ma tante could then retire to

Florida with mon oncle, ma tante drank her tea and snorted she already has a husband, why would she bother.

Ah, so, your aunt is shopping for a husband for your mom, la madame says en anglais, knowing the passengers are Eve's dropping.

We whisper like conspirators. Oui, I say. Ma tante always wants her to buy new sheets.

Non, non, ma belle poupée, la madame says. No need to rent rooms to find a man. Men are easy to find. The problem is, les hommes tiennent pas en place, she adds, flapping her arms like birds escaping.

Ma tante would not let go, insisting her sister buy modern sunny breakfast dishes to serve beans and eggs to foreigners to show them, not saying what she thought they should be shown, biting into another Petit Beurre, crumbs falling on the table, maman picking them with her index finger, telling ma tante it may be a good idea for other people, but it is not her cup of Salada tea to run une pension pour touristes, d'ailleurs, she has a full-time job, has no time to cook breakfast for people whose names she cannot even pronounce, la madame est d'accord, a working mother has enough on her plate without dishing out more beans, she offers me another cookie.

We talk non-stop, je ne vois pas le temps passer, the bus stops in villages and along the road, parfois, passengers get on and off in the middle of nowhere, the mystery of people's lives, my speaking mouth catches the burning cold seeping through the window, the white sun landscape of winter bleaches my lips, I tell la madame, one day in early summer, I catch the figure of an overgrown schoolgirl on the huge blue glass wall du Pavillon du Québec, variegated girls float by in silk-like polyesters and cotton prints, playful in bell bottoms and peasant skirts, daring in electric knits and open-weaves, carefree in minidresses and floppy hats, c'est moi, that drab schoolgirl drowning in a sea of colours reflected à l'infini on the blue glass sea, I blink, choke a little on a cookie crumb, that day,

things are beginning to exist, I am supercharged like la
Manicouagan, la Mani quoi? la madame asks, I am supercharged, don't know the names of my emotions, but things are
beginning to exist, I scratch and pinch my arm, who hides
under that skin, she tells me I'm too young pour avoir des
idées noires, at my age I should have the time of my life, not
waste my breath asking life questions.

Not so, I say. La jeunesse existe pour avoir des idées
noires, c'est connu.

She wants to know where maman works.

Dans un bureau. Elle est secrétaire particulière pour un
Anglais big cheese.

La madame tells me she too has a big shot Anglais for a boss,
he's a rat, but she knows how to handle him, in fact, that's why
she's on this country bus every Friday, I look out the window,
cannot miss Saint-Polycarpe, la madame is the best seamstress
dans toute la manufacture, her speciality is briefs, you know, the
kind with the opening in the front, she's so good at it and so
fast, her boss calls her the queen of briefs, she laughs her jellyfish laugh, her Friday trips aren't part of her official job, c'est une
entente privée avec son boss, for the past five years, she's been
travelling to the same institution in the woods for wild boys
nobody knows how to handle, she mends sheets and clothes,
brings those poor boys, lost and found, plenty of underwear,
clean and crisp, their road to salvation, her boss pays her normal
Friday wages on Friday and double-time on Saturday, he even
pays a babysitter for her six kids 'til she returns home Saturday
noon, she can't afford to refuse, and how else could she take a
country-air break and see trees instead of a brick wall through
a filthy window, and those boys with no family and big troubles, she tells her kids they don't have much, but they have each
other, I ask her how come her boss the rat is so generous.

Now, he's straight comme un manche à balai, she says,
mais dans sa jeunesse, oh oh, mon boss en a fait des vertes pis
des pas mûres.

Ah, so, that place saved him from hell, turned him from
a crackpot adolescent into a man capable of making pots of
money, now he supplies the institution in the woods with
cloth and manpower, la madame scolded her boss, non non,
sainte viarge, she told him, this is womanpower.

The sun strobes between the tall black spruce, I feel hot
and dizzy, queasy from the cookies, I ask la madame if we are
getting near Saint-Polycarpe, she does not know, I tell her
this is my first trip to visit a friend who has a house just outside the village, at Corona, Elizabeth told me her house sits
on the left side of the road, what does it look like, la madame
wants to know, I don't know, she did not describe it, sûrement, it is a house built solid en pierre des champs, with a
white gallery running around three sides, dormers in the
front, three chimneys high above the gable roof, a summer
kitchen in the back, I cannot be sure, Elizabeth told me
nothing, sauf, if I enter the village I went too far.

C'est ici! I shout.

Icitte, icitte? la madame shouts back.

Oui, oui, I say, getting up. The sign said, Saint-Polycarpe,
un mille, population 1,760.

I climb over la madame who does not move, she cannot.

Ah, so, c'est ça, Saint-Polycarpe. Sainte viarge, on en
apprend tous les jours. Bonjour, là, bonjour.

Au revoir, madame, I say, my coat getting caught between
la madame's thighs.

I tell her I may see her again next Friday, shout to the
driver to stop, stop that bus.

The driver brakes, my elbow hits the back of a passenger's head, the driver pushes the handle that connects to the
pipe that connects to the door, the door opens, I spill on to
the road, breathe a gulp of cold air, wait, when getting off a
bus never cross in front of it, maman braiding by the kitchen
sink instructed often enough, tu vas te faire happer par une
auto, okay, I wait, the bus wheezes into motion first gear, a

snort second gear, a hawk third gear, the bus rolls down the
hill toward Saint-Polycarpe, black smoke running behind,
like it is trying to get back inside the exhaust pipe. The cold
air keeps me from throwing up Petit Beurre in the ditch,
what if Elizabeth saw me.

Il est exactement midi, the church bell sonne l'angélus. I
stand in front of the only house on the road before a sharp
curve leads down to the village. I can see the first houses of
Saint-Polycarpe and the steeple of the church peeking
through the bare black trees. Hard-packed snow bulges down
the walk leading to Elizabeth's porch, like the tongue of the
glacier in my high school geography book, for sure no one
is home no one has been home since winter began. The
house is white clapboard with navy blue trim, the paint faded
in places, peeling in others, the white fence on either side of
the walk leans into the snow almost resting on two large
maples, pots with dead creepers hang from rafters on the
porch. I climb over the snowbank, slip on the two icy steps,
stand in front of a wooden door with a half-wheel-shaped
window, my finger searches for the doorbell, my fist knocks
three times like in tales with ogres.

I wait.

The door opens, Elizabeth appears in a brown sweater
with a hole over one shoulder and navy blue working men's
pants, comme ceux de mon oncle Joseph, and what underneath, boxer shorts, I cannot imagine that, her long blond
and grey hair piled on top of her head mimics the dead
plants on the porch, I don't remember her with grey hair, we
look at each other, she blows smoke, her hand holding the
cigarette rests on the open door high above her head.

Yes, dear?

Bonjour, Elizabeth.

What can I do for you?

I put on my cat's eyes, count to ten, no cheating, if at ten
she does not recognize me, I go and that will be that.

Ariane? she says on the count of four, scanning the road.
Who did you come with?

I took the bus.

All the way here?

It is Friday after, five after noon. You do not remember.

Of course, I remember. It's just. I didn't hear from you. I
figured you weren't coming.

I don't have your phone number.

She stands there searching my face. I glance at the butt
burning toward her fingers.

The next bus is at five, I say, putting my cat's eyes away.
That gives me time to visit your church. For my paper sur
l'art religieux populaire.

Get your ass in here, she says, grabbing me by the coat
collar.

I smell the inside of the house before I see it, apple cores
in ashtrays with cigarette butts, I feel drafts running through
like unruly children. My eyes adjust to the darkness, the walls
bulge, studded with bubbles of plaster begging to be burst
with a needle, my feet stumble on the warped floor, the
whole house stoops like an old woman. Elizabeth disappears
dans la pénombre, walls jut at odd angles into a narrow corridor that itself ends at a wall. Bien sûr, my eyes play tricks,
best to ignore the back wall, Elizabeth could not have walked
through it, it turns into a steep staircase hugging another
wall. Ah, le mystère des escaliers, all my life I wanted to live
in a house with a staircase, un escalier has more enigmas
stacked on its steps than all the crypts in the world, in our flat
on rue Sherbrooke a corridor a mile long runs front to back
connecting the rooms, nothing hidden, not even a secret
panel behind the fireplace, rien, but here lives un deuxième
étage ou un grenier, exciting mysterious. Non non, something is wrong, d'abord, my eyes, maintenant, my mind, from
the road, the house showed no second storey, et pourtant, je
ne suis pas folle, I stare at stairs, avec d'infinies précautions in

case this is another trick, I climb the first step, Elizabeth's call stops my foot, I follow her voice into the kitchen.

The back so different from the front, a house with a light side and a dark side, just like the moon. The kitchen, yolk yellow from floor to ceiling, swims in sunlight, the entire south wall pierced with small paned windows. The garden below and the rolling hills in the distance seem painted on the wall of glass that lets light in, and drafts too. The fat wood stove keeps the cold out when Elizabeth remembers to feed it, that day the stove rumbles, that day I do not know Elizabeth is immune to the cold, is she still immune to the cold, I want her to be warm in the dark earth, et puis, what will happen to her house, I must ask Gérard.

The table is covered with black and white photos, a sketch pad, pieces of drawing charcoal, I am interrupting, a brown teapot and two mugs, I am intruding, my legs want to run away, my curious brain makes my eyes look up. Raymond is standing in the corner of the kitchen between the last window and une armoire canadienne, his fists on his hips, his unlit pipe dangling from his mouth. He looks irrésistible in forest green corduroy pants and a bottle-green Shetland sweater, his brown hair grazes the collar of the white shirt under the wool, I glance at his crotch, what kind of underwear, look at his face again, what do I see in his eyes, not playful mockery like that night at the exhibit, non, what do I see, de la tristesse, oui, c'est ça, did Elizabeth tell him it is over between them, I am intruding, ça, c'est certain.

Salut, he says, taking his pipe out of his mouth.

Bonjour, tristesse, I mumble into my black turtleneck, like we did not have a nice talk on opening night.

Elizabeth asks Raymond to get me a mug, he does not move, she asks if I am hungry.

Non, merci, Elizabeth. Rien pour moi.

Je pense, what am I interrupting, l'atmosphère est à couper au couteau, like when I am little and spend Saturdays

at ma tante Rita's and mon oncle Joseph's while maman
works, parfois, I can hear them fight as I climb the stairs, it
will be one of those Saturdays when breathing and swallowing are difficult, alors, calling from the stairwell, allô allô, c'est
moi, the echo of my voice gives me courage, stumping my
feet, opening the flat door, ma tante and mon oncle standing
in the dining room, like petrified people in science fiction
movies after the aliens stopped time, not looking at each
other, Raymond and Elizabeth look at each other not in
anger, what is the emotion in their eyes, mon oncle and ma
tante greeting me, polite in their mouths, no smile on their
faces, moi opening my colouring book, spreading my
Crayola crayons on a small portion of the table, il ne faut
jamais prendre trop de place, mon oncle Joseph gathering the
sections of La Presse, in Elizabeth's kitchen, I feel like a
beached beluga, obvious and useless, could I take the charcoal, casually sketch Raymond and Elizabeth being blue with
la vie de bohème, mon oncle Joseph looking at my colouring book, saying, une vraie Picasso, Elizabeth lights a new
cigarette, Raymond stares out the wall of windows, mon
oncle rolling a cigarette, saying, crisse, cultive ça, ce beau
talent-là, has Elizabeth just scolded Raymond for not working on his songs, bits of tobacco falling on La Presse, mon
oncle running the tip of his tongue along the paper, flicking
his lighter, a strand of tobacco flaring up, crisse, les artistes, ça
meurt de faim, his eyes, sad sad, like he knows many dead
artists, I want to escape the heat in Elizabeth's kitchen and
take refuge in the cold damp of the village church, what style
of paintings fade on the nave walls, ma tante staring at mon
oncle, mon oncle retreating into the Sports section, moi
colouring barely breathing, mon oncle pretending to read La
Presse and ma tante to dust, should walk away, never come
back, Elizabeth's invitation meant nothing, like ma tante
telling us to come over for supper, not a real invitation, just
things women say.

See you, Raymond says, putting on his duffle coat, leaving by the kitchen door.

That could mean Elizabeth or me or both of us, impossible à dire, singular plurial, les Anglais only have one you for all occasions.

Elizabeth stands like a statue in front of the windows, looks at Raymond cross the garden, listens to his boots crush the snow, watches him disappear behind the garage, waits to hear the motor, he does not rev in anger I give him points for that, glimpses his car drive past her garage, only when the motor fades away, she moves, stubs out her cigarette in an ashtray on top of the fridge, that day I don't know there is an ashtray, it looks like she is stubbing out on Raymond's skull.

If you're not, she says, I am.

Bright cheerful Elizabeth, comme si de rien n'était. She frames my face with her cold hands, kisses me.

How about steak tartare, she says.

Okay, I say, like I eat steak tartare every Friday.

She sharpens a cook's knife on a stone, chops a slab of red lean beef, why doesn't she ask the village butcher to mince the meat, I want to ask but don't, peut-être, she hates butchers.

Ariane, dear, get me the plates chilling in the fridge, will you?

I cannot wait to go écornifler upstairs, en attendant, I take my time finding the plates, a fridge is not as good as a second storey, quand même, it has its secrets, Elizabeth keeps camembert and Velveeta, white wine and a bottle of vodka with the label glued upside down, a skinned rabbit on a blue platter, the rabbit's head still attached, I shut the door before mon oncle Joseph says electricity doesn't grow on trees. Elizabeth piles shavings of raw beef on the chilled plates, makes a well in the middle of each mound with the back of a wooden spoon, breaks an egg into the well. She garnishes the plates with chopped parsley and lemon wedges and what looks like mouse droppings in vinegar and skinned canaries' tongues in oil.

The phone rings. She clears the table, I do nothing not knowing what to do, the phone stops ringing, she makes an island of condiments in the middle of the table with black pepper, this is the first time I see un moulin à poivre like in Italian films, paprika, dark mustard, cayenne, a bottle of Worces that sauce. The phone rings again, muffled, like she keeps it wrapped in a blanket. She sets two places with normal knives and forks, tiny glasses like for playing house and the plates of meat. She lights a cigarette. The phone continues to ring, she finally goes, not looking impatient at all. Peut-être, it is a country party line like at mon oncle Joseph's chalet. Bien sûr, it is not, no more than she served mouse droppings in vinegar and birds' tongues in oil.

Pour ne pas être complètement inutile and because now I am hungry, après tout, it is past lunchtime, I find a frying pan, start to cook the hamburger meat, not on the wood stove, non, on the propane stove that is like a city stove, careful not to break the egg nested in each pattie, how does she eat her Velveeta. Elizabeth's voice so near like she is still in the kitchen makes me jump, the pan dances on the burner.

I like mine raw, Ariane, dear.

I scoop up the patties, put them back fairly intact on the plates, scrape off the layer of cooked meat, wash the pan, wipe the spatters off the stove, look at the snow-covered garden through different panes, the glass thick and wavy, like the house suffers from la grande myopie, I flick through the sketch pad, the house creaks, as if stretching her old frame, I put the pad back on the windowsill, sit, touch nothing, wait.

After the telephone call, Elizabeth no longer has her cigarette, she sniffs the air, smiles funny like mocking but caresses, her cold fingers on my cheek send tingles down my spine. She makes toast, cuts the bread into triangles, piles the triangles in a basket lined with a kitchen towel, pours chilled vodka, no orange juice, she must have run out.

Here's mud in your eyes, she says.

We touch our tiny glasses, elle fait cul sec, refills her glass but does not drink the refill right away, I sip, my lips go numb, I follow her every move, mix a little of the yolk into a portion of the meat, put a bit of raw meat smeared with raw egg on a piece of toast, bite, hold my breath, swallow, pauvre maman, she has difficulty with meat, she could not swallow, même si politesse oblige.

How do you like steak tartare Lausanne, Ariane, dear?

C'est délicieux. Do you always eat so, so unusual food? Steak tartare on Friday, snake kebab on Tuesday?

She laughs, not loud like la madame aux culottes d'hommes, non, an erudite laugh. Erudite laugh just popped into my head.

You have no idea, Ariane, dear, what people eat. Monkey's brain with a silver spoon, fried locusts with chili so hot it pops the top of your skull.

Sûrement, elle me tire la pipe, she is pulling my leg, mon oncle Joseph tells me never act surprised, crisse, never show you don't know something, peut-être, what Elizabeth says is true, she smiles, her eyes on me, her lips on the lip of her tiny glass. We eat, such silence in Saint-Polycarpe, outside, nothing moves, Window with Winter Stillness, like titles of paintings at opening shows, we eat, she says nothing about Raymond, I still feel his presence in the kitchen, pipe tobacco burning, in the sketch pad, his head, his naked foot, Raymond disembodied in charcoal, openings and closings, red dots on description cardboards, vendu, who is Raymond to Elizabeth, muse model lover, why does she go out with younger men, is he the exception, does she have a collection, does Gérard know, there may be clues upstairs, I chew raw meat raw egg, la madame de l'autobus has six children from six different lovers who all ran away, c'est la vie, la madame, so easy to speak to, Elizabeth, too sophisticated for chit-chat, will I give up ten coffees a month au Café de l'horloge for nothing, je pense, is Elizabeth the English pendant to la discrétion de maman, must I now discover la vie in the silences between the words of two languages, I drain my glass of vodka.

Of course, Elizabeth says, the best way is to let the spirit move you. Knock knock, Ariane, dear. Where were you?

Unusual label, I say, pretending to be interested in the bottle of vodka, so not to have to apologize for being lost in my thoughts.

Russian. A friend brought it back.

There was that American man at Expo, I say to say something. He was looking everywhere for the Plastic Eye. Imagine, Elizabeth, un œil gigantesque anchored high in the sky, peut-être, the eye of God, how could he not find it, I tried to help, it was hard not to laugh in his face, pauvre monsieur, bien sûr, there was nothing, my best friends Nicole et Diane, who were Expo hostesses, laughed, but they knew all about the Plastic Eye.

What was it? Elizabeth asks, her face crinkled with laughter lines.

La place d'Accueil à la Cité du Havre. Nicole et Diane said many Yew-Ess people made that mistake. Plastic Eye, that is how the words place d'Accueil sounded to them. Ah, so, I say, trailing my finger along the label, this is Russian. I walked every inch of la Cité du Havre, l'île Sainte-Hélène, l'île Notre-Dame, visited all the pavilions, continent par continent, rode le minirail et l'Expo Express, looked and walked, looked and waited, in queue after queue, mingled with skins of all hue, waited for hours pour aller dans l'ailleurs, got lost dans le Labyrinthe, saw Laterna Magika, got disoriented, so much to see, everything a blur of sounds and colours, like marbles in a blender, L'Homme à l'œuvre, L'Homme dans la cité, so much to learn, toutes ces connaissances nouvelles,

L'Homme interroge l'univers, lost in the dark, ah, l'immen-
sité du monde, Elizabeth, makes me gasp. And now, I add, my
nails raking the Russian label, and now, other people's alpha-
bets.

The world's a fascinating place, she says.

Her eyes, blue so blue, sparkling so bright, it almost
makes me cry the way she says, fascinating place. I can tell, I
touched her. Just like that.

I've been around, she continues. England, France, Greece.
Want to see more. You too, if you wish. India, Morocco,
Afghanistan.

Quoi! I shout. How come I did not see that? I was so
careful not to miss anything. After each visit to a pavilion, I
drew a star on my map. What was l'Afghanistan like,
Elizabeth?

In the real world, I mean. Expo was a teaser.

Un jour, me too I will travel dans le vrai monde, I say,
staring at the vodka label. Oui. I will see everything.

Tourists don't know how to travel, Elizabeth says, blowing smoke toward her yellow ceiling. As I just said, the only
way to travel is to let the spirit move you.

Let the spirit move us, that is how it began. An old desire
of hers, she told me, no assignments to hinder the free movement of the body. Little by little, that idea bore into our
heads. From June to December 1969, our project together,
Elizabeth and me. Can't believe it was only Labour Day
weekend last summer she surprised me with her incredible
invitation. Where would we go? Everywhere. England and
India, France and Morocco, Greece and Turkey, Afghanistan
and Kashmir, Borneo and Japan, Egypt and Etosha, the
Americas, and before coming home in December, she
wanted to make a detour to a mysterious place called the
Charlottes.

Wonderful friends, she said. Am dying to see them again.
Oh, Ariane, dear, you will love the Charlottes.

What kind of women were those Charlottes living together in a mystery place, bien sûr, I looked them up, les îles de la Reine-Charlotte, islands shrouded in mist, dans le hangar, leaning over the opening, I am shrouded in Montréal July heat, déjà, this morning, the brick walls are shimmering, la journée sera chaude, the spirit moving us, for six months asking a million questions, when I am little, les questions sont interdites, qui quoi, où quand comment, pourquoi, cesse de poser des questions, Claudette, elsewhere, questions are allowed, en français, in English, in Pashto, in the tongue of the Ibans, in Hindi, in Japanese, in Bantu, in December in the tongue of the Haida. For six months, nothing to do but move, Elizabeth Gold and Ariane Claude lifting red dirt, yellow dirt, the white powder of bones, for six months, searching for the cheapest room, bargaining hard, a game Elizabeth said we would play, eating in out-of-the-way restaurants, figuring out bus and train schedules, pretending to be lost to see what would happen, a game Elizabeth said we would play, June to December, nineteen years on rue Sherbrooke interrupted, what did I interrupt in Elizabeth's yellow kitchen that first Friday, Elizabeth never told me, I will never know, will not ask Raymond, ça n'a plus d'importance.

Maintenant, another summer stretches à l'infini like the sea like the Sahara, this Saturday in early July, maman chatting with Ana from downstairs from Bohemia, peut-être, a new friend, departures and arrivals, in my backpack, my genuine bona fide passport, dark blue leatherette cover with gold lettering, Elizabeth took my official photo, I ironed my hair, in the photo it hangs as straight as chocolate spaghetti framing my face, I look like a figure in a Byzantine painting, ancient and modern at the same time, my signature, Ariane Claude, a grown-up signature, and twenty blank pages, a virgin passport, valid for five years, in five years I will be middle-aged twenties, Elizabeth will be dry bones in the ground under her black granite, go, I could go on a solo trip.

Time to go, Elizabeth, or I'll miss my bus. Merci pour le steak tartare.

She says next time she will make sashimi, what is sashimi, I don't ask, sashimi means permission, sashimi means Elizabeth wants me to come back next Friday, c'est ça, l'aventure, not knowing. She holds me close, her sweater does not smell of cigarette smoke like mon oncle's shirt, it smells of wet country earth, we exchange phone numbers, like we are genuine bona fide new friends, she writes hers on the inside of a matchbook from la boîte à chansons Le Patriote, sans doute, Raymond sings au Patriote, will I become part of the in crowd, drink apple cider, go backstage, peut-être c'est fini entre Elizabeth et Raymond, Gérard put his foot down or whatever it is people put down in complicated bohemian relationships, I could have Raymond on the rebound like Pierre did with girls at Expo, I could go on a long trip into the real world, non, pas maintenant, I have my project, must finish what I promised, will show Virginia I mean what I mean, openings and closings, rush downhill to the village bus depot, my bladder like la Manicouagan holding so much water, have not peed since leaving home, am queasy, dans la ruelle, maman says, ah, cochonnerie, Ana agrees, I take deep slow breaths of winter air, feel flushed like in July, Ana laughs, the last rays of the January sun, blood smears over the long shadows in the snow, soudain, I vomit shavings of beef, keep my teeth clenched to muffle the sound of haut-le-cœur, retch fast, eyes closed, the stomach spasms may cause les globes oculaires to pop out of their sockets, plop plop in the snowbank, dans la ruelle, Ana helps maman dump something slimy drippy in a garbage can, I pile snow over the mess of red meat.

I am going down to help, but, as I close the wooden panel, their spontaneous laughter stops me.

Café de l'horloge

S uch an urge, see Pierre first thing, tell him about last night, ou peut-être, better say nothing 'til later, must not disrupt son rituel au Café de l'horloge, le temps sacré de l'écriture, he calls his morning writing, peut-être, all I want is to take refuge au café avec mes amis, cut fragments out of photos and work on Gold Rush, serious concentrated like Elizabeth in her studio, I arrive with ma valise de fin de semaine as Jérôme unlocks the door.

Ariane! Salut, he says, letting me in. Tu es bien de bonne heure, ce matin.

He kisses me on both cheeks, his goatee tickles, I hold on to him a little too long, what's wrong, his eyes ask, nothing, my eyes answer, when people say, rien, they mean, tout, he smells like Elizabeth, of damp earth after she worked in her garden, he must have just come up from the dirt basement where he stores his supplies, the way he glances at me, he knows I have not slept last night, have not been home, his eyes linger on the scratches on my left shoulder, I walk in, the café smells rich, how to resist, my first black coffee of the day, I put ma valise on the table between the counter and the brick wall, stand at the zinc counter, pour lots of sugar in the cup, the white hard grains dissolve in the black oily vortex the spoon creates, I sip the bitter sweetened potion, expect the racing of the heart, Jérôme tells me to dab peroxide on those raw marks, they look nasty, tu vas t'infecter, he says, how did I, he wants to know, just scratches, nothing to worry about, he worries plenty, regarde-toi, he says, meaning my not-so-white gypsy skirt, my sleepless face, meaning what, exactly, that I may go off the deep end, the deep end of what, I carry my cup to Pierre's table, open ma valise, wait for him to arrive.

I dip my hands in Elizabeth's photos like in black and white autumn leaves, start to cut precisely measured rectangles, three inches long by two inches wide, must not be sloppy, sinon, Virginia will reject, the work of an amateur, she will say, I cut, black clouds, the sooty brick wall of a factory, the close-up of a dead fish in sand, my hands search for cheery subjects, find mossy tombstones, mountains in mist, outside the café window, perfect summer light, dans ma valise, the carcass of a moose, never noticed before so many dark things in Elizabeth's photos, Elizabeth, so full of lifelove, here it is again, a woman's face blackened by years spent in the cold, why darkness, sans doute, it is required of artists, oui, le spleen, la mélancolie, beauty in sadness, quand même, Gold Rush 1969 must also reflect light lightness life.

Ma maudite chienne! a man yells.

The voice like a car backfiring makes my pupils dilate, outside, a man in beige shorts is shouting at a woman in a cotton dress huddling against an iron staircase, maudite folle, femme de cul, her body accepts his insults like a bunch of daisies, my hands find a city street at night with dim lights and long shadows, bien sûr, the shadows are menacing, what's the point of them if they don't mean fear, that man à grande gueule spits and hisses.

Deck him, I say, cutting.

My hands shake with fear anger, nothing to fear here, last night, why didn't I deck him, I touch the scratches on my shoulder, the woman walks away, the man screams, not looking back, she raises her hand, her hand commands silence, last night I wished.

Les habitués du Café de l'horloge begin to arrive, they all slept last night, faces glow fresh, jeans and tee-shirts not slept in, feet in sandals, pink and cool.

Salut, Jérôme, salut, salut.

Their words bounce bright between brick walls and tin ceiling, simple words said millions of times by millions of people, quand même, en ce si beau matin de juillet, they sound new, still no word from Pierre, he writes every morning at this table, he will become un écrivain engagé, un jour, he will, he will, un jour, the white pages wait for him, he writes in black ink or red ink or violet ink, in pencil or with the fountain pen his mother gave him when he graduated from university or with un stylo from la station Texaco where he goes quand il a des ennuis mécaniques, the mood dictates the writing tool, parfois, les mots ne viennent pas, he etches the paper with his nail, as if they were hiding in the fibres, les mots, visibles ou invisibles, lui donnent toujours du fil à retordre, words he read elsewhere, words he must steal, he rakes his fingers through his black hair, pulls on his beard, préoccupé par tous ces mots qu'il a volés, à quoi bon, he says, all the words have been taken, peut-être, he will choose not to write another word, but then, how can he become un écrivain engagé, pauvre Pierre struggling with le doute la peur le désir le dégoût, if Baudelaire could write about le spleen de Paris, sûrement, Pierre can write about la mélancolie de Montréal, sûrement, he can discover new angles hidden deep inside used words, as Elizabeth shot the beautiful dark corners of sad things, Pierre is late for work.

Each time the door opens, I squint at the newcomer who stands in the entrance to adjust his eyes to the dimness of the café before walking in to join the others, they drink their coffee, roll a cigarette, inhale exhale, read their newspaper, pay, they are gone, out of my sight and into the mystery of their lives, each time the door opens, I expect Pierre, hope l'homme from last night will not hunt me down. Who do you think you are, girl, cet homme a d'autres chats à fouetter, I laugh at myself. Jérôme works the coffee machine, butters toast, piles croissants in baskets, lights a cigarette, lets it burn in the ashtray under the counter, I tell him when Elizabeth was busy with things on her mind, par exemple, when I was talking too much and she didn't have time to listen, she said she had other fish to fry, he does not understand, I tell him en français we whip cats, in English they fry fish, what does he think the Chinese do, he leans over the counter and asks again if everything's all right.

Bien sûr, Jérôme. Apporte-moi un autre café. Tout va bien.

I must cut, no time to lose, newspaper pages turn at regular intervals, as regular as le tic-tac of the grandfather clock in its alcove between the window and the door, toutes les choses à leur place, Jérôme puts no music on, his customers like it quiet this early in the morning, le Café de l'horloge is full of guys, no girls at this hour.

It's a must with men, Elizabeth says, pushing smoke out of her mouth toward the yellow ceiling in her kitchen. They must read the newspaper. I tell you, Ariane, dear, for them, a day without a newspaper is like a day without a shit. Sure, they'll get through their day, but they won't feel satisfied.

It is true, I say. Mon oncle Joseph reads La Presse every day, and on those Saturdays I spent at mon oncle's and ma tante's when I was little, it is true he read aussi dans les toilettes.

See? A newspaper's a laxative.

You are so right, Elizabeth. Mon oncle keeps piles of old La Presse on a shelf dans la bécosse au chalet. I would never read a newspaper there, non, the smell of cold shit makes me gag, why would I sit dans la bécosse longer than necessary, but mon oncle says, crisse, pas pour lire, Claudette, pour t'essuyer, he tells me that while sawing firewood, so ma tante will not hear, je ris comme une baleine, bien sûr, he is joking, the newspapers are for lighting the wood stove, d'ailleurs, there is always plenty of toilet paper dans la bécosse, he says, crisse, what if you ran out?

Mon oncle's eyes sparkle, Elizabeth chuckles, I laugh and laugh, have to stop cutting, Jérôme looks up, a smile on his lips, imagine, I tell him, people walking with printed words on their bums, you would need a mirror to read the words, because la guerre, le hockey, un incendie would be printed behind your back and would be transferred in reverse, news like le Congo devient le Zaïre, countries too are allowed to change their names, news like le premier ministre du Québec déclare, but his name would be lost in the dark canyon between the cheeks, les habitués Eve's drop, they too have a smile on their lips, la mode du printemps, accident mortel, vente chez Eaton, I continue, all kinds of news printed sur le derrière des gens, the classifieds would make a herringbone pattern, there would be people's faces too transferred to people's bums, the faces of politicians, actors, businessmen, sports people, les habitués laugh at that, Elizabeth's accident-carnage, old news that will end up in someone's bécosse, I take a deep breath. Jérôme wants to know more about the accident, I tell him Elizabeth made me see things, I must continue to look sans Elizabeth, Jérôme goes back to his croissants, the customer at the next table watches me over the pages of Le Devoir, même si, I was taught not to stare not to squint, I must see, can't you see I must see. I go back to my cuttings.

Even in movies, Ariane, dear. Have you ever noticed? Elizabeth asks, sipping her wine.

Non.

Unless the character is pointing a gun at the camera or holding a woman in his arms or sitting in the saddle, she says, the poor sod is made to read a newspaper.

Maintenant, I see it all the time, I tell my cut-outs, in that movie, the man in his suit and tie reads his newspaper, across the breakfast table his wife in her white satin peignoir plots his murder, in another movie, a man lusts after the young woman visiting at his country manor, he feels lusty guilt, goes in his library full of books from floor to ceiling, what does he do, he picks up a newspaper, tries to read, it is no good, he rushes upstairs to make mad love to his wife's sister, I can tell, the guy next to me is trying to figure out the films, men in movies read newspapers on trains, carry stolen photographs of submarines in a folded newspaper, identify themselves as spies to other spies by sitting on park benches with a rolled up newspaper under their trenchcoated arms. It is all true. And here, au Café de l'horloge, my own generation takes over the tradition, la jeunesse qui dirigera, my Expo passport said, all those young males reading Le Devoir, Montréal-Matin, parfois même, Le Monde, no females.

Crisse, Claudette, tu dois t'informer, mon oncle says as he turns the pages of La Presse. Les ignorants se font exploiter.

Ma tante ne lit pas le journal, maman reads the newspaper after lunch, but she works in an office, ma tante stays at home, peut-être, girls of my generation prefer books, Elizabeth read lots of books, fat ones on history, art, photography, novels, modern and ancient, books she found all over the world in dark secret places, peut-être, women are allergic to newsprint, I open La Presse, my fingers itch 'til I wash the ink away, donc, for women it is an allergic reaction, for men a colonic affair, I glance at the toilet door, none of the newspaper readers has gone in yet. Coffee newspaper cigarette, a powerful laxative. Patience, éventuellement, they will evacuate the words.

Jérôme asks me if I wouldn't mind getting a can of confiture in the basement.

Avec plaisir.

He also asks if I wouldn't bring down that tray of sugar bowls to refill them.

Pas de problème, I say, too glad to help and to see the below.

The basement is low, the joists black with age, the dirt floor hard and smooth like cement, the old stone foundations may date from le temps de la colonie, peut-être, Radisson slept here, the space smells of ancient breath and centipedes, those English insects have fewer legs than their French cousins who are called des mille-pattes, Jérôme did not tell me what kind of confiture, I choose une grosse boîte de confiture de pommes et de fraises, set the tray on the floor, begin to fill each bowl with sugar, listen to footsteps, the front door opens and closes often, the toilet flushes, I smile, the water tumbles down the old pipe set against the opposite wall, hope it does not burst, the grandfather clock rings onze heures, eleven dongs in rapid succession, as if the clock wanted to get it over with and return to its quiet tic-tac, I have been cutting for four hours. At the bottom of ma valise I find happy photos, strange, as if light that should be light sank to the bottom and darkness that should be heavy rose to the top, I cut, a sunbeam across a park bench, a lit lamp, Pierre is still brilliantly absent, I cut, a woman's hand resting on a man's scrotum, a child splashing in a lake, the door opens on fierce light, I squint at the disembodied man in the bleached entrance, oh, to see again light-plated Sven as he must look right now in his wheat field, what if this is l'homme from last night, the café is empty, Jérôme stepped down into the basement, the man stares straight at me, he can see my face, I cannot see his, a standoff that takes an eternity of tic-tac of the grandfather clock, he spins around, shutting the door that guillotines the light out of the room, Jérôme comes back upstairs, carrying a crate of oranges, a white towel thrown over his shoulder, I touch my left shoulder, the skin cold and hot, the scratches throbbing.

The mirror dans les toilettes du Café de l'horloge distorts as if smeared with a layer of grease, I run my finger over the surface, it is clean, the glass is warped, c'est tout, I erase my print with toilet paper, polish the surface, Jérôme runs a clean café. I examine my shoulder, the scratches angry, red

and puffy, I could not go home last night, did not want to
worry maman, did not want to lie to her, elle est myope
comme une taupe, mais elle voit tout, she would have
smelled the eel under the rock, d'ailleurs, she is getting used
to my skipping home sleeps, après tout, je suis en voyage 'til
December, I soak cotton wool with Jérôme's peroxide, good
thing he keeps a first-aid kit, peut-être, the law requires it, I
stayed in well-lit places, did not run in dark ruelles like silly
frightened women in murder movies, dab dab, the wound
fizzes stings, went to la gare Centrale, did not pace up and
down dans la salle des pas perdus, acting nervous makes you
look suspicious, the gashes look like une étoile de mer who
lost an arm in a fight with une pieuvre, I could embellish
mon étoile de mer with orange and sapphire threads, catch
the thinnest layer of skin with my finest needle, draw no
blood, back into that room, people would agree this is body
decoration, they would think nothing of it, if I were alone I
would do it, pas maintenant, I cannot risk being interrupted
by someone needing to use les toilettes, what! a girl with an
ugly claw mark on her shoulder and a needle in her hand, no
amount of explaining would ever, I sat down quietly, looked
perfectly normal dans une gare avec ma valise, bought a
novel by Agatha Christie, Une poignée de seigle, it was
called, a sign said, Défense de flâner, I sat on the wooden
bench half the night, my back straight to show I was waiting
for a train, a traveller in transit, not une flâneuse a robber a
murderer, another sign said, Défense de cracher, I read half
the night, if a security man had asked I would have said, je
m'en vais à Distraction, au Manitoba, monsieur, Distraction
is as good a destination as any, if I would have had to buy a
ticket to prove, I would have, Sven, son of Duane, what a surprise to see me, still wearing the same skirt smeared with the
dirt of la Fête, what would he say, such a sweet Swede, even
with the pirate girl he was sweet, it comes from knowing
how to waltz, I bet l'homme last night a les deux pieds dans

la même bottine, his shoes so pointy, he could not dance his way out of hell, quand même, he seemed as gentle as Sven and look what happened, puis, in Une poignée de seigle, which I finished reading at dawn without any security man saying, circulez, circulez, the only character I had sympathy for turned out to be the one who did it.

I pee, endless stream, all that coffee, my thighs shake from squatting so long, never sit on public toilets, maman braiding, tu vas attraper des maladies, elle a raison, who wants to sit cheeks to cheeks with a stranger, I wash my hands, study my face in the wavy mirror, can I bring calm into my eyes, into my hands, I can, let's practice, a dry run, les Anglais say, as opposed to what, concentrate, take a deep breath, hold the breath, exhale, relax the jaw, relax the forehead, let the mouth hang loose, pinch the rim of the lips, upper, lower, pinch hard, harder, how does it feel, like the prick of a needle, not as painful as you thought, non, nothing to fear then, nothing to fear but what people will think, you cannot concern yourself, non, it'll be all right, oui.

Pierre speaks on the other side of the brick wall, I sneak up on him, kiss his cheek at the edge where his beard grows, where the skin is soft and smooth.

Je veux te parler, I say, trying to direct him to his table.

La lutte, la résistance, la conscience sociale, he says to Jérôme, c'est ça, le lexique-de-la-liberté.

He has taken off, his words strung together, as long as a comet's tail.

Jérôme polishes the zinc of his counter.

Quelle liberté? I ask. La liberté d'une femme est si fragile.

Ah! Tu as vu le documentaire, hier soir, he says.

Quel documentaire? I ask, telling him I want to talk about la vraie vie as it unfolded last night, a real-life story.

Le moment est venu d'agir, Pierre says to Jérôme. Il faut cesser de voir petit, il faut cesser d'avoir peur.

J'ai agi, I say.

Il faut se battre, lutter, he says to Jérôme, his finger tracing the red marks on my shoulder.

How to break through without getting burned, agir, c'est bien beau, but we must know what to do, how and when, he goes on, les ouvriers et les étudiants must unite now, talks about the crushing of la bourgeoisie, as if la bourgeoisie were a head of garlic, I want to know if that was le message du documentaire, because those words seem usés jusqu'à la corde, like the Persian rug dans notre grand salon, those worn-out words will crumble in his mouth, he will choke sur la poussière des mots, he thinks blood-spilling is unavoidable, what blood, I tell him it's all in the timing, he finally looks at me.

C'est la marque du destin, I say.

Bien dit, ma puce, Pierre says, squeezing my left shoulder. Il faut nous engager, Jérôme.

Lâche pas, bonhomme, Jérôme says to Pierre. Écris au lieu de parler. C'est ça, ton rôle.

Pierre wants to know what Jérôme sees as his role dans tout ça, as if running a café trahissait la Cause, Pierre's words and the black coffee Jérôme pours him splatter in the white stoneware cup, Jérôme tells his old friend not to spit on the working man, Pierre didn't mean, I tell him how can we feel good in the city if any minute we may be assaulted, Jérôme reminds him that les cafés et la révolution have always gone hand in glove, la fomentation in a coffee cup, the way Pierre slaps Jérôme on the back, he approves of that.

Pierre and I sit at his table, him not writing, me not cutting, he talks and talks about ce documentaire that so impressed him, the bright morning flattens into noon, people come in to eat, complaining how hot it is today, in winter, they come in saying, on gèle comme des rats.

Noon is a busy time au Café de l'horloge, I should order food, at this hour, the reasonable thing to do, Pierre doesn't have to, he and Jérôme went to collège classique together in the days before cégep, in the days when les Jésuites taught them le latin et le grec, Pierre can just sit at his special table, his head against the brick wall, order nothing and watch the place fill up, vieille amitié oblige, Jérôme puts music on, les chansonniers québécois chantent l'amour du pays, la solidarité.

Ça, Pierre says, c'est notre vécu.

Where is the girl who comes in to help at noon, I never remember her name, Jérôme prepares food, the girl with no name serves the customers, chats with les habitués, cleans the tables, sweeps the floor after the crowd has left, Jérôme slips upstairs for a rest, she sits behind the counter, counts her tips, Jérôme pays her once a week, she serves the rare mid-afternoon customers, habituellement, girls from la banlieue who come downtown to shop, at five, Jérôme comes back downstairs, she takes off her apron, goes aux toilettes, comes out, her eyes made up, says, à demain, she is gone, I never remember her name.

Jérôme dices and chops, sweats behind the counter, orders are lining up, I bring the plate of salade niçoise and the plate with pâté sur baguette avec petits cornichons to the tables, take orders from les clients who just came in, Jérôme inspects my feet in their leather sandals, should have washed them in the sink when I was dans les toilettes earlier, again, he looks at my skirt, wonders what is wrong with our washing machine.

Je suis en deuil, I say.

The noise prevents him from hearing, I repeat, he does not understand the connection, my hands try to flatten the wrinkles in the taffeta, the tank top cannot hide the scratches on my shoulder, quand même, Jérôme hands me the girl with no name's apron, a spotless white apron with a bib and a pocket for the order pad and pencil, I hope I don't mix up the orders, try to act like I have been a waitress all my life, je dois faire preuve d'initiative, that is what Elizabeth would have taught me en voyage, I will do her proud.

All the noon customers know Pierre, a few of them sit with him after their meal to drink their coffee and smoke their cigarette, they talk about Pierre's révolution sur papier, he has so many plans to write, has not decided in what shape, like trying on a dress pattern, making alterations, I serve a cucumber and avocado salad, refill a cup of coffee, Pierre struggles, not sure if the old words still fit, l'exploitation, l'indépendance, if they still have style, notre langue, nos droits, I know what he means, a dress is a dress, pants are pants, quand même, I too want to give the old clothes a new shape, even if body parts remain the same, la révolution et la création, Pierre says, comment réconcilier, lengthen the bodice and drop the waist, but that has been done by les grands couturiers, il faut écrire notre parlure, Pierre says, make buttonholes and sew buttons instead of following the pattern and constructing a fly zipper, but that too has been done, I bring a wild strawberry tart to a customer, a girl who eats nothing but dessert, Jérôme's grandmother picked les fraises des bois, I picked strawberries once in Saint-Pol's woods, Elizabeth was not into strawberry picking, Pierre picks words, la droite, la gauche, pure laine, les quartiers défavorisés, he pulls on his beard, what to do with la résistance, les remises en question, Pierre, on pins and needles.

Mademoiselle, a customer calls out with her index finger up in the air. Du pain, s'il vous plaît.

Le peuple qui demande du pain, Pierre says, we need more than bread, I write p-a-i-n on my order pad, show it to the woman and her friends, tell them, two languages, same spelling, but two meanings so vastly different, le pain du peuple, en français, the pain of the people, in English, how to reconcile, and that is just one word, they don't want words, I nod, du pain, tout de suite, I feel for Pierre's struggle with words.

No pain in Vivaldi playing. The afternoon lull au Café de l'horloge, Jérôme went upstairs, Pierre writes, I sit behind the counter, my tips counted, the dishes washed, the floor swept, the water topped up in the Mason jars holding fresh daisies on each table, my hands on my cottonaproned lap, in a lull. A good word, lull, nous on dit, les heures creuses, une belle expression, bien sûr, but a single word like lull pleases me, I see a slack sea stretched to infinity, feel the substance of the lull in le tic-tac of the grandfather clock, in the midday heat working its way through the brick walls, in the silence under the skin, I breathe, Vivaldi plays, Pierre writes, Jérôme sleeps dreams.

Pierre tells me Jérôme does not sleep, he dreams wide awake, he dreams of a chain of cafés des arts, how many coffees at twenty-five cents will he have to pour to build his string of cafés, he will exhibit young artists struggling with art galleries, will invite poets to read and chansonniers to sing, I told him about Raymond, Jérôme cannot pay anyone, it is always like that in the beginning, but he will give everyone a place to be seen, a place to be heard, Pierre favours l'art populaire actuel, Jérôme continues to lean toward l'Europe des Jésuites, Pierre keeps saying, on doit vivre notre culture, ici, en Amérique, on est des Québécois, Jérôme laughs, promises to leave l'Europe aux Européens, upstairs, Jérôme dreams wide awake.

Un fracas lops the lull, I jump out of ma rêverie, three girls with shopping bags crowd the entrance, I greet them, bonjour bonjour, they check the empty room, consult each other, finalement, sit at a table by the window, Pierre ignores the disruption, his head propped up against his left hand, his pale fingers splayed out in his dark hair, his writing hand runs across paper, the girls assess him, I brush invisible crumbs off my white apron, they order trois cafés glacés, avec beaucoup de crème fouettée, specifies the girl with the orange tank top, the girl with the white Indian shirt fans herself furiously, mon dieu qu'il fait chaud, she looks like she will faint of ecstatic exposure, je pense, are there smelling salts in Jérôme's first-aid kit, the girl with freckles at the corners of her eyes wants to know if we serve real whipped cream ou si c'est de la crème en push-push, she presses saliva bubbles between her teeth to imitate the sound of pressurized cream pushed out of a can, Pierre raises his head, the girl's friends make her stop, they giggle, Nicole et Diane et moi when we were that young going to A&W sur Sainte-Catherine, slurping our root beer through straws, the last drop making rude funny noises, sucking and giggling pour emmerder les madames anglaises who had been shopping chez Ogilvy, judging us, no class, sinking their teeth into their burgers, smearing ketchup over their redlipsticked lips, I tell her we use real whipped cream.

Now, they are hungry, will compete for the writer, order food from the blackboard menu above the counter, les chanceuses, none of them have to squint, I wait, pad and pencil in hand, like une vraie serveuse avec beaucoup d'expérience, peut-être, they think I own this place, du pâté et des toasts, hold les petits cornichons, for the girl in the Indian shirt, the girl with the orange top cannot make up her mind, I tell her everything comes fresh from the country every morning, Pierre lifts his head, smirks, I recommend the garden salad, the girl with saliva bubbles between her teeth and freckles at the corner of her eyes orders a smoked meat sandwich, I squint at the board, we don't have that, I suggest jambon sur baguette, I ask Pierre if he wants a coffee, he stretches.

Apporte-moi un expresso allongé, he says, rolling a cigarette.

I am busy behind the counter, the clock rings four, I search the fridge for the food, open containers, where is the mustard, where is the bread, look for the knife to cut a tomato, I am hungry, should eat a proper meal, peut-être une salade niçoise, I arrange the food artistically on the plates, saw

Jérôme do that often enough, bring the girls their late lunch, how to work the coffee machine, trois cafés glacés, un expresso allongé, the machine, a monster insect squatting on the counter, instructions in Italian and English stamped in black metal letters against stainless steel, the buzzing sound coming out of English mouths, like a cloud of maringouins in my ears, the English tongue, like the stages of an insect's life, d'abord l'œuf, ensuite la larve et la chrysalide, finalement l'adulte, we learned that in school, in the egg stage English was pure mouth noise, arrrr, awohhhh, I am Queen of Spain Queen of Olives, c'est jeudi, ma tante Rita and mon oncle Joseph had supper with us, habituellement, they visit only on weekends, today maman came home early to roast a chicken, I did not have to go to ma tante's after school, peut-être, it was une fête, because mon oncle opened a bottle of white wine, I had a sip, the wine gave my jaw cramps, the chicken skin was gold and crispy, I asked for a thigh, got a thigh, mon oncle took the other one, maman and ma tante ate breast, mon oncle and I pretended to cross swords with our thighs, we all laughed, now, they are talking and laughing in the dining room, I am moving my army of kitchen chairs through the great plain du petit salon, en avant, mes braves, marchons, conquérons, we are fighting the infidels, I speak command non-stop, the ships from England are sailing to invade my land, we embark on the Santa Maria, le grand salon, c'est la pleine mer, I put a cushion from the chest-her-field on the Persian rug, the burgundy and gold brocaded cushion, the rich ship of the Queen of Spain Queen of Olives, I spit speeches at my army, les Anglais, nos grands ennemis, one day the English wriggling larva will become a fully-grown insect capable of biting with words of meaning, pas encore, I am learning English in school this year, understand nothing, je pense, English is the contrary of French, black means blanc, old means jeune, death means vie, we meet les Anglais at sea, I throw tous mes antonymes at them, my mouth now full of soft caramel, je vous répondrai par la bouche de mes canons, I say like Frontenac said dans notre Histoire du Canada, we understand each other parfaitement, le capitaine anglais and the warrior Queen of Spain, mon oncle calls me into the dining room, must leave my ship and army vulnerable, must respond tout de suite when called, mon oncle wants me to get le bouchon de liège on the kitchen counter where he left it after he opened the wine, the kitchen smells of roast chicken, the pan soaks in the sink full of soapy water, eyes of grease float between soap bubbles, like insects drowned with their eyes looking up, I dip my finger into the pot of mashed potatoes, lick the leftover paste, find le bouchon de liège, run back to the dining room, mon oncle says, mets le bouchon dans ta bouche, blablabla, un moulin à paroles, crisse, cork it, maman and ma tante laugh, I rush back to my ship, the cork in my mouth, perfect, I really sound English, the words soft and muffled, better than caramel, the captain orders his ships to turn around, with le bouchon in my mouth and with mes antonymes, I cannot be beaten, I am fully bilingual, victoire!

Clanking of armour, the high-pitched scream of escaping steam, a black liquid comes out of the machine, the scent, strong and chewy, I am pleased, I conquered the machine, bring their coffees to my customers, wipe crumbs and tomato seeds off the cutting board, the girls eat and giggle, a chorus of seabirds, les folles de Bassan, I smile at that, Pierre writes, his tense shoulders show he tries hard to ignore them, the girls know they are having an effect, which one will take the prize, I don't care, just want to tell him about last night, the clock counts les heures creuses, Vivaldi has finished, I let Albinoni play, bunchofpricks rises in my head in rhythm with le tic-tac de l'horloge, a mystery word, sans doute, mon oncle Joseph said that once, probablement, he heard it in his machine shop, I am in grade seven, Nicole et Diane just transferred from another school into my class, they had to do grades five and six twice, I defy them to throw ma balle bleu-blanc-rouge like I do, as high as the edge of the brick wall where it meets the flat roof, but without losing it on the roof, hé! bunchofpricks, I invite friendly, they are older than me, will not want to play a kid's game, they do, after that, nous sommes inséparables, hé! bunchofpricks, venez danser à la corde, hé! bunchofpricks, allons nous promener au parc Lafontaine, we are best friends, une pour toutes, toutes pour une, that year, bunchofpricks is my favourite word, nobody knows where it came from, nobody knows what it means, Nicole et Diane do not know, our teacher does not know, certainement, if maman knows she does not tell, pour l'amour, Claudette, I'm voiding, she says behind the bathroom door when I knock and ask, bunchofpricks means nothing, a genuine bona fide English word with no meaning, mais bientôt, English will turn into une chrysalide, the full meaning will open its wings, the three girls talk about boys, clothes, the pill, their favourite bands, Pierre struggles avec les mots volés, notre destinée, le grand débat, maîtres chez nous, how to tell notre histoire au jour le jour, Jérôme comes back downstairs, his big curly hair damp from the shower, in tight white jeans and a white tee-shirt, he looks as fresh as if he had slept, I take off my apron, the lull is over.

Dans les toilettes, I dab more peroxide on my shoulder, the marks are scabbing ugly, not to worry, it will heal. When I come out, Pierre is sitting with the three girls, words spilling out of his mouth, parler, c'est si facile, customers occupy almost every table, evening has begun. The evening people, more animated than the morning people, chat and check the cinema listing, will they see un film à l'Élysée, au Verdi, what will I do tonight, I check the door, which of the three girls will Pierre take home tonight, is he doing research for his writing, he says he needs to listen to people's speech pattern, notre parlure, he calls that.

Jérôme puts on early evening music, jazz, I sit at Pierre's writing table, drink une citronnade, the light outside the

window has changed, une lumière rousse, oblique and full of
dust, la poussière des mots people spilled all day as they
walked along rue Saint-Denis, it is hot in le Café de l'horloge,
Jérôme turns on the ceiling fan, we are movie characters
stranded in the tropics, when the villain shows up, the sultry
adventuress will deck him right across the room with her
voice, deep and steady, her words, sharp and cutting, a girl
with a red headband reads a book, a pot of tea in front of her,
I squint, cannot read the title, Elizabeth's front rooms, full of
books, what will happen to her books, I must ask Gérard,
another girl in a miniskirt rose langue de chat sits sideways,
her legs wide apart, her fist between her legs pushes the hem
of the skirt flat against the seat of her chair, she talks intently
to a guy with a long beard sparse like cheesecloth, Pierre se
fait une rouleuse, he shows the girl with the Indian shirt how,
she piles too much tobacco on the paper, it falls on her shirt,
at another table, un jeune homme idéal in a suit and tie, how
can he breathe in this heat squeezed in polyester, his coffee
with the spoon standing straight in the mug so close to the
edge his elbow brushes against it, gives his newspaper a good
shake to remove creases, folds the pages backward three times,
keeping visible only the article he wants to read, like he is on
a crowded bus, he could be Elizabeth's Newspaper George
when he was young, ce jeune homme idéal reading the paper
au Café de l'horloge may also have a wife and a mistress.

    Men like George, Elizabeth says, the afternoon of the
newspaper talk, are newsprint addicts. Even on Sundays.
They scour the city to lay their hands on a copy of the New
York Times, then, spend twelve hours reading that.

    How many newspaper lovers did she have, l'homme who
scratched me last night wore black pointed shoes and a black
jacket, no tie, his room was full of old newspapers, un nid à
feu, ma tante Rita would call it, ma tante is right, that guy
smokes like an engine, worse than Elizabeth. Newspaper
George kept the Financial Times under the bed. After, he

reached under the bed, his fingers wet with Elizabeth's scent, gave the paper a good shake before turning the pages.

I told him to stuff it, she says. I told him, you won't share my flesh with the Stock Index.

Peut-être, if Newspaper George had played the game of transferring the Stock Index columns on his sweaty belly, Elizabeth would have found that sexy, a kind of exotic erotic tongue, like Chinese or Arabic, ou mieux, like the Dead Sea language of love lost, but he did not and Elizabeth left him. I stare at le jeune homme idéal, not long, I don't want him to get ideas. I eat ma salade niçoise, les tomates, les olives noires, les tranches d'œuf, like tiny suns with white halos, les anchois, bien sûr, les anchois live in the sea, but look like canaries' tongues, I rinse their saltiness by chewing pieces of buttery lettuce and strips of green pepper.

Vous êtes partie bien vite, hier soir.

His voice, so close, so sudden, how did he cross the room unnoticed, he appeared like the devil, I choke on green pepper, cough cough, tears run down my cheeks, drip on my lettuce, cannot breathe, Pierre rushes to my help, rubs my back, I know people are staring, my finger points at him whose breath smells of ink and smoke, the clock chimes six o'clock, l'heure entre chien et loup, the shadows lengthening, through my coughing tears, I see the tips of the devil's black pointed shoes, Jérôme brings me a glass of water, everything calms down, le jeune homme idéal stares over his newspaper, his mug with spoon still on the edge, people talk again, jazz is playing, the devil is gone.

Ça va, ma puce? Pierre asks, stroking my hair.

He squats beside me, I snuggle into his beard, we leave words out of this. After a long while, he speaks.

Qu'est-ce qui est arrivé? he asks, his finger following the red marks on my shoulder. C'est qui, ce gars-là?

I want to go for a walk, we talk best when we walk, why did l'homme say vous to me instead of tu, le vous qui met en

garde. Les Anglais only have youyouyou for all seasons, no big
deal. I said vous to Elizabeth only that first night at Corona,
la madame aux culottes d'hommes said vous to me only the
first time we met dans l'autobus, I continued to say vous to
her, mais ce n'était pas la même chose, a game we played. But
that man with the black jacket and the black pointed shoes,
vous, menacing, distancing, vous tue les relations amicales,
quand même, his voice, tonight, soft, his voice last night,
quiet, he approached grabbed me softly firmly, Pierre's finger
follows the red marks on my left shoulder, we talk best when
we walk, but he is in the middle of research.

Tu tu tu, I say.

Tut tut tut, he imitates.

Funny private song, I'm okay, he goes back to the girls, I
finish eating ma salade niçoise, count how many rectangles I
cut today, have a long way to go before I can begin assembling Gold Rush, this is like sewing without a pattern, no
Sewing Instructions to guide confuse me, when I learned to
sew, it took so long to break the code, gather, pleat, dart,
crimp, les Anglais de Montréal speak street words, not sewing
words, raw edge and nap ne courent pas les rues, life is full of
crimps, will I grasp well the language of images, so many languages to learn, après l'Expo, I go whoring in the west end
for more English words, did not learn whoring sewing, ça,
c'est certain, les étudiants anglais around McGill teach me
words like motherfucker and epiphany, shithead and serendip-
ity, they say fuck as often as mon oncle Joseph says crisse, but
crisse always stays independent in the sentence, les étudiants
anglais don't understand that, for them, fuck est un mot passe-
partout, it can replace a noun, a verb, an adverb, an adjective,
fuck can be used with a preposition or a pronoun, I ask them
why English has so many words if one word fits all, now, they
want me to teach them nos sacres québécois, cultural
exchange, I shake my head, in their mouths, câlice et tabarnac
are soft caramel, non non, I say, you have to sink your teeth

into those words, not nibble on them, les pauvres Anglais, they have no bite, quand même, they are surprised I don't swear in French, it's because, I say, I live on the hill just above le bas de la ville, so, I am in constant danger of catching la vulgarité, ce n'est pas la même chose for them, near McGill, they can say fuck and motherfucker all they want, they are in no danger of catching la vulgarité because they live far from le bas de la ville, the grandfather clock rings eight o'clock.

Jérôme's sound system plays rock québécois, le jeune homme idéal is gone, his newspaper in sections all over the table, Pierre and two of his friends decided to g᾿ see un Fellini au Verdi, do I want to come.

Pas ce soir, I say.

The girl in the Indian shirt is going, her friends will take le métro back home, I should go home, sleep 'til noon tomorrow, the black pointed shoes appear again, what was he doing dans les toilettes all that time, shitting newspapers, I bring my empty plate behind the counter, the devil grabs my arm gently, I yank, his grip holds, the plate slips hits the floor.

Vous êtes partie bien vite, hier soir, he says again.

The plate fragments litter far and wide, I cannot stand his touch, my skin bristles, the jaws clench, the hand makes a fist, the fist tightens into a brick, the arm winds like a spring ready to uncoil, the fist lands on the devil's chin, the body tension releases, he tumbles backward without losing his balance as if his black pointed shoes were weighed down with lead, fist, arm, shoulder vibrate with the force of impact, the knuckles feel bruised broken, people stop talking, the heart races, the music drumbeats hard, Pierre gets up like a cork, his chair scrapes loudly against the wood floor.

Hé! bonhomme! he shouts, pushing him away from me.

Eh eh eh, là, Jérôme says. C'est un café, ici, pas une taverne du bas de la ville.

The devil steps backward toward the door, palms open for all to see, the whole time, his eyes on me.

Vous êtes quand même partie bien vite, hier soir, he says.

He is gone, a bad smell lingers, I pick up the broken pieces, tell Jérôme I will pay for the plate.

Oublie ça, he says.

Pierre squats beside me, pulls on his beard.

Ariane, qu'est-ce qu'il t'a fait, ce type-là?

Rien.

Rien! Tu mets ton poing sur la gueule d'un gars qui t'a rien fait? Hé! ma puce, parle-moi.

I tell him the guy got violent in a soft kind of way, impossible to explain, try, Pierre encourages, I tell him his whole person became repulsive, where did I meet ce mec de France, Pierre wants to know, nowhere, on the street as I was coming out of parc Lafontaine, lots of people about, how did he find me here, on parlait de choses et d'autres, I told him je suis une habituée du Café de l'horloge, puis avec ma valise, le Français thought I was a traveller, I let him, girls en voyage have adventures, c'est connu, he invited me to his room, nothing unusual, Pierre strokes his beard, his room so hot, full of newspapers, full of the stink of Gauloises, Pierre rolls his eyes, I pushed him away, he insisted, speaking and speaking, tu sais, comme les Français sont articulés, Pierre nods, oui, les Français have a talent with words, well, that's just it, le Français kept rubbing against me and all those words kept pouring out into my face, when I pushed him away, he scratched me, it really hurt and his fingernails were filthy, he would give me le tétanos, I wanted to give him an earful, got tongue-bruised, all I could do was yell at him comme une fille vulgaire du bas de la ville, mon ostie de chien sale, could not find better words than those, and here was ce Français, snarky snarling superior, all the right words rolling off his tongue avec éloquence, and, when he said les Québécois ne savent pas s'exprimer, they have no words, I wanted to deck him like a man decks a man, Pierre approves, I just ran out comme une nana idiote in a French movie.

I want to say more, but Pierre hasn't the time now, so, I stop, each of us holding fragments of the plate.

Ce soir, tu as pris ta revanche, he says. Est-ce que tu te sens mieux?

I shake my wrist to show it hurts, he laughs arches his back like he does when he is happy relieved. The girl with the Indian shirt stands alone, Pierre's friends already left for le Verdi, I tell him to go, sinon, he will miss the beginning of the Fellini film, he should not make his date wait, he kisses me, a long kiss, like he has all the time in the world, it feels good, that kiss, I imagine when he kisses the girl later she, in a way, will also be kissing me, I don't know why, that makes me feel good too.

I cut, mouths kissing, Elizabeth shot many of those, little kids, sisters, friends, lovers, allsorts kissing, like she wanted to capture la physiologie du baiser. I cut, the evening stretches, not much to do after punching the devil, my punching the man wearing the black pointed shoes did not disturb the redheadbanded girl, I squint, still cannot read the title, so many letters on so thin a spine they dance in front of my eyes, my friend Elizabeth read all the time, I tell the girl, she kept most of her books in the two front rooms of her house, one room with a fireplace full of orange peel and peanut shells, no furniture, just books, the other, the reading room with one heavy maroon leather armchair and matching pouf, a reading lamp, un guéridon for cups of coffee and glasses of wine, a brass stand with a green glass ashtray full of cigarette butts and apple cores, and all around, books, from floor to ceiling, a labyrinth of old books with stained hard covers and dog-eared soft covers, le paradis sur terre, the girl says, they were also scattered all over her tiny crooked house, as Elizabeth read several books at the same time and never mixed up the words from a novel with the words from a history book, the girl can also do that.

Ah, oui?

Il faut lire dans le contexte, she says.

Exactement ce qu'Elizabeth disait. Same words, different meanings.

I tell the girl it must be practice, I did not grow up in a house full of books, une ironie, parce que I live next door to la Bibliothèque municipale.

Je n'étais pas un rat de bibliothèque, I say.

Moi, oui, she says.

Elizabeth aussi. Mais elle, elle était a bookworm.

We laugh at that, de toute façon when I was growing up, all the important books were à l'Index, she nods and tells me the nuns at her school kept their books locked in glass cases, they teased the girls, the books in plain sight but out of reach, I tell her, sans doute, the nuns had orders from la Bibliothèque municipale and they feared l'Index, as if to read les mots enflammés would cause the girls to catch fire, the girl raises her middle finger, we laugh, she tells me she and her friends used to break into the bookcases at night, picking the locks with a bobby pin, none of them became burning bushes, she goes back to her book, I to my cut-outs.

Elizabeth loved to hunt for second-hand books, with their distinctive smell of sweet rot, I cut perfect rectangles of people reading at the beach and on trains, imagine generations of readers' fingers imprinted on the paper, alongside their thoughts and their feelings forever mixed with the writers' words, sweet rot, les mots et les choses waiting to wake us up, the second-hand books waiting with stale cookie crumbs in their margins and hidden love notes and forgotten oak leaves between their pages, waiting for new readers to add to the manyvoices of the dead, I cut, discover books have infinite patience.

Une fois de plus, I try to read the spine as the girl closes her book, she holds it up in front of my eyes, I tell her no wonder I could not read this, it is an English title, she thinks I don't understand Intertidal Zone: A Survey of Marine Life.

Non, non, I say. Les Anglais font toujours les choses à l'envers.

Comment ça? she asks with an amused smile.

I tell her I first noticed that in Elizabeth's labyrinth of books, to read the English titles on the spines we have to tilt our head to the right, very disorienting for the eyes, she examines the spine, tells me in French we tilt to the left, because we must be left-leaning, that makes sense, après tout, I say, les Anglais sont fesses serrées, têtes carrées, donc, naturellement, they lean to the right, we snort and chuckle, I tell her not all of them, my friend Elizabeth was not. The girl gets up, I flick through her book, discover that les étoiles de mer live in the intertidal zone, she tells me she wants to become a marine biologist, will go to a university by the sea, probablement, on the West Coast, will she visit the Charlottes? her eyes light up, how come I know about the Charlottes? I smile shrug, she waves leaves, her sea creatures under her arm.

À la prochaine, she says.

She walks by the window, une sirène in the sea street, I touch mon étoile de mer, that girl is going places, outside le Café de l'horloge, the day is in full evening dress, a few customers come in après le cinéma for a last coffee and a last cigarette. I catch my breath. My hand went roaming in the interior pocket of ma valise and found snapshots of Elizabeth, I don't remember ever seeing those before, Elizabeth captured on camera, a rare sight, she hated being photographed, oh, how she hated it, did she slip them there secretly for me to discover one day, I catch my breath.

Elizabeth camping looks as young then as me now, these photos show her in her deep past, safe, so safe in her woollen trousers and matching short jacket over checkered shirt, Elizabeth showing a fish she just caught, Elizabeth's head poking out of a canvas tent, who was the photographer? Elizabeth rowing, in mon oncle's rowboat I caught a fever, I am eleven, j'ai les oreillons, difficult to swallow with my swollen cheeks, maman stays home, I should be in bed, non, I am camping in the wild tundra du grand salon, the coffee table is mon canot, my pillow, mon sac de couchage, my bedspread, ma tente, I brought a ration of Petit Beurre cookies and yellow cheddar, those are dried beans and pemmican, will not die of starvation, and an orange to keep my teeth from falling out, will not die of le scorbut, I know how to survive, row with my school ruler, the top of the trees in parc Lafontaine, a wild mountain range covered with les neiges éternelles, des glaciers étincelants au soleil, row row row on la rivière Toundra, bientôt, dizzying rapids, I am not afraid, I am Radisson La Vérendrye, le plus grand coureur de bois de toute l'histoire du Canada, down the rapids, mon canot shakes from side to side, deadly rocks, courage, crack, mon canot and I rise high in the air, crash splash sink to the bottom of the river, scrape my knees on the Persian rug, rise comme un bouchon de liège, bob spin churn, swim to shore, lost all my gear, sauf the paddle, will survive.

The sun setting fast, moi soaking wet, grabbing the paddle, crawling along the dark canyon of the corridor, passing maman's boudoir, on her Underwood she types letters she brought from work, dear sir, sincerely, must not play with her Underwood, it wears out the ribbon, in the cave of the kitchen, felling a pile of old La Presse, hunting a bag of marshmallows, killing it with one swift swat of the paddle, crawling back, pass le boudoir, the she-bear with cubs to feed does not see does not smell me, safe back to the campsite by la rivière Toundra, crumpling fuel, hands black with ink, pushing the paper into the fireplace, maman never makes a fire, she says, la cheminée fume, rubbing two sticks together, striking an Eddy match, the flames rising high inside the chimney, taking off my wet clothes to dry them by the fire.

Elizabeth squatting by her campfire, frying something in a cast-iron skillet, sans doute le poisson, my marshmallows roasting on the end of a straightened coat hanger could have been marsh swallows, did not know then a swallow is une hirondelle.

Chewing the marshmallows, whale blubber, black on the outside, white and oozy on the inside, shivering with fever, wolves howling in the distance, a great shadow blotting out the moon lamp, the she-bear grunting, elle va me dévorer, will keep a few pieces of my flesh pour nourrir ses oursons, the she-bear pouncing, a sudden downpour, raining buckets on my beautiful fire, will die of cold in the night, the tundra full of smoke, je pense, c'est vrai, la cheminée fume, water trickling down the brick walls inside the fireplace, maman with her empty bucket n'est pas contente.

Pour l'amour, Claudette. Tu es malade comme un chien. Qu'est-ce que tu fais toute nue comme un ver? Tu vas attraper ton coup de mort.

She throws my bedspread over me, she thinks je suis une sauvage, how to tell her I am Radisson La Vérendrye, better say nothing, she speaks very, very quietly.

Clean that up. You do one more silly thing, she says en anglais, sans doute, still in her letter-writing mode. If I can't raise you myself.

Maman leaves her English words suspended, who needs words when we have context. That day of the capsizing, I understood context very well. Maman is going to shop for a husband, peut-être, she will buy new sheets first, like ma tante Rita wants her to do.

Ce n'est pas ma faute, I say. C'est la fièvre.

I want her to understand, après la fièvre, I will be normal obedient again, she does not have to shop for a husband.

Elizabeth camping, was the photographer son fiancé? as they used to say à cette époque, peut-être, she also had a secret Dead Man in her past life, will not cut these up, cannot touch what is before our time together, I slip the series of snapshots back into the satin pocket of ma valise.

The grandfather clock counts the eleventh hour, Jérôme's closing time. He chats with his last customer, an old friend, I should go, can't bring myself to, would Jérôme allow me to sleep upstairs, how does his upstairs look, have never been dans une garçonnière, the friend leaves, ciao, Jérôme stops the music. He piles clean dishes behind the counter, stores empty bottles in a wooden crate, takes the garbage into la ruelle, bolts the door on his way back inside, taps his watch, I stack my cut-outs into ma valise. How will I pair them, careful construction or random design? Jérôme lights a cigarette, turns off all the lights except the one above the street door.

C'est l'heure de rentrer chez toi, Ariane.

Est-ce que je peux dormir là-haut? I ask, raising my eyes toward the tin ceiling.

He shakes his head slowly slowly, not taking his eyes off me, he thinks I'm a tough customer, as they say in movies, he thinks I'm going to seedy pot, I smirk, that's what travels'll do to you, he hands me ma valise, his lips leave a feather kiss on my forehead, he opens the door to hot sticky rue Saint-Denis, the day now en robe de nuit, sleepwalking, le jour et la nuit chasing each other, shadow trailing, I turn to tell Jérôme, he bolts the door of le Café de l'horloge, a motorcycle races downhill, rips tears past, people mill about.

Above, no sky.

Streets of Desire

Our flat, so hot tonight, like living inside a Chinese box, par les grandes chaleurs, the sun browbeating the stone walls of the house, cooking the tar and gravel on the flat roof, inside, not a breath of air, the plaster walls, warm to the touch, three eh–em, the body sweat-drenched in the bathtub, cold water slowly bringing down summer fever, waking up again at seven, the flat a furnace, the doors and windows wide open, au diable les mouches, the body astride a chair in the long corridor, catching whatever morning draft, battling afternoon heat with curtains drawn, iced tea, pillows cooling in the fridge, the body spread-eagled on the floor, the rabbit-shaped pink rubber bottle filled with ice cubes, the rabbit moving along chest, belly, thighs, face, oh, le délice of frozen skin in July, tonight, the body slouched on a kitchen chair, skirt hiked up to the crotch, faning myself with a page of La Presse pleated accordion-style, fan fan, maman comes home from work a zombie.

J'ai cru m'évanouir de chaleur, she says. C'est suffocant.

She lets her open-toed white shoes fall by the entrance door.

Pas des bas-culottes! I say.

She grins, a little embarrassed, I tell her we all go bare-legged, she sits on the ebony hall stand to remove her panty-hose, I never saw her do that before, she leans against the

full-length mirror at the back of the bench, she never did
that either, what if the mirror cracked, she unbuckles the
wide, soft yellow belt cinching her small waist, I can make
out the outline of her bra under the cotton, I tell her we go
braless too, half-moons of sweat stain the underarms of her
light-blue dress printed with small, pale yellow triangles, the
lines of sweat like dark lines under eyes, she looks exhausted.

Va prendre un bain, I suggest.

Par cette chaleur?

Un bain d'eau froide.

Oui, bien sûr, de l'eau froide.

She closes the bathroom door, the pipes make their rude
pipe noise, water splashes in the tub.

Water splashes in the kitchen sink, slides over my arms up
to the shoulders, maman keeps glancing at the scratches,
healing slowly, she asks no questions, but her glances are a
sign. She resents silly questions, but when the time comes,
même si elle mesure ses mots, elle fait son devoir, water
trickling in the kitchen sink, her hands braiding, I am eight,
something on my mind, have to ask, au diable les conséquences.

Comment ça s'appelle la chose que les hommes ont entre
les jambes? my little girl's voice asking, as clear in my ear
tonight comme si c'était hier.

There. Done. Must wait, quiet, for an answer, no answer,
punishment, maman pulling on my hair.

Ça s'appelle une verge, Claudette, her voice so clear I
turn around, bien sûr, she is in the tub.

Une verge! How can men store a thing thirty-six inches
long in their trousers? Pendant la récréation, staring at the
concierge's trousers, nothing, on Saturday, at mon oncle's
crotch, nothing, peut-être, it has hinges, like that special yard-
stick the teacher showed us, did not yet know Nicole et
Diane, could not discuss la verge des hommes with them, la
madame aux culottes d'hommes would have laughed her jel-

lyfish laugh and told me how it worked, I scratch my scabs, maman telling me what la verge is for, but never explaining the mystery of the three feet, I am eleven, waking up, blood on the sheets, a few months après les oreillons and my fire in the fireplace, she will never believe I did not play with needles in bed, mon oncle Joseph's story about needles, because a needle has no head, it can be pushed all the way into the skin, enter a vein, travel at breakneck speed all the way to the heart, peut-être, that is why I have des points au cœur, maman sighing, explaining the blood, must wear une serviette sanitaire between my legs, it does not look like a towel, but feels like a pillow, that is why men sit with their legs wide open, leur verge in the way, they must let it out of their trousers, la verge must breathe, pauvres flashers, they are embarrassed, that is why they let it hang out in out-of-the-way places, like doorways, quand même, maman never walks with her legs apart, sans doute, it is because of la discrétion, will we bleed together, a blood pact entre mère et fille, will I bleed learn la discrétion, learning about cramps, my belly, une pelote full of needles piercing my blood vessels, she gives me pink pills, telling me she had cramps when she was young, after she had me, the cramps went away, looking sorry for me, I will have to wait for a man to put sa verge inside me, thirty-six inches to heal my cramps forever and ever, cold water trickles down my armpits, maman saying time to shave, shave what? showing me how, not telling me why, putting a new blade in a silver-grey metal razor, soaping my armpits, the razor, cold scary against my skin.

Fais attention de ne pas te couper, she warns.

In movies, people in bathtubs slash their wrists with razor blades, the blood pumps out of their bodies, the water turns red, after the shaving, my armpits on fire, moi pacing, arms up in the air, singing, j'ai le feu aux aisselles, like mon oncle Joseph when he is angry saying, j'ai le feu au cul, refusing to shave, maman bringing me shopping for my first bra, back

home, telling me she was ashamed when la vendeuse measured and saw me, poilue comme une ourse.

On n'est pas des sauvages, Claudette. Rase-toi.

I dry my arms, je ne veux plus qu'elle fasse son devoir, I
want her to speak with her grown daughter about sex men
la vie, like I talk about sex men with Nicole et Diane, but
with her more sophisticated, like with Elizabeth, non, it will
never be like with Elizabeth, she will draw the line, will not
want to talk about Dead Man, about lovers, she must have
lovers, after all those years sans Dead Man, non, she will not
talk about that, peut-être, she is out of practice, we must learn
to start somewhere, I bring her iced tea.

Claudette! pour l'amour, she shouts, realizing her mistake, not correcting herself.

She never shouts, but I never visited her in the bathroom
before. There. Done. I have finally pushed my way in, the
walls are down. She lays in the pool of transparent water, her
arms resting on the edge of the high tub, elle me fait les gros
yeux, but does not try to hide herself, peut-être, things are
beginning to change, like a mutation, I give her the glass, she
holds it with both hands to keep it from slipping into the
tub.

Merci, Ariane, c'est très gentil, she says, taking sips.

In front of the mirror, I twist my hair into un long bou-
din, pile it on top of my head, pin it, watch her watching me.

Tu sors? she asks, sipping.

Elizabeth invited me in when she took a bath, I sat on
the toilet seat cover, my knees grazing the small tub, we
talked in Saint-Pol, I talk to maman on rue Sherbrooke.

Tu te souviens, I say, quand j'étais petite, tu te cachais
dans les toilettes.

Qu'est-ce que tu racontes? she asks with a tight little
smile.

Bien oui, I remind her I used to pursue the hem of her
dresses from doorway to doorway, when I caught her with

my questions she was in the bathroom the closed door
between us.

Tu disais toujours, pour l'amour, Claudette, I'm voiding.

She shakes her head, says she does not remember that, I
tell her I used to think she had a weak bladder because she
had me, c'est naturel, toutes les mères ont la vessie fragile, she
laughs, ainsi, mothers can escape their children's questions by
hiding in bathrooms and not feel guilty, in Saint-Pol, I peed
with the door open, I did not mind, Elizabeth peed when I
was putting on my eye makeup, she did not mind, we all pee
and shit, Elizabeth used to say, we all have bodies, maman no
longer laughs. What is she thinking, of Elizabeth dead or that
I should not tell her those things? She shifts in the water,
c'est l'heure du bain, I am so little, the high tub, as big as a
swimming pool, maman sitting on a low stool beside the tub,
moi shrieking, loving the echo of my shrieks in the vast
ceramic room, maman letting me splash her with my rubber
blue whale and yellow fisherman in his red fishing boat, I
stop applying mascara, tell her about that Saturday I wanted
to phone her au bureau, ma tante would not let me, would
not tell me why not, mon oncle puffed up his chest like he
was getting ready to dive, told me you worked elsewhere,
deflated his chest.

Je pense que ma tante et mon oncle pensaient que tu avais
un amant, I say, resuming brushing black over my lashes.

I squint at her, meeting men at work, pourquoi pas? sec-
retaries have affairs with their bosses, how else would she
meet men, she never goes out at night, what goes on inside
her, she swallows her iced tea slowly jusqu'à la lie, she does
not lie, she deflects, a master, pour l'amour, ce n'est pas poli
de poser tant de questions, only words, why are people afraid
of words, do you have a boyfriend, Ariane, dear? are you a virgin, Ariane, dear? Elizabeth asks, the day of the raw fish, just
words and bodies, maman holds the empty glass, the body, a
Chinese box, secret panels hiding secret compartments only

the very clever can discover how to open, Gérard has a Chinese box in his boutique of antiques, I tried failed, take her glass.

Je ne rentrerai pas tard, I say, closing the door behind me.

I put on a purple tee-shirt with a grinning black cat printed on the front and the backside of the cat printed on the back, its tail draped over the left short sleeve, nobody will see the red scratches, the day of sashimi, Elizabeth playful as a cat, wearing black jeans and a long striped shirt en laine du pays, the grey in her hair gone, before going out, I eat a handful of blueberries, bite into a tomato, red as that fish we ate, the day of the raw meat just a dry run, the day of sashimi the true beginning of our Friday ritual.

Mind the low ceiling, she said the first time. Duck when you get to the top of the stairs.

Every Friday after we finish hugging, I say, I'm going to the loo the can the john, as the spirit moves me I choose a word, a game we play, je canard at the top of the stairs not to bump my head on the low ceiling, look out the tiny window at the rolling hills in fog, in sun, in rain, the seat ice cold, my knees touching the side of the small tub, our bathroom, a sea of black and white ceramic tiles from floor to ceiling perfect for sashimi to play, it smells of the cold bath, the humidity lingers in the tub, clings to the towel, in Saint-Pol, the bathroom smells of incense and Noxzema, I listen, no screeching tires, no screaming sirens, a new kind of silence, deep and white, je tire la chaîne, long and rusty, attached to the toilet tank fixed above my head, water tumbles down the pipe, churns gurgles, clear water fills the bowl, I imagine swimming in water so cold it forces me to remain alert and think hard about things, on Sherbrooke, I brush my teeth, wash my feet in the tub, in Saint-Pol, the ceiling slants, but I can stand, explore the above, no access to the front of the house, the second storey hides over the kitchen, Elizabeth's bedroom and bathroom, away from the road and prying eyes, my hand follows the geography of her blue sheets, the ridges and valleys four legs carved, the scent of night lifts from the sheets, a blue night fog in the afternoon, a black hair rests on one pillow, straight and shiny in the sun, Gérard slept here, slipped out in the morning in his black and red Mercury, the blue sheets guarded by the heavy carved headboard painted jaune maïs, the face of a lion, serious and haunting, surrounded by vines and tiny deer with oversized but delicate antlers, Elizabeth's bedroom, a Chinese box, maman dans son boudoir reads Madame Bovary, I am pleased she reads my books from cégep, she always asks first if she may borrow, elle est polie, she put her cotton dress back on, without the belt, without the bra, her thick curly black hair stiff with Suave spray net, never a hair out of place, même par cette chaleur, her bare feet, white and perfect and tender because she never walks barefoot, lie motionless on the ottoman in front of the leather rocking chair, the chair not rocking, she looks calm cool, she reads.

Tu es encore ici? she says, holding her place in the book with her finger.

Her comment sounds like a reproach, bien sûr, it is not, quand même, it may be time for me to move on.

Tu aimes Madame Bovary? I ask.

It's a sad story.

Pourquoi? Je veux dire, pourquoi tu me dis ça en anglais?

Pardon?

Tu m'as dit, it's a sad story.

J'ai dit ça, moi?

I walk west on rue Sherbrooke, lentement comme une putain qui fait le trottoir, too hot to walk fast, the honkers throw silly words out of their rolled down windows, oh! le beau pussy, hé! ma belle chatte noire, viens ici que je te flatte, I turn north on avenue du Parc, Greek people sit, stiff and quiet, on kitchen chairs they dragged to the middle of the sidewalk, I smile say, il fait chaud, they nod say something in their language.

I will go au parc Jeanne-Mance at the foot of the mountain, will men leave me alone, tonight, a girl alone at night
can never be left alone, attention aux rôdeux, ma tante Rita
says when I am nine on my way to play au parc Lafontaine
in summer, attention aux rôdeux, ma tante Rita says when I
am twelve on my way to go skating au lac des Castors in
winter, selon ma tante, les rôdeux hide behind every maple
tree in the park, squinting at little girls and psst-pssting, les
rôdeux squat behind every bush on Mount Royal, rubbing
huge hands together and licking monstrous lips, maman does
not buy that, braiding at the kitchen sink, she tells me we
must call them des rôdeurs, she insists notre langue, c'est
notre respect de soi, n'aie pas la langue paresseuse, she advises,
braiding la langue maternelle, she may be right, mais les rôdeux do worse things than les rôdeurs.

Nicole et Diane have never seen un rôdeux, I have never
seen one, but we all know what they look like, des satyres in
filthy overcoats, men with filmy eyes the size of pumpkin
seeds, teeth the colour of licorice, they drink Varsol, sniff shoe
polish, black gives them the highest high, les rôdeux anglais
have mouths full of pebbles because they have gravelly voices,
les rôdeux français hold cheese graters between their lips
parce qu'ils ont la voix râpeuse, all of them, les rôdeux anglais
and les rôdeux français, have crooked fingers, they live by the
railway tracks au nord de la rue Laurier and they masturbate
masturbate, maman would say masturbate if she said masturbate, c'est ça, le respect de soi, Nicole et Diane say, les rôdeux
se crossent, maman would say, ne dis pas ça, Claudette, c'est
vulgaire, but we think les rôdeux n'ont pas le respect de soi,
alors, Nicole et Diane are right, les rôdeux se crossent, we
laugh and laugh, se crosser is so funny.

Maman is not laughing, she says, les rôdeurs sont de pauvres hères, they lost their jobs, their houses, their wives, their
children, but she lost Dead Man and she does not live by the
railway tracks au nord de la rue Laurier, peut-être, only men

can become des rôdeux. Quand même, ma tante thinks all
strangers are dangerous suspicious, ma tante is wrong. Pierre
is a good man and before I knew him he was a stranger,
Gérard is a good man and Elizabeth was not afraid of him
when he was a stranger to her, and what about Sven, bien
sûr, there are exceptions, the man with the black pointed
shoes is an exception with his tongue down my throat, his
nails dug into my shoulder, his other hand clamped on my
ass, sa verge de Français pressé pressed hard against me, but
with the score three for the good and one for the bad, le jeu
en vaut la chandelle. What does the pirate girl think about all
that? Whatever, she would say. Is she out there, tonight, hunting, the streets are full of people bobbing for air.

The fish in Elizabeth's kitchen lies in sweet repose, med-
itating on porcelain Black Sea plates, the red and white slices
garnished with pink and white strips arranged in a loose
clump like steel wool, Elizabeth pours saké in pottery tumblers the size of thimbles, we take a piece of fish with nos
baguettes chinoises, when I go to Chinatown with Pierre we
never use forks, we are eating raw fish, drinking hot saké, talking about lovers and boyfriends, girls my age have boyfriends,
women Elizabeth's age have lovers, lovers like Gérard, lovers
like Raymond, how many more, doesn't she get mixed up,
doesn't she have to deflect, I put a piece of fish in my mouth,
don't think about its rawness, chew stare at the winter garden
on the other side of the wall of windows, je suis une Esqui-
maude dans son igloo, je suis Iriook, la femme d'Agaguk.

Do you have to lie? I ask.

Not if you put your cards on the table. If they don't like
it, tough. Is Pierre straightforward with those girls you say
he's collecting?

I don't know what he tells them. He tells me everything,
but that doesn't count, I don't want to settle down.

Do you experiment with sex? Elizabeth asks, blowing
smoke at the ceiling.

My eyes follow the smoke, is Raymond waiting naked in her bed, I drink saké.

I meet a guy and we talk, I say. After an hour, if he invites me to his place, I go. I go, because talking more than an hour is a signal and if I just say au revoir and take le métro home, he will think I am une agace-pissette.

Do you want to?

Be une agace-pissette?

Go to his place?

I don't mind. I get to visit apartments in the west end.

Sex doesn't bother you, then?

I am on the pill.

Good for you!

It is maman's fault, I say. When mon oncle Joseph finished pulling strings and got me that job making pizza à La Ronde, she sent me to docteur Lamoureux tout de suite, he delivered me, you know, like I was a parcel, she wanted him to prescribe la pilule, tu comprends. Misère, Elizabeth, I think he took advantage, all he had to do was write a prescription and send me to the pharmacy, but non, he put that thing inside me like a shoehorn.

Speculum, Elizabeth says.

Ad vitam æternam, amen, I say, showing off my bit of Latin. I did not tell maman, she thinks docteur Lamoureux is a great doctor, nobody ever went down there before, except my finger.

Elizabeth smiles, I pinch my lips, never told anyone before, not even Nicole et Diane and we talk a lot about sex, and here I am, on a dark winter afternoon in the chilly mustard kitchen of a patched-up crooked house in Saint-Polycarpe, eating raw fish and drinking hot saké with a woman maman's age but with many lovers, telling her about masturbation et examen gynécologique.

Elizabeth bites a piece of white fish, waves ses baguettes chinoises.

Aren't you glad your mom takes care of things, Ariane, dear? Nobody ever told me one fucking word about fucking. How can people have sex and be so tongue-tied?

She shakes her head, flattens her empty pack of cigarettes, takes a new pack out of a drawer by the propane stove.

But for that fear of words, Elizabeth says, cracking open the cellophane, putting a cigarette between her lips, looking at me with those eyes blue so blue. The troubles I'd have avoided.

She lights, breathes the smoke deeply, exhales hard.

Tonight, hot, so hot, I cannot swear Elizabeth said that the afternoon of the raw fish or said it at all, peut-être, Gérard told me après les funérailles, peut-être, I heard Raymond talk about it, what is certain is that, years before, Elizabeth had her insides cut and crimped and sewn back par un charlatan de ruelle, she had to keep her legs raised above her head for five days, sinon, she would have bled to death. That is why maman made me take the pill the summer of Expo, she reminded me that, since it is the woman who gets pregnant, each woman must rely on herself for birth control, men are too distracted. Peut-être, Dead Man was not reliable.

My head spins with saké, Elizabeth feeds me the last of the fish, Japanese silk on the tongue. She swears, the shreds of white daikon and pink pickled ginger are not seaworms, I gobble the loose mass in one mouthful, a drop of vinegar goes the wrong way, I cough with my lips sealed to avoid spewing food on the table, a bit of fish swims up my sinuses, I blow my nose, the fish swims down into the Kleenex, trapped in thick transparent mucus, my face feels soft as a sea sponge.

More saké, please, I giggle.

You're samurai-tipsy, girl, Elizabeth smirks.

What makes you so happy, tonight, girl? the guy in the grass asks.

What is this? I say. La valse aux questions? What's your name, where do you live, what are you doing tonight, are you a student, what is the meaning of life, reciting the grammar of questions, qui quoi, à qui à quoi, lips singing, minds dead, de qui de quoi, par qui par quoi, the singsong of memorization, pour qui pour quoi, sans qui sans quoi, deep breath here, où, quand, comment, pourquoi, why should I give you my phone number, good question.

I touch the grass, fresh even dans ce bain turc montréalais, guys and girls lie around all over le parc Jeanne-Mance, they talk laugh smoke drink smooch, nobody is alone, I sway a little, the guy mumbles I'm on something.

Yeah, I say. I'm samurai-tipsy and Elizabeth wants me to talk about the summer of you-pho-ri-ahh.

The guy walks away.

I spin pizza dough à La Ronde, I tell Elizabeth, meet Pierre, Nicole et Diane play at being hostesses, we hang out, I stay out late, maman spends August au lac Memphrémagog, is she having an affair with her boss, I throw a party at our flat, my first ever, I show the yoots from Toronto l'hospitalité montréalaise, am getting tall bold seventeen, je grandis en herbe et en asphalte, I belong, Pierre is twenty-three that summer, he wants to become un écrivain engagé, but he too has to wear the pizza uniform, red pants, a striped red and white short-sleeved shirt, a red bow tie, a red and white cap, the prim Expo hostesses walk by in their Robichaud uniform, proud and snob comme des hôtesses de l'air, Pierre hates them, he says, elles se prennent pour des Parisiennes, he shoots pizza sauce at them, one day, bull's eye, a hostess with a pizza sauce shot wound right in the middle of her back, we canard under the counter, laugh our heads off, un monsieur asks for an all-dressed pizza, one slice, with his dark suit and black-rimmed glasses, what if he is un inspecteur, Pierre and I will get fired, pauvre mon oncle who pulled all those strings. After a week of slicing mushrooms so thin they look like dead insects, we could not eat pizza even on a desert island, after two weeks of slipping when-the-moon-hits-your-eye-like-a-big-pizza-pie pies in the oven, the smell makes us sick, we are bored, sauf when girl customers come to the stand, alors, Pierre brushes his manhood against my lower back to squeeze by to rush and serve the hungry girls with large breasts and pigtails, he asks all the redheads for their phone numbers, they always give them to him, when business is slow, Pierre and I warm up mode-za, that trendy cheese, and have contests whose piece stretches the longest, we hide beer behind the packs of raw dough, smoke a joint in the men's washroom, that's amore sixty-seven. What else? We make out for the first time one Saturday night at eleven o'clock pizza closing time, we jam ourselves under a shelf, in our red and white uniforms, deux cannes de Noël en bonbon doing the sixty-nine the summer of sixty-seven, sa verge is not thirty-six inches long.

What's that? Elizabeth cuts in.

I have to open une parenthèse for her, she laughs so hard, tears roll down her cheeks.

Anyway, I continue, it's shorter than I thought, but it is pink and purple with veins like des varices on an old woman's legs, I gag a little, cannot concentrate on what he is doing to me, his tongue not as agile as my finger, d'ailleurs, we are all contorted under that shelf, but we are daring, if we get caught, tu imagines le scandale, Pierre éjacule, it takes me by surprise, I swallow crooked, it burns my throat, try hard not to cough, how embarrassing, my first time and it has to go down the wrong pipe, I tell him to be careful, next time I might have the biting reflex.

I stop to catch my breath, my throat dry, Elizabeth blows her nose, I want more saké, the bottle is empty, she pours herself a scotch, I shake my head, non, merci.

I am seventeen, I say, my first boyfriend is twenty-three, what fun, we close the pizza stand, change into our normal clothes, Pierre in jeans and a white Indian cotton shirt, me in my new white gypsy skirt and a red halter top, we walk hand in hand, that night we started walking and talking, we talk best when we walk. Pierre will not rot making pizza 'til October, he wants to drive La Ballade, keeps his eyes peeled for the next opening, must jump on opportunity like it is a wild horse, he heard Americans are big tippers, give them some information and they slap fivers in your hand, just like that, je pense, how much would they tip Pierre if he brought them the Plastic Eye on a silver platter, for Pierre, shooting pretty hostesses with pizza sauce bullets is not revolutionary enough, he wants to live, sacrament.

What does he want to do? Elizabeth asks.

I asked him the same question. He said, tout, I asked, tout quoi? Tout, he says. Vivre, pas croupir dans la routine, aller au bout de tout, he is even willing to die young, if necessary, he wants to write, I ask him what, écrire notre histoire, he says, je pense, the story of Pierre and Claudette, two Expo yoots, the story of la jeunesse de l'Expo qui dirigera, I say, c'est une bonne idée, but he should change the names, il veut dénoncer les capitalistes, he says that, stroking my shoulder. Il faut unir la jeunesse, les étudiants, les ouvriers, les intellectuels, les artistes, les travailleurs, il faut se décoloniser, s'instruire, s'entraider, he says all that, his hand sliding down my ass, he wants to write le grand roman de la rue, avec notre parlure et notre vécu, he says, on doit sortir des salons et entrer dans les cuisines, tu comprends?

Elizabeth nods, she understands French, ah oui?

Well, I don't understand, I say. But I am lucky, wait 'til I tell Nicole et Diane, I just sucked la verge d'un gauchiste. I tell Pierre about mon oncle Joseph, he would be a good character for his novel, mon oncle works in a machine shop run by des Anglais, maman also works pour les Anglais, mais dans un bureau, he nibbles my neck.

So, it goes, we spin pizza dough, discuss Pierre's projects, we play in the woods of l'île Sainte-Hélène, Pierre's tongue is becoming more agile, I stand against a tree, he kneels hides under my wide gypsy skirt, his fingers push my panty to the

side, his tongue starts wagging silently, Elizabeth wants to
know if I come, you bet I do, I am pleased when Pierre's
body tells me my mouth is also a fast learner, I say, je le suce,
Elizabeth says, fellatio, je pense, sans doute, because we do it
to a fella, it is tricky because of Pierre's jeans, must be careful not to let the zipper scratch son pénis, Pierre says, pénis,
it looks pale and vulnerable, I watch the blue veins swell, we
are happy, we walk, he holds me by the shoulder, I hold him
by the waist, je suis la blonde d'un gauchiste, tout va bien, but
he warns me not to become too attached, he wants to go
places, study à la Sorbonne, travel to South America, faire du
cinéma, he knows un réalisateur à l'ONF, I am impressed, he
says, l'Onef, and he wants to write, Pierre says, he must
remain absolument libre, I tell him not to worry, I understand that no-strings-attached thing, give him the tongue to
prove I mean what I say.

I cannot believe I told all those details to Elizabeth, peut-
être, I did, après tout, she got interested in Pierre. Ah! moi,
une entremetteuse! That thought leaves me bouche bée, a
small fly flies right in, I try to cough it out, it hangs on for
dear life, bites burns my throat.

You all right? a guy asks.

His hand is getting ready to rub my back, decides against
the rubbing, too soon to touch the girl, I spit something,
clear my throat, he sits beside me, I glance, brown hair down
his back, a handlebar moustache, black shorts and a pearl grey
Moroccan shirt, as he lays his guitar in the grass it goes
tongggue.

Is this silk? I ask, fingering the edge of his sleeve.

How should I know? It comes from Morocco.

Did you buy it there?

Marrakech.

He stares at my lips, here we go, not ten seconds et déjà.

Elizabeth the kisser says I have a mouth that invites
kisses, voyons donc, a mouth's a mouth, but it took her

photographer's eye to point out the obvious to me, I examine my mouth reflected on her two-door toaster, c'est vrai,
j'ai les lèvres charnues, not maman's, hers are thinner, sans
doute, Dead Man's, mon héritage, j'ai les lèvres vermeilles,
the colour of lips in books, full, symmetrical, camera-ready,
Elizabeth did shoot my lips, my big mouth like merchandise
on billboards rising above elevated highways.

Do you smoke? I ask the guitar man.

He grins pulls a huge spliff from under his Marrakech
shirt.

So, you too.

Me too what?

The last one was from Lyon, I say. He knows all about
Québec history, he reads five newspapers a day, smokes three
packs of Gauloises a day, he is a researcher for a news agency,
he criticizes everything, la France et les Français, the way les
Québécois eat speak walk write, he says it is a disease, cette
haine du monde, he cannot help himself, I wanted to tell
him, he has a mind as clear as a winter sky, the right words
roll off his tongue like a waterfall, never a moment's hesitation, such flow, and yet, you should have seen his teeth, his
gums, he followed my lips with his nicotine-stinking finger,
his fingernail on my lips as yellow as a claw, he told me, avec
une si belle bouche, la parole est inutile, and his breath, man,
and his saliva, marinating in tobacco juice, his breath made
me gag, I came that close to be sick all over ce Français, when
I pushed him away and ran out, he thought je repoussais ses
avances.

You didn't want to put out, the guy in the grass says.

It was disgusting. Don't you think a person has a right to
expect a clean person, I mean, take a bath, brush your teeth,
we all stink given time, c'est normal, bad breath, sweaty
armpits, crotchy odour, smelly feet, shitty stink, it is not that
I pretend humans don't produce body odours, my friend
Elizabeth smoked like a chimney, Player's no filter, I never

smelled cigarette smoke on her clothes, not once, she never had bad breath, and she was a kisser, not a tongue kisser, but a kisser, I suspect my friend did not even have bad breath in the morning, she took care of herself, alors pour revenir au Français, if he wants to kiss a girl and go all the way, he should show a little consideration and brush his teeth.

Are you high on something? he asks, lighting the grass.

I don't know, I felt like merchandise, something snapped, I called him un câlice d'ostie de tabarnac de maudit écœurant.

It has a nice ring, he says, picking up his guitar and strumming. Say it again.

Non, too vulgar. My friend Pierre who is un écrivain says vulgaire means la langue du peuple, he wants to celebrate that in his writing, quand même, I wished I had said something brilliant to show ce Français I knew how to speak, au lieu, the only words that came out were les mots vulgaires du bas de la ville, maintenant, he will go back to France and bad-mouth les Québécois and it will be my fault, he has bad breath, c'est sûr, but it is me who spoke comme un charretier, I don't know why les charretiers are said to use bad language, in English when people use bad language, you say they have the mouth of a chicken, oui oui, you say they have a fowl mouth, where does that come from? For Christ's sex, stop staring at my lips.

I'm not staring at your lips.

Like hell, you're not, I've seen it before. Guys have one track in their mind, Pierre, le Québécois fleurdelisé, that man with the black pointed shoes, même Sven who was not pushy, don't tell me you're not, you all want the same thing.

There's a black spot, he points, smoking his joint.

What is it? I say, trying to brush off what ever it is.

In the middle. No, lower lip. It's stuck.

What is it?

Wait, let me. See? It's a small fly. Dead.

You let me speak with a dead fly on my lip!

No big deal, he says, strumming.

He sings, people watch, sans doute, they think I am his girlfriend, we grow grass and des courgettes on our balcony, we keep a goat at a little place dans les Cantons de l'Est, I wonder where cet Anglais lives, probablement, not far from here, on l'Esplanade or Milton, he has seen Morocco, he sings that song, Suzanne, Leonard Cohen did not write a song about Claudette, who would, Ariane, peut-être, Claudette, jamais. People sing along, I don't feel like un party impromptu, go to his place, smoke dope, listen to music, drink beer, he will want to do it, he seems nice, but my instincts are no good any more, peut-être sans Elizabeth, speak is becoming dangerous, too many words spill out helter-skelter, Pierre says, la langue du people, c'est la langue de la contestation, c'est vrai, everywhere the yoot protests, la jeunesse qui dirigera says ostie et câlice, worse than mon oncle Joseph, words of protest, I tried them on the other night, they didn't fit, why? peut-être, to fit well, the words must be used to protest against society, Nicole et Diane tried that out at Expo to protest against their parents, but I have no reason to protest against maman.

On their days off, Nicole et Diane dress the same in jeans, flat leather sandals, elasticized halter tops in orange dayglo, black leather jackets, they streak their long brown hair with henna, wear large silver hoops in their pierced ears, what a hoot we had the day of the piercing of Nicole's et Diane's ears, they wear silver and leather rings on every finger including their thumbs, smoke Gauloises, but chew gum, carry no handbag, handbags are too madame, they don't wear their watches because they don't give a damn about time, they speak with the thick accent du bas de la ville to protest against the years they had to take des leçons de diction because their fathers are businessmen who made a killing somewhere, I went to their houses a few times, everything in mint-green condition, their mothers did not go back sur le marché du travail, they don't have to, they think maman is a modern woman, la Femme nouvelle, they called her, I wonder if she knows about la Femme nouvelle, Nicole et Diane parlent joual to protest against the mint-green condition. On workdays, they wear their watches not to miss their breaks and to tell visitors the correct time, they slip back into their prim hostess uniform and improved montréalais, direct tourists to restrooms and pavilions, softening their tees and opening their aze, bien sûr, they don't say ostie tabarnac ciboire câlice, non, they sprinkle their English with gees and gollies.

L'Anglais sings another song, that summer of you-phori-ahh is over, Nicole et Diane are married, Elizabeth is dead, I leave, slowly walk back, would be nice to sit with the Greek people, Elizabeth said we would do that too on our trip, sit in the street, do nothing, the chairs are still in the middle of the sidewalk, but empty, I sense the people's shadows, imagine their feet imprinted on the stained ciment, soudain, I feel sad as if they had died, cette tristesse that pounces sans crier gare takes my breath away, Elizabeth's death fresh, oui, mais aussi, I feel for all the dead, peut-être cette tristesse, it is just the heat, la ville, a Chinese box, les rues, hot and close. Midnight, such a long night crossing in insomnia city.

I try to catch a breeze, walk across le carré Saint-Louis, men are drunk-sleeping on benches, I scoop up a bunch of flowers someone must have dropped, feet echo behind me, I stiffen, don't turn around, don't walk faster, my ears, alert, I zigzag in and out of streets the same way I did when I was twelve and that man tried to follow me home, every day after school his silly son standing in front of his flat, laughing at my cat's eyes, calling me an old maid, je ne suis pas une servante, making fun of my coat, the sleeves too short, my body growing faster than maman's paycheque, one afternoon, that stick in my hand to teach him to be polite, the boy bigger and older, no matter, the stick landing on the boy's face, blood trickling down, just a small gash through his eyebrow, quel pleurnicheur, his father coming out, follow me home, that boy laughing at my myopia, like laughing at maman's myopia, that boy laughing at my coat, like laughing at her for not taking good care of me, the footsteps follow me through the hot empty streets, my heart beats à l'unisson with the steps on pavement, the boy's father following, my legs turning in and out of ruelles, walking fast, leading him, him thinking I am not noticing, did a good job losing him, like a detective losing the villain who follows to discover where the heroine lives, I look, nobody, just blood rushing in my ears, at the end of notre ruelle, my eyes catch a shadow, danger city, I unlock the door, close it behind me, stand inside le hangar in complete darkness in the narrow suffocating space at the foot of the staircase, the steps sagging, I listen, nothing, stand in this sarcophagus of old wood, smell the phantom scent of flowers, I am holding des pivoines, wilting, Elizabeth whispers in my ear.

All he taught me was to hate cut flowers.

She says that the day of the minestrone soup we eat with village crusty bread and unsalted butter, maman buys unsalted butter only for her Christmas fruitcake, a luxury, Elizabeth's butter tastes like cream, not like our daily butter maman keeps in the cupboard in the red and yellow plastic dish, she likes it soft to spread on her toast in the morning, parfois, it goes rancid, but Elizabeth's lovers are on the table today, not les produits laitiers.

Were you allergic? I ask.

To George, she laughs slurps.

We are allowed in Saint-Polycarpe, Elizabeth says the Chinese slurp their soup, they don't consider that impolite, sur Sherbrooke, if I slurp my chicken noodle soup, maman me fait les gros yeux, I bite into the crusty bread with the thick layer of creamy butter, suck in the crumbs before they fall on the table.

Each time he wanted to break a date, Elizabeth says, he sent me cut flowers. Red roses were for cancelling get-away weekends. But he broke dates mostly with carnations. Those not important dates, you know the kinds. Staying home on weeknights, my place, of course, or casual encounters at the Forum on Saturdays when he had an extra hockey ticket and no one to take, but suddenly an important client showed up and so did the damn carnations.

She swallows her Bardolino, refills our glasses, mine, still half full.

Why did you go out with Newspaper George?

He wasn't a newspaper man.

You told me he hid the Financial Times under the bed and read the Stock Index, after.

You remember that? Newspaper George, that's a good one. What a schmuck. That's why I prefer younger men, Ariane, dear. They're too horny to fall into paralyzing habits. They need to do things, they haven't lost their sense of play. Besides, they have stamina.

You were à peine older than me then. He was as old as Gérard is now, I don't mean Gérard is old, I mean.

No, Gérard will never be old, she says, lost in her thoughts. She lights a cigarette, blows softly. Yes, I was young then, easy to impress. At first. You see, way back in the fifties, people's idea of exotic was to go to Chinatown for sweet and sour pork with canned pineapple in ketchup sauce. George ate escargots and avocado stuffed with crab. That was living high on the hog. He routinely travelled to those cities which names you see on bottles of perfume you can't afford. In the beginning, he took me to those places. He dazzled me. I expected he was a wise man who would teach me the ways of the world. Four years it took me to smarten up. When I finally realized he owned me as surely as his Corinthian leather chairs and his hunting guns, there was no turning back. He showed up one night, an hour late, barely bothered to talk to me, just blew his load.

Why would Newspaper George be angry with you? He is the one who was late.

What do you mean?

You just said he blew his top.

Oh, Ariane, dear, she says, laughing. You'll be the death of me. He was horny and in a hurry. I told him and his flowers to go to hell. Find yourself an Anne or a Catherine, I told him, because this Elizabeth isn't losing her head over you. And that was that. No more old geezers.

But Elizabeth knew that not all young men are fun and it is not only rich old men who can make you feel cheap. Why did he make me feel inferior, saying vous to me and tonguing me, in the sarcophagus of le hangar, it comes to me, he was nervous, did not know what to do, he only knows abstract words, he knows nothing about les émotions, I called him un maudit câlice de tabarnac de con, those were les émotions à vif speaking, what is wrong with that, if I meet him again, I will not blow my top, will not let him intimidate me, Elizabeth told Newspaper George to go to hell, she was not the cheap one, under the steps dans le hangar, the prankish monsters trying to grab my ankles sent the little girl running giggling, tonight, I rush upstairs, the kitchen door is wide open.

Maman! I say, startled.

Impossible de dormir, she says, fanning herself with my La-Presse-not-Chinese fan.

In her nightgown, she slouches on a kitchen chair, the light turquoise cotton open at the breastline, the hemline half-way up her thighs, her thighs not touching, the gap between showing through the cotton made flimsy by one hundred washes, she wiggles her naked toes, eats a slice of Neapolitan ice cream, row by chocolate vanilla strawberry row, I never see her skin, except her face, neck, hands, when I was little, she wore shorts at mon oncle Joseph's chalet, a bathing suit at the beach, but I did not notice her, maman was just maman, always there, mais ce soir, sans préambule, I saw her entire body in the bathtub, like a Bonnard painting, and now after midnight, it is as if she had said, this is my grown-up daughter, what is there to hide, nous sommes entre femmes, I put les pivoines in water and join her at the table, sit sideways on the kitchen chair, my left arm resting on the back of the chair, we eat Neapolitan ice cream together, row by row, chocolate vanilla strawberry.

In Elizabeth's kitchen I sit sideways, my arm resting on the back of the chair, the soft April rain melts the puffs of snow still pure white in Saint-Polycarpe, Elizabeth puts a bowl of steaming mussels on the table, brings thick slices of baguette in a twig basket lined with a linen placemat, we drink wine the colour of straw.

Gérard, Elizabeth continues.

Elizabeth pronounces the name lovingly. In her mouth Gérard sounds like j'ai rare.

Gérard, she says, smells people in the wood of his antiques. He can sense their lips on the metal goblets, their fingers on the brass candlesticks, their bodies in the beds, their heads on the plush chairs. He doesn't buy a piece because it's listed as priceless in some traders' catalogue or because the market will make its price rocket through the roof in six months. Not Gérard. He acquires it, because he sees in the piece the small history of men and women living in rooms. Gérard's a few years older than me, but he'll never grow old. He'll never see life in terms of old age pension. No paralyzing habits. Not Gérard.

J'ai rare.

Am I imagining this as I eat ice cream in the middle of the night? Elizabeth never said, I love Gérard, Ariane, anymore than maman ever told me, I loved your father, Claudette. Can't imagine her life with Dead Man. What goes on inside her, what went on inside Elizabeth? The ice cream feels like silk, cold and slippery, treacherous. Je pense, treacherous silk, how mysterious.

I suck on a few mussels, they taste of mud, Elizabeth says there will always be only Gérard for her, what did I see with all my myopia behind Corona, peut-être, Raymond upstairs waits for my visit to end, les draps en bataille, I never saw maman's bed unmade, as soon as we get up, we must bury alive the spirit of sleep between the sheets, smother the spirit of love under heavy bedspread, I look up at the yellow ceiling, feel the weight of the great big bed, swaying and shaking like Christophe Colomb's ship on the stormy sea, what did I see behind Corona, was she drunk that night, nervous about the exhibit, artists get nervous drunk, c'est normal, their lives exposed like raw meat, I dip chunks of bread in the mussel broth, drink my wine too fast, Elizabeth pours me another glass, she is distracted.

Je vais faire de la limonade, maman says.

She does not pick up her plate and spoon to rinse them in the sink. I don't understand, should I believe her? The day of the mussels, it was all Gérard. The day of the minestrone soup she talked about all her lovers, not Pierre, bien sûr, she did not know him then, later she would include him in her alphabet soup of men, George Gérard Raymond Pierre, plus tous les autres in her past, plus tous les hommes she would have met in her future had the silver Chrysler my silver tongue not stopped her in the middle of her love alphabet, would she have gone all the way to Zorro, she is the one with the stamina, Elizabeth's alphabet soup of men from Ali Baba to Zorro.

Maman squeezes lemons on a hot summer night, soudain je pense, elle a un amant, only that can make her behave so unlike maman, my eyes open wide, soudain je pense, all of us do it, have done it, will do it, want to do it, dream about doing it, Nicole et Diane did it before they got married, peut-être, the four of them do it together in their mirror-image bungalows, et moi à l'Expo with Pierre, the pirate girl, la madame aux culottes d'hommes, and Elizabeth all her life with men galore, grand galop petit trot giddy-hop aboard, et aussi ma tante Rita, pourquoi pas ma tante Rita, all aboard, never mind, là.

Ma tante Rita avec son amant, why not, a young intellectual living in a garret on rue Saint-Denis or a man her own age she meets Wednesday afternoons in a motel en face du Jardin botanique, Rita opening her legs in the afternoon in a motel, the window covered with heavy motel curtains to conceal deflect, where does maman meet her new lover, not in a motel, not her, we drink the lemonade, so many words left unspoken.

Elizabeth sucks the juice pooling in her mus el shells, leaves the bread to disintegrate on the side of her plate, dips two fingers in her wine, sucks her fingers, takes a sip of wine, lights a cigarette, looks at the April rain, breathes in deeply as if she could smell the outside inside. She looks at me with a tender smile.

Talk to me, Ariane, dear.

I am in first-year cégep, I say, I don't know what I want to do with my life, all I know is I don't want to get stuck like Nicole et Diane, they are going steady with two cousins, Robert for Nicole and Roger for Diane, like Nicole et Diane, Robert and Roger are best friends, they will get married at the end of the year, the four of them plan to be best friends for the rest of their lives. I don't want to settle down, I say, sipping my straw-coloured wine, watching the rain. Does that mean I should have many lovers? Is it what it means, not to settle down?

There's no law about numbers, Elizabeth says. We all have desires. Expressed differently. Take me, for example. I'm not obsessed, I just like sex. But that's me. You listen to your desires, don't let anything or anyone push you around, and you'll be fine. It's all quite simple, really.

We sip wine as April rain falls, the mussel shells shine in their shallow sea broth, like they are at low tide. Elizabeth tells me how she met Gérard.

George and I went to Boston. We spent a Saturday afternoon visiting antique shops. Gérard was in the second shop
we went to. I remember it was filled with chairs, only chairs.
He sized us up with one glance. As George was showing off
his expertise to the dealer, Gérard whispered to me, if you're
ever in Montréal, I've got much better antiques. Then, ever
so delicately, he slipped his business card through the opening in my blouse and into my bra. That was the most erotic
thing anybody ever did to me. When George and I got back
to the hotel, I was so drenched, the print had rubbed off. I
stood in front of the bathroom mirror, reading my breasts.
Gérard L'Heureux, Antiquaire, Anteannum, with the phone
number and an address in Old Montreal. Antiquaire sounded
less crass than Antique Dealer and Gérard's family name was
an omen.

Bien sûr, since Corona I knew Gérard's family name was
L'Heureux, but Elizabeth pronounced it Looroo. It sounded
like the name of a spirit in Indian mythology, a bird or a
small burrowing animal. The day of the mussels I had never
seen the name of Gérard's boutique and thought it was Ant
et un Homme. It sounded perfectly normal for an antique
shop.

Gérard was my first Francophone, Elizabeth says. My
Quebecker soul. Ah, Ariane, dear, the power of other people's
tongues.

Gérard. Elizabeth enunciates its full Frenchness with
great care, as if the name might escape her. J'ai rare. That was
Elizabeth's gee period in her alphabet soup of men, d'abord
George, ensuite Gérard, like Picasso had sa période bleue,
puis sa période rose. The April rain pushes against the kitchen
windows, Elizabeth pushes smoke out of her nostrils, slowly,
holding on to the words she leaves unspoken.

We have not slept, I go downstairs to check out the
mood, at five in the morning, la barre du jour is too bright,
the day will be fierce. At eight on the street, people's eyes sag,

their skin hangs like Lazarus's wrapping, the entire city tossed and turned on saltwater sheets. I come back up, a warm breeze runs through the corridor, maman is making toast, dressed for work in a pleated white skirt and a royal blue short-sleeved jacket blouse with breast pockets, dog days or not, she never goes to the dogs, never dresses à la chienne à Jacques. She shows me her pantyhose in her handbag.

Je vais les mettre seulement une fois rendue au bureau, she says with a smile.

Je vais prendre le métro avec toi, I say. Puis, j'irai voir Gérard. Tu te souviens de Gérard? Tu l'as rencontré aux funérailles.

Oui, bien sûr.

Gérard et maman, the thought forms slowly in this heat.

Peut-être qu'il pourrait venir souper à la maison, un soir, I suggest.

On verra, she says, rinsing her breakfast dishes in the sink.

On verra, that means no longer deflecting, last night, no words spoken between us, nothing like between Elizabeth and me, mais définitivement, a change, as if she realized she has done all the raising there was to do, the bread dough that I am can no longer absorb la levure, time to bake it, the loaf that I will become is up to me, I must rise to the occasion. Last night something happened. We are two women sharing the flat on rue Sherbrooke, she will continue to be discreet, c'est sa vraie nature, that will not change, mais elle n'a plus à se forcer à faire son devoir de mère. I can look after myself.

Dépêche-toi, she says. Je ne veux pas être en retard.

She leaves the flat bare-legged and, I can tell, she is wearing no bra under that blouse with the breast pockets. I never thought about her breasts before, or her legs, or her desire. Maman's body like a Chinese box with many secret compartments.

Surviving Sunday

Ariane! My half-asleep brain connects my name to maman's voice, is she accusing me of not minding my own business, what did I do? what did I tell Gérard? she wants to know, he phoned just now to invite her to a country antique show dans les Cantons de l'Est, what kind of idea did I plant in Gérard's mind? she is not into antiques, she doesn't care about things, new or old, my brain clears a little, she sighs, feels sorry for his loss, has no choice but to accept his gracious invitation, ah, pour l'amour, what a Sunday.

I open my eyes a crack, glimpse her slipping out of my doorway. Busiest Sunday in her life, she must be back in time for tonight's concert au chalet de la montagne, she and Ana are going, that day they met gathering the garbage dans la ruelle, they must have discovered shared tastes in music, two dates in one day, my eyes close, so sleepy in this heat, something I must do today, cannot remember what, Nicole et Diane dance in my head, hold hands with little children, they will get pregnant exactly at the same time, haven't spoken to them since they came to les funérailles, they weren't pregnant then, what do the children mean, I drift into sunny Sunday morning sleep, the doorbell jerks me wide awake.

I put on my cat's eyes, run to the balcony, spy Gérard leaning against his Mercury, he lights a cigarette, stares at the pavement, maman emerges on the sidewalk, wearing her white dress and a blue scarf wrapped around her hair for the ride in the convertible, carrying her old white and blue straw handbag, Gérard's eyes on her, she catches him, he looks away, they shake hands, he opens the passenger door, she slips her legs into the car, smoothes down her dress. Is Gérard comparing Margot Lalancette, née Joly, with Elizabeth Gold, née Gold, is this a true date, Elizabeth alone in her coffin, is he betraying her, she would push smoke out of her mouth, say, don't be daft, Ariane, dear, Gérard pulls away from the curb, checks traffic over his shoulder, drives off, serious sad, Margot by his side.

Mozart on Mount Royal, children dancing, what is the connection, ah, oui, c'est ça, I said I would babysit the two kids, but that is later, something else I must do, I crawl back into bed, my mind clears a little, is this the last Sunday in July, ah, oui, Nicole phoned yesterday to remind me about le 27 juillet 1969. My brain retraces the events.

Last December, I attended Nicole's et Diane's double wedding, their fathers-in-law, brothers who started a construction company together, built houses as wedding gifts for both couples, mirror-image bungalows they built side by side, the gifts could not be moved into 'til last month, aujourd'hui, the happy couples pendent la crémaillère. Nicole told me on the phone, from two to sundown, 'til the last of the wine, they expect a crowd of friends and family to visit their little nests, she gave me their addresses and phone numbers, they live in the suburb across the river on the north shore, Duvernay, it is called. Diane phoned a few minutes later to tell me they will have mountains of food, potato salad and a whole ham, tomato aspic and a baked salmon, stuffed hard-boiled eggs all in a row, peut-être, I did not sound enthusiastic about coming, she used the food as bribe, I told her I am not good company these days, will put a damper sur leur fête, unhook leur crémaillère, extinguish their house-warming fire. A few minutes later, Nicole et Diane were each on a different phone in Diane's house convincing me it was the best medicine, do come, I said I would think about it.

They are my best friends, I should want to see them now that I am not au bout du monde, mais c'est quoi, cette réticence? Nicole talked about a gathering of friends and family, it will be like at their wedding. I close my eyes, don't want to catch the bouquet, Nicole et Diane make eye contact, do they want me to catch both bouquets and marry two men parce que je suis bilingue? moi, Ariane polyandre, I keep my arms down, like Greek columns protecting my body that is no temple for any husband. Pierre ne m'a pas accompagnée, weddings are against his principles, I came by myself, the way the guests keep glancing at me, je pense, this is not done, peut-être, it is bad luck for Nicole et Diane.

I did not know my maroon velvet coat was not proper wedding guest clothes, it had great success at Corona the year before and it was not even lined, for this grand occasion, I lined it with saffron silk lampas, the coat worn open over a burgundy velveteen miniskirt and matching ribbed sweater and tights in pearl grey, and my knee-high brown winter boots I dyed burgundy with shoe dye I bought chez monsieur Savard, notre cordonnier. Je pensais, I am creative, what is wrong with that?

I went chez Marshall on rue Sainte-Catherine, going there is like mounting an expedition into the treasure cave of the forty thieves. Such glitter, Thai silks and Chinese brocades, such riches, moirés and Italian woollens as fine as gossamer, high quality cottons from Lilles, broché suisse, silk velvet, lace, such prices, in other countries, women and men, barefoot in the dust, go about their business in everyday clothes made of those fabrics, I went à la recherche d'idées pour la doublure.

I stretch between the warm sheets, fluff up my pillow, show the manageress the velvet remnant I brought, she says hmmm and the way she says hmmm, I know she knows her fabric inside out. She leans over the cutting table, examines the piece of velvet drape, like a newly discovered mummy, strokes it against the nap, suggests Thai silk with gold or silver thread, lays bolts on the cutting table, with one clean sweep unrolls a length, I am not sure, she shows me flowered silk from China, rich cream, have seen that kind of fabric before, she says, this weave in relief is called lampas, a French word. Lampas? my voice mounts with excitement, didn't know it was called lampas, maman's wedding cape! I bolt out of the treasure cave. At home, my fingers trace the raised weave of intricate flowers, white on white, that cape, my priestess dress when I was little, lampas from China will do justice to the antique velvet. After careful laundering, I dye it in an infusion of saffron threads.

Eyebrows raised at the wedding, but mouths kept shut, Nicole's et Diane's big day must be perfect, today, tongues will wag in their wine if I show up in my stained gypsy skirt, cannot make an exception and change, même pour Nicole et Diane, that promise to myself matters, better to stay away than risk ruining their special Sunday.

Guitar music dans la ruelle, Ariane! my name called again, must be hallucinating.

Hé! Ariane! Pierre calls.

That voice is no mirage, I slip on my skirt, Raymond strums his guitar, lui et Pierre, deux bouffons qui dansent dans la ruelle, the kids downstairs on their gallery holler and clap their hands.

Viens-t'en, ma puce, Pierre says. On s'en va à la campagne. À un festival folk à Verchères.

Raymond strums harder. Funny day, maman et Gérard dans les Cantons de l'Est, nous trois à Verchères, we are dispersing away from Saint-Pol, no one ventures north, not even to Nicole's et Diane's suburbia, south, we go. Have to be back at seven to babysit those kids, no problem, how are we going? in Pierre's Rambler, Raymond announces, Pierre explains Raymond's Pontiac had a driveshaft attack on

Métropolitain right in the middle of rush hour, Raymond plays dark notes, mourning sa pauvre minoune, he has no money to buy a better heap, we go in Pierre's Rambler that's no better that Raymond's Pontiac, mais au moins, she is standing on her four wheels, they laugh at that. Pierre and Raymond are pals, since when?

Viens-t'en! viens-t'en! they repeat.

Je n'ai pas déjeuné, I say.

Pas grave, Pierre says.

We'll buy things on the way at a farmer's stand, country bread and strawberries, Raymond makes up a song about that, Pierre suggests we could eat the strawberries dipped in thick cream, after, like those Swedish lovers in that film, we could shoot ourselves.

Quel bel acte révolutionnaire, n'est-ce pas? he says, in a fine mood.

On the narrow winding road qui longe le Saint-Laurent, a car passing a large truck is coming straight at us from the opposite direction, Pierre swerves on the shoulder, gravel flies under the wheels, the car skids, we will end up in the ditch, les quatre roues en l'air, the roof in the mud, my heart beats fast, the other driver in a suicidal-who-gives-a-hoot mood never budged.

Maudit cave! we yell.

We soon stop at a farmer's stand to calm our nerves, cows in the field look up, munching, une vache meugle, I breathe the chewy smell of freshly cut hay, the sky so blue it shines like a plate.

Salut, les jeunes, le fermier greets us.

We look at the loaves of bread, the shiny cucumbers and radishes, we don't dare touch, we have no expertise, I spot small baskets of strawberries, dark and fleshy, okay, my treat, I buy thick country cream and strawberries and a loaf of bread, maman delights in eating strawberries with chunks of bread dipped in cream.

Décadent, they say, licking their young chops.

The farmer says his wife does the same. We smile, nous, les jeunes de la ville, lui, le vieux fermier, connecting in the countryside in that single moment. When Nicole et Diane appeared at my school in May the year I was twelve, they were older, disconnected, I asked them how come they were in grade seven. When they arrived in Montréal from Rivière-du-Loup, three years earlier, they were in grade five, as they should be, they hated the city, failed their exams, had to start grade five over, the year after, they went on to the next level but in May, their parents moved, Diane failed her exams, Nicole did not want to go on without her, so she failed too, they repeated grade six together, now they were in grade seven, their parents moved again, they were getting too old for elementary school. Pierre hugs me.

Je suis très heureux, aujourd'hui, ma puce, he says, kissing my forehead.

We studied together, passed our exams without cheating, attended the same high school, after graduation, we insisted on going to the same collège, une pour toutes, toutes pour une, they were still older than me but no longer disconnected. I helped them throughout leurs études, mais non, I say, oui oui, they insist, c'est grâce à moi if they are not uneducated housewives, but une éducation collégiale is enough education, they want to play house, do come, they said. They don't have to thank me with an invitation, they owe me nothing. The crowd in the grass applauds the performer on stage, d'ailleurs, je pense, I am in Montréal only by accident, peut-être, I was not meant to see them today, a young woman in a long flowery dress plays the fiddle, I stretch in the grass, enjoy the music.

Raymond performs des compositions de son répertoire, he even sings Chanson pour Elizabeth, Pierre puts his arm around my shoulder, I listen to the words, don't cry, I am getting used to Elizabeth-on-my-mind.

Des raconteurs québécois tell crazy tales, scary tales, des histoires à dormir debout, stories about us, how we became who what we are, they invite les spectateurs to come up, share try out their tongue. Pierre urges me to go.

Je ne sais pas raconter des histoires, moi! I say.

He laughs, as if I said something funny, Raymond points at me, the crowd claps, I have no choice, moi, on stage. La madame aux culottes d'hommes pops into my head, I have not seen her since last summer, I draw a quick sketch of her on the green country bus, a messenger-of-good-will travelling to the woods with boxes of underwear for boys, la madame dreaming of riding le train incontinent-al, that draws laughs, on Good Friday, le 12 avril 1968, she shows up in a mauve spring coat and a mauve straw hat with a bunch of paper violets tucked in the mauve grosgrain band.

Vous êtes chic, aujourd'hui, madame, I tell the audience I say to her.

C'est mon outfit de Pâques, she says.

I tell the audience I am surprised to see her today. Doesn't she get the day off on Good Friday? She moves her hippopotamus hips to tell me her boss gave her a subsistential bonus on this holy day and he amused himself hiding chocolate eggs wrapped in metallic paper among the briefs. I tell the audience la madame's boss anglais uses her as a conduit to expiate a bunch of sins, which is perfect on Good Friday, he does not exploit her like les patrons anglais habituels, la madame put her foot down, he pays her as if buying des indulgences, she knows how to survive, that draws cheers.

I tell them I said to her, on l'a échappé belle, madame. How so? la madame asks. Dans l'autobus, I tell the people in the grass, I speak English in case some of the passengers take religious offence. One more day, I say to la madame, and this would have been Good Friday the thirteenth.

Sainte viarge, what could be worse than dying nailed on a cross? she says, also in English. And he was sans culotte.

Only a rag autour des reins. Le fils de Dieu. C'est scan-
daleux.

I ask her what kind of underwear she thinks Jésus should
have been issued, bien sûr, she favours briefs, the kind with
the slit in front, her speciality, but we try on all sorts, we are
in a good mood on this Good Friday that is no Good Friday
the thirteenth, a day full of gods parading in the bus narrow
aisle, in boxer shorts, long johns, briefs, bikini briefs, thongs,
Apollo prances about in a thong, ça, c'est certain, she thinks
Dieu le Père chooses long johns because he is old and, at that
age, les vieillards sont frileux.

People applaud, polite or pleased, impossible à dire, I go
back in the grass with Pierre and Raymond, voices rise in my
head, that Good Friday full of surprises, I open the back door,
because on the day of sashimi Elizabeth told me to come in
through the kitchen like everyone else, we don't stand on ceremony, I wipe my feet on the mat, the kitchen is full of people.

Ah, Ariane, dear, Elizabeth says. Come in.

She is leaning against the counter, the position making
her uneven hips even more uneven. She hugs me.

Gang, she says. This is Claudette Lalancette, my model for
Ariane 1967.

Claudette Lalancette in her mouth sounds like false iden-
tity, I smile a general smile at the chorus of hello salut bonjour, feel foolish with my basket displaying a tin of Earl Grey
tea, a box of English water crackers and a slab of Cheshire cat
cheese cradled in green straw, my Easter gift I bought chez
Ogilvy, slide the basket on the counter, where is Raymond
where is Gérard, une mer d'inconnus crashes Elizabeth's
kitchen, nobody stands on ceremony.

I find a chair, decide not to run upstairs, our private joke
ritual not for the crowd, people come in and out, like
Elizabeth's house is la gare Centrale à l'heure de pointe. At
the table, a man and a woman in black bulky sweaters drink
O'Keefe out of bottles.

Ariane, dear, Elizabeth says, meet Nancy and Mike.

Yeah, Nancy says to me. It's that April madness. I told Mike here, let's go for a spin in the country. We'll put our feet up and have a drink with old Liz.

Say, Mike says. Is your name Ariane or Claudette?

Claude. Ariane Claude, I say, exactly as I said it to Raymond at Corona.

People move about, un grand brouhaha de chaises, my stomach growls, Elizabeth banters with Nancy.

More people show up, what is this, villagers coming out of hibernation, I sit watch cette tombola de village. They arrive at the back door, stamp their muddy rubbers before leaving them on the mildew-smelling steps, walk in thick country socks, their country voices bounce off walls and ceiling. Elizabeth invites them to have a beer, they find a chair or sit on the windowsill, this is an impromptu Good Friday party, people crowd around, I hang on to my chair.

One woman with uneven bangs brings back a pile of books, threads her way through the kitchen like an explorer through a jungle, disappears to the front of the house, comes back empty-handed, everybody calls her Betty.

Marie Berthiaume, our schoolteacher, Elizabeth says to me.

L'institutrice helps herself to a beer, sprawls on the chair Mike freed for her, he shares Nancy's.

You look bushed, Betty, he says.

Il est temps que je prenne ma retraite, Marie says. Before those devils have my skin.

She bums a cigarette out of Elizabeth's pack, Elizabeth notices my basket, does not know how it got there, she cracks open the cellophane, sets the food on the table among the full ashtrays and empty bottles. Nancy gets a knife in the utensils drawer, in one quick move, I stand up grab four crackers cut a wedge of cheese sit back, eat watch.

Eh, Moffat, come in, Elizabeth says, brushing cigarette ash off her brown sweater, the one with the hole at the shoulder.

Lui, c'est un potier, Marie the schoolteacher says to me. Il a beaucoup de talent.

Moffat comes in wearing une chemise de bûcheron, his grey cords smeared with dried clay, his face hidden under a bushy beard a foot long with bits in it. He opens a cupboard, informs Elizabeth he is borrowing a bottle of rye to tide him over for tonight, he'll replace it next week.

Elizabeth winks at me. Moffat the talented borrower sits down, wedges the bottle between his thighs, accepts the cigarette Mike offers him, Mike offers me one, I decline. Moffat takes the beer Nancy got out of the fridge for him after it travelled from hand to hand, the cheese is all gone but for one lump the size of a pencil eraser, the box of crackers lies empty, soudain, I am attacked by un fou rire irrésistible, bite my cheek, please please, let someone say something funny, une chance, someone does.

A woman pokes her head into the kitchen, says she put the spade back in the shed, what is this, le rite du printemps à Saint-Polycarpe, the ceremony of returning things borrowed, I glance at the bottle of rye, the woman sees Moffat, says something accusatory, like, what a lazy shit, he should have brought back that spade he borrowed god knows how long ago, he smiles, Marie tells me this is his wife Pauline, a drop of beer falls in Moffat's beard, I wonder what the bits are, the company trades des bons mots, they say, returning it in spades, better call a spade a shovel, words crash in Elizabeth's kitchen like hail, I am out of my element, why would Pauline put playing cards in a garden shed, quel est ce jeu de mots that is so amusing, spade and shovel, I sit and watch, want a glass of water, but people on the counter block the sink. I am trapped in a log jam of chair rails and legs, trapped by the drop-in friends, this afternoon's visiting shows me another Elizabeth, she uses words I don't understand, different contexts, different meanings, it's up to me to jump in, the kitchen is getting sticky hot with human flesh and damp country socks.

The crowd shifts in the grass, the hot summer breeze brings une odeur de varech, le Saint-Laurent snakes shines nearby, time to leave, must babysit, I promised, cannot find Pierre and Raymond, they drank beer all afternoon, smoked joints, peut-être, they are sleeping it off somewhere, the field empties, hé! les gars, où êtes-vous? I have a job to do.

A job? I say, eyes opening wide.

After the last of the drop-in friends left, Elizabeth brought me to her studio.

We cross the garden dotted with mounds of hard snow, follow a narrow path of snow worn-out by persistent footsteps, slip in a mixture of thawing mud and yellow grass, hold on to the wire fence, I breathe in the wet earth, we enter the studio at the back of the garden.

Darkroom, Elizabeth says, pointing at a door painted black.

Elizabeth's studio, une improvisation in an old wooden garage, the smell of oil but not motor oil, everywhere, paint-smeared rags hang stiff on trestles, brushes crowd in large cans, the labels intact, Hunt's Tomatoes Fancy Choice, Les Confitures de pommes et de fraises Vachon pour les meilleures tartes maison, ashtrays full of cigarette butts, old newspapers, headlines and classified crossed out with red gold white paint, finished canvasses and gessoed canvasses stacked together against the one blind wall, the studio, the house's offspring with its floor slanting and buckling under our feet, this garage pierced with large windows on three sides.

Monsieur Labrie installed them eight years ago on a day of driving rain, Elizabeth says.

She holds me by the shoulder, we look out the windows, the April light floods the studio, the garden, brown with dead

leaves and dried flowers. I try to remember if monsieur
Labrie dropped in earlier, Cézaire Labrie, l'homme à tout
faire du village, I have seen his face on the billboard by the
road, non, he didn't.

His windows leak like crazy, she says, still holding me by
the shoulder, as if to keep me from leaving.

I keep looking for Pierre and Raymond, sense le fleuve
à l'horizon, so much water descending toward the sea, that is
what happens when you cut windows out of blind walls on
a rainy day. Water soaks into the glass, gets trapped for years,
slowly sweats out one droplet at a time, each one expands
and fuses to the next one, finalement, all the drops join to
form a film on the surface, the glass foggy in summer, frosty
in winter.

Tu n'es pas à l'abri des intempéries avec les fenêtres de
monsieur Labrie, I say.

Elizabeth gives me an appreciative tap on the back of the
head that proves she understands parfaitement les jeux de
mots en français, she refuses to speak French, because she
hates her atrocious accent. That is when she offers me the
job.

We're rolling, Raymond has crashed on the back seat, a
trumpet solo coming out of his gaping mouth, Pierre sits
beside me, his head bobbing on his chest, I am driving his
Rambler, clenching the steering wheel, knuckles white,
mouth dry, cat's-eyed eyes pinned to the white line, mon
oncle taught me to drive last summer, haven't had much
practice since, my foot on the gas pedal shakes shakes, as if
still tapping to the rhythm of the music.

Trop de soleil dans ma bière, Pierre said, handing me the
key.

I hope we get back in town before maman returns, I see
her riding in Gérard's Mercury, her back straight, what did
Margot and Gérard talk about while viewing the displays of
antiques, I steer along the tight curves in the narrow road,

something suddenly sounds strange, the car pulls in one direction, like a dog on a leash made crazy by the scent of a rabbit.

Pierre! Pierre! réveille-toi! On a un problème, I shout, swallowing hard.

Pierre and Raymond jerk up at the same time.

Stop! Pierre commands, visibly not knowing where he is.

The car swerves. We'll end up in the ditch.

Doucement, doucement, ma puce.

I steer the wobbling car on the shoulder, brake hard, we lurch backward. We are no longer moving, my heart is racing.

On a un flat, Raymond says.

We get out of the car, I check my watch, merde.

Maudite marde, Pierre says, raking his fingers through his hair and kicking the left rear tire.

On dirait que ta minoune est en train d'expirer, Raymond says, looking mournful.

It takes them an eternity, despite their male know-how, to get started on changing the tire, they circle the car, mumbling, as in a midsummer pagan rite, we will never get home on time now, I am nervous impatient, order them to do something, it's no good, they are too stoned too pissed. My first flat tire and in the middle of nowhere. Mon oncle showed me how, concentrate.

I search for rocks to block the front wheels, Pierre and Raymond are poking at things in the ditch, laughing their heads off, looking for frogs, pretending to be des batraciens themselves. It takes me an hour from jack up to jack down, but the tire is changed. I wipe the black off my hands in the grass growing in the ditch, command mes bouffons back into the car, they pile into the rear, I relax my shoulders, take a deep breath, start the motor, drive steady, no point racing, I am beyond late, I let Ana, et maman, down.

The setting sun blinds me. The last of the wine. Nicole's et Diane's party, over. Tomorrow, they will drink coffee at their new kitchen tables, after, they will help each other wash their dishes piled high in the sinks, non, they must have dish-washing machines. Last summer, they took a break from going steady with Robert and Roger, they wanted to go wild a little before becoming genuine bona fide madames, Robert and Roger understood that, better they get it out of their systems, whatever it was they had to get out of their systems. The road is bumpy, the traffic heavy, I don't try to pass.

We are walking along rue Sainte-Catherine, Nicole et Diane make plans for the summer of '68, the three of us will go camping à Val-David, peut-être même jusqu'en Gaspésie, they have their drivers' licences, I have my learner's permit, they make bolder plans. The three of us will drive to lac Champlain, possiblement, go all the way to New York, wouldn't that be wild, our last summer just the three of us, une pour toutes, toutes pour une, I tell them I will not be that free, I have a job with the art photographer I've been visiting every week. They holler with excitement right in the middle of rue Sainte-Catherine.

Three cars pass me, the drivers don't care about the dou-ble line, those fools, get back into your lane.

I let Nicole et Diane develop their own pictures, art pho-tography, we all know what that means, dans les Laurentides, we all know what goes on in those Swiss-style chalets. Let them imagine. In December, they will marry Robert and Roger and that will be that. They are disappointed I cannot hang out with them all the time, but I remind them that once they were the busy lucky ones, being des hôtesses à l'Expo, they say, oui, mais l'Expo, c'était pas la vraie vie, what waits for me dans les Laurentides, ça, c'est la vraie vie. Their smiles tell me they are happy for me, their eyes tell me Claudette Lalancette soon to become Ariane Claude has no right to be so fucking lucky.

We approach the outskirts of the city, cross streets in the deep southern reaches I never knew existed, like lifting her many skirts, Montréal la gypsy, I smile at that. In their mirror-image bungalows, Nicole et Diane will analyze endlessly why I didn't come this Sunday, je suis en deuil, they know that, quand même, they will say, Claudette est bizarre depuis qu'elle est devenue Ariane, peut-être, they will conclude our paths are separating.

Maman left a message on the kitchen table, with the key to Ana's flat. The kids are at Rita's, I'm to fetch them, Ana wants them in bed by the time she gets home.

I am in deep dung, mon oncle will tell me about mes responsabilités, ma tante va me faire les gros yeux, they are too old to babysit neighbours' children, I rush upstairs, happy shouts and giddy laughs, fried onions and simmering tomatoes, mon oncle et ma tante dans la cuisine with the two kids, I lean against the doorway, ma tante dishes out a medley of pasta, leftovers from her pantry, elbow macaroni, shells, wheels, and bows, says, tous les enfants du monde adorent les pâtes, the children eat listen, but mainly eat, they are starving, ma tante tells them she is not used to entertaining anymore, but in her days, oh oh, she could whip up spaghetti for fifty, cook it in the diaper pail, the kids stare at their food, roll their eyes, resume eating, ma tante butters bread for them, mon oncle tells them about doors becoming tables, oui oui, mes petits, very ingenious, you use two chevalets, he mimes what chevalets are, to rest logs on for sawing, the kids nod, not sure, they eat, tomato sauce polka dots the oilcloth, mon oncle shows how he unhinges a door, lays it flat over les chevalets, ma tante says she uses a bed sheet as tablecloth, she turns toward me, waves her butter-smeared knife, asks if I've been in a car accident. My eyes pop open, why so surprised, she tells me, that's the kind of thing a mother feels in her bones, I tell them about the flat tire, mon oncle is proud proud.

C'est un petit souper à la bonne franquette, ma tante says, serving me a plate of pasta.

Est-ce que maman était fâchée? I ask.

She reminds me her sister is not the kind of woman to show her feelings in public, d'ailleurs, Gérard L'Heureux had driven them here with the kids, was dropping the women off at the concert, that sudden exposure of her private life was painful for Margot, ma tante wants to know how long she and Gérard have been seeing each other, how come her sister goes out with a neighbour, what's happening? Heureusement, ma tante does not wait for answers, she keeps on talking, telling me Ana used to work at the Czech Pavilion at Expo, she didn't want to go back to her country, found work à l'aéroport, dans les bureaux, it wasn't too difficult to bring her widowed father and the children over, ma tante lowers her voice, but the kids stopped listening, they are speaking to each other in their language, ma tante tells me the children's parents died in a fire over there, her knife points somewhere overseas, a drunk had set their house on fire, si c'est pas épouvantable, that was three years ago, Lenka was eight and little Pavel only five, quelle horreur! quelle tragédie! ma tante shivers, her hand at her throat, leur gouvernement, les communistes, was glad to get rid of orphans and an ageing man, mon oncle jumps in, crisse, not much older than him.

What name your grand-papa? ma tante asks.

Karel, Lenka says, swallowing pasta.

Ma tante tells me Karel used to be un constructeur de décors de théâtre, quel métier original, hein! here, he can't find work dans le théâtre, so he has to work in the east end, dans les raffineries de pétrole as a night security man, si c'est pas une honte, what a waste of talent, that's why, Claudette, you had to babysit tonight, Karel doesn't usually work on Sunday nights, this Sunday is an exception, how come your mother is going out with a neighbour?

How come ma tante Rita knows so much? I bet she found out the life history of our neighbours in a few minutes, between frying the onions and boiling the water, what did she do? Sit the kids under a bright light to give them the third degree, l'interrogatoire en règle, ma tante has a talent for l'interrogatoire. All at once, I understand les silences de maman. Sa discrétion, un refuge. Discreet, but also discrete. Elizabeth taught me the difference between discreet and discrete, same pronunciation, different spellings, different meanings. Maman separating herself from us, talkers. She who loves silence, us, talkers, are exhausting her, our questions as poisonous to her as exhaust fumes. I smile a secret smile, stretch my lower lip, ma tante slaps my hand.

I tell her I don't know, probablement, on her way to work, she met Ana on the stairs, they exchanged un bonjour discret, Ana may have said something about being from la Tchécoslovaquie, about hearing our music, even though we keep the volume down, maman may have said she enjoys listening to piano concertos in the evening, tonight, they go to un concert en plein air. Margot shopping for a friend. Time to move on, for both of us.

Mon oncle reminds ma tante that the last time Margot set foot on Mount Royal was before her marriage when she went to a ball au chalet de la montagne. Je pense, Margot au bal with Dead Man, Dead Man not dead dancing with Margot.

Oui, mais, monsieur L'Heureux, ma tante says. C'est nouveau, ça, avec ta mère?

I shrug. How am I to know, quand même, what about Gérard? Will they start going dans des petites auberges pleines d'antiquités québécoises? I don't see her wanting to do that, today, she was taken by surprise, mais elle n'aime pas la campagne, I tell mon oncle and ma tante, I imagine one single mosquito travelling to town, flying to the top of Mount Royal, zeroing in on her like toward a light in the night, buzzing louder in her ears than the brass section of the orchestra, finalement, attacking her, ma tante shakes her head, les bibites au chalet always ate maman alive, biting her more than anyone else, mon oncle thinks she tastes better than other people to les maringouins et les mouches noires. Je pense, non, elle n'ira pas dans des petites auberges avec Gérard.

Back home, Lenka and Pavel put on their pyjamas in silence. The rooms are sparsely furnished. The few times I babysat in the neighbourhood, so parents could take a break from their children to see a movie or dance at a night club or go to a hockey game, maman told me, défense absolue d'écornifler, here, there are few drawers to open. I look at portraits on the wall, heavy secrets hide behind those eyes. Ana's niece and nephew watch me watching their ancestors, they don't seem to trust me, peut-être, they think I have no experience with children, will not know how to rescue them. Even in a new country, fires happen.

I used to babysit, I say. Maman gave me plenty of advice, check the babies regularly so they don't die in their cribs, when changing a diaper, be careful not to catch the baby's skin with the safety pins. The Christmas I was eleven, ma cousine Ginette and her husband came from Toronto, we were at ma tante Rita's like usual, but that year, Ginette brought a new baby boy who cried as soon as they arrived and went on crying, I talked to him lying in the middle of mon oncle's and ma tante's bed, his face a beet, the noisy baby beet squirmed between a hedge of pillows to keep him from falling off, I put my hand over his face so he would be quiet, that worked, he was getting paler, maman's hand removed my hand, she checked his breathing, the beet breathed fine, his mouth full of pink gums, she smoothed his baby blue baby blanket, took me by the hand without saying a word, he slept the rest of the evening, I was proud, I knew how to take care of babies, don't worry.

We're no babies, Lenka says.

And I'm too old to babysit. I'm visiting. How does that sound?

Okay, Pavel says, throwing himself against my skirt and hugging my middle.

His sister tells him something stern in their language.

You work, Ariane? she asks.

Last summer I had a job with a friend, an artist-photographer, I say. She had tons of black and white photos stuffed pêle-mêle in dozens of pastry boxes. My job was to sort out the mess. My friend said, this is not the National Archives. What I had to do was group pictures together, put as many in each stack as I wanted, mix and match subjects as I chose, my friend wanted me to be creative, she would use those groupings later to compose a new series of canvasses, like collages.

When I grow up, I want to be a surgeon, Lenka says.

And you, Pavel?

Fireman.

In the gallery of portraits, Lenka points at a photo of a young couple. She doesn't have to say anything. The young couple is on their minds all the time. In this flat on rue Sherbrooke, only one floor below my home, but filled with the spirit of elsewhere, I am beginning to understand what it means to be responsible for the dead. It means thinking about them all the time, bringing them along everywhere we go, like this Sunday, even to hear the music. The kids want a story.

What story? Twice in a day!

The still eyes on the wall continue to watch us, ancient portraits of people not forgotten, Pierre says, on doit retrouver nos racines, we are beginning to tell each other our stories, I stare at the faces of proud women in black dresses and high collars, the faces of unsmiling men, their faces brimming with mute stories.

Great-great-grandparents on papa's side, Lenka says. Do you have a babička, Ariane?

All my grandparents are dead.

Your dad? Pavel asks.

Dead too, I say, squinting at the ancestors from across the ocean and herding the kids to their small bedroom behind the kitchen. Okay, I'll tell you a story, I announce, sitting on the edge of Pavel's bed. Claudette Lalancette's grandparents who were Dead Man's parents had a huge tobacco farm near Joliette. When Claudette was small they no longer lived on that farm. They lived in a big house by la rivière des Prairies. A tower rose at one corner of the house. That promised many mysteries, as exciting as staircases. But inside, the walls met at right angles like in any ordinary room. The tower was a lie. The staircase in that house was also a tease, the children were not allowed upstairs. That was a gloomy house.

The gloomy house had a finished basement with a pool table and a bowling alley. Oh, yes, a bowling alley. Parfois, Claudette was allowed downstairs with her cousins. They play-fought on the bowling alley, but were forbidden to play pool. That was an adult game. The uncles came downstairs to play, they never bothered to teach the children. Claudette never called those uncles mon oncle, like mon oncle Joseph, non, she called those men uncles because they were shadows. Those shadow uncles had moved away in their yoot to seek their fortunes. They lived in places like Californi-Ah and Brampton.

The grandparents were gloomy people to match their gloomy house. Their hands were cold like the rooms, they wore clothes as black as the black drapes that kept the sun out. All the adults smoked, including the grandmother and her daughters and the uncles' wives. They smoked but did not drink, except one glass of sherry before dinner, they sipped that and nibbled on cheese straws the grandmother had made in her gloomy kitchen. Claudette and her cousins were allowed a small glass of ginger ale, no cheese straws, that was adult food, like pool was an adult game. D'ailleurs, the cheese straws would spoil the children's appetite, the grandmother believed children had no restraint and, if allowed one cheese straw, they would stuff themselves like geese, no control.

Those grandparents did not look like people with a name like Lalancette. En fait, they spelled their name not Lalancette, but La Lancet, two words, only one tee, and they did not even pronounce that letter. La Lancet. Nobody ever explained to Claudette why she ended up une Lalancette. Peut-être, Dead Man wanted to be un homme du peuple, pas un bourgeois, peut-être, he did not want to live stiffly in dark rooms with no air.

Beside Dead Man, the grandparents had other children, all married, with children of their own, that made keeping track and remembering who's who difficult.

Maman and Claudette had to visit Dead Man's parents à la Pentecôte. The seventh Sunday after Easter. Depending on the year, it fell between mid-May and mid-June. Maman didn't want to go, but Claudette was their dead son's daughter and they wanted to keep an eye on how she was turning out, donc, à la Pentecôte, she had to show off her daughter like merchandise. The gloomy people didn't seem to like maman, they acted as if she was responsible for Dead Man's death.

Every year, Claudette was excited to go back to the house by the river because she always remembered the tower. It grew mysterious in her imagination, but, as soon as she entered the house, ping! she remembered how much of a lie the tower was and wanted to go home. Every year, maman and Claudette arrived at two in the afternoon and left at eight after the women had washed the supper dishes.

It was toute une affaire for the uncles and the aunts and their children to come from places like Californi-Ah and Brampton, donc, the family met only once a year à la

Pentecôte, because there were no longer risks of snowstorms. As this was a celebration, they had turkey like at Christmas and ham like at Easter and mashed potatoes and Brussels sprouts to go with the turkey and beans baked in molasses and pickled beets to go with the ham. It was gauche to mix the fixings for one meat with the fixings for the other meat. Everybody was allowed seconds, but the rule was strict. Christmas was Christmas and Easter was Easter, the grandmother would have none of that mixing of birth and resurrection on the same plate.

For dessert, the grandmother served a thing called a tipsy parson, maman told Claudette it was a kind of bagatelle, which explained nothing since Claudette had no idea what une bagatelle was. The grandmother brought a crystal bowl to the table and, every year, everybody said ahhhh and ohhhh. Under a dome of whipped cream were layers of sponge cake, raspberry jam and slivered almonds with crème pâtissière that looked like vanilla pudding. The cake dripped with sherry, that's why the adults had only one glass of sherry comme apéritif, the rest of the bottle drowned that poor cake. Maman never had tipsy parson, she touched her stomach, said she was full. She only had a sliver of white meat from the turkey with a small potato and two Brussels sprouts, but everybody insisted she would disappear she ate so little, so, she had indulged in a slice of ham and a spoonful of baked beans with three small pickled beets. Donc, because maman had eaten so much, Claudette was allowed her own portion of tipsy parson and maman's portion. Claudette ate the tipsy parson slowly, wringing the cake between the roof of her mouth and her tongue to extract all that sherry, imagining herself drunk drunk, and rolling in her mouth the whipped cream and la crème pâtissière like velvet and silk. After the tipsy parson, she drank a large glass of cold milk and went to sleep in the tower on a couch the grandmother called a daybed 'til maman woke her up, time to go.

The gloomy grandparents died when Claudette was twelve and fifteen. When she was twelve she did not have to go to les funérailles, when she was fifteen she had to go. The grandfather died first of something of the liver. Maman went aux funérailles but Claudette did not have to go because it was a school day, d'ailleurs, she was too young to attend death. She did not mind not going, après tout, the grandfather had not said three words to her ever. Before supper, he sat in the living room in his armchair and smoked many cigarettes, sérieux comme un pape. At supper, he sat in the dining room at the top of the table and ate, sérieux comme un pape. In the dining room, he said not much more than he had not said in the living room and never spoke to Claudette. En fait, the adults never spoke to the children, except to tell them to eat and be quiet. The children sat at a card table set in the archway between the dining room and what was called the breakfast nook. Donc, when Claudette was twelve, the grandfather just disappeared.

Toute la famille continued to show up à la Pentecôte, comme d'habitude, for poor grandmother's sake, and everything was exactly the same, except that the armchair in the living room and the chair at the top of the table in the dining room were empty. Sometimes, Claudette smelled the grandfather's cigarette smoke, which proved he came back from the dead for the Christmas and Easter double celebration à la Pentecôte.

Three years later when the grandmother was on her deathbed, she asked maman to bring Claudette to her. That was the only time Claudette climbed the staircase. The blinds in the dying bedroom were not drawn, which surprised Claudette, in movies the dying bedroom is always dark. Through the lace curtains, she could see the river shimmer between the maple trees lining the shore. After a while, Claudette went vers la mourante, tried to take her hand into hers like people do with dying people's hands in movies, but the grandmother glared, donc, Claudette did not touch her, did not speak, just waited. She saw the dead grandmother in her coffin. She touched the dead grandmother's hand. The skin felt like the papery material covering lamp shades and the hand was as white as a lamp shade and as hard.

After that, Claudette and maman never had to go back to the big house à Rivière-des-Prairies. Have you brushed your teeth? I ask the kids, their eyelids heavy. Goodnight, then.

But they will not fall asleep, they whisper in their language words I cannot know, it sounds as if they were caressing each other's ears with their mother tongue. Barefoot, I pace up and down the flat, a third the size of ours, four rooms so small walls always seem to touch my face. Could we swap? Jamais de la vie, maman will say. No charity, those people are proud, they will find their own way. I pace.

What people do to live, to survive. Moffat the potter with bits in his beard, Marie the schoolteacher trapped with the little devils, Elizabeth interrupting her artist's work to shoot corpses for anatomy books, to shoot weddings, like she shot Nicole's et Diane's last December, what about the pirate girl, working in her hospital for incurable hearts, even the man with the black pointed shoes survives du mieux qu'il peut, and Sven, son of Duane, what is he doing at this very moment, is it also dog-days hot in Distraction, Manitoba. And me. Do you work, Ariane? Lenka asked. Must go back to work on Gold Rush. The kids are still wide awake, I pace, the other bedroom, je pense, for Ana at night, for Karel during the day. The way people live, survive.

I yawn a lioness yawn, what a Sunday for maman! Will she come home more tired than on weekdays, tellement fourbue, she has no appetite. The ritual of returning from work, exactement à six heures, of ma tante phoning lundi mercredi vendredi, exactement quinze minutes plus tard, has not changed since the days of elementary school when I would come home from ma tante's flat, since the days of high school when I would hear maman's key in the lock, even now, the ritual continues, unchanged. This is what I figured out when I was little.

People have office lives and home lives. Maman works in her office sur la rue Saint-Jacques and, at the end of the day, must transform herself back into someone I would recognize, alterations, like in sewing, take time, that is why she returns home only at six, at six, she is no longer secrétaire particulière, but always, elle est très fatiguée.

J'ai besoin de souffler, she says, every day hanging her coat on the hall stand, in winter sitting on the ebony bench to remove her boots, in all seasons touching her hair, looking at herself in the mirror, announcing supper will be ready soon, she simply needs to put her feet up for a moment, going dans son boudoir to stretch in her rocking chair that has her permanent imprint in the leather and to rest her feet on the ottoman, closing her eyes.

But on Wednesdays, elle est particulièrement crevée, because she spends those afternoons in meetings in the bored room, not only with her boss the Cheshire cat cheese, but in the company of the other big cheeses, and she says they are worse than les bibites at mon oncle Joseph's chalet, they go on droning and biting and droning. She has no appetite no inspiration to make supper, I offer to open a can of, non, Claudette, she tells me, her eyes shut, she will fry me liver, she will not eat it, but I must eat liver once a week, iron Wednesdays, she feeds me well, I need my calcium and all my vitamins, de A à Z, to grow up strong and healthy, the phone rings.

Ma tante Rita stays home all day, le téléphone, she says, c'est sa ligne de cœur, without it, she would be cut off from life, but maman does not feel cut off, she wants to cut off the line, the black phone rings beside her, I answer, pretend to be sa secrétaire, pretend to be surprised, ah! c'est ma tante! ma tante knows her sister is right by the phone, pretends she doesn't know that, I always say, un instant, s'il te plaît, hand the receiver to maman, leave le boudoir, so she can tell her stay-at-home sister all about transformation.

I dial Pierre's number, put the phone down, what's the point? Sans doute, he's dead asleep passed out pickled. I hear Ana's key in the lock. Look in, Lenka and Pavel close their eyes, fall asleep in an instant, their little kids' bodies cuddling their ghosts.

Montage

One seven seven six, that must be a mistake, figures don't lie, my calculations may, une erreur est si facile.

Dans la ruelle, the children enjoy their dog days, play, children, August is here, bientôt, summer will be gone, play. Lenka and Pavel avec les enfants du quartier, words in Czech, words in French, dans la ruelle, Lenka and Pavel adapting, games children play.

I eye the template of Gold Rush 1969 spread out on the floor, the bell shape of the caftan, ten feet long, three feet wide at the base, an elongated image of Elizabeth dwarfing the kitchen.

Let's go over the formula I devised to calculate the surface of bodice and sleeves. My elbows stick to the bright yellow oilcloth. Multiply, add, divide, go through the figures once more. The answer remains the same. Read that number in English, less daunting. In all, I need to cut one thousand seven hundred and seventy-six rectangles three inches long by two inches wide before I can start gluing and assembling. That is daunting in any language.

I sit back, exhale, will run out of everything, summer, photos, resolve, eyelets, stamina, glue, fishing line, will never finish in time to show Virginia next month. The children play, I cut. They run their race in the heat, I cut, one seven seven six, the task discourages. Every morning, wash my face, brush my teeth, drink coffee, maman goes to the office, I sit in the kitchen, cutting, one rectangle at a time, a chair, a turtle with her shiny shell in the sun, dans la ruelle, the children play, an apple hanging on a shoelace, a paintbrush in an iron cup, the rectangles pile up, chain production, I work alone. Last year, my summer job with Elizabeth, we worked side by side in her studio garage.

Six Fridays 'til June, then three days a week 'til Labour Day, my job with the art photographer. Elizabeth's back turned toward me, her right elbow moves like she is playing a violin set on the table in front of her. I adjust my cat's eyes, dive into the mountain of photos piled high on my table, will Elizabeth find inspiration in my geometry, maman has taught me neatness, il faut faire de l'ordre. Elizabeth's elbow paints, she is making mad music. I pick photos, classify the subjects at random into neat piles ready for collages, faces houses body parts ferns cars horses chairs. Elizabeth's back hunched over her work, smoke rises from an invisible ashtray. I wrap each set of snapshots in yellow foolscap, write a list of content on the lined paper, faces houses body parts, don't identify the body parts, let it be a surprise, ferns cars horses chairs, why chairs, why not chairs, tie the bundle with an elastic band, store it back in one of the empty pastry boxes. With practice, I become bolder and redo the early sets, ferns and body parts I keep together, put horses with houses, look for more chairs, all kinds, make one set exclusively of chairs.

We take breaks, eat rye bread and havarti with garlic pickles, outside monsieur Labrie's windows, it is sunny or it rains, we drink coffee the colour of China ink, Elizabeth smokes and paints, I sort out photos, mix and match, we drink a glass of wine at the end of the day's work.

Must not lose the thread, cut, a wrought iron fence, a broom made of twigs, I am not losing the thread, this is as it should be.

Elizabeth, may I keep this picture? I ask, the first time the thought occurs.

She looks through her smoke screen, like I woke her up from a trance, her cigarette hangs between her lips, her paintbrush high in the air, my question barely audible under the loud brass of jazz filling the studio that afternoon, monsieur Labrie's windows and my belly tremble.

Do as you please, Ariane, dear. As long as you're creative.

And so, I am, I cut, the corner of a dresser, a bit of mirror, a smile, an eye, this is as it should be. And then. A thought on this hot August day zigzags through my mind, une pensée fulgurante comme un éclair de chaleur, bright and brief, powerful. Gold Rush is the extension of that work we did last summer, j'étais sa collaboratrice, maintenant, I am Elizabeth's hands and mind and eyes and heart, I am doing her collages for her. This is as it should be, I cut.

A dog barks so méchamment, I go on the gallery to make sure the kids are not being ripped to bits, the humid heat makes me shiver, I don't see the dog, its rage calms down, the kids sit in a circle in the middle of la ruelle, absorbed with what, a turd, a piece of found gum, a dead bird, a firecracker, I go back to my own found objects, cut, the onion dome of an Orthodox church, a barge, a bear.

I took the habit of picking and pocketing photos without bothering to bother Elizabeth, she gave me distracted permission, but permission is permission. I picked and pocketed a photo here, a park bench with no one sitting on it, a photo there, a woman out of focus walking away from the camera, picking and pocketing, slipping snapshots in my handbag, ni vu ni connu, bientôt, ma valise de fin de semaine was full of Elizabeth's pictures. Was that stealing, big caper in vinegar! I chuckle, fingers cramping on scissors, what difference did it make, Elizabeth could not possibly have used thousands of pictures in her tableaux even if she had lived the full nine lives of an English cat, my hasty words did not give her the chance to live the seven lives of a French cat.

I go back outside for an orange-flavoured popsicle break, the children fight and argue, on her coffee break at the office, does maman drink coffee or tea, do machine shop workers like mon oncle Joseph have coffee breaks, does he have une entente collective, my work, artist's work, no pay, I lick. Dans la ruelle, the children capture the sun in a mirror, it blinds me like the flash of a camera. When Elizabeth explained the job and how my photo arrangements would influence her next compositions, it's as if, that Good Friday of the nailing on the cross, she took a crowbar to remove the nails out of my hands and soul. That day became my very own very good Friday.

I am so creative excited that day, I grab a camera, start shooting, move about the studio like that fashion photographer in the Antonioni film shooting tall skinny models in mod plastic dresses, I am so giddy on tremendous permission I don't care if Elizabeth starts to wrestle with me like the girls in pink tights who sex wrestled with the photographer and they all ended up naked on the paper backdrop, knocking down light spots and tripods, Elizabeth tries to yank the camera out of my hands, I pull this way she pulls that way, we let go at the same time, it flies across the studio, hits one of monsieur Labrie's windows, in slow motion I see the glass shatter in millions of pieces, see glass rain fall on Elizabeth and me, I blink, the camera hits the window with a dull thud, comme un frisson mouillé, it does not break the window but leaves a chip in the glass, on dirait une larme pétrifiée, lands on the floor. The black box lies between us.

Elizabeth puffs cigarette smoke out of her nose like she is a dragon. She stares at me, her hard-as-diamond eyes, like maman stared the hardest that time, I am eight, running through the dining room, on ne court pas dans la maison, I run anyway, my elbow knocks over the lamp she calls Tiffany, lamp glass, blue red yellow white green, covers the floor,

weeks later she still finds tiny pieces of glass under furniture,
her stare that day, worse than spanking, Elizabeth stares at me
with her blue Tiffany-diamond eyes, puffs smoke, breaks into
a slow smile, ça y est, she will fire me, juste comme ça.

I am the photographer, not the subject, she says in a neu-
tral tone. Remember that, Ariane, dear.

She shows me the inside of the camera, no film, puts it
back on the shelf with the others, like mon oncle Joseph
stores his hunting rifle, no bullets. Creativity or not, I discover spontaneity must be dished out in tiny spoonfuls.

I lick bite the orange ice, rinse popsicle sugar off my fingers, cut, a woman selling spices at a street market, a fisherman at sea. Out of the elasticized back pocket of ma valise, I
take the series of camping snapshots, had she not yet decided
she was not to be photographed, she looks young and slim
with her hair tied back, did she drown the camera in the lake,
who was the photographer? Elizabeth camping, a whole part
of her existed before I was born, Elizabeth, safe from my
spontaneity, I pinch my lips, hard. And then, I have to smile,
she did not smash the camera that took her passport photo,
but that is lost, she looked good in that picture, she said the
photographer lit her well. I slip the camping snapshots back
in the pocket.

Pierre phones.

Viens-tu prendre un café, ma puce?

Tu ne travailles pas? I ask.

Je pense, what about le temps sacré de l'écriture, if he
needs to talk, that means his battle with words overwhelms
him, like drowning in a stormy sea, wonder if I should go. I
tell him about the one thousand seven hundred plus rectangles
I must cut, if it weren't for all that work, oui, I would come
tout de suite, we would talk, plus tard, we would go to his
place, peut-être, come here, quiet in the afternoon, alone in
the flat, Pierre et moi, dans la ruelle, the children play, their
shouts climb up the brick walls, we are the yoot, it is summer,

I could be elsewhere, Pierre tells me, oui, he should be working too, peut-être plus tard, oui oui, we will get together, c'est promis, I hang up, should enjoy la canicule with Pierre, ou bien, with Nicole et Diane in their mirror-image backyards à Duvernay. I drink a glass of water, have a pee, cut, the hood ornament from a Rolls Royce, a whole afternoon of cutting, uninterrupted.

And then, that Good Friday, Elizabeth removes another nail.

Elizabeth, why did you tell your friends my name was Claudette Lalancette?

I can tell, my question jams the circuits in her head.

Isn't it? she says.

Those girls at school! I say. Like a flock of shrieking seagulls. Claudetttt' Lalancetttt', all those tees they threw at me, a picket fence between them and me, I was not allowed to belong, and just because of a stupid name. After Nicole et Diane arrived at my school, things started to change, but. The gall of those seagull girls, Elizabeth! They were no better than me. But they were strong, because they had that weapon. Bien sûr, I laughed with them not to show the hurt. I felt ashamed.

That kind of shame is a fabrication, Elizabeth says softly.

My breath makes a circle of fog on the studio window.

Peut-être, I say. De toute façon, I never felt like une Claudette Lalancette, ever. But I felt like une Ariane right away. J'aimerais ça if you continued to call me Ariane.

It's that important to you?

I shrug want her to forget what I just said, I wish we could erase my silliness as easily as my breath on the window. Elizabeth blows, the smoke fuses on the glass with my breath fog. She holds me in her blue so blue gaze, will not release me. I must answer.

Ariane Claude sounds just right, I say. I invented the full name that night at Corona when Raymond asked me my name. And earlier today when Mike asked and I told him, Ariane Claude, it did not feel like a lie or a fraud. It felt I belong in that name.

If you hate Claudette Lalancette, Ariane, dear, fucking change it, she says, her voice amazingly soft and kind.

And she turns away from me.

Donc, I fucking changed my name. At first, it didn't seem as easy as paille, but I did it. Bien sûr, maman helped. Misère! To thank her for her promise to help, I almost killed her with my experiment. Une chance, much water has since gone under that bridge.

Depends how badly you want something, Elizabeth said. Calling me Claudette Lalancette in front of her drop-in friends, was she hinting for change? I cut, an umbrella, books on a windowsill, dans la ruelle, the children bounce a ball, they shout play, nobody is arguing anymore, children adapting to each other in any language, they play, I cut, a tennis racket, dans la vraie vie, names can be changed. If I had known, I would have fucking changed mine sooner, I cut, a bottle of mineral water, je pensais, a name is given to you for life, inaltérable identité, carved sur la pierre des fonts baptismaux dans les siècles des siècles. Fucking change it, Elizabeth said, soft and kind. En fin de compte, a name is not carved on stone tablets, but stitched on skin and what can be stitched can be unstitched.

I will have to phone offices, speak to madames who could be mamans to girls who may or may not want to change their names, information will trickle down through telephone wires, do birds' feet dancing on the wires sometimes cut people off, the law allows me to get a new name, c'est ça, la vraie vie, a new name a new life. Strangers will send the forms, the envelope will go through its secret ceremony in the post office, one day it will fall in our mailbox. I will have to provide original birth documents, that means mon baptistaire, la preuve que j'existe, que je suis la fille de

Marguerite Joly et de. What is Dead Man's name, Adam, Apollo, Georges?

I cut, a lightbulb, a snake pit. A sudden breeze blows through the flat and the leaves in the trees applaud in the hot wind. The images, particles of Elizabeth's life, fish swimming in a bowl, lovers' lips kissing, I will not find her birth certificate, Elizabeth was born woman, Venus fully grown, papers that confirm you have a name, you are alive, papers that confirm you are dead, I cut, an ashtray full of butts with the one defiant cigarette burning above the extinguished ones, dans la ruelle, the children are quiet, peut-être, they went to play in parc Lafontaine, peut-être, they went to the public outdoor swimming pool, dog days of August perfect for a swim, I cut.

That Good Friday when I get home from Saint-Pol, I find a note from maman saying, elle est allée au cinéma avec ma tante et mon oncle, peut-être, they went to see Les Dix Commandements, hope she did not lose her olives, I chuckle, it doesn't matter, she has no appetite.

In her bedroom, on top of the chiffonier that was Dead Man's, I avoid him and his thick lips in his copper frame, but examine the man's ring with the blue stone in the copper tray next to the frame, that type of ring is called une chevalière, why the keys on the gold chain, as if Dead Man forgot them, is expected to come back any second, put them in his pocket, say, à bientôt, never to return, maman waiting for him to come back for his keys.

I open her jewel box on her dresser. On the royal blue velvet, I recognize son camée, a brooch and matching ring, I play with her necklace en strass du Rhin, for Christmas only, the matching drop earrings, non, she says, avec ses lunettes en chat, her face is sufficiently decorated, I examine the stickpin with the grey pearl she wears in the lapel of her grey work suit, and three gold chains I did not know she had. I recognize her wide silver bracelet inscribed with son nom de jeune fille, Marguerite Joly, and a date, 20 mai 1944, her eighteenth birthday, she changed her name to Lalancette in 1948, she was twenty-two, bientôt, I will be eighteen, should I take son nom de jeune fille, non, I want my own name, je pense, does she feel more like une Marguerite ou une Margot, does she want to use Joly again, will the law allow her to get her own name back. Wrapped in mauve tissue paper, I discover sa bague de fiançailles et son anneau de mariage, she says they hurt her finger, and also, Dead Man's wedding band. Did she slip it off his finger after he died, quel geste! My ears ring, I close the jewel box like a miniature coffin.

I open maman's closet, shuffle skirts and coats out of the way, look for her cardboard mute accordion folder where she keeps her important papers. At the back of the back of the closet, my hand touches three suits, Dead Man's suits, do I see a moth escape, did he leave home keyless, barefoot and naked, like a holy man, what do I smell, the breath of Dead Man in maman's closet.

What does she do with Dead Man's suits? Peut-être, she chooses one, lays it on her bed, did he sleep on the left or the right side? lies down beside it, wraps one sleeve of the jacket around her waist, folds the other over her heart, searches the tweed for the scent of Dead Man's skin, rubs la laine qui pique against her cheeks, one leg resting over one of the pants leg. Is she ashamed, pense-t-elle qu'elle est dépravée, wrapping herself in her dead husband's suits?

I find mon certificat de naissance et le certificat de mariage, squint in the gloom of the closet. As I am getting ready to change my name, I discover Dead Man's full name. Joseph Bourgeois Léonard Lalancette. It does not fit. It hangs loose on him. How can she worship that man's suits, moaning in the dark of her bedroom, oh, Léo, mon Léo, screaming when they tell her the news, pour l'amour, pas mon Léo. I raise my head into his suits, they smell of maman's scent, lemon and Camay soap. No death certificate in the accordion folder. How did Dead Man die? When I was little, he died in the war. I'm no longer little.

I cut, a suitcase, a train ticket to Berlin, nibble on pieces of cold chicken I dip in the jar of mayonnaise, munch cut, a paddle, a hammer, a wooden bowl, an Indian blanket hanging on a stone wall, am in a frenzy of cutting.

Waiting for maman to return from le cinéma, I make un pâté chinois for supper. She has more appetite than usual, I am famished, mix ketchup with the mincemeat, cream corn and mashed potato, eat the mess in delicious forkfuls, a ravenous raven, j'ai une faim de loup, le loup and the raven chase each other down my stomach.

Tu as toujours l'estomac dans les talons, she says. Tu dévores comme un ogre.

She talks, Guess Who's Coming to Dinner, I tell her I have no idea, we laugh, are in a good mood, she tells me more about the film, ma tante did not understand the dialogue, for the first time, I confess my Easter story about the lost olives in the dust, while Moïse parts la mer Rouge, she laughs à gorge déployée, should I risk it, now? I risk it.

Maman, est-ce que c'est toi qui as choisi de m'appeler Claudette?

I can tell, she does not understand. How does that follow olives and movie miracles?

I tell her in English, because I have good practice now speaking my real mind with Elizabeth, I tell her I want to change my name. My new name is Ariane. I tell her about Ariane 1967, Elizabeth and me in Saint-Polycarpe, my work for Elizabeth this summer, sorting out thousands of photos. I tell her Ariane cannot be une Lalancette, d'ailleurs, what is the point, the man who gave me that name is dead, maman may want to stay madame Lalancette, après tout, she knew Dead Man, I did not, she loved Dead Man, I do not, she married Dead Man, I don't remember him, I tell her I have chosen my full name. I will become Ariane Claude.

She says nothing. She lifts a minuscule portion of pâté chinois on the tip of her fork, has appetite deserted her or just habits creeping back as she is lost in her thoughts, quoi qu'il en soit, she pushes the food between her lips like Chinese poison, swallows. She says nothing, but behind the difficult swallowing I see an amused little smile. She sighs, also speaks English, our practice language for mother-daughter real talk.

He wanted to call you Claudette, because. Because. Oh, it's so silly.

I wait. Not a good idea to rush her, après tout, speak is new to her.

Because, she continues, because he was smitten with Claudette Colbert. A Hollywood actress! she adds, rolling her eyes. At his age.

Smitten? C'est quoi, smitten?

Il avait le kick sur Claudette Colbert, she says.

Dead Man? I shriek. And you let him?

She shrugs. It wasn't important. Just silly. And Claudette's not that bad a name.

D'accord. Claudette Colbert, okay. Mais Claudette Lalancette, ça, c'est niaiseux. By becoming Ariane Claude, I kill Claudette Colbert and you don't have to put up with her anymore.

Maman makes tea, and, bang, it hits me. A white flash in front of my eyes. At school, other girls like me had dead mothers or dead fathers, pauvre enfant, you heard people say about one of those girls, elle est orpheline. To be orpheline de mère was the worst, moi, j'étais orpheline de père, donc, it was not so bad. You heard people whisper about the dead mothers and the dead fathers, those things said not said, but later when we started to discover la vie, those things said not said meant the dead fathers and the dead mothers were not dead one bit, they had run away, donc peut-être, Dead Man is not dead after all, peut-être, he ran away with Claudette Colbert. It makes perfect sense, but I know better than bring this up, we cannot have too much spontaneity all at once. Quand même, one day, he will come back to get his keys, d'ailleurs, why else would Dead Man leave his tweed suits behind, only one reason, they would be too hot for Hollywood, il fait toujours soleil à Hollywood, c'est connu, en plus, sans doute, his suits were not fashionable enough for Claudette Colbert who would buy him expensive clothes at places with names like Jacques of Hollywood. Peut-être maintenant, maman could become Margot Joly. Ariane Claude, fille de Margot Joly. That pleases me.

Ariane Claude, she says, sipping her Salada tea to clean the meat out of her mouth. Ariane Claude, she repeats to try it on. C'est un beau nom, Claudette. Ariane.

I wrap my arms around her neck. She lets me.

I am so elated that she approves and that she will help me with the paperwork, she has vast experience with paper at work, I forget to watch spontaneity and let it run rampant. I announce I will cook Easter dinner, we will invite mon oncle and ma tante, I will take care of everything, she has no reason to say no, she does not.

Maman phoned. She and Ana will meet dans le Vieux-Montréal for a bite. It will give the flat a chance to cool down before she comes home. When Karel goes to work, the kids will come upstairs for a little while, they will have had their supper, they will bring a book to read, they will be no bother, I tell her not to worry, to tell Ana, no problem, have a good evening. I smile pleased, cut, a spider dangling from her silk, a rainbow, a full moon in winter. In high school, we tried on different names, like découpage of identities, Micky and Nicou and Ianick replaced Lucille et Nicole et Diane, but that was just girls' game. We also spelled our real names backwards, some sounded Norwegian, some sounded Eskimo, mine was Ettedualc Ettecnalal, I say that out loud, it still sounds like nothing, a nonentity. Ariane Claude backward, I bellow, now, that has a zesty zing ring.

Ariane-Claude-in-waiting checking the mailbox every day, spending hours practising her new signature, looking up the signatures of famous people, les grands personnages made sure no one could read their names, I want people to read my name, what is the point of going through the trouble of changing it if nobody knows what it is. Ariane-in-waiting choosing un A that slants to the right, high and strong as a sea cliff, followed by the manicured hedge of riane, le C et le L forming an umbrella over the playful aude. Je pense, I will have to sign Gold Rush. I stretch, time to make myself a little cold supper, wonder what maman will eat dans le Vieux-Montréal, wonder if she is ready yet for lamb brochettes.

That one, I say, pointing at the glass case. How much does it weigh?

On the phone very late that Good Friday evening, Elizabeth suggested her butcher on boulevard Saint-Laurent, donc, she does not hate butchers, she enjoys chopping her own raw beef for steak tartare Lausanne, c'est tout. The butcher lifts the leg of lamb, it looks like a real leg but without skin and wool, une jambe écorchée, this one weighs a little under five pounds.

Okay, I say, but hesitate.

Monsieur le boucher waits. Je pense, carving the roast with the bone in will be complicated, I ask if it is possible for him to remove the bone, I mean, can it be done?

Sure, he says. No charge.

En deux temps, trois mouvements, moving the leg on his butcher's block, wielding his sharp knife so fast it looks like an arsenal of knives in his hand, he removes the bone, it now lies outside the leg. He wraps the leg and the bone in butcher's paper, tied with white string.

At the counter chez Four Brothers, I ask a man with a black wart under his left eye if they have couscous. He nods a solemn nod like I asked for a piece of Brother André's heart, après tout, I am in the food cathedral. Once, Elizabeth talked about couscous with Gérard, I thought it was a bird, like un coucou in Switzerland, it made sense, après tout, we had steak tartare Lausanne, we had sashimi, why not du coucou grillé, heureusement, I listened to context and discovered couscous is not a bird but a grain. The man with the black wart guides me through the aisles stocked with cans and boxes printed in Arabic and Greek. He hands me a cardboard box with a drawing of a dromedary under a palm tree in the background and a platter of steaming rice in the foreground. Couscous must be the Arabic word for rice.

Look at those giant red two lips! a customer shouts.

Je pense, how rude, no manners, I walk through the store, head held high, hoot and catcall all you want, I don't care. I buy olives from Egypt, goat cheese from Greece, olive oil from Italy, dry Hungarian salami sliced paper-thin pour un petit hors-d'œuvre, lemons packed in brine for the couscous, pay the man with the black wart who is back by the front window so he can keep an eye on the cash register and the other on people bustling outside.

The leg of lamb lies on the kitchen counter, its bone simmering in our stockpot to make a broth, maman sometimes makes soup with beef bones she buys chez monsieur Lebœuf. As Elizabeth recommended on the phone, I cut slits in the right side of the meat, who would have thought meat had a right side and a wrong side like fabric, push slivers of raw garlic deep inside the cuts, Elizabeth said, it's like fingering a cunt, she said, cunt. I flip the meat over, its wrong side facing me. I cooked the couscous following the illustrated directions on the box, easy to make, that Moroccan rice, but it does not look like rice, does not taste like rice. I look it up. Wheat! what a surprise!

I mix chopped pickled lemons with the cooked couscous, season it with pepper and cinnamon, pack le couscous au citron on one half of the slab of meat, fold the other half over, sew the two flaps of flesh with white cotton thread, it feels strange interesting pulling a needle and thread through red raw flesh, poor lamb, maman went to church with ma tante and mon oncle, ma tante asked her if she would mind very much, she did not mind, as I sew the lamb, I see the church full of Easter-dressed people, the priest in his rich clothes of silk and gold bends over the altar, cuts open the belly of the sacrificial lamb, Elizabeth in her midnight blue silk caftan with silver threads shoots priest and lamb, the meat is sewn, it looks like a leg again, I followed Elizabeth's instructions à la lettre. I put the meat in a roasting pan, salt and pepper it, dust it with cinnamon, stuff the leg in the oven, is maman going to communion this Easter Sunday, will she mind if ma tante asks, what if l'hostie tastes of goat cheese in honour of the resurrected sacrificial lamb, I wipe the counter.

Ah, cochonnerie, maman says as soon as she returns from church. Quelle est cette odeur?

Ça sent le mouton mouillé, mon oncle Joseph says.

C'est vrai, ma tante says. Veux-tu me dire, Claudette, qu'est-ce que tu nous fais pour dîner?

De l'agneau, I say, my heart sinking.

Ma tante looks at the djellaba I am wearing in honour of the dromedary on the box of couscous.

Qu'est-ce que tu fais encore en pyjama? she asks. Il est passé midi. Va t'habiller.

I tell her I am dressed, this is called une djellaba, I made it a while ago, using that tablecloth she bought maman on sale, the design with its squares of gold blue yellow paisley too busy for the table, perfect pour une djellaba.

Crisse, Claudette, mon oncle laughs.

I set the table in the dining room, the salad plates into the dinner plates, the salad already served, a pinwheel of thin slices of tomato and cucumber, scattered with onion rings and drizzled with Italian olive oil. We sit dans le grand salon to sip un rosé d'Anjou, ma tante's eyes sparkle.

C'est jour de fête pour vrai, she says. Oh! quelles belles tulipes! Tu les a achetées où?

Dans une épicerie sur Saint-Laurent.

Ma tante leans over the oversized lip-red flowers to smell them, tulips have no scent.

Ça fait rien, she says, like she reads my mind. C'est un beau bouquet de Pâques.

Mon oncle speaks at the top of his voice, makes jokes about the paper-thin Hungarian salami, ma tante nibbles on an Egyptian olive, discreetly leaves most of it on the side of her plate, hidden under her Easter paper napkin, yellow chicks and mauve Easter eggs, maman sips the wine, eats a slice of salami.

C'est très bon, cette charcuterie, Claudette, she says.

Nobody touches the feta cheese but me, I eat it all I am that nervous.

Maman opens the balcony door.

Quel beau dimanche de Pâques, comme une journée d'été, she says, taking deep breaths of rue Sherbrooke air.

Ce vin fancy-là, crisse, mon oncle says, c'est pour les femmes. Moi, je vas me prendre une petite bière, okay, Margot?

I jump up to fetch mon oncle a beer. The kitchen smells strongly of roasting lamb, I open the kitchen window, the kitchen door, all the bedroom windows, the dining room windows don't open.

Je suis désolée, Claudette, maman says. Cette odeur me rend malade.

She is brave, tries to eat, in the end, the lamb defeats her. All the windows and doors are open, nothing more I can do. She has to lie down with a wet cloth over her mouth and nose, repeating, je suis vraiment désolée, Claudette, vraiment désolée. Ma tante cannot eat, too worried about her sister, mon oncle drinks a lot of beer, says the meat is good but it tastes like sucking on wet wool, crisse, ma tante says the meat

is tender but too rare for her taste, I tell her this is the way
to eat lamb, rare. Mon oncle and ma tante leave before we
have Turkish coffee and halva.

For days afterward, maman complains she smells something rotting, je pense, phantom smells, peut-être, the lamb
himself feels his missing leg. Every day, she comes home from
work, insists something is really rotting in the flat, it is not
her imagination, peut-être, a dead rat. I hunt for the rat, in
the bottom kitchen cupboards, in the dark corners between
the wall and the stove, between the wall and the fridge, nothing. Peut-être, a rat died inside the walls and its death smell
is escaping through a hole, I inspect the walls, inch by inch,
move the light furniture, peek behind the heavy furniture,
nothing. I pour down the toilet the lamb broth I had stored
in the fridge, clean the toilet bowl, burn incense sticks in the
bathroom, still the smell persists. One day toward the end of
the month, maman opens the oven door to roast a chicken.

Ah, cochonnerie, she says, running to the bathroom to
vomit.

I run out of my room into the kitchen, see smell the
cause of her distress. The lamb with its couscous stuffing is so
faisandé the odour makes me gag, easy to imagine maggots
and things writhing in the dark oven.

Ah, cochonnerie, I say in complete agreement.

How did the lamb limp back into the oven, a complete
Easter mystery. I spread layers of La Presse on the floor by the
oven, half-close my eyes, hold my breath, lay the decomposing mess on the paper, wrap the poor lamb tightly, throw the
lot in the garbage can, une chance, les vidangeurs are collecting tomorrow. I clean and disinfect the roasting pan and
clean the entire oven with Easy Off.

I feel faint, ate nothing all day but a popsicle and a couple of pieces of chicken dipped in mayonnaise. Maman is
fully recovered. During her lamb illness, I took care of her,
brought her bouillon in bed, tea dans son boudoir, felt the

ancien fear that gnawed at me when I was little and she lay down dans le petit salon Sunday after lunch, like she was lying down in the afternoon to die, ne meurs pas, she smiled, pour l'amour, I rested my head on her chest to listen to her heartbeat, un deux, she stroked my hair, I listened to the whoosh whoosh of blood, the alive heart. I was terrified her heart would stop if I stopped paying attention, marvelled how the pumping machine kept the whole of her alive, even when she slept. I kept vigil at the foot of her bed to watch her chest rise and fall. Le cœur de maman. Solitaire. I never think about my own heart because I never heard it. And Elizabeth's heart, not organic, but ethereal to give away, to those lovers she loved, to those friends she loved and liked, et surtout, to Gérard, j'ai rare. Elizabeth's heart. Desire, seduction.

The kitchen soudainement so dark, I have to turn on the light, the evening sun gone in an instant, black clouds twisting the sky, thunder rolling into town, a knock at the front door, Lenka and Pavel come in, I lean over the railing, Karel waves from the bottom of the staircase, thank you, young lady, no problem, monsieur, he is gone to his nightwork, we are waiting for the thunderstorm, the dog days ready to bark their full heat rage.

The kids want to know why I am cutting all those photos, I tell them, can they help? non, something I have to do by myself, I store the day's work into ma valise, rain starts to spit spatter on the roof, we run to close windows, lightning and thunder getting close, Lenka points at a stain on my skirt, then another, then Pavel points too, like they play connect-the-dots, what fabulous beast will emerge, thunder cracks the air, they glance out the window at the muggy restless darkness, huddle close to me, they will not read their books, rain crashes down, why don't I wash my skirt? I tell them why, they understand, I tell them this skirt I made out of maman's wedding dress, she said yes? I didn't ask, they

shriek, didn't my mother want to kill me? I can tell, muti-
lating wedding dresses is not done in Bohemia either, not
mutilation, I tell them, mutation transformation, they are
waiting for the story.

For Expo, I want a billowing white gypsy skirt, I have no
money yet, so, I explore the flat for fabric. Let's go on the
grand tour, I say, they giggle, we run through the rooms.

Dans le grand salon, the maroon velvet drapes that used
to hang in the window, what a great gypsy skirt they would
make, non, for winter wear only. Where are the drapes? That
is another story for another day. The sheer curtains, oh, non,
too flimsy, and not the Persian rug, I will not be the thief of
Baghdad. Venez.

Dans le petit salon, as you can see, nothing but apple
green and pearl grey furniture and the beechwood hi-fi.

In the oval dining room, the cotton doilies on the ebony
sideboard and on the glass shelves inside the corner display
cabinet. Let's pin them together. Barely enough for a sleeve-
less microdress, great daring for parties, no good for gypsy
garb. Let's unpin the doilies and slide them back on the sideboard under the crystal bowl with the fake fruit, under the
black and white plaster cats, back in the display cabinet under
the cut-glass tumblers and the silver bowls we never use, all
that tarnish. What do we have in the sideboard drawer? Oh,
non, will not cut the formal Irish linen tablecloth with its
twelve perfectly pressed napkins. The busy paisley tablecloth
is no good. Where is it? Ah, that tablecloth too has mutated,
but, you're right, that is another story. And la nappe de Noël!
Who has ever heard of a Christmas gypsy?

The kids giggle, we rush on through the storm.

Dans le boudoir, no more fabric than dans le petit salon.
Let's flick the floor lamp on and off, bulb flashes may give me
material ideas. No idea yet. Continuons l'exploration.

In maman's bedroom, the pink chenille bedspread faded
in spots with lines of chenille worn off as if les chenilles

walked away, no good. I will not look through maman's things, she wears size petite. Dead Man's clothes in his chiffonier, drawers full of socks, underwear, sweaters, shirts neatly buttoned up and folded, ties rolled up, wool scarves, leather gloves, a shoehorn, a felt hat, white shirts, with a wide belt over a miniskirt or tie-dyed, am I crazy! Not his clothes! Let's slam those drawers shut.

This is maman in the double silver frame on her dresser, in the right frame, she stands alone on a sidewalk in front of a fenced garden, a young woman I never knew in a suit from the forties, high heels, a pillbox hat avec une voilette that covers the upper half of her face. See the white dots scattered over the mesh making fly shadows on her skin. She smiles broadly, like the fly dots tickle her. In the left frame, in a pale dress with long soft sleeves, she stands beside Dead Man in pleated pants and an Argyle sweater, he holds her by the waist. They look straight at the camera, peut-être, ma tante Rita took the photo.

Let's sit on the floor to study the vanity bench covered with the tapestry cushion embroidered au petit point. Those are three eighteenth-century marquises picnicking in the woods. We know they are marquises, because their breasts are puffing out of their dresses and they have fat fingers holding their gold goblets of wine. We know this is a picnic, because there is a tablecloth spread on the ground and a pear has rolled in the grass. See the deer, the wolf, and the lion watching les marquises from the leafy shadows. What do you think will happen?

This is my bedroom. I will not cut my gold bedspread, yes, now, it's gone, but is still on my bed the summer of Expo. You're right! That too was transformed, but later. Come along.

The television room. Let's dig through the trunk where we store our winter clothes. And where the wedding clothes used to be stored too. They are gone, oui, but let us imagine.

When I was nine, I played with the cape. It had a mother-of-pearl oyster-shell clasp at the neck. See, I sewed it on the waistband of my skirt. Maman wore the cape over her wedding gown, no veil, but a cape to fly away. So? I ask myself that day of the fabric search, where is the wedding gown? On the floor, the silk cape in a heap, the woollies in a heap, the trunk empty, oh, but the mind suspects a trick. Ta-dah! yes! A false bottom. And under the false bottom, here she lays, undisturbed all those years in her wrapping of tissue paper. Quelle étoffe! Miles of shimmering silk taffeta, what a gypsy skirt I will cut out of that dress! I am beyond asking permission. This is inspiration.

She lays in full splendour on maman's bed, sheltered under the headboard shining like peanut brittle, even on that dark morning, as dark as tonight. Late June '67 after my high school graduation and before my summer job à La Ronde, c'est la deuxième lune de miel de la robe de mariée. Imagine. The dress is la baronne Frankenstein's creature lying on the marriage bed, waiting to be dissected transformed, electricity in the air, my skin bristling. Nine yards of silk taffeta and organza, taffeta sounds like taffy, organza like a baroque instrument. What is the conversion for a gypsy skirt cut on the bias, three yards, three and a half, tops, but the skirt of this dress is cut sur le droit fil, the grain, in English, comme si le tissu était une céréale.

I finger the dress, you may touch my skirt, on the wedding day, Dead Man's fingers all over his bride, the silk gave him the first illusion of skin, all kinds of skin all kinds of silk woven by le ver à soie, soie grège, shantung, crêpe de Chine, surah, faille, peau de soie, grenadine, satin, la robe de mariage en taffetas et en organdi, a pool of slippery silk.

Imagine the gown. Designed in the forties, floor length extending nearly to the foot of the bed, a high neckline with a silk organza yoke covering the shoulders like a short cape, a fitted bodice with a dropped waist, the bodice lined with its own fabric, long sleek sleeves with pleats at the elbows and a shaped edge forming a point over the hand, like the tip of a heart, each sleeve closed at the wrist with three pearl buttons and taffeta loops. I turn the dress over to look at her back, rearrange the flowing fabric over the chenille, extend the sleeves flat on the bed, the lined bodice has side seams and a back opening with twenty-one three-eighths-of-an-inch pearl buttons and taffeta loops cascading from the neck down to the small of the back, the flared skirt, unlined, the back panels extend into a train.

I lean over the dress, one knee on the bed, fingers follow-ing seams, fifteen pieces to unstitch, so much thread to snip without ripping the fragile fabric. I name the pieces out loud, comme dans une leçon d'anatomie, bodice front, bodice back, front band, back band, yoke front, yoke back, upper back facing, lower back facing, sleeves, twenty-seven loops when removed from the bodice and sleeves will lie on the bed like white crescent-shaped nail clippings, skirt front, skirt back, skirt side back, extensions for the train, miles of unstitching to do.

But first, I must give the yellowing dress a bath, a wise move to wash her before dissection, sinon, quel cauchemar! The raw edges of each unstitched piece would fray mon-strously in the bathwater. We're out of Tide.

I run to monsieur Lebœuf's grocery store, the day, sticky muggy, how was her October wedding day, bright and sunny, cold and rainy, I pay monsieur Lebœuf, the clouds burst all at once, let's look at the rain from the balcony. I am in the wash, soaked in a flash, no point running, impossible to get any wetter, I walk giggle, the box disintegrates in my arms, je suis trempée jusqu'à la moelle, imagine the marrow oozing out of my bones the way the white soap swells out of soggy card-board, the white froth spreads on the black smoking pave-ment, bubbles float, burst under the wheels of cars, the hard rain churns laundry soap, la rue Sherbrooke, a giant washing machine, I cross, slip on suds, the pavement treacherous comme en hiver, I stop traffic, lean on the hoods of cars to regain my footing, swirl in the frothy street, a train of white flakes follows me, cars move cautiously after my passage, motorists smile smiles of dismay, ah, la jeunesse d'aujourd'hui, laughter and honking, what fun, après tout, c'est l'Expo, il faut bien se défouler.

Confetti melting in the pelting rain, the high tub full of cool soapy water, on the roof the rain drums, the dress takes her bath, my hands push her under, press her train, her hem, her sleeves, massage the cloth in soapy water, gently rub silk against silk, should I beat the yellowed taffeta against black slippery pavement, the chore of thousands over countless years of beating rubbing cleansing cloth against stone, hands red, hands chafed against perfect white, the white laughter of a morning rain, the new Montréal summer, soggy warm as the inside of a washing machine gyrating a full load, my hands pick up the wedding dress, rinse, empty the tub, rinse rinse, the foam churns down the drain, rinse the dress, must remove all traces of soap, gently press water out, no wringing, this, a wedding dress, one must be gentle, I enter our building, drip soaking wet, trail whiteblue soap on the cold stones of the lobby, strip in the entrance of our flat, jeans and tee-shirt in a wet heap on the floor, after the rain the sun, the dress dries on the clothesline in June sunshine, every ten minutes I go on the gallery to check, is she dry yet is she dry yet.

In my bedroom, come on, gang, I lay the dress on my gold bedspread. On my desk, I line up all my scissors like surgical tools, les authentiques ciseaux de couturière maman gave me for my fourteenth birthday, the big pinking shears ma tante Rita calls des ciseaux à pinker, I call pinky cheers, those shears, like the mouth of a Nile crocodile impatient to bite velvet cotton silk polyester, the straight blades, different sizes, and the thread snippers, all ready, stainless steel gleaming, edges sharp, once a year, monsieur Savard sharpens the blades, along with my skates.

No need to undo the top, will detach it from the skirt and unstitch the skirt panels and train extensions. For the gypsy skirt, I will need extra fabric for two side seam pockets and a wide waistband, peut-être, I can use remnants of the train, if not, I will have to mutilate the bodice. I lean over the body of the dress, the stitches so small, the thread snippers won't do, better use a razor blade like a scalpel. Cat's eyes on, hands clean, deep breath, begin. Once the first cut is done, once begun I must go on.

I snip for hours, quarter-inch stitch by quarter-inch stitch, pull break, pull break, the first knuckle of the left index finger has deep thread cuts, must not bleed on white taffeta, the heart pounds for fear the silk will rip near a seam, le tissu est mûr, fragile from years of neglect, after hours of thread breaking, the neck aches, the back burns, the eyes swell up with fatigue, enfin, the bodice separates from the skirt, the body stretches on the floor, flashes of red and white shoot across the eyes, must begin to separate the skirt into its parts, snip pull break again, the stabs of pain in the back sharpening, the cuts in the finger opening like fish gills, but no bleeding, bits of white thread catch on clothes, stick to hair, fly into mouth, snip pull break, fingers full of cramps.

The bodice lies intact on the bed, the skirt, dissected, one front and one back panel, both cut on the fold, two side back panels, two extension panels for the train. The sewing thread left tiny holes along the edges of the cloth, permanent scarification, this is no virgin silk, will this wedding tattoo show on the finished gypsy skirt, I put the razor away.

I sew, church bells ringing, when I'm little, I think I am at maman's wedding, in her belly, moi, la petite espionne, hearing the bells, the music, puis, la nuit de noces, bien sûr, it was all imagining. I counted on my fingers, substracted on paper, l'arithmétique ne ment pas, eighteen months between wedding day and birth day, maman is not une éléphante, quand même, cette nuit-là, the bride and groom are in the bedroom next to mine, I sew.

Dead Man stands behind his wife, his head numb from the immensity of the night, they watch themselves in the mirror of the dresser, like later they will live inside the portrait silver frame, I sew. His butter fingers attempt the challenge, the seduction of undoing twenty-seven tiny pearl buttons, first the three buttons on each sleeve, ensuite, the twenty-one buttons from the nape of the neck to the small of the back, at the shoulders he slides the dress off, kisses his wife's neck, brushes his lips along her spine, the dress hangs off her, still caught at the wrists, he slips the sleeves off one by one, the dress slips falls in a swish of water taffeta at her feet, I sew. Did ma tante Rita advise her sister on lingerie pour sa nuit de noces, did maman choose pure soie pour la séduction, fine batiste pour l'élégance, simple coton pour le confort, I sew. Dead Man peels his bride like a grape, twenty-seven pearl buttons to unloop, moi earlier with the razor blade, snipping stitch by stitch 'til the wedding dress was no more, I sew.

Instead of a zipper, I cut a placket for the back opening and, because this is the summer of Expo et j'ai dix-sept ans, I use seventeen loops and seventeen pearl buttons from the bodice to fasten the skirt.

Tomorrow, I begin my summer job, I am impatient to finish, guess the seam allowances, no time to mark them with chalk first, make long stitches, sew in feverish haste.

Last detail. I fasten the oyster-shell-shaped clasp from the wedding cape in the centre front of the waistband. See? A permanent sea jewel.

The kids are sleepy.

I tell you what. Why don't you sleep here, in our guest bedroom. Tomorrow, we'll have breakfast together. What do you say?

Their eyes light up, this is adventure. They soon settle into the twin beds, but don't want me to go, not yet.

How did your dad die?

I don't know, Lenka. My mom never told me. When I was little, I invented different deaths for him.

Like what? Pavel asks, leaning on his elbow.

One was a hunting accident. Dead Man walking in the woods, the November trees bare, his boots crushing leaves, the air smelling of mushrooms. Il est prudent, Dead Man, cradling his rifle in the crook of his elbow comme un baron in a French movie out to shoot un sanglier, a young city man in the woods, following a moose. His buddies hearing a shot echoing through the woods like in a cathedral, the hunters rushing, the sound of crushed leaves deafening. A circle of men around Dead Man, is it his blood painting the fallen leaves, he is lying face down, shot in the face comme un sui-cidé. That's one death.

Another death. Il était un ethnologue, he studied tribes deep in the steamy Amazon jungle, he wore his tweed suits only when he taught l'anthropologie à l'Université de Montréal. He disappeared during one of his expeditions, sans doute, he was eaten. For months, maman woke up scream-ing, her fist in her mouth to muffle the sound, les murs sont minces, she did not want the neighbours to hear, pain is pri-vate. She had nightmares full of grimacing faces. Léo Léo, she called his name, the more she called the more his face faded away behind thick jungle-green leaves. Léo Léo, she called, only long-tailed red birds in the canopy answered with long piercing shrieks.

The most likely death is this one. Dead Man dies en vrai Québécois. He drives his Blue Chevy on the winding road ten miles from mon oncle Joseph's chalet. Sunday night, warm summer evening, he rolls down the window, props his left elbow on the window frame, hooks his fingers over the edge of the roof. The two brothers-in-law play horseshoes all afternoon, it is hot, they drink des petites Labatt 50. Later, Dead Man drives fast, not because he is drunk, but because he is young, with a young wife and small daughter in the city, his eyes grow heavy with sleep, he closes his eyes, one tiny second, his foot pushes the accelerator to the floor, the car hits a cement wall at full speed, the blue Chevy crumples like a mute accordion, Dead Man's fingers imprint into the metal at the edge of the roof, the impact is terrific, he doesn't have a prayer. Later, maman weeps, Léo non, non Léo, pour l'amour, comment est-ce possible, pas mon Léo. Later, people pay their respects to a closed casket, ma tante Rita explains a hundred times to distant relatives, on a dû fermer le cercueil, vous comprenez, would have cost a fortune to reconstruct his face in wax and what for, ma tante and the relatives hang their heads, mon oncle Joseph mutters, crisse crisse crisse, an incantation that sounds like a priest's blessing sending Dead Man into the forever after.

I wish I never knew how our parents died, Pavel says, settling into his pillow.

But they died heroes' deaths, I say, honourable deaths saving you and your sister. You see, I don't have a dad, not even a father, to remember. I call him Dead Man, because he doesn't matter. Maman never speaks about him. Peut-être, he died a silly death or a shameful death and she doesn't want me to know. That is a terrible burden to bear alone.

We say no more. We listen. The downpour on the roof lulls them to sleep.

Maman and Ana are late coming home. Not to worry. Sans doute, elles n'ont pas vu le temps passer, and when they checked their watches, they were startled, look at the time! happy in each other's company. Sans doute, they are having difficulty finding a cab in this dog days storm. Nothing to worry about.

I cannot resist opening ma valise and cutting a little while longer, rain taps on the kitchen window pushed by a strong west wind, I cut, a pig from the sign of a butcher shop, carrots in a basket, old bricks with weeds growing between the clay shards. The night is young, I cut.

Only one thousand seven hundred more to go.

Bed & Breakfast

Gérard shows a client furniture, in French we say, meubler son temps, the client buys meubles, I furnish my time, and how, you may ask, très bien, merci, and not just looking, touching too, in Gérard's boutique of antiques everything tactile and odorous, the scent of things occupied, sold, reoccupied, maman's wedding gifts are here too but where, I don't see her silver coffee and tea sets, those, the first things I brought Gérard last year, the things he sells, we never see again, the things he rents to film and television people come back after their adventures in front of the camera, peut-être un jour, the silver coffee set will appear in a toothpaste commercial, notre dentifrice rend vos dents étincelantes de blancheur, the actor in the lab coat hired to make that promise will say, while madames enjoy their coffee, knowing their teeth are safe from stains, ou dans un téléfilm, the well-known blond actress playing une bourgeoise will pour tea out of la théière d'argent, while a cat burglar enters her bedroom window, each time I brought him one of the wedding gifts from le hangar, Gérard thought she had nice things, did they hit it off, the other day in the country, comment ont-ils meublé leur temps, the client buys nothing, no furniture reoccupied today, quand même, Gérard slaps him on the back, calls him, mon vieux, the special relationship client-merchant like the ancient mystique penitent-confessor, go in peace, my son, and sin no more, but the client will be back, like penitents become sinners again, he has bought before, will buy again.

Notre logement est plein d'antiquités, I say to Gérard.

Je sais, Ariane, je sais.

So, that's how they spent their time, Gérard talked shop-furniture, why would maman tell him about her things in the flat, that is not like her, what if she told him she never gave me permission to sell him her wedding gifts, my heart skips a beat. Non non, not true, I did not misread her, those things dans le hangar, carefully packed years ago, le trésor caché de Montecristo, bon débarras, like I rid her of Claudette Colbert.

Ta mère est très sympathique, Gérard says.

His tone means, no more hints, Ariane. D'accord. Après tout, if I want to see him, I see him, if she wants to see him if he wants to see her, I will not put my nose into their business, maintenant, I want to put my nose into my own business. I want to talk to him, he wants to talk to me too. He takes me by the shoulder. I need to know what will happen to Elizabeth's photo collection, because I may need more snapshots for Gold Rush, puis, what will happen to her house, il est l'héritier d'Elizabeth, she said, Gérard is my sole heir, he's also the executor of my will, like Gérard is to shoot execute her mind, she took care of things before our trip, if anything should happen, she said. We sit in the green velvet armchairs separated by a low table where important clients sip coffee, while Gérard fills out papers for them or makes telephone inquiries behind the oak counter, we sit in those important-client chairs.

Ta mère s'inquiète à ton sujet, Gérard says.

He crosses his long legs, places his elbows on the arms of the chair, the tips of his fingers touching to form a roof, rests his lips against his middle fingers, looks at me, the four lines on his forehead fully creased. Wearing black jeans and a black jersey in the full of summer, he looks like le jésuite who ran the house of la Jeunesse étudiante catholique on rue

Sherbrooke where I went a few Saturday mornings when I was fourteen, not to share similar interests with people my own age dans un environnement sain, as ma tante Rita suggested, but because the old beautiful house promised many staircases and mysteries. Gérard le faux jésuite better not give me a lecture in mon oncle Joseph's voice about maman not getting any younger, that house inside looked and smelled like a school with dull green walls and staircases cordoned off, un environnement sain always forbids curiosity, I don't need lectures on getting a job.

I tell Gérard I am responsible, last year, I kept my summer job with Elizabeth, the summer of Expo, I lost my job making pizza through no fault of mine, d'ailleurs, I did not want a job, I did well in high school, deserved one last summer to play before continuing my studies and becoming a genuine bona fide adult and then that would be that.

Gérard opens his mouth to speak.

Je sais ce que tu vas me dire, I say. Mon oncle Joseph m'a déjà tout dit sur la vie.

I tell him mon oncle told me, when he was my age, he was already working at Angus, that was not l'Eldorado, but it does a man good to work, his high school chums, en chômage, wasting their lives shooting pool, mon oncle was learning English, his foreman could not pull the lamb's wool over his eyes, crisse, he became a machinist, skilled work didn't grow on trees, best experience in the world.

Le patron m'a pincé les fesses, I say. Donc, j'ai démissionné.

I can tell, Gérard is confused. I tell him that's what I told the family. Tout de suite, mon oncle puffs up his chest, crisse, tu te défends, he says, making two fists like a boxer. But, I tell Gérard, that was not true, le patron did not make a pass at me. I lost my job making pizza, not because I was slow stretching garnishing cutting serving, non, the boss's niece wanted my job, elle avait le kick sur Pierre, she was hot,

Pierre did not fight for me, he just stared at her breasts, I tell Gérard Pierre said, elle a des seins comme des pis de cinq heures. As un écrivain engagé, Pierre has to store many kinds of details like the time of day cows have to be milked, five in the morning and five in the afternoon. I could not tell the family why I got the sack, mon oncle would have had a fit caused by that grave social injustice. Maman was not worried I lost my job. Comme d'habitude, she picked the crumbs off the tablecloth with the tip of her index finger and put them on the side of her bread plate.

Gérard nods and smiles a tender smile, that means, he has already seen her do that, that means they had a meal together that Sunday.

I tell Gérard I managed to make a few pennies that summer by hanging out outside le Pavillon de la Jeunesse and sewing, people talked to me because I sewed, they had never seen that before, a girl my age sewing, they thought I was an Expo exhibit, la jeunesse au travail. I practised my English, offered to guide visitors, I knew where everything was, to prove it, I named all the pavilions, restaurants, fast food counters, bars. I could direct anyone in both Expo languages to any Expo washroom, in a few days of people asking, where is the, où sont les, I collected several words, some I knew some were new, bathroom, toilet, petit coin, toilettes, latrine, bog, cabinets, can, privy, restroom, vespasienne, john, pauvres Johns, lavatory, loo, urinal, pissoir, pissotière, even closet like in broom closet and double-you-see, un mot suggestif que maman trouverait vulgaire.

People asked how much to guide them through Expo for the entire day, more fun to visit with a companion, they said, I said, free if we speak English. We walk and talk and visit, they ask questions, I translate in my head, answer, trip a little over grammar, but learn fast, they say, I speak English very well, I don't believe them but say, merci, they say, I am a great ambassador, they buy me a meal, give me tips at the end of the day, they say, take it, you're a student, sometimes they give me five dollars, sometimes twenty dollars, huge money.

Gérard's assistant comes downstairs, she slips behind the oak counter, tells him she needs to look up some customers' cards, she can do that later if he prefers, he indicates it's all right, do your work, he turns back to me.

What will you do in September? he asks.

Michelle looks up from the index cards, goes back to work, disappointed. When I was small, if maman and mon oncle Joseph switched to the caramel language, that meant they were having a serious private conversation.

Is that what you and maman talked about that Sunday? I ask.

We talked about many things. Of course, your mother understands you didn't want to look for a job this summer.

I have a job. What do you think Gold Rush is?

Will you go to university? If you think it's too late to apply, explain the circumstances to the Registrar. I'm sure you'll get a dispensation and will be admitted. Besides, the money you saved for the trip could be your university fund. You won't have to apply for loans, you're set. Or do you want to travel? Or work for a while? You could also work overseas. You have many options.

Travailler à l'étranger, I say.

Michelle glances at us, her eyes like a mare's ears pricking up, searching for the source of the sounds she recognizes.

Many young people gave me their home addresses, I say. We would write, they invited me to visit them in Vancouver, Colombie-Britannique, Portland, Orégon, Sydney, Australie, Inverness, Écosse. Bien sûr, we never wrote. A brother and a sister at place d'Afrique said I would love African fabrics. Peut-être, I could go to Africa to study fabrics. Did maman ask you to talk to me?

She asked nothing, Gérard says. I'm telling you she worries.

I don't believe that, I say. That summer I lost my job, she did not worry.

He takes an important call, Michelle goes back to her file cards.

Maman drinks her Salada tea, tells me she will be going to her boss's country house on lac Memphrémagog. I am surprised, she never goes anywhere, je pense, une fin de semaine, she says, un mois, I holler, un mois! she smiles in her cup, tells me it is a working holiday. The next day, mon oncle and ma tante come over, she tells them about her month of August au lac Memphrémagog, ma tante rolls her eyes, the only answers to my queries are the usual never mind, là and l'expérience la vie. Ma tante thinks it is not a good idea to leave a seventeen-year-old girl alone in the city for a month, maman tells her not to make a fuss, elle a confiance en sa fille. Je pense, this is a test, I will not disappoint her. Ma tante suggests I have supper with them every day, maman fait les gros yeux, ma tante keeps quiet. Maman leaves me enough money to buy food, to pay the gas, electricity, telephone bills, she explains how that is done, she gives me extra pour mes petites dépenses à l'Expo, I will prove to ma tante I can be trusted, I will show mon oncle I can handle l'expérience la vie.

I'm curious, Gérard says, sitting back, but still tying up loose business ends with Michelle.

The next next day, ma tante comes back without mon oncle. The sisters sit dans le boudoir, their words travel through the brass vents cut high in the walls, they go from le boudoir through the bathroom and maman's bedroom before reaching my bedroom, by then, the familiar voices are distorted, difficult to tell them apart, and though the words, une vraie honte, tu te trompes, tous ces samedis, un homme marié, c'était fini, coming out of the brass vents like out of a meat grinder have meanings, they lost all context. Puis maman's voice rises on the words, mettre ton nez dans, but fades on the rest of the sentence, as she remembers not to shout, leaving me to learn that ma tante is nosey, but without knowing what about. Finalement, an explosion of laughter. Je pense, they invent stories, because they never go anywhere, this time is different, maman is a guest at her boss's country house for a whole month. Laughter and whisper out of brass vents give me no answer.

What will you do with yourself? Gérard asks, giving me his full attention. The danger, Ariane, is that you have money in your pocket, but no goal.

Are you sure maman worries?

She didn't say she was worried.

You said she worries.

I infer that from our conversation. And why not? She's afraid Elizabeth's death unnerved you.

I stare at him. Je pense, how did Elizabeth's death unnerve you? I breathe, he speaks.

You may use that as an excuse to waste your time and money. Many people your age are drifting, they become disenchanted.

Maman said that?

I say that.

Don't worry about me, Gérard.

I want to ask him how he is coping. I can't. Too scared Pandora crouching in the dark will spring up, eager to open her box.

The silver bell above the door rings.

Michelle and Gérard look up at the same time, I squint at the tall woman in purple pants and paisley turban and silver hoops in her ears and many bangles sliding along her wrist.

Ah, Nina, Gérard says, uncoiling his legs.

Bonjour, Madame Lambert, Michelle says.

Mes amis, the woman says.

How do you deal with it? I ask Gérard, not understanding my mouth betraying my common sense. I didn't know Elizabeth long. But you.

We look at each other for such a long time, Michelle scurries away, sensing qu'elle est de trop, does he know, c'est ma faute, c'est ma grande faute, that elegant older man's gaze digs deep into little me, what are his thoughts, he looks away as he rises to greet Nina Lambert, a client with clout, time moves again, his hand on my shoulder squeezes gently, he could be stabbing.

Michelle has to run an errand, Gérard and Nina Lambert must go upstairs to the office, do I mind keeping an eye on the shop, if clients ask anything, I am to come up and tell him, Michelle will not be long.

Compte sur moi, I say.

He knows I worked last winter in that madame clothing shop at Place Bonaventure. He and Nina Lambert climb the marble steps to the third floor. I wear my cat's eyes to look more antique-businesslike, a good thing too, because outside, I spot trois madames dressed like tourists, they examine the building, put their faces up against one of the shop windows, hands shielding their eyes, peut-être, they think they may shop by appointment only, I watch them, as if they were on stage in the sun spotlight flooding rue Saint-François.

They study the metal sign hanging below one of the second-storey windows. Anteannum. The name puzzles them, they see it before they hear it, I heard it before I saw it. The day of the mussels, Elizabeth telling me about Gérard's boutique, the name printed in reverse on her skin, she said, Anteannum, I heard, Ant et un Homme, sounded like une fable de La Fontaine, L'Homme et la Fourmi. Anteannum looks like the singular of antenna, quand même, ants don't have anything to do with antiques, d'habitude, woodworms bore holes into old furniture, maman would burn her antiques if she ever spotted such holes, Gérard told me some people make new antiques, boring holes themselves and not telling their clients, maman would prefer the fakes, if she cared at all about any of that.

La madame in the navy pantsuit tries to photograph the sign, la madame in the floral print dress and canvas shoes signals the light is no good, la madame in the beige twill pants and long shirt and the black laced shoes puts her face against the window again, la madame in the floral dress pulls her away, they look at the sign, what a puzzle, finalement, la madame in the navy pantsuit opens the dark wood door that looks like a Caramilk on hinges, the silver bell startles her.

Bonjour, I say.

Bonn-djour, she says. Pardonnez-moi, do you speak English?

Yes, I do.

She points at the sign outside.

Last year, I say.

La madame touriste stays on the threshold, peut-être, her mind and her eyes need time to adjust.

Anteannum means l'an passé, I say. Latin for last year. This is an antique shop.

We know, dear, she says, holding up her camera. We were wondering if you'd agree to have your picture taken in front of the building. It would give perspective. Add human interest.

My heart pumps like I spent the morning boring holes into Gérard's antique furniture, my arms and legs, four jujubes, who is that woman appearing out of nowhere, I follow her in a daze out of dark and cool into light and heat.

See? the woman with the camera says to her friends. She doesn't mind.

Where are you, ladies, from? I ask.

My voice startles me, comme si, someone else spoke, peut-être, a giant woodworm. Ladies, that is how les Anglais speak to and about women.

Medicine Hat, the woman with the camera says.

I did not mean to mock them. Why is she kidding me?

Alberta, the other two women say.

We are sisters, the woman in the floral dress says, as if that explained everything.

I know a man from Distraction, Manitoba, I say.

They look at me, as if they didn't care for my attitude.

If a place called Medicine Hat, Alberta, can exist, I say, so can a place called Distraction, Manitoba. The man made me waltz once.

I bet, the woman in the beige pants and black walking shoes says.

We stand in the flat light and the humid heat. I tell them, earlier, deep creases of light and shadow revealed more details in the stone façade, I point out elements of architecture, the four storeys of grey flat stone slabs, the large windows, on the first floor the windows framed in stone arches carved with grapes and leaves, the glass etched with tiny owls and squirrels. The original building housed a wine import company, later, a furrier, later, a toy factory, in the forties, une coopérative d'artisans, that means, potters working all together, they nod vigorously as if in Medicine Hat, Alberta, they knew everything there was to know about pottery.

It looks very old, la madame in floral print says. Everything in Old Montreal is so old.

It would be older, I say, but there were always fires in Vieux-Montréal and the old old buildings had to be demolished and replaced with newer old buildings.

We are baking on rue Saint-François, if I invite them inside, they will think I am a crass merchant greedy to exploit tourists. La madame in navy aims her camera at the building, but the narrow street prevents her from framing the whole façade in her viewfinder.

The light is no good, she says.

Quand même, she asks again if she can take my picture in front of the shop.

Okay, I say.

Je pense, what are the chances I will visit her Friday afternoons, this is a one-shot deal, I take off my cat's eyes.

No, no, she says. Keep your glasses on, dear. You look very Mont-reealeese.

The street spins, I bend down, head between my knees.

Are you all right, dear? la madame with the camera asks.

It's the heat, la madame in the beige pants says. Just take the picture, Myrna.

I am in mourning, I say, showing my dirty skirt.

Oh, dear, they say in a chorus.

Does it mean I can't take your picture? la madame with the camera says.

It's okay, I say. Go ahead.

She moves backward, the street deserted, but what if a delivery truck came tumbling down out of nowhere, her sisters would scream, the tires would screech, in Medicine Hat, Alberta, the newspaper headline would read, Local Woman Killed By Truck in Montreal, comme si c'était la faute de tout le Québec, I lean against the window frame, la madame in the flower dress touches my wrist, la madame with the camera crouches on the pavement like she is rehearsing the accident, I keep my cat's-eyed eyes glued on the corner of Notre-Dame and Saint-François, she wants a high angle shot to include Anteannum and as much of the façade as possible, like squeezing History into a Chinese box, Elizabeth never did acrobatics when she shot, she just shot, I hear, click, enfin, c'est fini, invite les madames inside, tant pis if they think I am trying to make a sale, I need cool, open the door and the silver bell rings.

Here, we are, I say to les trois madames from Medicine Hat, Alberta.

Here we are, I say, unlocking the door to our flat.

Maman enjoying ses vacances de travail au lac Memphrémagog, moi bringing five yoots home for the weekend.

Three guys and two girls sit outside le Pavillon de la
Jeunesse, I am not sewing that day, je fais l'oreille indiscrète,
but squint in the distance so they will think I am not listening, I patch their words together to make their story. They are
from Toronto, mon oncle calls it la ville des morts, he and ma
tante spent a weekend in Toronto once to visit Ginette and
Georgette, nobody could pay mon oncle enough to live
there, even to be near his daughters, people are so dead on
their feet dans la Ville Reine, the City has a special work
crew to remove cobwebs at important intersections, particulièrement, on Monday mornings, the cobwebs are so thick,
like a snowstorm blew overnight, traffic can barely move
through them.

It took the five yoots two weeks to hitchhike from
Toronto to visit Expo, bien sûr, they could never hitch a ride
all together with their backpacks, en plus, one of the guys
carries a guitar, at the end of each day, they waited for each
other in campgrounds and truck stops, parfois, not connecting for two three days, it took them so long to get to Expo
they ran out of money, their sleeping bags got stolen in the
first campground they went to after crossing into Québec,
they wired their parents for money, peut-être, they will beg
for food, sleep à la belle étoile à l'île Sainte-Hélène 'til the
money arrives, they look dirty from the trip, tired, hungry,
they also look like nice Anglais with their long blond hair.

Are you brothers and sisters? I ask.

They laugh, no, they are not. I tell them, I am an only
child.

I'm Peter, one of the guys says. This is Paul and Mary.

The five of them laugh like it is a joke, peut-être, an in-
joke, the two others are called John and Sylvia, it does not
matter what their names are, de toute façon, I mix them up
all weekend, they look like carbon copies with their wool
ponchos from South America, one of them, Paul, peut-être,
plays the guitar and the five of them sing folk songs, one they

call, Early Morning Rain, that attracks a crowd of yoots, they have sweet voices, je pense, they are real hippies from Toronto, I don't believe mon oncle's story, even though he said, c'est la pure vérité, wiping the spit of excitement off his lips. It is Friday evening the banks will be closed 'til Monday, they got robbed, if it rains early in the morning, their ponchos will not keep them dry, they may get arrested for camping in the woods, they stop playing and singing, the crowd disperses, Nicole et Diane arrive, tell us, the spit of excitement shining on their mouths, they played a trick on visitors this afternoon, made everybody cry.

Au Pavillon du Québec, they removed the rock collection from the glass case and displayed a hostess uniform, complete with gloves, shoes, and hat, like a body in a glass coffin, they managed to shed real tears, telling visitors their good friend had drowned the previous weekend. All afternoon, visitors expected rocks from le bouclier canadien, only to find the couture uniform of the dead hostess. Nicole et Diane kept adding layers to the story, comme des strates dans le roc. People hung their heads, observed a minute of silence, a woman crossed herself, another kissed the glass. People hoped for miracles, like blood squeezed out of the stones from le bouclier canadien. Nicole et Diane étaient mortes de rire, which sounded like crying, but when a man asked what was the name of the victim, alors, they tripped over each other's tongues. At that point, they thought they had been caught and would be fired. But no. The man said, it doesn't matter if she had a thousand names, a young life wasted, is still a young life wasted by any other name.

That's when we lost it, Nicole says.

The visitors thought Nicole et Diane were hysterical with grief.

That story cheered up the Toronto yoots. I introduce everyone as best I can and, juste comme ça, my mouth invites them to stay chez moi on rue Sherbrooke. Nicole et Diane me font les gros yeux, trop tard, my mouth spoke, my mouth said, come to my place, d'ailleurs, I want to show Peter and Paul and Mary and John and Sylvia not everybody in Québec is a thief, jokers, oui, thieves, non, après tout, on sait vivre.

Why don't you come too? I say to Nicole et Diane. We'll have a party.

Sure, Diane says, quelle bonne idée. This is our weekend off.

On va téléphoner à Robert et à Roger, Nicole says, wisely.

The Toronto yoots are impressed they will party with two genuine bona fide Expo hostesses, we take le métro, Nicole et Diane et moi chip in for our out-of-town guests and when we get to my flat, I say, unlocking the door, here we are.

Here we are, I say, closing the door on the heat.

Les trois madames from Medicine Hat say they are sisters, c'est possible, they all have big noses with large nostrils, but they look like friends, alors que, the five yoots from Toronto were friends, but they looked like brothers and sisters. Les madames examine the marble floor cracked in places like we had an earthquake, the five yoots crowd into the bathroom, I give them towels, they jump in the high tub, Robert and Roger arrive with cases of beer, I make tomato and mayonnaise sandwiches, Nicole and Robert, Diane and Roger neck in the kitchen under the lit plafonnier like they are on stage, les trois madames look at the high ceiling with its plaster mouldings, I tell them it is representative of the era, I say, era, the walls and the ceiling are painted green in a kind of wash to imitate vert-de-gris, they understand the word but say, verdigreez, they run their hands along the dark wood railing of the staircase, climb the first marble steps, I tell them the upper floors are made of the same dark wood as the railing, they creak with every step, a mouse cannot sneak in or out night or day, they laugh, the two girls in long loose dresses, walk barefoot along the long corridor, their blond hair drips on the floor, the three guys in shorts, go barefoot bare chest, everybody eats the sandwiches, drinks beer, says thank you a lot, Nicole et Diane relax, the five yoots think my flat is far out, they say, far out, they want to know if I am rich, I laugh, les trois madames want to know what's upstairs, as they can see, I say, the first floor is for furniture and household accessories, the second floor is for costumes and personal objects, the third floor is where the owner's office and private apartment are, that impresses them, the fourth floor is le capharnaüm, they don't understand, I say, un débarras, their eyes are blank, I say, a kind of warehouse, they nod, I tell the five yoots I live here by myself, maman is away at the lake with her boss, I don't mention Dead Man, they think it is a cool arrangement, they say, cool, the flat is hot again, Paul, the guitar man, asks if we could have music, sure, I say, and wait for them to play sing again, he says, no, records, he asks if I have Ravel's Boléro, I go look.

Les trois madames look around, I tell them they may buy anything they want, I tell them if l'antiquaire, l'antiquaire is the owner, they nod, if l'antiquaire does not sell the objects right away, he rents them as props to movie people, commercial photographers, advertising agencies, theatre companies, les madames say, how interesting, the two girls ask if they can have a look at the fantastic rooms, they say, fantastic, I say, sure, follow them, follow les madames without seeming to, il faut être poli, not insult the yoots from Toronto, not insult the sisters from Medicine Hat, ma tante would be suspicious, she would expect the girls to slip the silver vases under their dresses, ma tante would not think les madames would snitch silver salt shakers, but the yoots, ma tante would keep a sharp eye on the yoots.

With les madames, I really look as if for the first time at those things Gérard never seems to sell, with the girls, I see with new eyes the objects that have always lived in the flat, the girls think our place is like in the movies, dans le petit salon, they shriek with delight when they spot the four over-sized modern birch frames with the paintings of the same house viewed through the four seasons, one of the girls' mothers, is it madame Sylvia or madame Mary, has similar paintings in her ordinary living room, les trois madames don't care about the five-panelled Chinese screen, even after I point out the recurring theme of the cherry tree in winter spring summer autumn, and the cherry tree in bloom printed on the reclining courtesan's silk robe.

I sit with les madames on the Mediterranean blue plush sofa with the asymmetrical backrest.

What is this couch for? la madame in the pantsuit asks.

To sleep in the afternoon, I say. It is called une méridienne. The word also means siesta.

Ahhhh, they say in a chorus.

Cette méridienne is from la Restauration française.

Ahhhh.

They trail their hands along the back which is low at one end and rises higher at the other end, they run their fingers along the pale wood carved into a swan, wings open, its long neck turned sideways and resting on its body.

The swan is having a méridienne, la madame in the beige outfit says.

He's sleep-flying, la madame in the floral dress says.

We laugh, they do bons mots, those sisters. Their eyes open wide when they check the price tag, eighteen hundred dollars, we sit on la méridienne in front of the window looking out at rue Saint-François, I sit on the brocaded chesther-field with the two girls, we study the columns flanking the archway to le petit salon with their plaster of vine leaves and grapes, one girl, Mary or Sylvia, distractedly fondles the lid of one of the Wedgwood candy boxes, the other girl, Sylvia or Mary, asks if my mother is an actress, I shake my head, play mysterious, the girls examine les bergères from Dresden, the crystal doorknobs, les trois madames tour the boutique cluttered with mahogany bureaus, gilded clocks, black iron farm implements raised from the dead of la Nouvelle-France and transformed into lamps and table frames, Tiffany lamps, I should buy one to replace the one I broke when I was little, maman serait contente, non, she would not want me to spend my trip money on things, les madames pick up copper drinking glasses, pewter plates, crystal bells, silver spoons, the girls pet the bronze horses rearing running on the bookcase, stroke the maroon velvet drapes, they say, the window treatment is dramatic, like the window is on stage, sit at maman's vanity, brush each other's long blond hair with the silver-plated brush, hold the silver-plated mirror, ask one another who is the fairest of them all, I remove the blond hair from the brush, roll the hair into a tight ball, in the kitchen, Peter, Paul, and John laugh with Robert and Roger like men do, loudly, I smell smoke, we join them, I throw the hairball in the toilet bowl, flush, pick up the damp towels off the bathroom floor, hang them on the clothesline to dry, Nicole et Diane are on the gallery, they come back inside with me.

Il fait chaud, Nicole says.

I open the door to the gallery and the door to the balcony, the sheers move in the draft, not the velvet drapes, they are too dramatic, les trois madames are interested in a set of lace curtains, the label says, guipure de Flandre, Bruges, 1918, one hundred dollars, the five guys sit at the kitchen table, pass a fat joint around, Ravel plays son Boléro, the girls sway to the music, Nicole et Diane giggle, I cough, les madames whisper among themselves, is it vulgar to bargain in an antique shop, this is not a rummage sale, everybody has the munchies, the tomato sandwiches were not enough, I raid the cupboards for chips and pretzels and cheesies, tell Nicole et Diane to look after things, they understand, I run downstairs, tell les madames I could go upstairs and get Gérard L'Heureux, l'antiquaire, he is with a client right now, they say, no, no, don't disturb him, they are not sure they can afford the curtains, what lovely needlework, but one hundred dollars, they don't want to bargain, chez monsieur Lebœuf, I buy un pied de céleri, a jar of Cheez Whiz and a bottle of paprika, I will make celery stuffed with cheese dusted with paprika, like ma tante Rita makes at Christmas, I buy un pain croûté and strawberry jam, an expensive jar of olives stuffed with pimento, a ten-pound bag of potatoes and a pound of Crisco, at the counter as monsieur Lebœuf punches the prices sur sa caisse enregistreuse, I select a dozen chocolate bars, Caramilk, Oh Henry, CoffeeCrisp, MaltedMilk, I did not bring enough money, how embarrassing.

I promise, juré craché, I will be back first thing in the morning with the rest of the money, monsieur Lebœuf nods not worried, I run out of the grocery store with my bags, it is nine o'clock Friday night, my first party, my gypsy skirt brushes against bunches of dried mauve hydrangea and dead red roses, les trois madames examine table mirrors and strings of amber beads the size of Fabergé eggs, a Turkish coffee pot on a Chinese lacquer tray, a cut-glass decanter with a stopper shaped like a fish standing on its tail, two enormous snifters with gold filigree, the monogram says they belonged to le cardinal Villeneuve, when I close the street door behind me with a thud, I can hear Ravel playing son Boléro à tue-tête, les murs sont minces, I rush upstairs, my guests are dans le grand salon, they rolled the Persian rug under the window, are racing the twenty-four bronze horses across the oak floor, they make horse sounds, crowd noises, they bet cheesies and pretzels, les trois madames make up their minds to buy the curtains, they say, let's throw caution to the wind, le Boléro is reaching its crescendo for the fourth time and it is not nine-thirty yet, I cannot turn down the volume, this is a party, tant pis pour les murs minces, ce soir, nous sommes des sauvages, I hope les voisins sont à leurs chalets pour la fin de semaine, I wrap the curtains in tissu paper, slip them in a bag that says Anteannum, Antiquités, Vieux-Montréal, les madames beam with joy, they say thank you very much several times, they are having a ball in Montréal, if ever I am in Medicine Hat, everybody knows the Brown sisters, in the kitchen, a draft scatters ashes from the ashtray on the yellow oilcloth, I start making french fries, this is a test, I will not burn down the house, my guests dans le grand salon laugh like demons, my party is a success and it is only nine-forty Friday evening, pourvu que ma tante and mon oncle don't decide to stop by to visit check on me, I am a little stoned, wolf down a Caramilk, open the door, the silver bell rings, les madames laugh, I drop the potato strips in the hot Crisco, the fat sings along with the full orchestra du Boléro déchaîné, I stir the fries, sold the lace curtains from Bruges, 1918.

How was I to know? Michelle went on her errand, I took care of things, now, Nina Lambert makes telephone calls and Gérard avoids me. There was a price tag, I filled out the bill of sale like a pro, la madame who took my picture gave me five traveller's cheques, she signed them on the bottom line, her signature was the same squiggle as on the top line, les madames chipped in with change from their purses to pay la taxe de vente, Gérard examined the cheques, he agreed I did everything right, quand même, he is unhappy. What did Nina Lambert want the curtains for? I came to ask Gérard about the photos, now, that will have to wait, and what if things deteriorate sérieusement between us, cela va compromettre maman's chance at happiness, better slip upstairs, out of sight.

The second-storey floor creaks like it is screaming with pain, how to be lighter on my feet than a mouse, I dip my arms deep into the racks of costumes, the velvets, the brocades, the nylon mesh, the tulle, the boas, a soothing sea of softness, I smile at that. My maroon velvet coat with saffron lampas lining! Who wore it, I wonder, intimacy with a stranger. Magnifique! Gérard says, the day I bring him the coat after Nicole's et Diane's wedding. He examines it sous toutes ses coutures to show he does not buy cheap merchandise, he nods, my first transaction, I am une comtesse in a Balzac novel visiting the trusted dealer as discreet as a confessor, always a helping hand to titled characters who have lost their shirts playing whist. I sniff fibre dust, ammonia in the stage fright of actors, could I sniff out the caftan by tracking down Elizabeth's sweet earth scents. Where did Gérard put it? The night of la Fête, the black mannequin with the ostrich feather was wearing it, my hands search the silk racks, even dry cleaning cannot remove all the smells the silk soaked up, Raymond with Elizabeth at the back of Corona working hard at crushing their scents into each thread, le 17 novembre 1967, an archeological time ago. I sniff my skirt, qu'est-ce que j'exsude? On the first floor Gérard's voice rises, the phone rings Michelle answers, enfin, my hands touch the water-slick silk, squeezed between the blood-red satin of a mandarin robe and the rosewood shantung of a fifties strapless ball gown, I bury my face in the caftan, the aroma lifting, woodsmoke and dead leaves, shattering.

My weekend guests race the twenty-four brass horses down the long corridor into the kitchen, I could get the cookie sheet breastplates, we could play war, Montcalm contre Wolfe, our armies evenly matched, cinq Français assiégés contre five English invaders, the war would be a draw, the night is drawing to an end, we ate ten pounds of french fries with plenty of ketchup, smoked more fat joints my mouth drying out like the Sahara, drank too much beer my head pounding like a herd of buffalo, Ravel continues to revel in his horns and violins and percussions, les voisins in the flats below must be away, sinon, they would have spent the evening knocking on their ceilings with broomsticks, voisins of the world, unite! against all parties.

The caftan turned inside out, I know where to snip, Gérard must never discover l'ablation, a mere few threads at the junction where the seam of the sleeve meets the side seam at the armhole, the small scissors bite the silk, the stairs creak, I hang the caftan back where I found it, fluff up the costumes, bientôt, time to sleep, Nicole et Diane both want maman's bed, Nicole with Robert, Diane with Roger, I tell them, okay, je vous donne le lit, which twosome gets it is up to them to decide, in the morning I find the foursome, sheets legs arms, mixed together, the chenille, in a heap on the floor, but we are still in the middle of the night, I make the twin beds in the guest bedroom, tell les Anglais to decide the sleeping arrangement, to be a good hostess, I offer my bed, the three guys holler play fight, je veux dire, I will sleep on the couch dans le petit salon, do we have enough sheets, maman should have listened to ma tante's advice.

Gérard arrives with Nina Lambert. Sitting quietly on a windowsill out of sight, I watch them between the racks. Nina examines a gown in a heavy brocade of old gold and red paisley, the Voltaire robe, Gérard calls it. Scrooge wore it five times, Marat, once in the bathtub scene, le marquis de Sade lounged in it the morning after his release from prison, and Sherlock paced up and down his room in Baker Street dropping ash over it, and now, Othello will suffer in it. Gérard's and Nina's words go through layers of costumes, that is why, je présume, I receive their meanings in disguise. Nina holds Elizabeth's caftan, I hold my breath.

Sorry, chère, this is already reserved, Gérard says, draping the tunic over his arm.

He takes Nina by the elbow, shows her my velvet coat.

For your Desdémone. Size eight.

It's gorgeous, Nina says. Yes. For full effect, I see Desdemona in a vaporous gown under the open coat.

Gérard reveals provenance of silk and velvet, his words, words of praise I am not meant to hear, I slink away.

Paul follows me to le petit salon where I arrange my sheet, pillow, and blanket on the couch, he wants to listen to le Boléro one more time.

It is three in the morning, I say. We listened to that thing one thousand and one times tonight.

The horniest music ever composed, he says.

What is horniest music, sans doute, music with lots of horns. There are plenty of those dans le Boléro.

You're so heavy, he whispers, leaning heavy on me.

And les Anglais are supposed to be so polite, je pense, merci bien, I take you into my home, feed you, show you l'hospitalité québécoise and what does this one do, he insults me.

I am not fat, I say.

He laughs, says, that's not what it means, je pense, sure, bonhomme, what does he think I am, ignorant, everybody knows heavy means lourd, he kisses me, here we go, in no time he tries to get inside me it will not go in I am too tight, he tells me to relax, je pense, I am relaxed I want to go to sleep, he tells me to concentrate on the soaring music, je pense, more soaring and my head will burst, he rubs sa verge d'Anglais against me, whispers, concentrate, okay, I concentrate on Pierre.

He would not enter me, mon écrivain révolutionnaire, did not think une pucelle de dix-sept ans knew how to protect herself, je prends la pilule, I say, we walk, he keeps talking about la responsabilité de l'individu, la conscience sociale, we walk, he stops dead in his tracks, did he hear right? tu prends la pilule? Soudain, I am different, la responsabilité et la conscience turn me into what, we walk faster, in search of a hidden spot in the trees of l'île Sainte-Hélène, he does not bother with the seventeen pearl buttons I sewed instead of a fast zip zipper, quel romantique érotique! what about the slow motion of foreplay, he lifts my skirt, takes me fast, as if the magic spell of the pill would wear off, pouf!

Pierre changed into a toad, since that initiation, he has learned to slow down.

Paul tells me to absorb the notes, peut-être, cet Anglais is overdosing on le Boléro, my mouth dry like the Sahara, why doesn't he go down on me like Pierre does, peut-être les Anglais sont trop timides to use their tongue, Paul whispers, it's out of this world to come at the climax of the music, climax sounds like cymbals banging together, that word climax increases my headache, quand même, he is my guest, the music is making me queasy, I close my eyes, plan breakfast, do we have eggs, should buy baked beans to show les Anglais, like ma tante suggested if maman wanted to run a bed & breakfast during Expo, de toute façon, I have to bring monsieur Lebœuf the money I owe him, the music soars comme un cataclysme, I fall into a deep hole just before the horny climax.

Tout d'un coup, Gérard's boutique of antiques is full of people, first floor, second floor, people mingling, slapping each other on the back, kissing this cheek kissing that cheek, the shop looks like a hoot at a gallery opening, some people I vaguely know, others I recognize as theater people, cinéma people, I should mingle make connections, I finger the silk graft in my pocket, should think about my exhibit, le reste de ma vie. I sneak away to the third floor.

My first visit. In Gérard's apartment, no doors no walls. To delimit the idea of rooms, Persian rugs, thick and soft, like walking on sleeping cats. On this rug, the living room with leather sofas and floor lamps and low pale wood tables, on that rug, the bedroom exposée aux regards indiscrets with a brass bed and une grande armoire de pin, the bathroom has no rug, no walls no door, the bathtub in the middle and the sink and the frame of the free-standing mirror and the toilet, all blue, set on large squares of blue ceramic tiles, exactement la couleur des yeux d'Elizabeth, the kitchen, bright with cushy yellow and white linoleum and shelf units crammed

with dishes and pots and pans and food like des pâtes alimen-
taires et de la farine d'avoine in blue glass jars and a deep
sink, a butcher's block, a fridge, a gas stove and a black bistro
table with two red metal chairs, Elizabeth and Gérard drinking café au lait, le lit encore défait, the last morning.

On the third rug by the front windows, an old-fashioned
oak desk, the weight of a whale, with a green leather top and
brass handles in the shape of lions' heads, and wood filing
cabinets and bookcases. I run my finger along the spines of
antiques and art books, peut-être, Gérard will add Elizabeth's
books to his collection, peut-être, he will hawktion them.

Ah! the Chinese box, I say, like to an audience. And look
at this. An old book lying open on the desk, the pages stained
with yellow brown circles and black fingerprints in the margins, quel dommage! The text, peut-être de l'hébreu, oh, mais
non, look, I say, holding the book up for everyone to see, the
characters, so small and crowded together, at first glance, they
appeared to be woodblock prints of geometric forms, but
now, the language emerges slowly, English. Ah, an arrow in
pencil draws my eyes to a line, it says, and I read, the
Orientalists investigated the tradition of demolishing the
houses of the dead. How interesting! I shout, echoing les
madames de Medicine Hat.

Beside the open book, des dessins au fusain, sans doute,
the sketches of the set for the play. I saw that play once made
into an old movie, the actors wore eyeliner, Othello, such a
sucker, he believed anything he was told, pauvre Desdémone,
he will carry her limp body to the crypt, heavy music will
play, he will trip on the uneven papier mâché stones, will stag-
ger under the weight of Desdémone étranglée and his own
foolishness, Desdémone's long red hair, une perruque bien
sûr, will sweep the floor, my coat will open on her filmy gown
to reveal my hand-dyed saffron lampas lining, Nina better put
my name in the program. Still cannot figure out how to open
the Chinese box. If I did, would Pandora pop out?

We pop out to a store to buy gold hoops. Sylvia shrieked when I told her I pierced my ears myself, in June for my seventeenth birthday, I said, c'est facile, Mary shivered, it must hurt, not really, Nicole et Diane asked if I would pierce theirs, certainement, now, Sylvia and Mary also wanted to, like going back to Toronto, branded with le sceau de Montréal in their earlobes. We bring home the hoops, small training ones for newly pierced ears, the four girls giggle nervous, we are going to have un party de perce-oreilles, John Peter Paul and Robert and Roger hastily beat a retreat, say they are going to check out downtown, we hoot at them, peureux, poules mouillées, it's not that, they say, they have better things to do than chick things, we hoot and whistle, chicken, ils prennent la poudre d'escampette, no guts.

My patients sit at the kitchen table, watching me gather the things I need for the operation. A more sterile-clinic-professional look will give them du cœur au ventre, donc, I lay a white linen towel over a portion of the yellow oilcloth. Mary wants to know if I need hot water, we burst out laughing, this is not accouchement ni avortement. On the linen towel, I put the bottle of rubbing alcohol, a fresh bar of Camay soap, one large sewing needle, they stare at the needle, serious silent, a small white porcelain candy dish with the earrings, a box of Kleenex we don't have cotton wool Kleenex will do, a metal bowl with ice cubes, a white face cloth, the silver-plated mirror. I pour alcohol over the jewellery, drop the needle in the dish. I wash my hands carefully like a movie surgeon, dry them on a clean towel, walk back toward the table, hands in front of me. Who will be first? The silence in the kitchen is deep.

Had to climb higher to avoid the crowd inching its way toward the apartment. Dans les limbes du capharnaüm, les trouvailles de Gérard, pêle-mêle, years of searching the countryside, chairs and fur coats, coach lamps and cut-glass perfume atomizers, mirrors framed by gilded cherubs and sea serpents, orphan things waiting to be occupied again, I trip. Oh, pardon. Ah, bonjour, madame, black mannequin. How is your ostrich feather faring in this heat? I take my sewing kit out of my bag, smooth out the piece of silk, expose my navel.

I place two ice cubes, one on the front and one on the back of Nicole's earlobe, cover each cube with a corner of the face cloth, ask her to hold that in place, I have no rubbing alcohol and no ice to numb the navel area, I pinch the skin, not overly sensitive, I thread the needle. When I think the area is numb, I hold the bar of soap behind the lobe, grip the sterilized needle near the eye, the point touching the centre of the lobe and, very straight, I am precise, push the needle through the flesh 'til the point enters the bar of soap, pull the needle out, my hand steady, sewing the few strands of silk like skin graft over my birthspot, a sapphire in a belly dancer's belly button, the needle hurts, only a little, aucun point au cœur, the heart beats, steady, just a few stitches to hold the dime-size patch in place for a little while, drawing not a single drop of blood, Ariane with a needle, une virtuose.

Nicole's face, convulsed, a drop of blood forms on the surface of the lobe. I soak a Kleenex in alcohol and dab to stop the bleeding. The others ask if the needle hurt, Nicole tells them, the worst was the crunching sound. I put the hoop through the hole, repeat the procedure with the other lobe, in five minutes, Nicole has brand new pierced ears. Now, she must turn the earrings around and dab her lobes with alcohol several times a day 'til the holes heal. She looks at herself in the mirror, hollers with joy.

Mouth screaming, legs gliding down two flights of stairs, hand flinging open street door, feet running into street, body kneeling beside blood silk, she looks awful.

Are you all right? I shout over the commotion.

We will miss our plane, ça, c'est certain, blood bubbles out of her mouth, I cannot see her eyes, all the blue washed away.

It would appear even to the casual observer, she rattles, that I am not.

Don't worry, Elizabeth, the ambulance is coming. Can you hear it? Everything will be all right. We're next door to the hospital, Notre-Dame is just.

With surprising strength, elle m'agrippe par la peau du cou, pulls me down, this is not Elizabeth. I am in the grip of an amazing force.

What was your rush?

In the kitchen, they all speak at once, I cut the thread after the last stitch, make a knot over my navel, her words become tangled in the street noises, who can be sure what she really said, the others can't wait to go through with it, Diane's earlobes, thicker tougher, resist the needle, she says, it sounds like écraser des peanuts en écailles, but feels no pain. I start again, leave the ice longer, what if I give her frostbite in August, what if she ends up at Notre-Dame avec une infection ou la gangrène. Finalement, the needle goes through, un lobe, deux lobes, her ears are tomato-red and feel like wood. Mary and Sylvia have small delicate ears, against them, the needle looks like a Medieval torture device. Their flesh pierces easily, but les Anglaises are bleeders. I soak balls of Kleenex, pink alcohol drools down their necks, the bleeding stops. I hook the hoops in, dab and dab with more alcohol to make sure, their earlobes must be drunk drunk.

We all light cigarettes, pleased with ourselves. They pass the mirror, smile big.

People paint their bodies comme le Québécois fleur-delisé, temporaire, people tattoo their bodies like that man in mon oncle Joseph's machine shop who showed les ouvriers the multicoloured garden growing on his back, permanent, people all over the world pierce scar their bodies. Animals shed. Renewal. Muer, changer de peau. Mutation. Sailing alone. Why not decorate skin with cloth, why not filigree with gold thread, like those snifters that belonged to the cardinal, why not? What would be so sick crazy about that?

The tiny piece of silk stitched over birthspot, not carried in locket like relics of saints, this is not ecstasy of Medieval nuns, this is not mystic vapours, this is not silly sacrament, la flagellation never brought back the dead, this is silk in remembrance of beginnings.

Did Elizabeth know you took all those photos from her studio? Gérard asks in English.

As if Elizabeth sat between us sur la méridienne. The visitors are gone, Michelle has left for the day. Gérard and I watch rue Saint-François, quelques promeneurs walk by, disappear like off a movie screen.

Elle m'a donné la permission.

After permission, what can he say, I may tell the truth, I may not, if Gérard chooses to doubt me, what can I say, Elizabeth will not rise from the dead to say, Gérard, Ariane is a liar, she will not wedge herself between us, Gérard, Ariane is telling the truth.

I tell him more about Gold Rush, every line in his face speaks of doubt, the laughing wrinkles at the corner of his eyes we call des pattes d'oie, the four horizontal lines on his forehead, the two deep creases on either side of his mouth, his doubt makes me doubt.

Tu as peur? I ask.

De quoi?

Le pouvoir des objets. Le pouvoir des mots.

Ne sois pas absurde.

I tell him, if he goes to her house, her things will speak to him, it will be painful, the fridge bare, the bills paid, the laundry done, the house, unoccupied, waiting for her to come home, her things will say, Elizabeth does not live here anymore. I tell him, he doesn't have to go, he can give me the key, I will go, I know where the snapshots are, will not disturb a thing, will just get more photos, nothing more.

He lights a Player's unfiltered, draws slowly deeply, pushes the smoke out of his mouth like he is Elizabeth, his smoke in front of the window makes the shimmering street shimmer even more. He reminds me about something Elizabeth used to say. She used to say, the last words a person says are always the most important, even just, see you.

See you, my Toronto friends say, as they climb down the stairs, their joyous voices echoing between the terrazzo walls of the lobby.

Monday morning, the party is over, the banks open, the money waits for them, Nicole et Diane put on their hostess uniforms, Diane's lobes are a little crusty but she feels fine, they will give our friends a special whirlwind tour of Expo before they take the train back to Toronto this evening, I stay home to get rid of the evidence, squash the bluebottles that flew in through the open doors, wash the dishes and the ashtrays, wash the floors, check under the furniture, inspect the mattresses, hang the washed sheets on temporary cords along the corridor so the neighbours will suspect nothing, the flat, a tall ship ready to sail à la découverte du Nouveau Monde, the yoots from Toronto ride their train, I go to bed, crash instantly, dream dreams so complicated in the morning I remember nothing. See you, they said. We know we will never see each other again.

Savais-tu, Gérard says, not looking at me, savais-tu, juste avant son départ, Elizabeth et moi, on s'est querellés. Oh, nothing serious, he continues in English, as if not wanting to speak behind her back. Not a row, merely a spat.

À quel sujet?

That's just it. I'm the one who was sore about something, but, for the life of me, I can't remember what it was. She gave me one of those loving, mocking looks of hers that just defeated me every time, and said, see you later. Do you remember the afternoon of the funeral when I asked you? You told me her last words were, I can't bear Gérard to be sad. A-t-elle vraiment dit ça?

My navel throbs. How does it feel to be in an earthquake, not the catastrophic kind they have in California or Japan, non, the kind of earthquake people are not sure happened, thinking it was just a truck rumbling by, the kind that leaves no marks, but a vague malaise, a vibration that may be an illusion. I touch my navel. Elizabeth said, but did she? Was rage on her lips or Gérard on her mind? She told me we may be in an earthquake in Turkey or in Nepal or even in the Charlottes, and here, on the Mediterranean blue plush méridienne in Gérard's boutique of antiques, here in Anteannum l'an passé, even if he remains perfectly still, his whole body quakes. The convulsion of the superficial parts. I don't move, my heart beats fast, my navel throbs deeper, we are not touching, and yet, we are linked by a tectonic disturbance of immense magnitude. I don't have to peek to know the lines on his face have widened, violence contained, oui, but the lines, cracking open.

We rest sur la méridienne. Wondering. What were her true last words?

Bouillabaisse

Would you pick up a few things for me?

Elizabeth never phoned before. J'en suis bouche bée.

Would your mom let you spend the weekend in Saint-Pol?

Elizabeth never invited me to stay over before. That takes my breath away.

Hello? Have you dropped off the twig?

Sure, Elizabeth, I say, not exhaling, to keep my voice steady.

Sure, what, Ariane, dear? You're dead? Your mom'll say yes? You accept my invitation? Or you'll run my errands?

I am two-day-old eighteen, I say. I can vote, now. No need to ask.

I know. I was on a shoot. Horrendous schedule. Happy birthday, Ariane.

I want to know why I was not on the horrendous shoot and what is the point of being her assistant if she does not let me assist, I don't ask, but am grateful for ceilings, sinon, je monterais au septième ciel.

Merci, I say, to her birthday wishes and invitation.

As soon as I tell maman about the weekend plans, she brings me a small case I never saw before she calls une valise de fin de semaine. All those years, it lived dans le hangar, hidden in one of the many boxes stacked against one wall, I never thought of peeking, that is how maman raised me, to be discreet even when nobody is looking.

La valise de fin de semaine resembles an attaché case but larger and deeper, is made of strong cardboard covered with a thick cream and caramel checkered cloth, each corner reinforced with triangles of brown leather, it has a brown leather handle and brass hinges and clasps. Bien sûr, maman says nothing about the mystery of la valise, donc, I have to imagine her going places on weekends before she married. Margot Joly does not travel by bus, jamais, she travels by train, toujours. My favourite imagining is when she takes the train at la gare Centrale early Saturday morning en route to Québec City and, later in the afternoon, she drinks cocktails au Château Frontenac with friends she now has lost touch with. Margot jeune fille also travels once as far away as New York, a long time ago when she had a life. She never got rid of sa valise, as if she hoped to escape la rue Sherbrooke and find her own life again, secret and exciting, today, she takes it out of its prison box to give it to me, as if she wanted me to have my own life, secret and exciting.

Inside, the satin lining is the colour of old roses, with a large elasticized pocket in the lid and a smaller elasticized pocket on the bottom and brown leather straps criss-crossing over the main compartment to keep the weekend clothes in place. I touch the satin, detect a faint scent, the scent of maman jeune fille before she married Dead Man, did she go out with other men. A man, amen, many men in one man, love mystery, I touch the satin.

Merci, I kiss her. C'est une très jolie valise.

I don't know what I will bring. On the phone, Elizabeth said, come as you are, je pense, a test to see if I travel like women in old movies, with hat boxes and parrot cages, portable record players and picnic baskets, and wardrobe trunks, porters in caps stack on hand trucks, or like Elizabeth who never brings more than what she can carry on her back, including her photo equipment. She calls that, no hindrance travel. Sounds like fire hydrant, peut-être, for emergency escapes from hot spots.

Donc, I picked up a few things, fish and shellfish, Elizabeth will make une bouillabaisse, maman n'était pas contente, she said nothing, but her eyes feared Elizabeth would conveniently forget to reimburse me, maman is not mean, oh non, she just does not trust all those strings attached, lending borrowing, elle n'était pas contente.

Elizabeth gives me a precise list, I write everything down, what is diable de mer, will le poissonnier have diable de mer, will la bouillabaisse be ruined sans diable de mer, another test, I smell it, this diving into la responsabilité la vraie vie.

Go to Waldman's, Elizabeth says. Best fishmonger in the city.

I look up Waldman's address in the phone book, fishmonger in the dictionary.

Chez Waldman, voices bounce off the white-tiled walls, counters piled high with ice float like icebergs on the red-tiled sea floor, on each ice bed lie gigantic red, white, black fish, huge octopuses, their tentacles hugging their ice mattress, as if afraid of falling, mounds of oysters a man in a white coat picks one by one for a woman customer who knows her oysters, the man knocks each shell with a wooden peg, throws the ones with the good sound in a plastic bag, the ones with the bad sound back on the oyster bed, like this is an audition for singing oysters, knocks throws, knocks throws, mon oncle Joseph says we must not eat oysters in months with no ars, piles of mussels and clams, cockles and periwinkles, squids in a heap, their arms braided together like they are having group sex, carpets of shrimps from pale grey to fiery pink, from huge to tiny, shark fins, I touch the gelatinous white cartilage, skate wings resembling corrugated fans, from the bottom of the sea animals sticking out of

iridescent shells the sign says are abalone. Live crabs and lob-
sters take a stroll on the bottom of basins, in green muddy
tanks carps swim mute, and tiny jars of caviar wait in locked
glass cases, safe from le tumulte. Fishmongers, les poissonniers
d'Elizabeth, scale and gut mackerel and salmon with the
speed of les prestidigitateurs, wrap them in sheets of The
Montreal Gazette, joke with the knowing customers, everybody speaks in fish tongues, fish guts spill out of buckets on
the floor, a skilled hand waters the red tiles with a black hose.
Beside a school of whole flounders resting sur leur banquise,
pairs of eyes bunched up together, sad and resigned, ah! le
malheur est sur nous, I read my list, raise a drowner's hand,
help! a man in a white coat, not the oyster man, hears my call
over the din like the wind at sea and comes to the rescue. We
are going to make une bouillabaisse, Elizabeth and me.

Après la poissonnerie Waldman, Elizabeth's list in hand, I
explore la Main maman prefers to call properly le boulevard
Saint-Laurent, I enter the food cathedrals with their stained
glass windows made of giant jars of pickled red peppers, their
ceilings chandeliered with strings of sausages, their stoups
brimming with cheeses in holy brine, I close my eyes to
breathe in not l'encens et la myrrhe, this is not l'extase
religieuse, but le café et la charcuterie. Entering sacred mysterious places, that Saturday, maman, at work comme d'habitude, I am brand new nine, my first time sur le boulevard
Saint-Laurent, ma tante Rita taking me chez Eaton, the bus
moving slowly, people crossing the street without looking,
men in long black coats and women with fringed black
scarves crowding stalls set along both sidewalks, buying live
animals in cages, a man in a black hat sitting on a low stool,
pulling the feathers off a dead hen, white feathers flying, like
he is having a pillow fight, his black coat will be full of white
feathers, his wife will be angry, she will have to brush and
brush his coat, they will have a fight, moi expecting dancing
bears and des funambules in red and white tights like candy

canes walking across a wire strung high above the street, ma tante Rita saying, seigneur, on se croirait au Moyen Âge.

C'est vrai! Now, we are in that movie avec des jongleurs and des avaleurs de feu and Esméralda in her gypsy skirt and off-the-shoulder blouse to make men drool telling la bonne aventure with tarot cards, always drawing les amants et le pendu. Elizabeth's list, my guide my map to buy things I have never tasted, never seen. Regarde! I shout point, so ma tante will see. A woman in a black coat and scarf gets on the bus carrying two live ducks inside a brown paper bag with handles, the bus driver does not say, les animaux sont interdits dans les autobus, the bus is crowded, people stand in the aisle, the driver says, avancez en arrière, avancez en arrière. I cannot take my eyes off the ducks, so cute with their heads sticking out of the bag, their flat beaks turning this way and that way, they will bite people's knees, sans doute, they are pets for the woman's children, ma tante tells me it is their supper, duck is so fat, she shudders, I jump on my feet, must save les canards, but I am caught between the bus window and ma tante, ne mangez pas les canards, madame, I shout, s'il vous plaît, ne mangez pas les canards. The passengers look at me, the duck woman frowns, a man whispers in her ear, she laughs, they are mad, mad like Middle Ages people in movies, dans la vie and in movies, the sane people are the ones sent to the madhouse, le boulevard Saint-Laurent is called la Main, maintenant je comprends, la Main means la maison d'insanité, we live nearby, what if la folie is as easy to catch as la vulgarité. À l'automne, mon oncle will bring les canards from his annual hunting trip, slap the dead birds on ma tante's kitchen table, I will sob, my face buried in the soft blue feathers, ma tante will refuse to clean cook eat them, les canards sauvages taste like liver, dans l'autobus, people laugh, the ducks quack, ma tante pushes me back into my seat, I try hard not to cry, I am eighteen, have never tasted du canard sauvage ou du canard à l'orange. Peut-être après la bouillabaisse, Elizabeth will teach me.

What to do with les poissons et les fruits de mer, I don't want maman to see the fish heads pour le fumet, not after the rotten lamb still fresh in her memory. I repackage everything in layers of waxpaper and plastic bags and store the food dans le hangar. The rain tonight will make the fish feel at home, the mussels will open their shells and sing, the shrimps will kick their ten legs and dance in the rain, I cannot sleep, cannot wait to be in the green country bus.

Sainte viarge, t'es chic, à matin, ma belle poupée, la madame aux culottes d'hommes says.

She rubs the burnished gold polyester weave between thumb and index finger, a fun jumpsuit I sewed fast fast for my birthday, je pensais, Nicole et Diane will throw me a party, nothing, they did not phone, Pierre did not phone, all my friends forgot Tuesday I turned eighteen. Maman, mon oncle Joseph, and ma tante Rita were excited to take me to le Nanking in Chinatown, Pierre and I go to tiny restaurants full of Chinese people, on my birthday, we ate egg rolls and pineapple chicken in red sauce, mon oncle and ma tante ate with forks, I asked for chopsticks, maman did too, she handled hers with skill, mon oncle and ma tante were impressed we knew how to, mon oncle asked the waiter to bring him des baguettes, crisse, he's not so old a dog he can't learn new tricks, he made a mess of rice on the table, ma tante laughed, her hand over her mouth full of red chicken, the Chinese waiters watched and spoke in tongues, that was my eighteenth birthday.

I tell la madame I am wearing my bedspread, a veteran seamstress like her appreciates such transformation, the long sleeves and legs, flaring wildly at the bottom, I cut with abandon, used the entire bedspread, left not one scrap.

C'est extravagant, I say.

À ton âge, she says, l'extravagance, c'est permis.

Permission. Mon oncle gives me permission, saying, crisse, on ne vit qu'une fois, mon oncle and la madame are happy for me, but, I can tell, they wish, ah, so many regrets behind the sparkles in their eyes.

Nous jasons non-stop for fifty miles, as we do every Friday since January, la madame says tu to me, I continue to say vous to her. She knows about our flat on rue Sherbrooke, I know about her bare-bones flat in Hochelaga, her second-hand furniture, the hand-me-downs, and the clothes she makes on the sly on her industrial sewing machine during her lunch breaks, every Saturday night, she goes dancing, her hippo hips pinned in her seat, she moves her shoulders to show on a dance floor she is as light on her feet as any skinny ballerina, she picks up men, screws on the side, but takes precautions now, the only weekly pleasure she can afford, we speak freely and openly, but don't know each other's names, we are friends strangers, a game we play on Fridays on the green country bus.

She glances at ma valise on the rack above our seats. I tell her I am spending the weekend with Elizabeth, she knows I am Elizabeth's collaboratrice since the Friday after the Good Friday that was not a Friday the thirteenth, peut-être, she imagines herself on her dream train, I tell her about les amis de jeunesse de maman in Québec City, I catch myself, warn her those are stories.

T'en fais pas, ma belle poupée, she says. Je sais quand une histoire est cousue de fil blanc.

What if I told her ma valise de fin de semaine is full of fish and shellfish, fennel bulbs and insanely hot red peppers, shallots and leek and thyme, she would laugh her jellyfish laugh, would never believe that fishy story, ça, c'est certain. Tout de même, in the small pocket, I packed une petite culotte, la madame would understand the need for an extra pair of underwear, my toothbrush, hair brush, eye makeup, and, bien sûr, my anticonstitutional pills, as she likes to say. She knows I take the pill. I ask her if she and her sister from Longueuil will soon go on their train trip.

Un jour, ma belle poupée, un jour, she says, patting my hand.

And the next thing I know, I am waving to her from the road.

Allô allô, Elizabeth, c'est moi, I say, using my trademark entrance.

Elizabeth never locks up, even when she spends a few days in Montréal with Gérard or when she shoots weddings and corpses, I open the back door without knocking, wipe my feet on the tattered coir mat, Elizabeth told me it is made with the husk of coconuts, each time my feet touch the mat I imagine standing on a minuscule island shaded by a single coconut tree and say, allô allô, Elizabeth, c'est moi.

Out here, dear.

She rakes behind the lilac tree, leaves burn in a metal drum by the wire fence.

Look at you, she says, dropping her rake, holding me at arm's length.

We spin like witches, les herbes folles catch on the wide legs of the jumpsuit, the June black flies try their luck, the smoke from the burning leaves saves us from their bites, I tell her this is my bedspread, she throws her head back, her face full of light.

Where's the food, Ariane, dear?

I indicate the back door.

I have to finish raking this corner and burn this pile of leaves. If you're hungry, grab something. You want to make a pot of coffee? I could use a cup.

Okay.

I lay ma valise on the table among dirty whisky glasses and coffee cups and a plate with not yet dried smears of egg and toast crumbs. The kitchen holds no more secrets, I have fixed sandwiches, uncorked bottles of wine, made tea, Elizabeth says I make a great cup of tea, I watched the ritual at home hundreds of times, boil water furiously dans le canard, as ma tante Rita calls the kettle maman insists is une bouilloire, pour an inch of boiling water in the brown stoneware teapot, swirl swirl, throw the water in the sink, use two Salada tea bags, orange pekoe, fill the warm pot with boiling water, let the tea seep five minutes, remove the bags, I never brewed coffee in the contraption Elizabeth calls a Silex, standing like a glass spaceship on the propane stove, maman uses un percolateur électrique en acier inoxydable.

Mon oncle says we must figure out how things work before taking them apart, sinon, we can never put them back together whole again, crisse, where does that nut go. Okay, mon oncle, I am figuring it out. The bottom part is a round glass jug with a Bakelite handle, the top part is a glass funnel fitted over the bottom jug with a black filter sitting on the glass tube going into the bottom jug. Okay, mon oncle, how does it work?

Leftover coffee in the bottom jug, used coffee grounds in the upper jug. Where do we pour the fresh water, sûrement, in the bottom jug with the handle, sinon, an empty glass container will explode as soon as I turn on the gas. Where do we put the grounds, sûrement, they cannot lift into the glass tube and pass through the filter to rest in the upper part of the funnel. And if we put the grounds in the upper jug, how does the water below turn into coffee, I don't get it, mon oncle. There must be a principle of physics that escapes me dans cette contraption diabolique.

Elizabeth rakes, soon, she will come in, misère, Ariane, do something. Okay. Take the thing to the sink, twist to release the rubber filter, the glass jug and funnel separate like the two halves of a spaceship. A chain dangles down the glass tube of the funnel and is hooked to the edge of the tube. Don't touch that. Wash both containers, with the filter still attached to the funnel. The grounds mess up the white porcelain sink, go down the drain, better not clog the pipe. Fill the clean jug with water, find the measuring cup, measure the water, the jug holds four cups of eight ounces each, seal the funnel back on, the clean alien coffee maker sits on the burner.

Elizabeth carries dead leaves to the fire in the metal drum. Find the metal canister with the drawings of coffee beans, measure four rounded spoonfuls of beans, non, make that five, Elizabeth likes her coffee strong, find le moulin à café, that old block of wood Gérard gave her a long time ago, fitted with a little drawer in the middle and a brass cup and handle on top she uses to grind the beans, look and look, cannot find it. Okay, improvise. Open the tools drawer.

Elizabeth leans on her rake, talking to Marie the schoolteacher on her daily lunch hour walk to get away from the little devils who are slowly driving her nuts. Put the beans in a brown paper bag, close the bag, hit the beans with the hammer, Elizabeth looks at the house, can she hear the banging, she turns back to speak to Marie the schoolteacher, bang 'til the right grind of coffee is achieved, pour that in the top jug. Take a deep breath, turn on the knob, put a match to the propane gas burner, we have a natural gas stove at home, maman taught me to respect gas, make sure the silly Silex sits over the blue flame, wait for the explosion, shattered glass, wait.

Done, Elizabeth says behind my back.

I jump to the ceiling, grip the plaster and hang upside down like a cartoon cat. Elizabeth washes her hands, I put the hammer away, throw the crumpled paper bag in the garbage pail by the wood stove Elizabeth stops lighting in early June, go to the window.

I love the smell of burning leaves, I say.

Me too, she says, lighting a cigarette. Hmmm, don't tell me I'll have to buy a new coffee mill.

I turn sharply on my heels. She is holding le moulin à café, where was it hiding? points at the uneven grounds in the coffee maker, she is not panicking, it means I loaded the outerspace contraption correctly, nothing will explode shatter.

Fuck me gently, she says, examining le moulin. It worked fine this morning. I guess objects expire like people, sometimes, quite suddenly. I hate shopping.

Probablement, I did not use it right, I say. Maman does not make coffee often and when she does, she uses factory-ground beans.

The water is starting to form bubbles at the edge of the jug.

Let's have a look at that fish, she says, searching for store bags.

I open ma valise, she laughs with delight.

Like an old-fashioned picnic basket, she says. This is so clever, dear girl. What have we got here? she says putting the herbs and vegetables on the table, starting to unwrap and inspect les poissons et les fruits de mer. The mussels look good. Great scallops. They'll taste quite sweet. Fine shrimp too.

She does not say shrimps like I do, are shrimp like sheep, I am learning. The water makes its boiling noise, nothing is spilling over. She unwraps each bundle of cod, sea perch, sea bass, grouper, turbot, opens the package of salmon heads pour le fumet, nods approval, but is a little disappointed. On the phone yesterday, she said the true bouillabaisse needs diable de mer, but the chance of finding that fish was slim. Keeping an eye on the coffee contraption, I smile a Salada-tea-cup smile.

What have you got up your wide sleeve? she asks.

Ta-dah, I say, presenting her with the hidden package.

Is it? Marvellous.

In chunks, without its head and poisonous spines, ce diable de mer could be any fish. Hogfish, le poissonnier called it, the ugliest thing in the sea, he said, I said, that cannot be diable de mer, he assured me hogfish is diable de mer, he showed me a poster on the wall with colour pictures of fish, their names written underneath, hogfish, he pointed, c'est vrai, it is ugly with long thick spines on its dorsal fin, it still does not prove hogfish is diable de mer.

Le poissonnier said it is not hogfish from la Méditerranée, I warn Elizabeth. But hogfish from le golfe du Mexique. Will it do?

It will do.

Why is diable de mer so important dans la bouillabaisse?

According to my concierge who was from Marseille, Elizabeth says, flicking her ash in the ashtray on top of the fridge, diable de mer, she called it rascasse, acts as a kind of catalyst in the broth. It brings out the flavours of the other fish. Her bouillabaisse was sensational.

Concierge, diable de mer, rascasse, Marseille, bouilla-baisse, je pense, how brave of her to use so many French words all at once, she enunciates to compensate for the atro-cious accent she hates so, the way she enunciates Gérard's name lovingly.

I hope I can pull this off, she says.

You never made it before?

Just came across the recipe the other day. I plain forgot about it. Where did I put it?

She goes through bills on the counter. The water comes to a full boil, will Elizabeth remember to reimburse me, I leave the receipts on the table, watch the water rise through the glass tube into the funnel through the filter, it will spill over, Elizabeth shuffles paper, she made me promise to tell her how much the food cost, the water grows like a black blob from outer space, when there is but a little water left in the jug, without looking, Elizabeth takes the whole thing off the burner, turns off the gas, still searching through the mess of paper on the counter, I am about to tell her how much the food cost.

Ah, here it is, she says, calm.

The coffee in the funnel holds in a kind of unstable position 'til it falls back through the glass tube into the jug, like it was shot out of a cannon, reached its maximum height and now starts its descent back to earth. Elizabeth gently shakes a brittle sheet of paper in my face. The kitchen smells rich with coffee.

When will you make la bouillabaisse? I ask.

Tomorrow. Let's have a cuppa.

She separates the funnel from the jug, pours, I put the fish in the fridge, it is quite bare, she has not shopped ahead like ma tante does when her daughters visit from Toronto with their husbands and children. On those occasions, ma tante always invites maman and me and her fridge is so full, she balances plates and bowls on top of each other. If I yodelled, this fridge would send an echo, the empty metal shelves would sing vibrate. Elizabeth pours coffee, we sit at the table. The recipe for la bouillabaisse is handwritten in French in faded violet ink, an old-fashioned handwriting of curlicues and wings difficult to read, a long list of ingredients, no instructions how to proceed, the blue-lined paper fragile like an artifact. Elizabeth had une concierge française who knew bouillabaisse intimately. Où? quand? I ask.

In the mid-fifties, she says, I lived in Vence for a couple of months. Are you sure you wouldn't eat something? How about olives and cheese?

Okay, I say, expecting green olives stuffed with pimento and cheddar and crackers, which would be fine, what else could she offer me from her bare fridge.

Elizabeth feeds me olives from Sicily and goat cheese from Greece. I get the saltines from the cupboard where she keeps cans of soup and the soup bowls.

What did you do there? I ask.

Elizabeth pronounced Vence like fence with a vee, je pense, she meant Venice. I press the goat cheese with my tongue to turn it into a pungent paste. I cannot ask, what did you do in Venice? that would be impolite to correct her.

I tramped up and down the coast of Provence, shooting Roman ruins on a shoestring.

Why did you stay in Venice? I ask, je pense, that was far to travel to Provence each day, surtout, on a shoestring.

When? Oh, that was later. With Gérard. Sixty-three. Camera-less in Venice. I swore I wouldn't be a slave to the shutter. I used my eyes, my hands, my nose. No machine. What a holiday, that was. No mail and every night we had chocolate mousse.

Je pense, I am glad there were no males in all of Venice to distract Elizabeth from Gérard's affection. And how inventive of Venetians to make chocolate in the shape of moose, or is it meese, like goose geese.

What are you grinning at? Elizabeth asks.

Oh, chocolate moose. I am trying to imagine.

You never had it?

Non.

I am dreamy, imagining. Eating cheese and olives in the South of France. Touching Roman ruins. Listening to les cigales scream in the fierce afternoon heat. Smelling la lavande, le thym, le romarin. Chanceuse Elizabeth. I am imagining the house she lived in, sûrement, it was pittoresque.

Tell me all about la Provence.

There's not much to tell, except I got very interesting shots. I published them later. Must have a copy of that book somewhere in the front room. It rained almost the whole time. Winter is not the best season to see Provence, although, bad weather has its charm. And the stone ruins in rain and mist came out better than in the ubiquitous sunshine.

Where did you stay?

In a shed. The roof was not leaking, but just. Animals were kept there, once. As the rain persisted, the smell of goat became stronger and stronger. I caught the worst cold in my life. Madame Artaud made me bouillabaisse especially. I ate it for five days. Each day, it tasted better. A little miracle in a bowl, Elizabeth says, laughing, pushing smoke out of her mouth. And tomorrow, I'll try to reproduce that miracle.

Cannot wait to see how miracles are done, don't have to, miracles and wonders begin now, this afternoon. No work. Au lieu, we go for a walk in the woods. I rush upstairs to la vespasienne, in honour of la Provence, Elizabeth lends me a pair of baggy pants, a shirt, heavy socks, rubber boots.

We smear ourselves with Off, I understand maman's refusal to visit the country at the height of la saison des mouches noires, the woods are alive with them, but Elizabeth does not notice them, she picks fiddleheads, says, they are late, this year.

We reach a small lake, she lies in a patch of sun, I churn my arms like a windmill, sit close to her cigarette smoke. The sun is hot, she wants to swim, I was never allowed to swim before the beginning of July because, avec la fonte des neiges, the water had a higher level of bacteria.

Is that so? Elizabeth says, taking off her clothes.

She throws herself in, breaks through the mirror, destroys the reflection of the serious firs climbing the hills, thick like the ribbed stitches in a knit. Elizabeth swims, strong, her body glides just below the surface. In no time she is in the middle of the lake.

I go in too, so she will not think que je suis une poule mouillée. My feet sink into thick mud that looks like water rising through coffee grounds, I throw myself in water so cold, it freezes my breath. Je pense, sûrement, le lac vient juste de caler, last night, skates would have been de rigueur. I swim fast to warm up. The sensation is thrilling, the water, a silk cocoon cold hot. I never swam naked before, when I was lit-tle, mon oncle talked about les jeunes who went skinny-dipping after sundown, he said, skinny-dipping, not, tout nus comme des vers, I did not know the word skinny-dipping, knew the context, what I did not understand was how les jeunes could stand the biting. Les brûlots are worse than les mouches noires which are worse than les maringouins, at sundown, les brûlots come out in clouds, devouring any bare skin they can find, like those movie piranhas who eat a cow in five minutes flat. Mon oncle swore, the next day, he could tell who went skinny-dipping by their swollen eyelids. I swim, the blue sky high above, now I understand why les jeunes took their chances with les brûlots.

Une chance, no swollen eyes. In the bathroom, I am gluing on my false eyelashes, we are going to the village inn for dinner. I have been to the village only once, the day I vomitted raw meat in the snow, afterward, I flagged down the bus outside Elizabeth's house, Elizabeth says the village is quaint, peut-être, quaint is the same as pittoresque. This weekend is opening weekend for many things, what a hoot, le vernissage de mes dix-huit ans.

Elizabeth, I call out, why don't you wear your caftan?

I lean in the doorway of her bedroom, glance at the recess between les deux lucarnes, c'est approprié in a bedroom to call les lucarnes dormers, that recess, not a real closet, but a space closed by a panel of heavy fabric printed with Japanese brush strokes representing cranes in flight. Elizabeth is putting on brown cord pants and her long shirt en laine du pays qui pique.

Oh, that wasn't mine, she says. It belongs to Gérard. He rents costumes, did you know that?

C'est pratique.

A blessing, she says, buttoning up her shirt. I absolutely hate shopping for clothes.

I could make you clothes.

She is tying her hair into a French twist, stares at me through her mirror on the wall.

Only if you want to, I add.

That's sweet, but really, Ariane, I don't care for clothes. For social functions, okay, I make concessions. Otherwise.

Quand même, I know I will not stop thinking about what I should make her, what size patterns I should buy, how to adjust compensate for her uneven orange-crate hips and her small chest. Mon oncle is right, think things through before taking anything apart, the same principle applies in reverse, think things through before offering to build something from scratch.

Everything here is made from scratch, Elizabeth said, as we sat down.

Notre bœuf bourguignon with boiled potatoes est délicieux, full of robust flavours, as the menu promised, flavours I don't identify, but the rich blend dances on the tongue, makes les papilles bristle with excitement. Elizabeth says L'Auberge du lac is renowned, people come from far and wide, she is right, the dining room is full, the fire blazes in the immense stone fireplace, cette cheminée ne fume pas, a woman in a long black dress plays discreet piano, the big lake, not the small hidden lake where we swam this afternoon, shines under the reflectors set above the deck, this is a genuine bona fide adult evening, I drink mon vin de Bourgogne that le sommelier poured in glasses that resemble the top of Elizabeth's coffee pot from outerspace. Those glasses are called des ballons.

Everybody knows Elizabeth, except the people who come here only because le restaurant est réputé, those diners stare at her, wonder if she is une vedette, they stare at me, wonder who I might be, dining with une vedette, everyone else stops by to kiss Elizabeth on both cheeks over her plate of bœuf bourguignon, to shake her hand, she gets up to hug a good friend, says, long time no see, they are all dying to know when she will exhibit next, and where, and what, they make her swear to let them know or they will kill her, Elizabeth introduces me as Ariane Claude, her new assistant,

I shake hands, bonsoir, enchantée, bonsoir, a pleasure to meet you, one woman is a lawyer, a man an impresario, does he know Raymond, another a publisher, should I tell Pierre, another one a politician, the painters and weavers and ceramists of Saint-Polycarpe wave as they are heading for the inn bar, a popular watering hole, as Elizabeth says, je pense, we had our own private watering hole this afternoon, I drink mon vin de Bourgogne, je suis l'invitée d'Elizabeth Gold, j'ai dix-huit ans, la vie est belle.

After we returned from our skinny-dipping, I changed back into my jumpsuit and went in the garden to brush my hair in the last of the sun. I am amazed we swam, while in shady corners of the garden snow persists. It strikes me the light of June refuses to die, that pleases me, I was born in the month of light.

Don't move, Elizabeth says, like a gunslinger in a movie.

I stop brushing my hair, she shoots me, ou plutôt, she shoots my long shadow she says looks like a giant Indonesian puppet you work with sticks. She directs me, move that way, open your arms, kick one leg high, make slow movements like a shadow mime.

I applied to have my name changed, I say, one foot up in the air.

No kidding. Keep that pose. Raise your right arm a little higher. Slowly. Very good.

She clicks clicks in rapid succession.

Bientôt, I say, I will be official Ariane Claude for the whole world to know. Thanks to you. I am Ariane Claude 'til I die. Changing my name is like me marrying me.

Click, click, she shoots my shadow in her garden.

Click, she touches my glass with hers, asks where I was.

Madame Gold, le chef says, kissing her hand. Toujours un plaisir.

Le chef came out of his kitchen to kiss Elizabeth's hand, je vais pouffer de rire, chefs and couturiers are so extravagant.

Elizabeth introduces me, I don't catch his name, keep my hands busy with bread and ragoût.

Bonsoir, I say, chewing slowly. C'est délicieux.

He bends at the waist, a little more, he will hit his forehead on our table, I swallow very very carefully, cannot choke on le bœuf bourguignon in front of le chef de cuisine, he leaves.

You know everybody, I say.

It's a village.

Quand même, I say, my fork piercing a piece of potato. I have lived in our flat on rue Sherbrooke all my life, people move in, move out, stay a long time, stay a short time, it does not matter, our neighbours are shadows.

In a village, you can't live like that, she says, sipping her wine. Ten years ago when I arrived here, people were suspicious. You keep your distance, their suspicion grows. Right away, you're the cliché of the eccentric woman living on the hill, frightening the children away. As soon as I was settled in, I put up my shingle, so to speak, and announced I would shoot weddings, baptisms, first communions, fiftieth wedding anniversaries, school, community, and religious fêtes. I left no celebration unturned. At first, I charged just enough to cover costs. Instead of money, I accepted payments of food, hardware, firewood, whatever they could provide, whatever I needed. They no longer perceived me as a greedy city bastard, but as a decent woman down on her luck. You see, that's the only way they could explain why I would live in their backwater village. I let it be known I wanted solitude, but I was no snob. I have no family, which is not a lie since I don't want to talk about family, nothing sordid, nothing tragic, I just want to live on my own terms. They didn't understand that, but they had great photo albums for the cost of a chicken or a hammer. And I showed I trusted them by never locking my doors, got chummy with everybody, spoke like them, made the effort to say a few words in French despite my unspeakable accent, called everybody monsieur and madame, except the kids, of course. They got used to the idea of a so called artist living in their midst, realized artists eat eggs and soup, use toilet paper and catch colds. In the last few years, potters like Moffat and his wife Pauline, sculptors, painters, weavers have been setting up shops, the inn was renovated, the village prospered, people always like that. I figure in another ten, twenty years, this place will no longer exist. It will become a suburb of Montréal. People will buy new houses in subdivisions and commute to work. When that starts to happen, I'm out of here. I might be six feet under. In that case, nothing will matter. But right now, this is where I want to be.

She drains her glass, lights a cigarette. This is her universe.

How come Saint-Polycarpe? I ask.

I was looking for a cheap place to live. Not right in a village, too many eyes, you understand, but not in the woods either. I wanted peace and quiet. That was paramount. Gérard found the house. Dear man. You see, he had been scouring this area for antiques and kept driving past this old house that had been for sale forever. We checked it out, the notaire's son had inherited it from an old aunt, the son no longer lived here, wanted to get rid of the house, but refused to spruce it up, so it didn't sell. Not the most idyllic location either, right by the road. I made an offer. Talk about lowballing, she laughs.

What's lowballing?

Got the house for a song. I fixed it up a little with monsieur Labrie's help, but that was it. None of that endless round of renovations that traps you. As long as the house doesn't fall down on my head, who cares how it looks.

The waiter asks if we want dessert. They don't have chocolate moose tonight, the waiter est désolé, I say, ça ne fait rien, Elizabeth says the chocolate tart and the crème brûlée are excellent, the waiter says they have those, I say, non, merci, and touch my stomach. Même si, I only had one glass of wine, I want fresh air. Elizabeth asks for the bill.

The walk back will do us good, she says, reading my mind.

We pay half and half, I say.

This is my treat. Didn't I say?

Non.

Well, I say it now. This is my treat. But haven't you forgotten something, Ariane, dear?

The fish, I say. No, I am not forgetting. I left the bill for the fish and the bill for the grocery on the kitchen table. Why do I have to remind you if you remember?

You have to look after yourself.

That would have sounded greedy.

To look after yourself?

To remind you. Isn't it your responsibility to remember to reimburse me?

Of course, it is. But don't count on it. If people think you're a cheapskate because you remind them to pay you back, let them. But don't let them get away with the easy way out. The lame excuse, oh, sorry, I forgot.

For an eccentric artist, Elizabeth, you sound like maman and mon oncle Joseph sewn together.

Is that so? I don't live on much, because I don't want much. But I always manage to have enough money to do what matters to me. And I get paid for work done. Saint-Pol is a bit of an exception, but that too is changing. A few villagers continue to barter, but most of them now think it's more sophisticated to fork out the dough. With all my other clients, I lay down my terms. I don't care if a few skinflints think I'm a bitch. Everybody pays, and on time.

Okay, Elizabeth. You owe me twenty-three dollars and forty-nine cents.

She puts the dinner money in the little plate on top of the bill and slides twenty-five dollars toward me. I get my wallet out and count the change.

Forget it.

Jamais de la vie. Les bons comptes font les bons amis, as the proverb goes. Tiens. Exactly one dollar and fifty-one cents, I say, pushing the change toward her. Nothing shadowy between us.

I wake up in complete darkness, total silence, an itch on my elbow, les mouches noires had a nibble, my foot asleep, my brain wide awake. I listen for Elizabeth's breathing next to me, nothing, the silence of the countryside swallowed her sleep breath like a giant amoeba, I open my eyes wide, cannot see my hand, when it brushes against my nose it startles me, ah, oui, Elizabeth gave me her bed for tonight, she is sleeping in her labyrinth of books on the living room floor because of her back.

When we returned from the inn, we got down to brass tacks, Elizabeth called the business we had to do. She said she was going to take a bath to ease the pain in her lower back, would I bring her a glass of brandy, have one myself, I said, non, merci, and to bring the glass in the bathroom, would I mind if we had our meeting there, I said, bien sûr que non, I was not sure, this afternoon, we swam toutes nues comme des vers, Elizabeth did not look at me in any particular way, but now, inside her house dans l'intimité de la nuit, I was not sure.

I sit on the toilet cover in my extravagant jumpsuit, Elizabeth lies in the small bathtub, knees bent sticking out of the water, arms stretched on the porcelain edge, head resting on the sloping tub, eyes closed.

That damn back, she says. I hope to hell it doesn't act up again. I'll be crippled all summer.

She sips her brandy without opening her eyes. I swallow hard, have to learn not to be passive, with Pierre I learned to take l'initiative, he loves that, peut-être, Elizabeth also expects l'initiative, she said I have to look after myself, she wants to live on her own terms, I swallow hard.

Do you want me to massage your back?

No, she says, her eyes still closed, her hand up in the air. Thanks, but it doesn't really help. I shouldn't have gone in this afternoon. The water was way too cold. I'll be fine.

She opens her eyes, lights a cigarette, pushes the smoke toward the tiny window.

I want to talk to you about your summer job. I can't afford to hire you full time.

It's okay. We discussed everything on Good Friday. D'abord, six Friday afternoons 'til June, ensuite, three days a week for twelve weeks starting next week, oui? Euh, my work is not satisfactory?

Je pense, peut-être, Raymond needs money urgently, she will give him the job, like the pizza boss gave my job to his hot niece.

On the contrary, dear girl. I'm wondering though, she says, exhaling smoke. Are you looking after your best interests?

What do you mean?

Money, that's what I mean. You'll make five hundred dollars working for me.

That is more money than I ever saw in my entire life. What's wrong with that?

She flicks her ash in the small glass ashtray she keeps in the metal soapdish hanging off the edge of the tub, a speck of burnt paper falls between her breasts, I try to concentrate.

If you get a full-time summer job in Montréal, you could double that amount.

Will you deduct income tax and unemployment insurance?

She sips her brandy, takes a last draw, stubs out her cigarette, pushes smoke out of her nostrils.

Don't worry about that.

It is settled, then, I say. In any other job, there will be deductions. Et puis, unless you change your mind, I already have a job. Un tiens vaut mieux que deux tu l'auras.

She smiles nods, I may have scored points with my proverbs, two in one evening, but cannot tell for sure, the whole of Elizabeth is fuzzy, the bathroom, full of steam.

Any question?

I trust you.

This is a business arrangement, Ariane. Don't trust me.

Okay. Will you pay me every week? I'd prefer that.

Every week, it is.

Which three days did you have in mind? And I will have to find out about earlier buses.

Here's what works best for me. Early each week, I'll be in town. On Wednesday mornings, I'll pick you up, sometimes at your house, sometimes at another location. I'll let you know the night before. We'll drive back here early, seven or so. Then Saturday mornings, I'll drive you back to town on my way to shoot weddings. How does that strike you?

She looks at me through the steam that is dissipating, droplets clinging to the window, the high toilet tank, my face.

This is a fine satisfactory job arrangement, Elizabeth.

She laughs at that, we shake hands, I trust her même si she does not want me to.

In complete darkness, in total silence, the smells, old wood, musk, damp earth, fir sap, darkness itself has its own smell, rusted iron, its own fabric, thick felt, in the bathroom, a faint light, the body walks toward the window, like a ship lost at sea sails toward a lighthouse. The studio is full of light, Elizabeth comes out, carrying the same wooden box she used to bring dead leaves to the fire, in the kitchen I hear sounds of glasses, dishes, utensils, drawers and cupboard doors, what is she doing, son ménage du printemps, je pense, she is an eccentric living on her own terms, it is normal to clean house in the middle of the night, she crosses the garden again, the box looks heavy, she is holding a flashlight, a gigantic firefly guiding her. I pee, drink water, go back to bed, sleep float between layers of dark and light, touch felt, black, follow fireflies, white, night shifting, black light, black light toward Saturday morning light.

In Elizabeth's house, everything normal. I eat toast with strawberry jam, homemade, bartered, Elizabeth is reading in the front room, I dangle my bare feet under the chair, the morning sun, the colour of honey, and une mésange singing her shrill i-u woke me up, ten o'clock, I jumped out of bed, smelled Noxzema in the bathroom, the breath of the firs coming in through the open window, I made Elizabeth's bed she will have a fit, tant pis, an unmade bed looks sick, finish my coffee, rush upstairs, miss by a hair the low ceiling on the landing, je canard in the nick of time. Grocery shopping in Saint-Polycarpe, no customers bumping into each other's carts through the aisles.

Dans ce magasin général, we stand in front of the counter, crowded, this being Saturday morning, give our list to la propriétaire, a big woman, not fat like la madame aux culottes d'hommes, je pense, la propriétaire est plantureuse, she smiles chats with the customers, all honey, barks orders to the store boys, all bile, the boys run, arms loaded with the customers' items, la propriétaire packs the supplies in cardboard boxes lined up on the counter, no grocery bags, I move to the side, the store smells of woodsmoke laundry soap leather, she writes the price of each item on a pad, one column per customer, the sun streams in through the large store window, the shadow of the lettering painted in an arc on the glass lies upside down on the worn wood floor, she adds fast fast, chats, money changes hands, she gives the correct change, chats barks, she never makes a mistake, Elizabeth says to me loud enough for la propriétaire to hear, the woman takes the compliment like a pro, no giggling, no false modesty.

I carry the box. Sans doute, Elizabeth buys provisions for an entire month, too busy to shop every week like maman. I work my way through the undisciplined crowd, pardon, excusez-moi, people stare at my jumpsuit, we put the box in the back of Elizabeth's huge station wagon, brown and old like her clothes, the five doors creak like the hinges are full of sand, rust polka dots the body, holes in the floor let us see how fast we are going, we leave the beat-up beast to rest in front of le magasin général and walk to la boulangerie, on a side street beside monsieur Labrie's lumberyard.

Bien sûr, la boulangerie smells of freshly baked bread, Pierre would say, ah, le bon pain de nos ancêtres, mon oncle would say, crisse, by now it would be as hard as a rock, la boulangerie is as quiet as a church. A half-dozen customers line up, but words are few and barely audible. Behind the counter, la femme du boulanger is young and pregnant, Saint-Polycarpe is luckier than the village in that old French movie where la femme du boulanger leaves le boulanger her husband for another man and le boulanger refuses to bake bread, sans doute, the baby in the woman's belly is le bébé du boulanger de Saint-Polycarpe, sinon, the bakery would not smell so good.

I had no idea Elizabeth ate so much bread, two dozen vol-au-vent, two baguettes, sûrement pour la bouillabaisse, four large round loaves, like the kind ma tante Rita calls du pain sur la sole. When I was little, I thought du pain sur la sole meant bread on sale, ma tante fait parfois des fautes de français, I thought she meant en solde but said sur la sole, to make sure, I asked mon oncle Joseph who knows everything, he did not know, maman said the bread is not baked in a pan, but placed directly on the base of the oven, which is called la sole, we put the bread in Elizabeth's car, she looks at her watch, lights a cigarette.

Let's take a walk through the village, she says.

Je pense, the car must be hot sitting in the sun, the bread will ferment again and rise, the bacon will grow maggots.

Women kneeling in their yards plant geraniums and tomatoes, men fix windows, put a new coat of paint on their houses, salut, bonjour, Elizabeth, they greet her, she blends right in with her paint-stained jeans and lumberjack shirt, kids skipping rope ask if I am a clown, will there be a show this afternoon.

We go in a small art gallery, a woman Elizabeth's age greets us.

Jo, c'est Ariane. Joséphine paints these, Elizabeth says to me.

Ah, Ariane, Joséphine says. C'est toi?

Oui, I say, shaking the woman's hand. Ariane, c'est moi.

She stares me up and down, disapproves of my bedspread, Elizabeth sits with her, they drink coffee. I look at the post-card-size paintings depicting everything there is to depict in Saint-Polycarpe in all seasons, from bird's-eye views of the entire village to extreme close-ups of doorknobs. One post-card shows an old man leaning on his cane, looking at his shoes, the right side of his body missing, like in a badly framed photograph. Joséphine does pointillisme, what Paul Signac called divisionnisme, I learned that in my art history courses. She must spend long winter days hunched over her paintings, hypnotizing herself dot dotting, emerging in the spring, dizzy, incapable of focussing on the wider world, dots dancing in front of her eyes. Elizabeth looks at her watch. Je pense, is she bored with me?

Are you Waiting for Godot, Elizabeth? I ask, as we leave dotting Joséphine.

Let's get some beer, she says, laughing.

We drive to the inn as Elizabeth explains there is no booze shop in Saint-Pol, she says, booze shop, the inn has an off-licence. The owner of l'auberge near mon oncle's chalet sells beer to special customers, out of sight, mon oncle winks, I know it is illegal, sans doute, that is what an off-licence is, off the law. In Saint-Pol, the owner of L'Auberge du lac sells his illegal booze in plain view, peut-être, he knows the right politi-cian and pays him des pots-de-vin, peut-être, the politician

who talked to Elizabeth while we were eating le bœuf bourguignon is the one who gets les pots-de-vin and he came to
the inn last night to collect. Elizabeth buys two cases of
twenty-four, one case of Molson and one case of O'Keefe.
We carry that to the station wagon. A man leans on his car,
the kind with long fins that stab distracted pedestrians.

Hé! les petites mères, ça va fêter à soir, he jokes, eyeing
the beer. Est-ce que vous m'invitez?

Elizabeth flashes a smile at him.

Who is he? I ask.

Haven't the foggiest.

I need a pee. Let's go home.

Let's drop by the diner. Are you hungry?

I need a pee.

Okay. You have a pee, I'll have a BLT.

I pee, wait outside for Elizabeth to finish her bee-el-tee,
she sits at the lunch counter, her figure and the leafy trees
reflecting in the window overlap, she smokes a cigarette,
chats with the waitress. She keeps glancing at her watch.
Does the day go by that slowly, does she regret inviting me
for the weekend, does my extravagant jumpsuit embarrass
her, did la madame aux culottes d'hommes give me permission because it cost her nothing?

The church bell chimes twelve.

Let's go in, Elizabeth says.

I relax. Peut-être, the church is locked 'til noon on
Saturdays, that is why she kept looking at her watch, sans
doute, she has to go inside to prepare things for a wedding
shoot, I'll be damned. When Elizabeth does not say, fuck me
gently, she says, I'll be damned. I'll be damned, I was right.

She walks around the church with her light meter,
checking how much light comes in through the coloured
glass set in the row of windows along the lateral walls, peut-
être, she will shoot a solstice wedding, what a pagan idea, this
old country church belongs to a time when people still

danced in fields under a full moon and came to church on Sundays only to avoid being burned sur le bûcher de l'hérésie. The interior smells of cold wax, but the wax from les cierges smells sweeter than the wax from normal dinner candles, peut-être, that is l'odeur de sainteté, that sweetness the corpses of saints are said to exude as they do not rot like normal corpses.

I stopped going to mass when I was fifteen. Maman was sitting at her vanity combing her hair, I told her I did not believe and, if I continued to go, I would be une hypocrite. We looked at each other through the vanity mirror, she asked if that was my idea or if I was going through the phase of une adolescente en rébellion. I assured her I thought about that all by myself and was a little hurt she presumed I could not have my own thoughts. She said, d'accord, si c'est ta pensée profonde. I wanted to hug her, but this was too solemn a moment for effusive childish demonstrations. That Sunday and forever after, we stopped preparing for church.

Elizabeth measures the light, I examine the paintings of le chemin de la Croix hanging between the stained glass windows, les scènes exécutées dans le style de l'art naïf, squint at the painted angels flying high sur le plafond en ogive, contemplate the red and white carnations in thin silver vases on either side of the tabernacle, I hope Elizabeth with her hatred of carnations will not go crazy and crush them, the white flowers symbolize the pure souls of the Faithful and the red ones the tainted souls of the Damned who danced under a full moon, I feel like dancing, a pagan priestess in a gold gown. Instead, I notice covering the wall behind the altar the fresco of a very old bearded man, in clothes not unlike mine, tied to a stake, eyes blue so blue raised to the heavens, flames licking his naked feet.

Is he un hérétique? I ask Elizabeth.

Meet Polycarp.

C'est saint Polycarpe? Oh, non! Pas un autre martyr.

In the Church's crowded pantheon, he was one of the first.

Who was he?

The Greek bishop of Smyrna, now Izmir, in Turkey.

What did he do?

He grew old.

That was une hérésie?

He was at the wrong place at the wrong time and died for his Christian beliefs.

You mean, like the Christians who got eaten by lions in Roman coliseums?

Something like that.

I thought only les hérétiques were burned sur le bûcher de l'Inquisition.

The Church didn't have exclusive rights on that procedure.

Was he as old as he appears in this painting?

That's the consensus. But the record is not consistent about his age. He could have died at 86, 95, or 108. Eighty-six is remarkably old for the second century, 108 is unlikely. Also, sources diverge about his Feast Day, either January 26 or February 23. Here, they chose January.

At least both dates are in winter. It keeps the poor man cool.

Elizabeth chuckles.

How come you know all that? I ask.

I painted him. Moffat posed for me.

You did that! I shout, my eyes opening wide.

I stare at the long white beard. Ou bien, Moffat washed out the bits, ou bien, Elizabeth was not aiming at realism.

Granted, she says. This is not my style, but I thought the painting should reflect the same folk art as the Stations of the Cross. Monsieur le curé, she enunciates painfully, is a modern priest, but he agreed with me. A Rouault-like Polycarp in this nineteenth-century country church would have been out of place and, although he is a fan of the Automatistes, a stream-of-consciousness Polycarp would have been an affectation.

Are you a Catholic, Elizabeth?

I told you, monsieur le curé is a modern man. And he has a sense of humour.

Ses paroissiens were not offended a non-believer painted a Christian bishop burned by pagans?

The few who objected raised the question of language, not religion. They wanted a French-speaking Québécois to paint their saint. I told them, quand je peins votre saint, je peins en français. They must have bought that, because they let me work in peace. For crying out loud, Ariane, the man was Greek and he died in the second century. What difference does it make who, in the twentieth century, holds the brush?

We stare in silence at the poor martyred bishop, Elizabeth sneaks another peek at her watch.

I thought les Anciens had great respect for old people, I say, trying to ignore her preoccupation with time.

Do you realize, she says, if he had had a normal lifespan he would not have been burned to a crisp and chances are he would have been completely forgotten.

On our way home, Elizabeth announces her gas guzzler needs fuel and she has to make a call. She disappears inside the gas station, the attendant in greasy overalls tucks the nozzle inside the gas tank opening, washes the dust off all the windows and the squashed bugs off the windshield, leaves streaks of grey water, checks the tire pressure, checks the oil, lets the hood fall with a twank, je pense, fais attention, cette vieille minoune will fall to dust, Elizabeth comes back, pays, we drive off. She looks excited, the phone call must have been good news. What is it?

Surpriiiiiiiiiiiiiiiiiiiise!

The word explodes in both languages.

I stare at a sea of faces. See everybody. Recognize nobody.

Even to the casual observer, I hear Elizabeth's voice far away, I'd say it's clear we succeeded in surprising her. Happy birthday, Ariane, dear, she says, hugging me.

Nicole et Diane shout, bonne fête, Claudette, euh, Ariane, bonne fête. Diane explains they were so excited about the surprise party they did not phone Tuesday to wish me happy birthday, because, Nicole continues, they were afraid qu'elles vendraient la mèche and the surprise would be ruined and it would be their fault, but they felt so bad for not phoning, they press in my hands a small box with a big bow, from the two of them, earrings for pierced ears, I can tell.

Pierre kisses me full on the mouth, tongue and everything, catcalls and whistles from the company, the corner of Nicole's et Diane's box stabs me in the ribs, he also gives me a present, books, I can tell.

Bonne fête, ma puce, he says. Es-tu sûre qu'elle ne se doutait de rien? he asks Elizabeth, staring at my party clothes.

Joyeux anniversaire, Gérard says, kissing me on both cheeks. J'ai apporté le gâteau, he says to apologize for not bringing a present, showing the large mocha cake on the table.

Elizabeth lights a cigarette, takes a puff and lets it burn in the ashtray on top of the fridge, she looks at the cake, says something about birthday wishes to be written on the icing, she bangs cupboard doors, à la recherche of tubes of decorating jelly.

Bonne fête, Raymond says, kissing me on both cheeks and on the mouth and giving me his present, records, I can tell.

Robert and Roger wish me bonne fête, say they brought themselves, if I want to unwrap them, this is my day.

My ears ring, everything, a blur.

I don't remember la bouillabaisse. We cooked it, fish heads swimming drunk in white wine, we added the herbs and shallots, Diane said fennel tasted comme de la réglisse, I peeled shrimp, never done that before, fingers smeared with le jus de crevette, Elizabeth put the shells in the freezer, je pensais, garbage conservation, kitchen chaos, food booze, voice crescendos, beer drinking, wine sipping, fish heads simmering, Elizabeth made the broth, the flesh of the vegetables sang screamed in the hot oil, we chopped tomatoes, dusted with saffron, Gérard said saffron is more expensive than pot, botanical debate, we looked in the stockpot, like a sunset in the bottom of a crater, we made la rouille with the hot peppers and garlic and olive oil, we ate la bouillabaisse with des croûtons toasted in the oven, not burned to a crisp like saints, not rock-hard like ancestral bread, we ladled la rouille, did le diable de mer act as the anticipated catalyst, cannot remember tasting, eating, much white wine drinking to kill the fire of la rouille, words fired across the long table set in the studio, a jumble of words with roots still attached, soupe, in old French, meaning bread in broth, sop, sup, soup, soupe, so many soups, bortsch or bortscht, take your pick of spellings, gaspacho, panade, minestrone, miso, gibelotte, garbure, mulligatawny, everything depends on region, culture, language, time of year, high tide low tide, la marée culturelle, Pierre's voice rising, Pierre diving, this is right up his bowling alley, he inhales le fumet de la discussion, is la rouille an aïoli or an ailloli, that is the question, are grammarians as extravagant as chefs and couturiers, language shift, cataclysme linguistique, langue de morue, Elizabeth smokes, her hand on Pierre's thigh, fish soups, la bouillabaisse, la bourride, la matelote, la pauchouse, la gibelotte du Québec, Moffat insists, on est au Québec, pas en France, vive la gibelotte de Sorel, he yells, seconded by Pierre, we are in the language soup, an endless wave of words points of view, un raz-de-marée, as long as there are fish in the sea, fish everywhere, in lakes and rivers,

Moffat, a blur across the table, bits of wet bread and speckles of saffron broth in his beard, fiery Moffat en Polycarpe, la rouille burning his tongue, did they give a last meal to the poor bishop of Smyrna, sans doute, bread and fish, his last food avant de se faire immoler sur le bûcher, I drink, a mussel shell flies across the table, mussel fight, someone shouts, I don't remember la bouillabaisse.

Vaguely remember crowding around Ariane 1967. Déjà vu. The birthday girl as gallery opening, in November '67, wearing drapes, in June '68, a bedspread, what a hoot, friends and strangers connected by la couturière in the b&w photograph on board with gold thread, 24 x 60 in., $800.00, sold, not to a client on opening night, the red dot, a ruse, never sold, but kept for me, a birthday gift from the artist to her muse, the main players from Corona in Elizabeth's studio see le tableau for the second time, Raymond looking like un intellectuel français avec pipe, will he and Elizabeth do it in the daffodils tonight, Virginia mourning a lost sale in her glass of wine, Gérard, toujours sophistiqué, even in the country, Elizabeth wearing the borrowed caftan, Pierre saying, l'histoire se répète, non, this is faux déjà vu, the new players crowd too, seeing that Ariane for the first time, Elizabeth's village friends, Moffat, the martyr nibbling nuts, crumbs catching in his beard, his wife Pauline, nails painted rose corail, Marie Berthiaume, the walking schoolteacher, Mike and Nancy, the drop-in friends, and my friends, this afternoon, setting up camp for the night in the garden, anywhere, Elizabeth said, except in the daffodils, Nicole and Robert and Diane and Roger erecting a canvas tent, sleeps four, Pierre helping Raymond with his pup tent for a lone camper, peut-être, he writes songs in his portable monk cell, Pierre and I spreading his sleeping bag on a stretch of floor in the living room, between the columns of books, everybody camps, Nicole et Diane will spend their last wild summer camping, they discovered Elizabeth's Swiss chalet overlook-

ing a lake is a rundown house by a dusty road, I should buy
a sleeping bag, go camping with them when not working on
the photo collection.

We crowd around Ariane 1967, Elizabeth puts her arm
around my waist, Elizabeth and Virginia lock eyes, déjà vu.
Ariane 1967, the catalyst pour une bouillabaisse of party-
speak, two coins' worth cling clanging into the pot, art analy-
sis, did they say, avant-garde or crazy, peut-être, same thing,
political action and yoot awakening, feminists rising and
Virginia defending the art merchant, money versus creativity,
words criss-crossing, French and English mingling, the plates
of nibbles plundered, party locusts buzz buzzing, Ariane
1967, une diablesse de mer bringing out the flavour, we
breathe the bracing sea air of freedom imagined, ideas
thrown to the four winds, monsieur Labrie's windows vibrat-
ing with words shouted 'til sun-up, white balloons and
streamers, candles everywhere, the studio tables put end to
end to end, covered with sheets of rice paper, glasses and
soup bowls and plates and utensils borrowed, the jumble of
mismatched chairs, I drink le désordre de la vie, cette fête qui
est la mienne, great bang.

We suspend words, listen. Elizabeth and Virginia slipped
out to fight in peace, a tiff over Ariane 1967 will spoil la
bouillabaisse, ça, c'est certain, we turn to Gérard, he opens his
hands, he is not their keeper, they argue all the time, a game
they play, he pours booze into any glass presented, I drink
two glasses of wine coup sur coup, will pay for this, we hear
more noises, like cookie sheets dropped from great heights
on a concrete floor, Raymond cranks up the music, the door
opens, Elizabeth and Virginia carry trays of vol-au-vent filled
with fiddleheads in herb sauce, tender shoots from Saint-Pol's
woods we eat before the soup.

Don't remember the cheese tray, don't remember the
mocha cake, there was dancing in the garden, tripping over
tents, Raymond played his guitar under the lilac tree, there

was pagan singing, dope smoking, smooching and groping, the stars spinning, landing on my face, each time a star shot down I shouted, timber! someone vomited in Elizabeth's daffodils, dawn caught us off guard, Virginia drove back to Montréal in a stupor, Mike and Nancy staggered to Moffat's and Pauline's, Marie shuffled home alone, we crawled into beds, tents, sleeping bags on vacuumed floor.

Daylight stabs my eyelids, blind spots, sunspots, bad breath, clammy skin, dry mouth, cold sweat, fuzzy tongue, pounding skull, burning stomach, mal de mer, high tide low tide, the famous morning after, what a hoot, ma première gueule de bois, happy birthday to me.

I open one eye, a slit. Pierre watches me die in our fortress of books. I open the other eye, a slit.

J'ai mal à la langue, I mumble.

My jaw hurts, my lips hurt, my eyeballs hurt, oh, mourir, Elizabeth, shoot me, de grâce, par pitié, shoot me, I see double, close my eyes, drums beat dull against skull.

Plus jamais, I say, hair dripping.

I feel a tiny bit better, that dip in the lake saved me from terminal gueule de bois.

Plus jamais, I say again.

They laugh at me. Not loud. Elizabeth and Gérard look pale, holding on to each other, Mike and Nancy look stale, saying goodbye before driving back to Montréal, Nicole and Robert and Diane and Roger look shaky, undoing the tent in slow motion, Elizabeth says, green around the gills, Raymond lies on top of his collapsed pup tent, staring at the sky like a dead soldier in a poppy field, Pierre staggers, making exaggerated sounds of distress.

We try to shove Ariane 1967 into Pierre's Rambler, no go. We stand helpless. The large asymmetrical shape defeats us all. We think we broke off the upper left corner of the board. Elizabeth reminds us that's part of the design.

Keep her, I say.

She's yours, take her home. Vamoose, already.

We say our goodbyes, slowly, my party bedspread feels slept in, I crumple into the passenger seat of Gérard's Mercury, all the way to Montréal, she rides in the back seat of the black cat convertible, in her frame of black and white, forever sewing with that gold thread that gold needle, I feel Gérard's foot on the accelerator, the cleansing wind on my face, sense her behind my back, queen of the ball waving her gold needle from her blood-red seat.

I close my eyes. Ah, to hang my self in maman's flat. Such a thought, fleeting on the wind.

Rush

If I rush like the wind I may just catch the ten-thirty to Saint-Pol, haven't been on that bus for fifteen months, I rush run, le métro crawls from tunnel to station to tunnel, mon nombril élance, je suis peut-être atteinte de nombrilisme, I smile at that, quand même, pinpoints of pain shoot through my navel, I touch my birthspot through my gypsy skirt, behind the oyster-shell-shaped clasp, it feels hard and swollen, an angry pain, je m'élance dans les corridors, pardon, madame, run up the escalator, excusez-moi, monsieur, must finish Gold Rush in a rush, bring it to Virginia, Corona is open again, the art season, soon in full swing, in Elizabeth's studio, I will fill ma valise for the last time, après, should be starting something new, September, the month of kick-starting, back to school, back to work, September, the month of fresh beginnings, new jobs, new selves, I run across the street, new things are happening, I don't pay attention, Pierre tells me to be aware, this is our future playing in the streets, the man at the ticket counter tells me the bus is leaving now, the passengers crane their necks to see who is late, the driver recognizes me, we nod, I bump ma valise against the edge of seats.

Ici, ma belle poupée! Ici! la madame aux culottes d'hommes shouts waves.

C'est vendredi? I ask, surprised to see her, surprised not to know the day of the week.

Encore un vendredi, she shouts laughs.

I put ma valise on the rack, slide past her fat jolly body, plonk myself down into the window seat with un ouf, I am a zeppelin deflating. What a rush!

Outside the green country bus, time in a vortex, tossing swallowing us, inside the green country bus, time in a lull standing still, non non, not still. Linear and constant. How did the pirate girl put it, that night au Vieux Fanal? Small deaths visit us long before the Big One shows up, small cracks in the lifeline, à peine visibles, but watch out, the beginning of the end. Not in this old transport, non. No matter what, it goes on without me, same driver, same passengers and, toujours, la madame aux culottes d'hommes. The green country bus, une présence constante, like the cows in the fields on our way to mon oncle Joseph's chalet, I was little but I knew, I knew the cows would always be chewing in their fields, year after year, they looked up as we drove past, promised nothing would change, I sat deep in the back seat, maman would be there beside me, toujours, I sit deeper in my seat, la madame would always be dans l'auto-bus. She touches my arm, I touch my throbbing navel.

J'ai des nouvelles, she says, her excitement high getting higher.

She turns sideways as much as the narrow seat allows her hips to move, puts both hands on my arm, her eyes shine brighter than mon oncle Joseph's getting ready to tell a story.

Eh bien, ma belle poupée, c'est fait! Me and my sister, we did it.

Ah, madame! Racontez.

She sits back comfortably.

C'était comme dans un rêve. Very polite young black men in white jackets served us tea in the dining car in silver teapots. Imagine si c'était chic. They answered all our questions, saying ma'am this and ma'am that. Sainte viarge, I felt like the Grand Duchess. We went to New York, you know la fameuse gare à New York? Grand Central Station, they call it. We walked and walked in that place bigger than l'église Notre-Dame.

What did you visit in New York City?

Nothing. Hé! ma sœur et moi, on n'est pas folles. Non non non non. We would not step outside that station, pas pour tout l'or du monde. We waited for our connection and rode the train to Virginie. What a pretty name for a province, hein? Much better than Saschewan and Ontario. Terre-Neuve, par exemple, that's a nice name, but not as pretty as Virginie. En tout cas. We stayed in one of those houses with white columns and slept in four-postal beds and drank mint julep. A little sweet for my taste, mais c'était bon quand même. But the houses! Oh my oh my! Those are the most beautiful houses, you should have seen them. People down there call them antibelles. Maybe because the white people who used to live in those houses a long time ago had slaves and now, that past makes the houses ugly. Qu'est-ce que tu en penses, toi?

Antebellum, madame, c'est un mot latin. Ante veut dire avant et bellum veut dire la guerre. Donc, antebellum veut dire avant la guerre civile américaine.

Bellum? Ah, so. Now, they say war is beautiful? she says, shaking her head and pinching her lips thin as a pencil.

I see imagine Elizabeth climb the bus, shoot la madame and prepare an exhibit dedicated to her triumph, enfin! she sat in a seat wide enough to accommodate all of her exuberance, her survival instincts as stretchy and resilient as the elastic bands she sews on men's underwear, a thought flashes through all that stretching, I jump out of my seat.

La maison d'Elizabeth, I gasp.

What what? la madame asks.

I tell her about the oriental practice of demolishing the houses of the dead.

Quoi? Quels morts?

I had forgotten about that. What if Gérard? I tell her, the big bad wolf himself would only have to blow a little on Elizabeth's house for it to collapse into a heap of rubble, not much of a house, been falling apart for years, the roof may not last another winter, you couldn't heat that place if your life depended on it, a sick house, almost a cadaver house again, like when Elizabeth bought it, la madame is confused, her eyes slide down my dirty skirt, she tells me I look a bit pale. I tell her I need more snapshots, if the house is down, so is the studio, and and, I wish that bus would move along faster, I have work to do, September already, Virginia is expecting Gold Rush.

Stop! la madame says, putting her foot down on my words. There's no gold in Virginie. C'est au Klondike, la ruée vers l'or. Même moi, je sais ça.

She glances at my skirt again, sees me touch my belly. She narrows her eyes.

As-tu fait des folies, toi? she asks, staring at my belly.

I frown. Can she see through silk and sea jewel? She reminds me of her teenage pregnancies, unlike me, she didn't have the pill, did I forget to take it? I shake my head.

Good. Don't you let any man, she says, wagging her finger. I'll tell you something, ma belle poupée. Nous autres, les femmes, we're supposed to do our duty and populate this province. Sainte viarge! Only men would come up with an idea like that. J'aime mes enfants, but you know? I wish I never had children. Tu sais ce que je veux dire?

Oui, madame. Vous êtes brave. Most women would never admit that.

C'est vrai, ça. They think it's a venial sin to think about it and a mortal sin to say it out loud. We should say what we think, hein? Keeping everything bottled up inside is no good. It's like a fat boil, it hurts, but it's best to lance it.

Donc, vous et votre sœur avez fait un beau voyage en Virginie?

The best, ma belle poupée. The best.

I tell her about the past year in a nutshell. Last June, June '68, that is, the last Friday I saw her, she nods, that weekend, I tell her about the surprise party Elizabeth threw for my eighteenth birthday, the summer of lazy days in Montréal and driving lessons with mon oncle Joseph, the three days a week sorting photos, Elizabeth and I working side by side in her studio, on Labour Day weekend last September, Elizabeth's invitation to travel the world with her for six months, my last year au collège and preparing for the trip, my part-time job at the madame's clothing boutique at Place Bonaventure, I even tell her Pierre, she remembers my ex-boyfriend? she nods, he had it off with Elizabeth at a swanky hotel, no hard feelings, we laugh at that, then, two days after my nineteenth birthday this past June, departure Friday, three months ago. I catch my breath. La madame puts her hand on my arm. She waits.

Elizabeth, I say. Elizabeth died on the day we were leaving.

Sainte viarge du bon dieu.

I don't know if this is a lancing of the boil, but I break down sobbing, nothing sober about sobbing, passengers turn their heads, stare, la madame waves them back to their own business, she wraps her arms around my shoulders, I cry in her rich bosom, soft and warm, her polyester dress smells of the violets printed on the fabric, je pleure à chaudes larmes, she says chu-chu, ma belle, chu-chu, she sounds like a train on rubber shoes, I sob weep, say nothing more.

Something hard and cleansing, ma détermination, is forming inside, I shall not waver, sounds pompous, but is not, joy and excitement at the prospect rise through my tears, I kiss la madame's soft cheek, she pats my hand, as if giving me permission. That, the lancing of the boil.

I sit back, take a deep deep breath, the best ever, watch my resolve stretch in the September light, like those elastic bands she sews, la madame and I feel no more need for non-stop talk. The bus takes us.

I stand by the side of the road, wave to her, déjà vu, no more, watch the green country bus disappear down the curve toward the village, the September sun warms my shoulders, Saint-Pol air cooler than Montréal air, I stand. Elizabeth's house stands. Crooked and intact.

Pauvre maison abandonnée, I say, stroking her peeling clapboard. You don't know, do you? You are waiting, waiting to hear Elizabeth say, here I am, so good to be home after a long trip. Waiting for me to walk to the back? Don't. I will never again wipe my feet on your island coconut mat, will never again call out, allô allô, Elizabeth, c'est moi. Things are on the move, House. Better brace yourself. You're in for the change of life.

I rush to the studio. Locks cannot be that difficult to pick, never picked one before, but saw movie detectives and burglars pick plenty, Gérard forgot to give me the key or ignored my request. I brought a long pin specially, insert the pin into the keyhole, listen like a skilled burglar for the tell-tale click of the safe, aha, la rivière de diamants is mine, the burglar thinks, I hear no click, the doorknob turns. Sésame, ouvre-toi? Wouldn't Elizabeth lock up for a long absence, she told me she would, did she forget? Pin or no pin, the studio door opens. Tire la chevillette, la bobinette cherra, the grandmother-wolf waits for Little Red Riding Hood. I go in, gasp.

Empty.

The studio, empty. Someone broke in, the good people of Saint-Pol took their cue from Elizabeth's death, they barged in, fought over her things like those women in that Greek film, nothing left, not even a rag, they even took the smells of oil and paint thinner away, nothing left, except the chip on monsieur Labrie's window where the camera hit that day Elizabeth did not let me shoot her, I touch the scar

on the glass, cette larme pétrifiée, the studio, empty, the echo
of my steps, non, someone else's steps.

Marie Berthiaume. Despair in her hair, despair in her
eyes. The beginning of another school year, the furthest point
from les grandes vacances and the end of torture, September,
the month for kicking ass kicking heads, one long year
teaching the brats, her hair brittle and wild, she may not survive this pain, her eyes wide and wild, she may die in classroom captivity, no more walks. Marie and Elizabeth got to
know each other because of the noon walks. They had con-
versations like in a serial cartoon in the newspaper. Parfois, it
took weeks before they reached the end of an anecdote. The
teacher talking slowly, her voice taking a break from morning yelling. Some days when Elizabeth was deeply engaged
in her work, Marie watched, l'anecdote du jour could wait
another day, her mouth resting, but never enough for the
afternoon assault. No more walks to restore daily sanity, ten
long months with her parasites. A she-moose harcelée by so
many ticks, Marie will bleed to death.

Gérard est venu, she says. J'ai oublié le jour. Il a tout
emporté.

I ask her if he also emptied the house.

Je ne sais pas. Gérard a vidé le garage. Il a tout emporté.

I ask her if she spoke to Gérard.

Nous avons échangé quelques mots. Quels mots? C'est
vague, tu sais.

A brief but sharp pain shoots through my belly, I break
into a sweat.

Je crois que je vais prendre ma retraite, Marie says.

I ask her if Gérard looked strange to her.

Non. Enfin, pas plus que d'habitude. Tout le monde est
bizarre, ici, tu sais.

She thinks for a moment and tells me it's not people who
look strange, but things.

Les choses? I ask.

She shrugs. I ask her if she will continue to walk to the studio at lunchtime.

Pourquoi? Il n'y a plus rien, ici.

I tell her she has no reason to change her habits. Her hair bristles with intense despair, I imagine lightning inside her skull.

Mes habitudes? Why did I become a teacher? she asks herself in English, her eyes wilder than wild.

She looks around, as if committing the scene to memory. À la mémoire d'Elizabeth. She tells me, at lunchtime from now on, she will walk in the other direction, toward the little river, across the bridge, up the faint path winding to the top of the mountain. If she is lucky, she may lose herself, hear the school bell ring the end of lunch recess, hear the little devils shout, out of reach. If she is lucky, she may break an ankle, be eaten by a bear, miss the whole dreary afternoon, never again to be trapped inside that sickly-sweet-sweat-soaked room, the unbearable smell of generations of cloistered children.

Les après-midi sont interminables, she says. Ab-so-lu-ment. In-ter-mi-na-bles.

That's what she should do, she tells me, start walking and never stop, walk north 'til she meets les caribous, walk with the herd.

The school bell rings, she closes her eyes, takes a slow deep breath, flares her nostrils, opens her eyes, starts walking.

Demain, Marie, I say to encourage her. Demain, c'est samedi.

She raises one arm high in farewell, not looking back. Marie disappearing.

Spectacular pain, reappearing, forces me to curl up in the foetal position. J'ai la nausée, je suis malade, body fighting an infection, peut-être, my birthspot is swollen with pus. Under the skin, flesh silent, oozing.

Prends sur toi, Ariane, my voice echoes back to me. Check yourself. What have we got here? I say, unbuttoning the skirt. Pink as the day you were born! See? No swelling, no smell of putrefaction, no malady. You are intact, ma fille. Prends sur toi.

The forked tongue of pain. Phantom but real. Paradox. The odour of grass coming in through the open door soothes a little. I undo the stitches to free the silk graft, resistance of skin healed in white thread. The grain of sand encased in nacre. Ringing the navel, eight points of the needle. Eight dots dancing on the edge of the birthspot. Am dizzy, feel fine. Pain pleasure. Paradox.

Last summer, Elizabeth teaches me paradox. The artist photographer who smokes like an engine, plays music à tue-tête in the studio, concentrates so hard her face is made of stone, her mind locked elsewhere, if I interrupt, she explodes in anger, frightens herself shattering like that, I learn not to interrupt. The ugly woman, with the beautiful lover friend companion, drawn to younger men, these days, Raymond, how many before, sooner or later, Pierre, I saw the signs at my birthday party, she put her hand on his thigh, he let her, that is the sign, later in the garden they danced closer than close, Pierre was ready to explode with lust, she was making him desire her, how does she do that, she would have him anytime she chose.

Elizabeth's cupboards teach me paradox. Did Gérard empty them? Marie did not know. Like maman, Elizabeth buys Ajax and Tide, Javex and pink Scotties, Homestead white sliced bread and Velveeta, Campbell's cream of tomato and McCracken saltines, unlike maman, she buys cheese from Sweden, whole coffee beans from Kenya, she cooks fresh rabbit and lamb chops, like maman, she cleans toilets and washes floors, not as often, but she does, unlike maman, she does not want me to help.

I don't pay you to be my charwoman, Ariane, dear, she says, her voice filling the deserted studio, flattening against the windowpanes.

Unlike maman but like mon oncle Joseph, she chops wood, Moffat came to help saw whole trees into bûches, but Elizabeth chops her heating wood, no help, one must be self-sufficient. She may be up half the night chain-reading chain-smoking, at six she is chopping wood, she knows how to swing an ax and avoid opening her shin, she chops kindling into the smallest sticks, holding them up on the chopping tree stump, the blade falling dangerously close to her fingers. One day, she takes apart the things inside the toilet tank, brings a ladder up the steep stairs, bangs it against the low ceiling on the landing, pieces of plaster fall on the steps.

Ayoye! maudite marde! I shout, in the ladder's voice.

She almost trips down the stairs laughing.

I hate a leaky toilet, she says, perched on the bruised ladder. A mere trickle keeps me awake all night. Pass me that new seat, Ariane.

I hand her a round piece of black rubber, she is still shaking with fits of laughter, as she works up to her elbow inside the toilet tank, she keeps repeating maudite marde under her breath, sinking her teeth into the French words, she giggles, my tongue's orality that so defeats her, but to her ears, those are the funniest words in the world.

The horny woman, she says, horny, teaches me body paradox. One July day, I come back from the village with tomatoes and canned tuna, she is shooting Raymond, where did he spring from, Raymond, in the nude at high noon dans le jardin d'Elizabeth, Marie no longer visits, never in summer, what would she think of Raymond's whiter than white body javexed by flat light, when he moves, he seems stabbed par cette épée de Damoclès qu'est le soleil de midi.

Elizabeth shoots close-ups of his muscles straining under the task of raking the ground, digging the iron teeth into the earth. She captures a section of his back, his upper arm, a shoulder, his thigh, a buttock, all the disembodied parts of Raymond's body in the noon sun. Elizabeth is using a slow

film to overexpose, she is experimenting with harsh light and
flattened angles, later in the middle of the night, in complete
silence, she will manipulate the pictures in her dark room,
later in the middle of the day, in the studio flooded with light
and music, she will add texture to the prints, des détails à
l'encre de Chine, will glue the photos on rice paper, dab
watercolour, use woodblocks, concentrating into oblivion.

Rake harder, she says. I want a close-up of your sternocleidomastoid.

Pardon? Raymond says, worried.

Flex that neck muscle. Hold it tight. Hold it. Come on,
Raymond, dear, you're not concentrating.

C'est Ariane.

We're losing the light. Concentrate on the job.

Elle m'empêche de me concentrer, he says, trying to hide
his crotch.

Je m'en vais, I say.

Stay, Elizabeth says.

Je pense, oh, non, she wants more noon nakedness.
Elizabeth naked in the bathtub talking business, I can take.
Elizabeth barging in the bathroom while I am having a shit,
I can take. Photo nakedness with Raymond, I am escaping,
sandwiches to make, limonade to stir, crisse, le corps humain,
c'est naturel comme la tarte aux pommes, justement, mon
oncle, I am on my way to make lunch.

That night, a warm night, Elizabeth builds a fire in the fireplace, no garbage, just her own chopped wood. She props a
full-length mirror against the portion of wall free from books.

Look at your body, Ariane, dear, she says, steering me in
front of the mirror. Strip and have a good hard look at your
body. See? No camera.

Voyons, Elizabeth. It is silly. I have seen my body.

Are you sure? Strip.

I strip, pourquoi? because I don't have a good argument
not to, Elizabeth pokes at the fire.

Don't be a voyeur, she says, studying the flames, and don't be an exhibitionist. You hide inside that shell, it'll compress brain and heart. It's only a body. Look at it.

I am looking. You want to see my sternocleidomastoid?

She chuckles, I am surprised I can remember that word, it has been playing in my head all afternoon, iniminimennimo, cache ton sternocleidomastoid-oh.

Be serious, she says, smiling. Your body, one of the infinite variations on the body universal. You've seen my variation. Not beautiful, according to the Western canon, but the only one I've got. Functioning, healthy. All mine to do as I please. I've shot so many faces, so many bodies, so many body parts, I should be numb or put off, I'm not. No more than I am eating breakfast every day. What are you escaping?

I don't want to have sex with you, I say, feeling silly.

She bursts out laughing.

Ah, Ariane, dear, you will be the death of me yet. What do you take me for? A female satyr?

I heard things.

Opportunity knocking, she says, grinning. I was willing, not coerced. True. I went with women on occasion. Once, in Tunisia, I also had the opportunity to taste roasted locusts. It doesn't mean I made locusts part of my regular diet. The rule is simple. Don't do anything you don't want to do and don't let anybody push you into anything you don't want to do.

What about group sex?

You're into orgies? That's your business.

Oh, non, Elizabeth. Non non.

Look, she says, reading my mind. Raymond models for me from time to time. But we were lovers first. This is not a case of photographer and model screwing after each photo shoot, because photographer can't control herself when exposed to model's skin.

So, you sleep with Raymond? I ask, getting dressed.

From the first time we met. We screwed our heads off. He completely turns me on. You see, Raymond and I are lovers. You and I are friends.

And Gérard knows?

Of course, Gérard knows. Fuck me gently, Ariane. Do you think I'd sneak behind his back?

Elizabeth teaches me my body. I go for runs in the woods, feel thighs, buttocks, breasts move with the running motion and it is not embarrassing. I am careful not to flaunt, I am careful not to hide, the brain the heart breathe, we are becoming pals, my body and me, we learn, my silent partner and me, to be, to occupy space, to move in that space, such a simple thing. I am glad about my navel, I am glad about the whole of me. The positive and the negative, the forked tongue of our being. Elizabeth teaches me my living body in front of the camera, tells me about the diseased body, the dead body. Over the years, she took so many pictures of corpses for medical books and anatomy classes, corpses intact and with their chests and bellies open, with the skin of their faces rolled back. She looks at them with her naked eyes, she looks at them through her camera's eye, each time, she takes a good hard look, never forgetting that once those corpses were dancing and loving and daring and hating and fearing and farting. She tells me she has shot healthy living bodies and healthy dead bodies, she has taken close-ups of maladies devastating living parts, no voyeurism, simply looking at life in its infinite variations. She loves the human body for its obviousness and for its mysteries, but some days, the body overwhelms. She spends those days on the neighbouring lakes, sitting in a borrowed rowboat, looking at nothing at all. Oui, Elizabeth taught me paradox. But she explained nothing about the relationship between the constants Gérard and Elizabeth and the variables young lovers. Sans doute, she wanted me to work out the equation myself. The forked tongue of love. Pleasure pain. Paradox.

I chew the strands of silk from the caftan 'til well soaked with saliva and wedge press flatten the blue paste into the chip in the window.

The day is splendid, not quite autumn, no longer summer. The light, gold. Marie m'a donné le goût. Moi, aussi, je veux marcher. Marcher à l'infini. Oh, the thought rises, joyful. Silent walking. That appeals. Light stepping, I weave through Saint-Pol's woods, nous sommes outre-saison, the air has a rarefied quality, I am out-of-life, falling through a crack in the earth, joyful.

Wednesday through Friday, in Saint-Pol's studio, we work side by side, in silence, serious, moi trying to catch Elizabeth's intensity, watching spontaneity closely, parfois, she tells me not to be a stick-in-the-mud, to do things by myself. I go for swims alone, but she means I should do things with people, I invent my own adventures, bring back stories to tell her at supper. On Friday nights, she takes a bath, pours herself a scotch, she says, I need a stiff one, we go to the bar at the inn, she says, let's have a blow-out, I say, il faut se défouler, we come home late, my hair my clothes stinking of cigarette smoke, Elizabeth drinks hard, she never has la gueule de bois.

Saturday through Tuesday, in Montréal's workshop, I practise being Ariane inside her own adventure. In the morning, I stretch in bed, listen to maman's ritual. After she leaves for work, I drink café au lait in a soup bowl and roll my peanut butter toast in the shape of un croissant. I take a bath, the bathroom door open, listen to music, the volume up, au diable les murs minces, I play them, one after the other on the hi-fi, Claude Léveillée, Renée Claude, Claude Gauthier, Claude Dubois, Raymond's eighteenth happy birthday gift to me, peut-être un jour, he will have his own albums to give, Claudette listened to le Boléro de Ravel, Ariane listens to les chansonniers québécois.

In the afternoon au Café de l'horloge, I drink coffee, read Cocteau's Les Enfants Terribles and Ducharme's L'Avalée des

Avalées, Pierre's birthday gifts, peut-être un jour, he will have his own books to give, we discuss la littérature des autres, I ask Pierre about his own writing, he says, ça va. I wear Nicole's et Diane's silver hoops, their birthday gift for my pierced ears, I wear a leather ring on my right middle finger and a thin leather anklet on my left ankle, made from scraps monsieur Savard gave me with a conspirational smile, holding nails between his lips, hammering them into the soles of shoes, his hands stained with street dirt, his fingertips black with shoe polish.

Au parc Lafontaine, I transform clothes, lengthen or shorten hems, add or remove sleeves, open the inner seams of corduroy pants and sew A-line panels of contrasting print cotton to turn the pants into skirts. Everywhere, I let Ariane speak to everybody, show off her fabrications, build her reputation, but keep her from being pushy, après tout, maman raised me well, I don't want la nouvelle Ariane to unravel her life's work, at the same time, I don't want that Ariane to be a stick-in-the-mud.

I sew for Elizabeth. At first, small things, a tie-dyed scarf, a velvet vest. I know she likes that I make things for her more than the things I make. One day, I bring her a long top I embroidered with geometric patterns in bright primary colours, I can tell, that top she likes for real, she says it looks Mexican, I tell her I used ma tante Rita's kitchen curtains she removed because they were sun-bleached, I can tell, Elizabeth no longer thinks I am a stick-in-the-mud.

In Saint-Pol's woods, the leaves are changing their colours, the insects are gone, nature yawns, ready to go to sleep, I walk in gold September light, rushing back to Gold Rush, that can wait a little.

Last summer, I bought a sleeping bag au Surplus de l'armée on boulevard Saint-Laurent and went camping with Nicole et Diane to Mont-Laurier. C'était au diable vert. We leave Saturday noon, it takes us so long to get there, because they thought it would be a hoot to hitchhike, I panic, we will never come back to Montréal in time for Elizabeth's Tuesday night phone call, I keep asking Nicole et Diane why we had to go camping au diable vert. Enfin, we arrive in Mont-Laurier, the best camp sites are taken, we have to pitch the canvas tent near les bécosses, all of Québec's biting insects, les maringouins, les mouches noires, les brûlots, les mouches à chevreuil, live in Mont-Laurier, I am eaten alive more than the yoots who skinny-dipped after sundown. I want to start back right away, Mont-Laurier is no fun, Nicole et Diane say, okay, de toute façon, il n'y a même pas de beaux gars, what do they need beaux gars for, they are getting married in December, they remind me this summer is for going wild, the last freedom fun. We hitchhike back, stand on the side of the road for hours, my thumb numb, Nicole thinks it is because there are three of us, it's raining, what fun. We pretend we love camping, après tout, this is the thing to do, Nicole et Diane don't invite me again. In Montréal, when I am not camping, my sleeping bag lives on my bed. On hot nights, I camp on our gallery, listen to les matous mités fight fuck dans la ruelle, pretend they are cougars in the night. In Saint-Pol, I camp in Elizabeth's living room, in her studio, in her garden. I camped here once, à la belle étoile by the small hidden lake, but did not sleep, because I kept thinking about the wild beasts creeping up to sniff me. I squint at the lake, one last swim. But am interrupted. Noises in the woods. Sleeping here one night last summer, beasts. A moose on the loose? A bear hunting? Footsteps. Je me cache dans les fougères. What is he doing here? I watch him through the fronds.

Gérard wastes no time. In one motion, he drops his towel in a heap, takes off his sandals, sunglasses, and watch, walks straight into the water. Where did he leave his clothes, sûrement, he did not drive from Montréal in his swim trunks. À moins que. He changed by the Mercury. He changed at

Elizabeth's house. What if he saw me dans le studio, moi, the spy being spied on. I watch.

He does the crawl. Perfect. Strong. Deliberate. How we swim. Maman sideways as she has always done, moi teaching myself, underwater first, ensuite, above, doing the crawl, not well, lying on my back, the water cradling me. The water cradling Gérard en deuil, drowning his sadness, he goes for a long swim across the lake, comme une méditation, peut-être, Elizabeth swims with him, peut-être, he will meet her on the wild shore, where the firs climb north, uninterrupted. His love for her, multiplied and refracted.

My belly throbs in sharp waves, but that is no longer pain. Ostentatious, a word Elizabeth used. She said, I abhor pretenses. Gérard's love is ostentatious. He will not apologize for that.

Ah! I say out loud. Les grandes amours sont terribles. I don't ever want to love like that.

Missed the bus. Went walking Marie's intended new route. Standing on the mountain in the fading light of this September afternoon, watching Saint-Pol breathe, listening to the church bell ring l'angélus de six heures, not seeing but feeling the churchyard, the bell rings for the dead and the living. We are responsible for the dead. Let them hear our voices.

Along the road at night. Ma valise, empty, light. Could walk fifty miles back to Montréal. Fourteen hours. Would be home for lunch. The only problem, Gérard will drive by, will want to give me a lift. Elizabeth picking me up at seven every Wednesday morning, parfois, in front of my house, parfois, near le Terminus du Nord, parfois, on boulevard Dorchester, phoning every Tuesday night to tell me where the next day's pickup will be, last summer, all over Montréal.

Elizabeth driving her rusty station wagon in silence, weaving in and out of traffic, a cigarette between her fingers, steering smoothy, on the open road, driving fast, focussed, taking sharp curves steady as a rock, glancing regularly in the rear-view mirror, in the side mirror, swinging into the other lane, accelerating, my feet pushing against the floor, the road whizzing by through the rust holes, I squint at the dark clarity of the September night, the rare headlights come at me from great fuzzy distances, the drivers, startled, sans doute, by my white skirt reflecting the lights back at them, Elizabeth's heap travelling in the wrong lane, passing, swinging back into our assigned lane, moi swallowing, Elizabeth smoking, every Saturday early, turning the car around, travelling in the opposite direction, bumping along the cracked surface of that killer road.

Now, I walk, returning to town, Elizabeth no longer on her way to shoot that day's wedding, no longer returning to Saint-Pol alone after the wedding to work all night and all day Sunday on her own projects, no longer speeding back to Montréal to spend Sunday night with Gérard above Anteannum, no longer staying over Monday and Tuesday to take care of business, the wedding photos, billings, supplies.

So, Elizabeth? I ask her on this country road. What did you and Gérard do on those summer evenings? What did you talk about? What was your life together like? Staying home together alone? Going out alone together? Meeting friends I never met? You told me nothing about your life in the here and now with Gérard. No need to feel obliged. If he drives by, that is. Non, merci, Gérard. Je préfère marcher. You swim, I walk. Deal? Deal.

Peut-être, he will spend the night in the house, sleep in Elizabeth's bed if the furniture is still inside, on the living room floor if the house is empty. Marie did not know.

I was not really hitchhiking, my thumb lifted. Old habit from last summer. Could not tell le monsieur who stopped, c'est une erreur, monsieur, excusez-moi, could not tell him I want to walk to Montréal, non, he would have thought I was afraid of him, that may have triggered the chase.

Le monsieur drives with his face set, his lips tight, when he lights a cigarette with the car lighter, his face glows red, I inhale deep to take in the first smoke, watch the headlights eat the tar, sit with my hands on my lap, my feet crossed like a goody two-shoes, shoo shoo, goody two-shoes. A yellow Beetle passes us, I squint at the girl my age driving alone, should be Ariane Claude driving at night going places, last summer, mon oncle offered me driving lessons for my eight-eenth birthday.

I study the road booklet, we practise shifting dans la ruelle, driving at rush hour, stopping at traffic lights on steep hills. As soon as the light turns green, I shift into first gear, step on the gas and release the clutch in a two-step choreog-raphy, must not stall, must not peel rubber. Au début, I stall, a chorus of horns gets me flustered, mon oncle waves the cars to go around, sticks his head out the window, tells the impatient drivers to go hang themselves, crisse. He makes me practise parallel parking 'til I can park on a dime, he makes me back up into tight spots with one hand on the steering wheel and one arm draped over the back of the front seat, I keep looking at the windshield to see where the car is going, he keeps telling me to look out the back window, crisse, and not to worry, le hood va suivre.

What is the story of the girl passing us in the yellow Beetle, she swings back into our lane in front of us, the red of the tail lights grows fainter, like life fading out of a beast's eyes. Le monsieur seems lonely, so, I tell him how I learned car basics in the language of mechanics.

I tell him mon oncle taught me to change un flat, showed me where to put le jack, how to pop out les hub-caps, explained the workings of la clutch, when to pump and when not to pump les brakes, we went to the corner gas sta-tion, I filled up, he reminded me not to forget to check l'air dans les tires, demonstrated how to change les windshield wipers when le caoutchouc became cracked, let me look

under le hood, told me where to clamp les jumper cables if I
needed un boost, au cas où l'auto est stallée parce que la bat-
terie est à terre, gave lessons in how to change l'air filter, how
to clean les spark plugs, how to check if la fan belt est tight
and how to change it when it wears out, where to check
l'huile avec le dip stick, told me to make sure there is enough
water in the battery cells and dans le radiateur in summer and
where and when to put l'antifreeze in the fall. If the car over-
heats in summer because I forgot to check the water level, he
warned me never never never to unscrew le cap du radiateur,
la steam will burn my face, crisse, he heard stories. Dans la
ruelle, we crawled under the car, changed the oil, he showed
me la pan à huile and how it can be pierced if I drive like a
maniac on a gravel road. We touched everything, my hands
became black with oil, grease, road dirt, I scrubbed with mon
oncle's Snap and ma tante's nail brush. He looked pleased
with my progress, didn't know my friend Elizabeth let me
drive on my learner's permit, she chatted, smoked, watched
the road, never criticized, never seemed impatient when I
drove below the speed limit or when I stayed behind a slow-
moving truck, trop poule mouillée pour dépasser. Soon, I tell
le monsieur, I was ready for my driver's test, I memorized the
book of driving rules cover to cover, I would ace the written
exam, mon oncle taught me everything there is to know
about driving, I learned right downtown Montréal and survived that, will never be afraid of anything, could dive with
sharks, no fear, would impress the examiner with my driving
skills, show him how I can parallel park like a Montréal pro,
I would get that licence with gold stars. Mon oncle took time
off on a Tuesday morning, the examiners are less fussy in the
morning, except Mondays when they are cranky demanding
and Fridays when they are impatient distracted.

In the middle of country darkness and whooshing wheels,
le monsieur rakes his throat.

Ils sont allés sur la Lune en juillet, he says.

En juillet?

Oui, en juillet.

Je ne savais pas, monsieur.

Je pense, I was spaced out, j'étais dans la lune, how can I say that to le monsieur, he would not understand, peut-être, he would think I am laughing at him. I let a little bit of silence grow between us before speaking again.

Je suis en deuil, monsieur, I say, hoping that will explain my ignorance of moon travels.

Out of the corner of my eye, I see him assessing me out of the corner of his eye, a girl in a filthy skirt, walking along a road at night, carrying a suitcase, everything to make me suspicious, but my hair is neatly tied on the nape of my neck, I said merci when he stopped, call him monsieur, articulate well, sans doute, he decides je suis une belle jeunesse bien élevée distracted by a death in the family.

Je suis désolé, mademoiselle.

Vous êtes bien aimable, monsieur.

And we say no more 'til we have a flat tire. Le monsieur says, crisse, under his breath.

Je m'excuse, mademoiselle.

I tell him I can change the tire to thank him for giving me a lift, I will never be a helpless woman standing by the side of the road, the hood of her car open, not knowing what to do.

Woods on either side of the road. Downhill, a farmhouse in a clearing makes a bulky shadow box against the sky, the house breathes with the people sleeping in her rooms. The flashlight in my hand aims at le monsieur changing the tire, the shadows push hard against him in the pool of light, what is this human doing in the middle of their darkness, he looks strong and competent. I feel nothing but infinite patience, watch him jack up his big car, remove the hubcap, unscrew the nuts, take the wheel off, put the spare on and do everything in reverse.

I tell him the story about the man who was always looking for deals. That man had une crevaison in winter on an iso-
lated road, he realized his spare was also flat, so he rolled the
wheel down the road to a garage he had passed earlier, he had
to wake up the owner, le garagiste n'était pas content, but it
was his duty like a country doctor who has to deliver a baby
in the middle of the night to repair the man's flat, while le
garagiste worked, the man with the flat poked around in a
mountain of second-hand tires, soudain, the whole mountain
tumbled down and he was crushed to death.

Le monsieur tells me he vaguely remembers reading
about that. I start to cry and my tears take him by surprise
and my tears take me by surprise, because I don't want to cry
one bit and I am puzzled he remembers a story I just made
up to entertain him, but it is too late to backtrack.

Calmez-vous, mademoiselle. S'il vous plaît, calmez-vous.

He wipes the grime off his hands with a rag, taps my
shoulder lightly, what is a man to do with a girl in mourning in the middle of the night, I plan to stop crying, but my
nose brushes against his chest and I smell a bit of sweat, a bit
of soap and that mysterious male scent, muskus animalis, and
I can feel his erection grow against my thigh, he moves away.

Partons, he says.

He puts the flat tire in the trunk, we get back into the
car. He does not start the motor. He sits, hands on the steering wheel, stares at the darkness through the windshield,
looking sad and ashamed and undecided. I have enormous
compassion pour l'homme taciturne et timide, not just pour
ce monsieur, mais pour tous les monsieurs who will live and
die without allowing spontaneity to move them. Je pense,
that man wants it, he is afraid he will become angry for
wanting it, he will become angry, because he is afraid and he
will blame me for his fear, he will call me une agace-pissette,
une garce, but he will still hate himself and me for his two
minutes of ecstasy and weeks of full-blown guilt. But I want

the man to like me, I am not une agace-pissette, monsieur, but unlike him, I am not embarrassed by sex, scared of it, obsessed with it. What difference does it make, in less than an hour we will arrive in Montréal and I will never see him again, what the hell.

I grab his crotch, he goes wild, pushes me into the back seat, we bump into ma valise, he throws it on the front seat, fucks me so fast my head spins, no foreplay, nothing. Just stick it in, blow his load, wipe, tuck it back in, get back in front, turn the key in the ignition and step on it all the way to Montréal and all that in complete silence, except for the Groan. I bite my tongue, must not laugh, must not emasculate le monsieur, his rage might leave me dead dans le fossé, Jeune femme trouvée morte étranglée, and the newspaper will say I was raped, I clamp my mouth shut, hope not to laugh. As soon as we cross the bridge into Montréal, I ask le monsieur to let me off, I will take le métro from here, don't forget ma valise back on the back seat, don't forget to say, merci, monsieur, it is too much, my mouth bursts wide open, it sounds like sobbing again, le monsieur, poised between anger and guilt, rend son jugement, it is my fault, today's yoot, no morals, it is me, the yoot, who is the ice hole, not him, I know that's what he decides, because he peels rubber and leaves me laughing silly in the middle of the night.

Time to deal with those lips of mine. Bien sûr, priority one, finish Gold Rush.

Needlework is no laughing matter, the expert says.

I nod. The special woman chez Marshall knows all about needlework. Goldwork is her specialty.

Goldwork is a very ancient craft, she says, as if uninitiates like me need not apply. Gold thread came from China, is mentioned in the Bible, merchants brought it to Europe. Alexander the Great had his tent adorned with gold thread. As you can see, gilt thread is made with a fine silver wire coated with gold.

Real gold?

Ah, yes. This wire is hollow to enable the stitcher to pearl the sewing thread through. Your sewing thread should be yellow silk. Come here. I'll demonstrate on this sampler. You do goldwork after all your other embroidery is finished. Now, thread a length of silk, push the silk through the fabric from the wrong side toward the right side, cut a length of gold, pass the needle through that length of gold and slide the gold over. See, it now lies flat against the surface of the fabric. Careful not to crack the gold. Now, push the needle back into the fabric, so it comes out on the wrong side, to secure the length of gold in place. And you keep going.

Ah, oui! Je vois. This is like sewing beads on clothes.

That's right. Another technique is called couching. The silk thread goes over the gold at regular intervals.

Ahhhh! So. The gold cannot hurt. The fabric, I mean.

She raises one eyebrow.

The silk thread, she says, holds the lengths of gold in place against the surface of the fabric, like a string of pearls. But the gold does pierce the fabric. Once, at the beginning and, again, at the end of the work. What do you want to use the gold thread for?

Artwork. A large collage called Gold Rush 1969.

She shows me a small, but intricate phoenix she did in gold superimposed on a garden of fire in silk stitches.

It is dazzling, I say.

If you want to be properly dazzled, go to the Museum of Fine Arts to view the goldwork version of an old Chinese painting. It's a large tapestry of silk stitches on silk, adorned with gold thread. It's called The Poet and the Courtesans. Goldwork is a labour of love, she adds. It can't be rushed. Do you need sharps?

Sharps?

Yes. The name for fine sewing needles. Come here, I'll show you. The higher the number, the smaller and shorter the needle. So, you have a great choice.

I see what you mean. My beading needles are too long and my embroidery needles too fat for the work I want to do.

This one's a gold eye number ten. It's made in England. The diameter is point zero one eight of an inch and the length is one point three one inches.

I stare at its stainless steel sharpness shining in the store light, imagine its effectiveness. Not too long. Piercing neatly cleanly.

Oui, I say. That will do just fine. I'll buy a pack of those and a spool of yellow silk thread. Also, a threader to help me thread the silk through the small eye of those needles. Now, for the gold, madame.

She shows me different thicknesses and textures. Flat, round, crimped, spiraled.

This one is smooth purl, she says. You can bead that. See? The gold is hollow.

I find it difficult to choose, après tout, I am a gold novice. Beading less scary than couching, I decide on size number seven smooth purl. The thread is sold by the single strand, eighteen inches, each stored in a small clear plastic box, like a preserved insect. Expensive too, après tout, c'est de l'or. Now that I bought it, I can touch it. Smooth purl feels slinky between fingers, looks like a ray of sunshine in the palm of my hand.

The play of light is greatly enhanced, the expert says, if you do your goldwork on a padded surface instead of a flat surface. As you'll see in that tapestry I just told you about.

Oui, I say. This will be done on a padded surface.

I rush home. Une chance, I will manage with the photos I had already picked and pocketed, despite my loss to the valise thief, donc, my last trip to Saint-Pol, inutile.

For two weeks, je travaille jour et nuit. The kitchen table, mon atelier, covered with b&w photos, brass eyelets, fishing line. One thousand seven hundred and seventy-six cut-outs that I glue in pairs recto verso to make eight hundred and eighty-eight rectangles that I pierce at each corner to insert three throusand five hundred and fifty-two eyelets that I link together in the shape of the gigantic caftan with short lengths of fishing line that I cut from rolls long enough to fish deep in the deep blue so blue sea. Maman comes in for breakfast, eats her toast and drinks her tea, using a corner of the table.

Ne me laisse pas te déranger, she says.

Bientôt, she is gone, I glue, pierce, tie, she returns from work, looks at my progress.

Ça s'en vient bien, she says.

She cooks supper, soup and bread or a small breast of chicken with peas and potatoes, she leaves food for me on the stove.

Tu n'auras qu'à réchauffer, she says, knowing I will not eat 'til midnight.

Some evenings, she reads dans son boudoir, ma tante Rita phones to hear the day's news, other evenings, she goes out with Ana to catch a film and I keep an eye on the kids, or they stay downstairs for a cup of tea and a chat.

Tu fais du voisinage maintenant, I tease her.

Oui, mais pas avec n'importe qui, she says.

It is not her fault we now have distinguished neighbours. Not nosey for a penny. With miles of ocean and miles of land between them, maman and Ana grew up not knowing each other's existence, elles sont devenues femmes chacune de leur côté et, tout à fait par hasard, they found each other. Similar interests, Ana in her language, Margot in her language, each on her side of the ocean. Ana suggested they go see plays this fall, she loves the theatre, not surprising, with her father a set designer, little Ana, sans doute, grew up dans les coulisses, now, she wants to discover le théâtre québécois, Margot could explain la culture du pays. Maman says she used to go to the theatre too, but has not seen a play since her wedding, knows nothing about le nouveau théâtre, Ana suggests they could discover that together.

At my fabric store on avenue du Mont-Royal, I depleted le monsieur juif's small stock of eyelets, I told him I needed more, this was a rush, he asked what they were for, I explained, told him it was art, he winked, told me, time to call in his eye-oh-yous, the next day, when I picked up the order, we bargained a special price and he waived the sales tax.

One evening, mon oncle Joseph stops by to fix the light fixture dans le boudoir. He leans against the kitchen doorway, says crisse a lot, he is that impressed. In case I run out of fishing line, he runs home and brings me two spools of his special super strong line for catching des achigans, crisse, feisty fish, his contribution to art.

The hardest part of the project was to decide how to assemble the rectangles, in a well-thought-out narrative or at random, comme le hasard de la vie. Because I am in a rush to finish, I chose le hasard, après tout, random is truer to life. Par exemple, maman. She now has a neighbour who escaped her country who is becoming a friend, peut-être même bientôt, Margot et Gérard. C'est ça, le hasard de la vie.

Time to sew the strips of coloured cloth I ripped from Elizabeth's travel clothes, tatters of colour breaking the severe symmetry of black and white. I rush back to my fabric store to buy bigger brass eyelets, as I tell le monsieur juif, to articulate the sleeves at the wrists and elbows in a joyous pose to imitate the last dance of life, he donates those eyelets, wishes me luck, I promise to let him know the exact dates of the exhibit, peut-être, he can come to le vernissage, openings are always a hoot.

Fini. Gold Rush, on the kitchen floor, ready to be hung at Corona Gallery, ready to spin from floor to ceiling, the multitude of brass eyelets ready to catch the spotlights, as people walk around, absorbing meaning. Should the ramp Virginia will build be painted gold? Peut-être, that is excessive.

Le dernier détail. Near the hem of the caftan, I sign my name twice. First, on the right-hand side recto, across a paintbrush in an iron cup, second, on the left-hand side verso, across lovers' lips kissing. Ariane with her slanting A sea cliff and riane edge, and Claude with her CL umbrella shading playful aude. Ariane Claude etched with the point of a needle.

La Cité l'Underground

Virginia said no. Not, I'll think about it or maybe next season. She said no. Flat, blunt, sans équivoque. No means no. She practically throws me and Gold Rush out of Corona, I fold mon collage monumental into ma valise, slinky brass eyelets singing flashing gold in the October gloom, open the door a crack.

I guess it means you won't build the ramp, right?

Close the door before she can respond, start walking and, all at once, menstrual cramps and another of Montréal's cloudbursts assault me. Ma foi, c'est le comble du rejet!

No point running, this downpour, much more violent than the one that caught me with the box of Tide, this, a tempest of tropical grandeur, an October typhoon with a poor sense of direction, powerful enough to lacerate the body to strips of bloody flesh, the raindrops as hard as nipples in lust changing to un déluge, le fleuve swelling, buildings reeling rolling, the streets, waterblasted, as shiny as convent floors, the thousand rain fingernails scratching exposed skin, bulky brown sweater over ruined gypsy skirt offering no protection, feet chilling in leather sandals disintegrating, breasts belly crotch throbbing under water fury, at red lights, rain pounding the pavement breaks into a multitude of droplets, when I'm little, they are des petites bonhommes qui dansent dans la rue, cars hit the water men, scatter them into ethereal mist, walls of water spash me, drivers honk, I bow as if untouched, don't tell me, any of you, dry as a bone inside your metal bodies, don't tell me you never had une liaison érotique avec une ville sous la pluie, this city any city, oh, come on, it happens all the time, I bow, wait for green, cross, walk. But. This is no longer water erotica, this is rejection, the end of the affair. Virginia said no, Montréal's having a hissy fit, my body, shedding her lining.

Before the period comes, I have no body, no sweat, no odour, I play. The period comes, the body be-comes a wired basket caging my freedom, electric current jolting the senses, fingers feet tingling, nose smelling things being singed, lips tongue distending, I can no longer soar, trapped inside the bodycage, am ordered to be-have, don't run, don't talk so loud, now that the body bleeds, I must watch la vulgarité closely. The period comes, I be-come invisible, I slouch, maman warns about the danger of bad posture, but I am not allowed to flaunt non plus. The trick is to achieve perfect bal- ance between slouching enough not to flaunt and not slouching so much as to develop un dos rond. The period comes, body denial. Last summer, Elizabeth showed me my body is just a body. She also fed imagination rising. As long as you're creative.

From Virginia, no such feeding. Mais je comprends Virginia. She thinks I took her bread and butter away, d'abord, Ariane 1967 slipped through her fingers, ensuite, Elizabeth died going away with me. Peut-être, attempting to practise creativity with Virginia wasn't in the best of tastes.

So, what's a girl to do? Shut your mouth and keep on walking.

All the way to Pierre's rue de la Montagne apartment. Sous l'averse.

He brings me thick socks and his bathrobe, gives me a rub down with a ratty towel 'til my skin glows, his bathrobe smells like it needs a wash, he opens the door of his kitchen the size of a closet, makes coffee in his Italian coffee pot he calls une napolitaine.

C'est un déluge, he says, looking out the kitchen's œil-de-bœuf.

I tell him the streets have turned into torrents, there could be a flash flood. I wring my skirt in the bathtub, hang my clothes on the shower curtain rod. This being the last floor of the four-storey walk-up, the rain crashing on the flat roof fait un bruit d'enfer. Pushed by the wind, it sounds like hail hitting the windows. We wait for thunder, listen to the moaning of the wind, the wind really moans as if ripping itself against the sharp corners of the roof. Hail Mary hail and Holy Ghost wind, water percolating, drip dripping on coffin lid, pauvre Elizabeth, submitting to the Chinese water torture, she who hated leaky plumbing.

Il pleut décidément des clous la tête en bas, Pierre says above the whoosh of the gas flame catching under his expresso coffee pot.

I tell him it rains nails in French, cats and dogs in English. What rains on people's heads in other languages?

Pourquoi des chats et des chiens? he asks as he puts on a Bach sonata.

His writing is scattered all over the living room, some sheets with only a few words punctuating the white space, others filled from edge to edge with writing as tight as his anguish. I smell coffee, he brings two tiny cups of mud.

We sit on the floor, he brushes my hair, wet overcooked chocolate spaghetti, he brushes, Bach plays. Such a fine afternoon, Montréal raining on October, outside the living room window, le mont Royal rising behind a curtain of rainfog, a shadow, notre montagne dans la ville. Bach plays, Pierre brushes my hair, ce tableau d'intérieur makes me fidgety.

Je te dérange, I say, getting up.

Au contraire, ma puce, he says, sipping his expresso.

I should go, but he won't allow, not in wet clothes, what if I caught une pneumonie.

I open the window, the air sharp as in the country, back down into the street après la pluie d'octobre, I'm on my way to see that goldwork tapestry the expert chez Marshall recommended.

La rue Sherbrooke smells of Saint-Pol, a mix of decaying vegetation and old stones. Devant le Musée des beaux-arts, the smoke from une Gauloise destroys the scents, unravels the thought of gilt thread on padded surfaces, the body stiffens. Like a shadow, the man with the black pointed shoes appears in my field of vision. I stop walking, watch him materialize in stages, d'abord, the tip of his shoes stained darker by the rain, ensuite, a shapeless trench coat comme celui de l'inspecteur Maigret, finalement, his Gauloise dangling from his lips. Automatiquement, I hold my breath. We say nothing, we don't move, un homme et une femme facing each other devant le Musée des beaux-arts. We could be statues standing on either side of the monumental stairs under les colonnes ioniques, un homme et une femme separated by les beaux-arts, la vie, tout.

He offers me un café. In a public place, he must talk to me, nothing to fear. I fear nothing. We go. He pushes the door of le café Prag, we're on rue Bishop, I pay attention, never been so focussed. We sit in the dark at a dark wooden table, he says Dvořák is playing.

Pourvu que ce ne soit pas Ravel.

Vous n'aimez pas Ravel?

Son Boléro, quelle orgie!

He leans over, touches my skirt and tells me le Boléro represents the rising excitement of a crowd watching une gitane qui danse, he leans back.

Vous préféreriez sûrement Pavane pour une infante défunte.

Je pense, does he imply I like death? I feel zen calm. The waiter brings our coffee, deux cafés crème, the man with the black pointed shoes ordered. The place is empty, except for two girls and one boy, their faces turned up toward the music. Stone angels in a gothic church. I could be elsewhere with Elizabeth, peut-être, in the city of Prague, squinting at stone angels in dark churches. The afternoon is perfect, même si, I'm not with the right person.

He pushes something across the table. A relic. Elizabeth's clutch bag lies between us.

Je ne comprends pas, I say.

C'est simple, he says.

He tells me he was there. The day of the accident. I narrow my eyes. He didn't see the impact, seulement les conséquences. He remembers me well in my white skirt soaked with the woman's blood. In July, he recognized me instantly. Donc, that night, he didn't meet me by chance encounter near le parc Lafontaine. He tells me he invited me to his room to give me the bag. I don't believe him. He swears he had no dishonourable intentions. Why did he kiss me?

Un baiser volé, he says. Cela ne veut pas dire baiser.

En général, I say, un baiser est un prélude.

He maintains a kiss was just a kiss. He smokes. I want to tie those unlikely loose threads together.

C'est mon boulot de lire les journaux, he says. Comme une grande bête sous un microscope. Je récolte, j'étudie, j'analyse, je synthétise, je conclus.

He tells me I said a lot of things that day. Mainly, I kept asking where Elizabeth's clutch bag was. I spoke French, sauf pour les mots clutch bag. He didn't know what that meant. He scanned his newspapers, counting on the French press pour clarifier les faits. Nothing. He scanned articles in English, but his command of that language is poor. D'ailleurs, the English press doesn't write like the French press, even in this city.

Comme si les journalistes francophones et les journalistes anglophones, he says, n'appartenaient pas au même pays.

Bien sûr, I say. Le contexte est différent.

He thinks about that, nods. When he finally cracked the mystery, he went searching for the bag.

Pierre won't believe this, anymore than I do. Quand même, it looks like Elizabeth's bag. Seems unlikely. Quand même. Une chance sur mille? Après tout, the man with the black pointed shoes is used to combing newspapers. Why not places? Peut-être, he can also sniff like a dog and find missing objects. Une chance sur mille.

C'est possible, non? he says, playing with the mother-of-pearl clasp.

I open the bag. Empty. I look at him, he looks at me, sûrement, he knows how to cash traveller's cheques illégalement, I look at the bag, look at him, sûrement, he knows fringy groups to whom Elizabeth's passport would be de l'or en barre, he looks at the bag, looks at me, he shrugs.

La pochette était vide lorsque je l'ai trouvée dans les buissons, he says.

Dans les buissons? I say, raising an eyebrow.

Dans les buissons. Je vous assure.

Je ne vous crois pas.

He repeats, ses intentions sont honorables. He tried to return the bag to me, because it seemed important. After I ran from his room, he tried to right things au Café de l'horloge, but the situation turned nasty. And now, he finds me again. I ask him if he walks the streets with the bag under his coat in case, une chance sur mille, he bumps into me. He admits he has kept an eye on me, I'm not hard to find. Ha! To be the object of cloaked observation.

Vous m'espionnez? I say. Vous vous prenez pour qui? Un agent d'Interpol?

Je pense, et s'il était un agitateur? We're perfectly capable of agitating ourselves ourselves.

Je n'aime pas que des étrangers viennent jouer dans nos plates-bandes, I say. Après tout, c'est notre destinée qui est en jeu, pas celle des Français.

Vous avez l'imagination fertile, he says.

Je pense, what if he's not what he says he is, what if he's drawing up a file on Pierre and is using me to get to him? What if Pierre's reputation as un écrivain engagé is ruined, because he slept avec une Anglaise last winter? And I followed them to the hotel. Probablement, with my shadow in tow. Misère, quel imbroglio! What will worry Pierre isn't that he'll be shot as a traitor like in war movies, non, but that son nationalisme has several doors.

I tell le Français the bag wasn't meant to be found, not to put his nose where it doesn't belong, I won't play his cloak-and-dagger game.

Que voulez-vous dire?

And he better get out of the habit of tailing me. He protests, I say nothing more. He tries to lure me into his debate. I don't take the bait. My word lull shakes him. It feels strong, that mighty silence damming his brilliant speak flow. I stand firm. He gives up, leaves. With a grand gesture, he throws the bag into the lost and found bin by the door. I watch his black pointed shoes disappear.

From November to April '69, I watch people's shoes criss-cross the corridors of the underground city, wet with rain, white with snow, salt-crusted with slush, from November to April, busy people meeting busy people.

Elizabeth, wearing a sweeping black cape like Zorro and, underneath, the pants and jacket I altered for her in September, one of Dead Man's suits, my most ambitious project, looks elegant dans la version au féminin of a man's suit. We hug, go to a bar in l'hôtel Reine Elizabeth, men in suits and women in miniskirts drink talk in semi-darkness, a trickle of music seeps out of the ceiling, waiters in black pants and white shirts bring drinks avec de petits hors-d'œuvre chauds. Elizabeth orders a martini, I order un café, s'il vous plaît. She brings up the question of money, I tell her not to worry, I saved most of the money she paid me during the summer.

That won't be enough, she says, lighting a cigarette. You need about four hundred.

For a plane ticket! I shout whisper.

It's more expensive, because it's an open ticket. And one thousand dollars.

For pocket money! I shout whisper.

For at least six months. We may want to travel longer. If you know how, you can stretch that money. Besides, there'll be expenses before we leave. Oh, and it's a good idea to see your dentist, and your physician.

Where will I find that kind of money? I ask, toute découragée.

You have seven months. Why don't you go around the shops in Place Ville-Marie and Place Bonaventure? Christmas's coming, surely, they'll need part-time sales clerks. Besides, if your work's satisfactory, the manager may keep you through to June. I'd bank on clothing stores. With your sewing experience, you'd have an advantage, she says, showing her suit. Get cracking, girl.

We have lunch à la gare Centrale, like we are practising for our trip. Elizabeth says there's much to do 'til June. She has to renew her passport, I have to apply for mine. We have to secure visas and get our international driver's licences, go for various vaccines and buy plane tickets and traveller's cheques.

Also, she says, you'll need to buy a backpack and a few necessities. We'll travel light, so we want to pack carefully.

I am already making a list, I say. Everything from passport number to safety pin. That way, if the train or plane or bus people lose our luggage, we can show them exactly what they lost.

We won't always travel on official transport.

C'est vrai. We may go downriver in a fishing boat or, in Afghanistan, travel in the back of a truck, like you said.

Lorry. In Afghanistan, Ariane dear, they say lorry.

Lorry, I repeat.

My first Pashto word.

We won't check bags, she says. Too much of a nuisance. Light and free, Ariane, dear. As the spirit moves us.

That bright day in January '69, I meet Elizabeth sur la rue Crescent at an English pub below street level, we eat hot roast beef sandwiches, drink dark stout, talk about the cost of living. I don't go to Saint-Pol anymore. She has too much work, I am too busy with cégep and my job at the madame clothing boutique at Place Bonaventure. Elizabeth was right, la madame my boss kept me after the Christmas rush. We meet in the city, here and there and everywhere, as the spirit moves us. Today sur la rue Crescent, she is late, I don't mind.

Hi, Ariane, dear, her voice makes me jump to my feet.

Allô, Elizabeth, I say, as we hug over the large wooden table.

For you, she says, slapping an animal skin on the table.

All at once, she sits down motions to the waiter for a beer gets a cigarette out of her pack lights it draws pushes smoke out of her mouth, all at once.

What is it, Elizabeth?

An Afghan coat. Very warm. Too tight in the hips for me. It'll fit you like a glove.

Pour moi? Merci.

In a cloud of cigarette smoke, she tells me she is getting rid of things in Saint-Pol.

This is my annual give-away-get-rid-of-things event. Every January. A cure that clears the air, cleans the mind. Possessions! Like bacteria, they grow on you unnoticed. Amazing, Ariane, dear, how much junk piles up in drawers and closets in the course of a year. If you don't watch out, all that clutter will choke you to death.

We want to travel light and free, I say.

Damn right.

The more I think about our money talks, the more je dois
me rendre à l'évidence that my part-time job won't earn me
enough. Bien sûr, I considered Ariane 1967, but could not sell
Elizabeth's gift right under her nose for cold cash. Ce n'est
pas poli. And then, it hits me as I walk home in the crack-
the-brain cold. Elizabeth's yearly closet-cleaning cure gives
me an epiphany of epic proportion, not surprising, January
being epiphany month. Maman's wedding gifts dans le hangar. C'est ça, la solution. Peut-être, she packed them away,
mon héritage. Gérard est antiquaire, sûrement, he will give me
a good price, he is a friend, a fair man, he won't cheat me. I
am so excited, I walk double fast. Je vais faire d'une pierre
deux coups. The sale will finance my trip and will free maman
from the slavery of possessions forever and ever. Because she
thought she had no right to enjoy her wedding gifts sans
Dead Man, she stored them dans le hangar, because she could
not get rid of them without betraying him, bien sûr, he had
no way of knowing that, but, since she is a moral person, she
simply could not go all the way. I will finish the job for her.

At supper, to test the water, I ask her if she is keeping my
toys for any reason, no reason in particular, would she mind
if I sold or donated them, no, this is not important, I wade in
deeper, ask if the wedding gifts dans le hangar are important,
she does not answer. That silence territory I know comme le
fond de ma poche. We have an understanding, what is that
understanding? I cannot tell, it is unspoken. C'est ça, une
entente tacite. Between evasive answer, pour l'amour, I'm
voiding, and a smile in her cup of Salada tea, my job is to fill
in the unspoken blanks with anything I choose, it has always
worked. La preuve? She said nothing when I transformed her
wedding dress into a gypsy skirt, when I used her wedding
cape to line my maroon coat, when I took down the living
room drapes to make my velvet coat. Even after she saw
Elizabeth in Dead Man's mutated suit, she said nothing.
When I asked, she only said something like what's the point

of being upset. I asked about the wedding gifts, she said nothing, the coast is clear.

The first box I open contains a silver tea set and a silver coffee set. I bring those to Gérard. How much? He is interested, but wonders if I have permission, oui, maman is no butler, she has no time to polish the silver. How much?

From January to March, every Friday before going to work at Place Bonaventure, I pick a box dans le hangar to bring to Gérard. I can tell, he looks forward to the opening of the Friday box.

He carefully unwraps the heavy cut glass decanter and the twelve tiny but very thick matching glasses.

Du verre de Bohême, he says, environ 1920. Pour le whisky.

Another Friday, he lifts un grand compotier de cristal so heavy you need three butlers to pass the compote to dinner guests, maman would find that impractical, no wonder it lives dans le hangar. Gérard has a client in mind for the ponderous vessel.

Another Friday, he finds a delicate dish with a cover and fragile handles and its own small ladle with hand-painted pale roses on white porcelain so fine we can see the outline of our fingers when we hold it to the light.

Ça vient d'Allemagne, Gérard says, reading the bottom of the bowl, like a Gypsy reads the lines on the palm of a hand. C'est pour la confiture.

Another Friday, he is happy to discover the steel salt and pepper shakers are Bauhaus, I know le Bauhaus, we studied that school in my art history courses.

Friday after Friday, porcelain vases from Sèvres and Limoges, lead crystal bonbonnières, silver bells, they all move from le hangar to Anteannum. I make a tidy sum, as they say in movies.

Le 19 février 1969, Ash Wednesday, my official name arrives through registered mail. My wedding gift to my self received on that day makes me uneasy, as if I am watching my amputated birth leg burn to ashes while learning to walk on a new artificial leg with no feeling in it. The disconnection makes me question the ethic of selling the wedding gifts for my benefit, but is not strong enough to make me distrust my instincts. Quand même, I keep a list of all the objects Gérard buys, with detailed descriptions and provenance, and deposit that money in a separate account at ma caisse populaire. Wedding-widow money. Sounds like blood money.

Qu'est-ce que tu vas faire, Ariane? Nicole asks. Maintenant que Elizabeth est morte?

Vas-tu aller à l'université? Diane asks.

Je ne sais pas encore, I say.

We bumped into each other in the underground city. After leaving le café Prag, didn't feel like going to le Musée, needed air, started walking again. I came in out of the rain, Nicole et Diane came downtown by métro pour faire du lèche-vitrine.

Being a student is a political job. Les étudiants descendent dans la rue, ils protestent. There's always une manifestation somewhere about something, I know what's happening, let it happen at the edge of my myopia. Nicole et Diane placed themselves in the eye of the storm, un jour, when they get bored playing les femmes traditionnelles, they may look for a job or become des féministes de cuisine or they may continue to live happily next door to each other, comme des religieuses cloîtrées. The pirate girl comes to mind. What is she doing this afternoon dans son hôpital pour les incurables? Washing sheets, preparing that pap the chronically ill eat. The pirate girl in a white uniform and white shoes that squeak on highly polished floors, her green plastic parrot perched on her shoulder, his plumage of red and yellow and blue floating behind her, with her yellow eye patch and her cropped red hair caring for the incurable hearts, herself, tough and hurting, jumping over the cracks in her lifeline, saying, whatever.

Peut-être, I say to Nicole et Diane, je vais voyager.

They approve. Pourquoi pas? I have the money, a virgin passport.

Où irais-tu? Diane asks.

Je pense, in May, I was so sure, practising packing, the first rule of travel, ne pas s'encombrer de bagages, stretching in bed, déjà, I was lying on a straw mat in Nepal, a wool blanket in Guatemala, a mud floor in Etosha, the sirens of rue Sherbrooke, night birds in the Borneo jungle. So sure, in May. Where would I go now?

Peut-être à Distraction, au Manitoba, I say.

They don't know where Distraction is. I tell them about tall, thin, pollen-plated Sven, son of Duane, the waltzing wheat farmer in the white suit, I would arrive by train, we'd live in his log house, him tending his wheat, moi tending the vegetable garden, the people of Distraction might think that a sin, mais je serais toujours polie, bientôt, they wouldn't mind us living together, the women would teach me prairie things, like how to survive in winter without catching cabin fever or setting the cabin on fire.

Nicole thinks that would be a waste of a good passport, because I don't need one to go to Manitoba.

C'est vrai, I say.

I tell Nicole et Diane, quand même, I'd like to see prairie geography, drive there and back in mon oncle Joseph's Buick. Alone in the open, between the vast sky and the vast land.

Je pourrais devenir une raconteuse itinérante, I say.

I tell them about ce festival folk I went to with Pierre and Raymond.

Je suis montée sur scène, I say.

Non!

I don't tell them it was the Sunday of their open-house party.

We walk through the underground city, wasting our
time, talking nonsense. Mon oncle needs his Buick to go to
work, he's getting old, but can't afford to retire, mon oncle
est un ouvrier, struggling for his rights, he should march in
the streets avec les étudiants, but he has no time for freedom
fighting, il doit gagner sa croûte, as he says. Pierre's right, I
should get involved, get a job. I have my trip money, am
going nowhere.

The afternoon lull is nearing its end, Nicole et Diane are
thinking about the long métro ride to Henri-Bourassa, the
crowded bus crossing la rivière des Prairies. They don't want
to see the gloomy sky sooner than necessary, donc, we walk
from Place Ville-Marie through le Passage toward la gare
Centrale through to Place Bonaventure to take le métro
directly on the north line, I'll get off at Sherbrooke, they'll
continue to the end of the line, tout le monde descend, le
monsieur on the loudspeaker will say at Henri-Bourassa.
C'est la sortie des bureaux, we walk with the crowd. How
many of those men and women are going for a quicky at
l'hôtel Bonaventure or for a lovers' drink in the discreet bars,
everybody so worldly.

I bump into une femme pressée, pardon, madame, I bump
into Elizabeth with Pierre that Thursday night last March.
Business is slow, la madame my boss asks me to run an errand
for her at Place Ville-Marie, that's when I see Elizabeth, but
don't believe my eyes, she hates shopping, à cause de la
myopie, les yeux can't be trusted. I hide behind a column, put
on my cat's eyes. The woman in the black cape est un sosie
d'Elizabeth, same thin lips, blond hair in a French twist, pock-
marked skin, potato nose. Her friend arrives, l'homme est
aussi un sosie, so many store windows reflecting so many
faces, the stage for a baroque play full of mirrors, we are repli-
cated in the criss-crossing corridors of the underground city.
The woman smiles, same perfect teeth, the man wraps his
arms around her waist bunching up the black cape, kisses her

full on the mouth, my lips part, as if to receive that mouth, she kisses him back like a mother like a friend like a lover, my lips know that soft hard pressure. Pierre takes Elizabeth by the shoulder, she does not wrap her arm around him, they walk toward la Place Bonaventure, I follow, what else can I do.

Her boots clack clack on the terrazzo, my boots are cat's paws. Only last week when we had lunch dans le Vieux-Montréal, she said she would be too busy in March to see me, did not say what kind of busy, je pensais, all those jobs to wrap up before our trip, I did not mind, having my own kind of busy avec le collège, mon emploi à temps partiel, mes amis. Is Pierre only one part of her too busy in March or the whole of her too busy? Elizabeth se tape Pierre en mars before the long trip with Ariane. Pierre, la lettre P in her alphabet soup of lovers, Pierre and Elizabeth, a whole city in which to play, underground and aboveground, Ariane shadowing Elizabeth with Pierre, we are in a play.

Dans le Passage, the carpet mutes Elizabeth's boots. We walk by le marchand de journaux et cigares, wise of Pierre not to stop to read the headlines, bien sûr, he read Le Devoir this morning, he doesn't need to read stale news, this evening, he has better things to do, happy hour for romantic interludes from newspapers, Elizabeth stops, I flatten like a cockroach against the wall, catch my sweater on the rough ridges in the concrete, she buys a pack of Player's and two cigarillos, for later, she says, Pierre smiles his knowing smile, she flings a panel of her cape over one shoulder and reaches for her wallet in the inner pocket of the jacket of the suit I altered for her, my proudest sewing moment, passer du masculin au féminin by softening the lapels, replacing the drab buttons with fancy glass ones, sewing une martingale, that suede half-belt pleating the back of the jacket, streamlining the long jacket, she does not look manly butchy at all, she said I was getting so ingenious, and, tonight, she is celebrating my ingenuity with Pierre on her arm, like men wear une boutonnière.

Where were you? la madame my boss whispers annoyed.
There was a lineup, madame.

I give her the coffee and turkey on rye, hold the mayo,
and the small package I picked up for her at the jewellery
store. The boutique is busy, she cannot drink her coffee, eat
her sandwich in front of her customers, she suspects I dilly-
dallied in shops, I cannot tell her I had serious business to
attend to, no personal business can possibly be that urgent
when I am on her time, she sends me in to the portion of
the dressing room we keep for making alterations.

I trust you can shorten the hem of Miss Van Horne's skirt
by closing time, she says, indicating une jeune fille idéale
anglaise.

Bien sûr, madame. This way, Miss.

La jeune fille unbuttons her coat, smooths her green tartan skirt, changes in one of the cubicles, comes into the alteration room, carrying her green skirt and her coat. The hem
of the new red tartan skirt hangs below the knee.

Mother wants the hem to graze the knee, she says. No
higher.

So, if you kneel, the edge of the skirt will touch the floor.

Yes, she says, rolling her eyes. I don't care what Mother
says. Turn up the hem two inches above the knee.

Okay, I say, measuring and pinning.

I see your mother lets you wear your skirts pretty short.

Six inches above the knee is normal length for a
miniskirt, I say, clenching the pins between my teeth.

Your mother lets you do anything you want?

Pretty much, I say, taking the pins out of my mouth.
Maman gave me plenty of advice when I was young, she
thinks I am now responsible enough, euh, I don't mean to
imply your mother did not raise you well or that you are not
a responsible girl, it's just, when Expo came, I turned seventeen, maman thought it was time I learned to make my own
decisions.

You visited Expo often?

I practically lived there.

Mother wouldn't let me go without a chaperone. She won't even let me choose my own clothes, for Pete's sake. Mother says I have no taste. How can I learn to have taste. Well.

Next June, when I turn nineteen, I say, pinning the hem, I am going to travel with my friend, a woman maman's age but my own friend.

You're going abroad? she says, a break in her voice. Where?

Oh, everywhere. Europe, Asia, Africa.

All that in a month?

Why a month?

Package tours don't travel much beyond a month.

Oh, non non non non. No package tour. Non non. Just Elizabeth and me. For six months. Done.

She looks at herself in the full-length mirror.

Hmmm, she says. I hate to be a bother, but would you mind an awful lot to turn up the hem two and a half inches?

No problem. Two inches plus one whole half inch.

Thanks. You're lucky.

You think so? Just now, I saw Elizabeth and my boyfriend go up to l'hôtel Bonaventure, I say, repinning the hem.

You did not! What will you do?

Nothing.

Are you sure they?

Oh, oui, I made sure.

How? she asks, sitting on the bench next to me, still in her slip.

Easy, I say, threading the needle. After they went up, I took the elevator to the lobby. One minute, I am dans la ville souterraine, the next, dans le ciel de Montréal. Bien sûr, I don't have my coat on, I pass the reception desk without looking at the clerk to show I am used to hotel walking, spot the lounge that opens to the corridor leading to the rooms, opposite the cozy lounge, through the large windows, I see the famous roof garden, full of snow at this time of year, but a few people swim in the steaming pool, and with the surrounding highrises blinking in the evening, c'est féérique.

I know. Mother and I go for swims there. Regularly. But don't let me interrupt.

Elizabeth with Pierre sip martinis in the lounge, not a breath of weather to upset the mood, la fête intime des amants sous la ville now above the city. Where will they dine? Not eat, non, not in a place like that. Dine. Alone in Elizabeth's room or surrounded by others in the posh restaurant? Peut-être, Pierre is doing research for his writing, infiltrating the life of la bourgeoisie anglaise, so his main character will know how to throw the rotten rich, I don't mean you, and give le peuple, something. But, you see, Elizabeth in her crooked house in Saint-Pol is not la bourgeoisie. She is too suspicious of possessions. Peut-être, she too is doing research.

I stop to pull another length of red thread from the spool, thread the needle, continue to sew the hem, two and a half inches above la jeune fille idéale anglaise's bony knees.

Skin so alive, I say, absent-in-my-mind. Pierre's lips on my skin, his fingers on my skin, Pierre's lips, Pierre's fingers playing on Elizabeth's skin.

You and your boyfriend have?

Oh, sure. We still do it, but we are not actually going out together, at least, not steady. Right now, as I sew your hem, he sees Elizabeth's body, the bow legs, the large uneven hips, the small breasts, the body white with butterscotch freckles. Oh, I know what you think. In movies, sensuality always comes packaged in perfect bodies. Pas dans la vraie vie. Donc, I pick up the hotel phone, the woman's voice says, switchboard, I articulate well, say, bonsoir, I can tell by the silence travelling through the telephone line, she is uneasy, in

French, I ask her to ring Elizabeth Gold's room, expect her to say, sorry, there is no one by that name in the hotel, the phone rings, my heart beats fast, after six rings, the woman asks if I want to leave a message, I say, non, merci, she disconnects, sans doute, relieved I did not dictate a message in French. I wonder if the man at the reception desk will help me, it may be forbidden to give room numbers, what if a jealous wife, what if an enraged husband. I am cool as an English cucumber sandwich, say, bonsoir, the man says, bonsoir, we belong to the same language, I tell him I am from out of town, madame Elizabeth Gold asked me to meet her in her room, I got lost in the corridors, could he, aucun problème, la chambre de madame Gold, suivez ce corridor, en haut du petit escalier, tournez à droite, la chambre 2211 est à votre gauche, he gives me the number not to give me the number but as part of his sentence.

What did you do next? she asks, excited, her elbows resting on her knees, her chin cupped in her hands.

Since I didn't have my pearl-handled gun with me, I couldn't very well shoot them, could I?

We burst out laughing, I knock over the sewing box, the spools roll out of the alteration room, we are on all fours, chasing a thread rainbow.

What's going on in there? la madame my boss asks, her voice overflowing with English annoyance.

Nothing to worry.

Miss Van Horne? You're still here?

Yes. I'm learning professional stitchery.

Oh. Oh, very well.

When Mother walks in, Miss Van Horne refuses to try on the skirt. Mother runs her fingers along the hem, turns the skirt inside out to check the stitches, tiny, invisible, Mother approves. Miss Van Horne smiles a smile of conspiracy as I wrap the new skirt in tissue paper, Mother pays, I insert the purchase in our posh bronze-coloured bag with the name of

the boutique in swirly white script, Saint-Germain, and
below in smaller sober script, Fine Ladies' Apparel, I close the
bag, Mother snatches it with an icy hand, she marches out,
head held high.

Don't worry, Miss Van Horne says to me. Everything'll
turn out all right. I wish I had your guts. That was a hell of
a story.

Wendy! Mother barks.

Miss Van Horne follows, in no hurry, sans doute, their
limousine waiting, no métro for them.

Dans le métro, a man jumps sits on the single seat as soon
as its occupant gets off, letting his legs open wide like men
do, his knee brushes against Diane's knee, she doesn't squeeze
in, maudit! she was there first, elle fait les gros yeux, Nicole
et Diane seated side by side try not to laugh, they look tired.
They invite me to their houses next Saturday. I've no reason
to say this, but tell them I can't. Will be in touch. À la station
Berri, I get off with the crowd.

Je descends ici, I say, on impulse.

I can tell, they were planning to say their last-minute
words in the tunnel between Berri and Sherbrooke, I robbed
them of leur au revoir. This afternoon, we bumped into each
other, they think I've changed, the weight of the dead
between us, non, that's not it, not anymore. They're the ones
who've changed. Non. That's not it either.

In soft rain, in fading light, I swing my arms, the rain feels
good on my face. I endured the constricted arteries too long.
La vulgarité isn't a terminal disease, too much discrétion
sucked the air right out of our lungs. Maman is about to sur-
render her responsibilities to the dead, is unlocking the compartments of her Chinese box, we're opening the windows,
not on noise, but on bustle, oui, un accident est si vite arrivé,
mais la vie continue, we're agitating ourselves at last. Can
things come back the way they were between Nicole et
Diane et moi? Bien sûr que non. I hope they're happy.

I'll no longer endure the constricted arteries. Pierre dreams of la révolution dans les rues de Montréal shaking things up from the east end to the west end. He writes speaks of kidnapping the system, torturing it 'til it swears égalité pour tous. Pierre speaks writes of making war, because the love people have is rotten, broken down, scooped straight out of a can. Not all of it. Gérard and Elizabeth, was that love out of a can? We're on pins and needles, Pierre's mouth full of words, my mouth full of pins, I never swallow pins, we swallow words, swallows are hirondelles, Elizabeth thought mon bon mot funny, Pierre doesn't, because he doesn't know swallows are hirondelles. Elizabeth and Gérard played together, two can play with two languages, deux langues qui se touchent, deux langues qui s'embrassent, two tongues intertwined create a new language, the private langue à deux. I was learning that language, Pierre doesn't understand, he speaks la langue solitaire, fights battles on paper, crosses swords with words, crosses words with swords, refuses to swallow words any longer, les hirondelles s'envolent de sa bouche, quand même, see how deep Gérard's grief cuts, that's not love out of a can.

That night in March Miss Van Horne follows Mother to the family limousine, I emerge from the weatherless underground city into a white-howling blizzard. Une giboulée de mars s'abat sur Montréal, mars joue à saute-mouton, the lion jumps over the lamb, the lamb jumps over the lion, who will arrive first at the finishing line, the number twenty-four bus is late, at the top of the stairs, the crowd grows, no one wants to exit la station Sherbrooke, the sky roils, clouds shiny like crumpled foil, from the seventeenth floor of l'hôtel Bonaventure, Pierre with Elizabeth in room twenty-two eleven, naked, before or after, watch the same aluminum sky.

Behind my back, the crowd thickens with the arrival of each rame de métro, am I allowed to phone Elizabeth? pretend I saw nothing, ma tante Rita would say, il ne faut pas réveiller le chat qui dort, but Elizabeth is a straight shooter, she will tell Gérard about sa nuit avec Pierre, shouldn't she know I know, bien sûr, I will not tell her I followed them, do the people waiting for the bus have complicated lives, that first afternoon I visited her, what did she and Raymond fight about, will she fight with Pierre, he will debate les grandes questions, they will have words about la société, ça, c'est certain, what does Gérard think about all that, peut-être, he feels guilty himself, après tout, he stole Elizabeth from Newspaper George that day long ago in the Boston shop of chairs, bien sûr, Newspaper George was a scumbag, quand même, how much does Gérard know about Elizabeth's alphabet soup of lovers, behind my back, people smell of wet wool and impatience, I dive into the blizzard.

No hat, no gloves, the fat flakes stick to my face, plaster the front of my coat, I slip on a patch of ice, fall square on my right shoulder, hear a crunching sound, the pain so sharp, it crescendoes through my body, what if there are complications, there are always complications, when the heat of the flat hits me full blast, the throb in my shoulder and in my heart becomes unbearable.

I collapse on the ebony hall stand, maman helps me remove my slush-soaked boots, take off my snow-crusted coat, she wants me to go à l'urgence à Notre-Dame, mais non, on a night like this, they have more urgent emergencies than a sprained shoulder, no broken bone, I know that now, she helps me undress, makes a sling with one of her polyester scarves, brings me cream of tomato soup with crackers and strong sugared Salada tea, sits by my bed.

I thank her for being there when I had la rougeole, la picotte, les oreillons, my first menstrual cramps, I thank her for explaining la verge des hommes, she smiles, I tell her I love her, I never said that before, je t'aime, maman, the words, spoken, so wrench my heart my mouth wants to cry, but cannot cry and swallow at the same time, so, it spews out soggy crackers on my sleeping bag that has replaced my gold bed-spread, I cry with my mouth open for fear cracker crumbs will go down the wrong pipe, not a good night for choking, I cry and laugh, must look absurd, in three months I will be nineteen, travel the world, look at me now, je braille comme un veau dans les bras de ma mère on a night when the lion of winter pursues the lamb of March, between sobs, between fits of laughter, I tell her, tonight my heart is broken, I inhale deep, sip a spoonful of soup.

Pauvre petite fille, she says.

Now, she thinks Pierre broke her daughter's heart. I tell her my broken heart is like la giboulée de mars. C'est exas-pérant. It comes out of nowhere.

J'aime Pierre, I say. Mais je ne suis pas amoureuse de lui.

I tell her I don't love him like being in love, I love him like liking him, ce n'est pas la même chose. Les Anglais know the pitfalls of love, and, being fesses serrées, they are cautious by nature, so, they invented two distinct verbs, to love and to like, les Anglais don't mix love with friendship, moi non plus. Alors, why am I tingling all over when I think about Elizabeth? She is too busy to see me, but not too busy pour baiser mon chum, my heart cannot be broken if I am not in love with him, ou bien, I am in love with him and don't know it. Must discover my true feelings. I tell maman I know Pierre and Elizabeth are lovers, I am not in love with Pierre, I am pretty sure about that, donc, I cannot be jealous, quand même, that broken heart thing feels real, I ask her if it is possible for me to be in love with Elizabeth. It takes my breath away to say that.

Je suis toute mêlée, I say.

Maman explique les choses de la vie. Elizabeth's new rela-tionship with Pierre is threatening, because she may change her mind about the trip. I should not worry. Elizabeth is not the kind of woman to break her promises.

Maman a raison. She sits in the chair, I lie in bed, the two of us, alone together in semi-darkness, outside, the storm rages, the lion runs after the lamb, inside, we breathe together in the best silence ever.

The lion roars a little more, but is out of breath. March moves from snow to slush to ice back to slush, I walk like a Japanese woman in a samurai film, small steps not to slip, my torn stretched shoulder hurts, but less, I continue to work for la madame my boss in case the trip is still on, the ice melts, Elizabeth does not phone, I don't phone Pierre, I skip classes, phone Nicole, we talk 'til my left ear is red hot, phone Diane, we talk 'til my right ear is red hot, I tell them about Pierre and Elizabeth, they compare notes, no secrets. I drink the peach brandy, a sticky-sickly-sweet digestif maman's boss gives her every Christmas, the bottles sport a fine coat of dust, I smoke cigarettes I bought not chez monsieur Lebœuf, drink smoke, pretend to be Elizabeth with Pierre, pretend to be anybody but me, doze off tipsy on the couch dans le petit salon, wake up from a horny dream, in the kitchen, open and close the cupboard doors one after the other, like chorus girls kicking their legs in turn, the days are getting longer, but the flat remains dark as terminal depression, my shoulder is mending slowly, but the days are running me raggedy doll, dull day. I pace up and down the flat, a zoo she-bear pacing around her enclosure, putting her huge paws in the same spots again and again and again and again, the packed dirt in the shape of her prints has sunk a few inches, the sign of her boredom, the tracks, the memory of her freedom, I feel in my bones in the soles of my feet the full weight of the expression, tourner comme un ours en cage. The level in the brandy bottle I cracked open is getting low, my breath reeks, I flush the butts, dream about the bear brushing her thick fur against my leg over and over, shaving off thin layers of skin, new skin grows, pink and smooth, like beginnings, the she-bear never looks at me. I throw away the empty bottle, brush my teeth, wash my hair, the right shoulder never mended completely, the left one bears its summer starfish scar, a cool October wind rises, Nicole et Diane ride home to suburbia.

I choose not to endure the constricted arteries, but can't imagine myself putting on la chemise à carreaux de la révolution. When I sew thread to my fingertips, rainbowed fingers, oui, c'est joli, but that's not the point. The point is to learn to pierce the thinnest layer of skin and draw no blood. Can we fight a revolution without drawing blood? Pierre doesn't know. The true challenge is to sew with the left hand and still draw no blood. We must learn patience to become ambidextrous. Bilingual, la langue à deux. What will I do, now? Nicole asked. Go on the road, collect our stories. La raconteuse Ariane Claude en spectacle solo. The one-woman show. Speaking for the many. What will I do, now? Enter a desert, climb a mountain, run through streets pockmarked with bullets, make love to men with fenugreek and hashish breath, men who reek of muscus animalis. But first, need silence to listen. I swing my arms, the rain feels good on my face.

Au Café de l'horloge, water has percolated through the dirt basement. Jérôme spent the past two nights building extra shelves to store his supplies off the floor, pauvre Jérôme, his flagship in his shoestring of cafés des arts sinking into underground Montréal, he shrugs, c'est la vie. He points at the brick wall covered with black and white photos.

La première exposition? I say.

I put on my cat's eyes. The pictures show the yoots in the streets, les jeunes revendiquent, believing they'll prevail. It's happening au Café de l'horloge, it's happening in the streets. The noble tradition of coffee houses as ferments of revolts, where art and politics collide, cette exposition, c'est notre parlure. Bientôt, Jérôme will exhibit paintings and that new art form, l'art vidéo, très d'avant-garde, de Vancouver, he says. Bientôt, Pierre will read his first finished piece. Bientôt, tous les verbes seront au futur. It will all happen.

Peut-être, Jérôme will exhibit Gold Rush, moi aussi, I'm an emerging artist, the ceiling's too low. Elizabeth was no longer an emerging artist, artwork goes through the roof after the artist's death. Who'll buy Gold Rush? Two hundred dollars, two fifty, who says three hundred, ladies and gentlemen, the muse honouring the master, three fifty, thank you, sir, four hundred, collectors are bidding in a frenzy, five thousand dollars, gasp, sold. What a hawktion!

C'est lui! I shout point at one face in one of the pictures. Jérôme and his customers look up.

Lui, qui? Pierre says, coming in.

He embraces me from behind, his bearded chin resting on my neck.

Tu aimes mes photos? he says.

Tu es photographe, maintenant? Comme tu es engagé, Pierre, I say, in the tone of Little Red Riding Hood to the grandmother-wolf.

C'est pour mieux t'impressionner, mon enfant, he says, biting my neck. Ton tour viendra, ma puce.

Tu te souviens? I say, pointing at the face in the crowd. Le Français aux souliers pointus? Je lui ai mis mon poing sur la gueule en juillet.

I tell him about the man with the black pointed shoes following me, about the clutch bag, I tell him that guy doesn't just read newspapers in his room, il est un agitateur, for or against, that's the question, he could be closely watched. Je pense, doesn't Pierre know photographs can be dangerous documents for any of the real people he shot? I don't have the heart to open that can of fat wriggling worms. Moral dilemma. What if the man with the black pointed shoes is un agitateur who dissects words to manipulate context, what if he distorts facts to manipulate l'opinion et les émotions du peuple, what if he's all that, but what if he's not and gets targeted? Why doesn't Pierre fight le grand combat in his novel? That way, he doesn't risk playing with people's lives. I don't have the heart. We look at his pictures documenting la jeunesse marching in the streets.

We spend the day together. He wants to talk about Elizabeth, we've talked a lot about Elizabeth since l'aventure à l'hôtel Bonaventure. We go for a long walk sur le mont Royal, the sun shines, enfin! C'est vraiment l'automne, things are ending things are dormant, we walk and talk, we talk best when we walk.

Pierre rakes his fingers through his hair, he's fired up, tells me about un opéra rock contestation he'll write with Raymond, they'll feature fishermen and factory workers and unwed mothers and young intellectuals and, well, they have many things to work out.

Hé! he says, stopping in his tracks, grabbing me by the shoulders. Tu pourrais faire les costumes.

Tu crois?

Absolument, ma puce. Tu seras géniale avec les costumes.

He tells me il est grand temps that I hang out with people my own age, do my own thing. I did my own thing, I remind him, and Virginia said no. What's the point of imagination growing, what's the point of initiative? Virginia said no. No point wallowing, a little setback, c'est tout. When Jérôme noticed his supplies drowning in his basement, he didn't tear his clothes and grind his teeth, c'est la ruine! c'est la ruine! non, he said, c'est la vie, and built shelves. Simple. Initiative and imagination, the two eyes of life. Pierre's fired up, tells me he'll write un scénario dans le style cinéma-vérité about the relationship between a young girl and an older woman, explore the dynamics, the personal and the political, the implications are huge.

J'aimerais que tu me parles de ta relation avec Elizabeth, he says.

Et toi, ta relation avec elle, I say. Tu faisais de la recherche?

Je te l'ai déjà dit, Ariane, he says. Elle avait envie de moi. J'avais envie de cette expérience-là. Rien de plus.

He doesn't understand what bothers me, he's always told me about his flings, I've never reacted so strongly before, he suspects that Elizabeth and I were lovers, but that I'm too embarrassed to tell him.

Ce n'était pas comme ça, I say. Je te jure.

He teases me with his tongue, I push him away, we play-fight on the path to le chalet de la montagne. I try to understand my feelings, tell him, peut-être, I didn't want to share her with my usual friends, peut-être, she meant a new life for the new Ariane, a special relationship, special in ways I never knew before. He puts his arm around my shoulder. We walk, dead Elizabeth between us.

Pierre thinks Gérard can't forget as easily as we can, c'est normal, après tout, they were not just lovers, they were life-long companions, but there's something else. Gérard is old. At fifty the mind calcifies, he has nothing left but his memories of her, Pierre can't deal with her death on the same level as Gérard, he wants to use the idea of Elizabeth and create his own film. Does that make him a ghoul?

I ask him if he'll collaborate with the filmmaker he knows à l'ONF. He doesn't remember telling me about him. Non? Non. The first time we made out at Expo. He shakes his head, tells me ce réalisateur no longer works there. How will he make his film? He'll find a way.

As we tumble down le mont Royal toward the west end, he speaks pêle-mêle about his projects. Like mon oncle Joseph, il a le verbe haut, like mon oncle Joseph, he has many desires, many dreams, mon oncle has reached la fin de sa conjugaison, no more verbes au futur.

Ton oncle est d'une autre génération, he says. Les pauvres écroulés de la grande noirceur. Nous autres, on prendra notre destinée en main. Tu verras, ma puce. Tu verras.

Pierre conjugating full steam ahead. The power of will.

We go to his apartment, drink expresso, he rolls a ciga-rette, I roll one, tobacco falls on the table, I don't want to smoke. He asks if I'm happy being back with my own kind, I'm not sure if he means people my own age or people of my own language, I don't know what to say. He looks at me with pleading eyes.

On est bien ensemble, hein, ma puce? he says, lighting sa rouleuse.

Oui, I say.

Virginia said no. Pierre wants me to create the costumes pour son opéra rock contestation with Raymond. Pierre wants to do research with me pour son film cinéma-vérité about an Elizabeth-and-Ariane-type story, bien sûr, he'll add lesbian sex, ça, c'est certain, his film must shake people up. Entre nous, he wants us to move forward. Where? We don't know. But forward. Peut-être, to go forward, we must go underground a little. Imagination and initiative, the two big eyes of life. To see in the dark. Underground. Who needs her? Virginia is establishment. I can do anything I want.

Tea Ceremony

We're doing research.

Regarde-moi, he says, his speaking lips brushing against my silent lips.

In his rue de la Montagne apartment, he wants me to kiss him with my eyes open, not to shut ourselves off from one another. Where did he learn that?

Je pense, the camera never blinks, a trick Elizabeth taught him, he wants cinéma-vérité, mais se faire du cinéma et se dire la vérité, ce n'est pas la même chose.

Parle-moi des jardins suspendus de Babylone, I say.

We touch each other's bodies. He tells me, on one side of the hotel, the pool steaming into the Montréal March sky, that, I saw through the glass door, on the other side of the hotel, through another glass door, that, I didn't see, the gardens with stone-paved paths crossing small streams, basins with aquatic plants, a rooftop landscape supporting pines and firs growing high above their native ground, climbing plants covering stone walls surrounding the basins and the paths, le promeneur makes his way to sheltered patios, watches ducks swim in summer, sleep in winter.

I make my way to le Musée des beaux-arts, research interrupted by the man with the black pointed shoes now resumed. The embroidery expert chez Marshall said, go see. I see. Large goldwork tapestry in the Oriental Room.

Panels painted with landscapes enclosing a courtyard, le poète half-reclining on a platform, les deux courtisanes standing on either side of him, in the foreground, a rectangular vase with an intricate floral arrangement, in the background above the panels, on the left, an elaborate, twisted branch, on the right, three columns of Chinese characters. What the poet said? What the courtesans said about the poet?

Ouvre les yeux, embrasse-moi.

He slides inside me, we look at each other, pupils dilating, skin blushing, laying on his living room floor, linked by body parts, katydids in the mating ritual, peut-être, in that species the female holds down the male, female insects are assertive, our bodies rotate, I'm on top. My lips feel the fragile fluttering skin of his eyelids, my eyes feel the texture of the tapestry based on the painting by T'ang Ying, the stitcher, unknown, silk on silk of all hues, brilliant slickness, he wants to open his eyes, I kiss his mouth, my lips parting the raised flesh of his lips, on the raised surfaces, the robes of the three figures, the hair of the women and the hat of the man, the writing and the branch, the screen and the flower vessel, on all those padded surfaces, gilt thread, couched, fluid fire running on top of silk stitches, catching the light. My lips press on his body, my fingers want to touch gold, défendu de toucher dans un musée, imagine the living effect of gold couched across skin, can't resist, walk up close, nose to the needlework, furtive fingers feeling la tension du fil d'or sur la peau, a soft roughness, hear goldsilk rustle, taste silkgold on tongue, walk back, fingers across lips, sit and watch, the giant katydids lay motionless, the artery at his temple pulsates, could watch gold running for days, for days, mating katydids mimicking twigs, what are their odours? foul to their predators, sweet to each other, what's Elizabeth's scent up close? Why did they go to Babylon? Why call it Babylon? his throaty voice wants to know. Why not? The rooftop gardens remind of the aerial gardens of antiquity. He moves inside me.

Est-ce que Elizabeth avait mauvaise haleine le matin? I ask.

Je n'ai pas remarqué, he says.

I tell him it's not good research not to know, bad breath's important, it can lead to scratches, a punch in the face.

Ça n'a pas d'importance, he says.

Bien sûr que c'est important, I say.

I tell him we're doing research. What's the point of exchanging body fluids if we ignore each other's scents. Does only performance matter, did Elizabeth give him a gold star?

In May, I told Elizabeth I spotted her at Place Ville-Marie, wearing a cape I had never seen before. She blows smoke that dissipates around my face, we are having coffee at that café on rue Saint-Paul. She knows I know, two equals, hyphenated by the same man.

Le poète et deux courtisanes, the original, ink and colours on silk, by T'ang Ying. The stitcher, unknown. Her work, a triumph.

Est-ce seulement une question de performance? I ask him.

I tell him how easily people expose themselves, like film to light. When they were in the hanging gardens in room twenty-two eleven, was he performing to impress Elizabeth? He didn't have to for a pro like her. Quand même, it was all action, no scent. If he wants cinéma-vérité, that contradiction, he must deal with Elizabeth's sweet foul smell as she rots underground.

He grows big inside me, research is exciting, someone blows his horn outside, he groans, nostrils dilating, mouth opening comme un noyé, his body in distress pleasure, he isn't interested in smells, that of lovers or insects, he cares nothing for gilt thread, couched, lips on fire, he wants action, he wants to know Elizabeth's last moments, like Gérard, they all do. What happens to a life slipping away in front of your own open eyes? Was she aware?

Oh, oui, I say. Elle savait.

I tell him she had amazing strength. She pinned me down so close to her I smelled her blood, like smelling her soul. Is that the smell of Gold? It was painful for her to speak. Peut-être, she said she was in no rush. She pushed me away.

He rolls me over, his flushed skin pinned to my skin reddening, gold thread, couching, beading, runs on the surface of the fabric, we move in rhythmic consent, palms perspiring. Careful not to crack the gold. His eyes lock into mine. What's he thinking? can he know what I'm thinking? what's that thing of looking into each other's eyes? We never know what the other is truly thinking, when we kiss, when we speak, when we come, Elizabeth said, come, when we say we don't want to die. We arch à l'unisson, bodies gorged with lifeblood, nos visages se convulsent, our voices pierce the silence, the bodies release. He smiles with his eyes, the tip of his tongue drinks the bead of sweat pooling dans mon sillon naso-labial, right at the edge of the upper lip.

I sleep a little. He moves in the apartment, autumn light slants across the living room. Everything quiet. He sits cross-legged beside me.

On est bien ensemble, hein? he says.

I remind him about those strings to which he never wanted to be attached, that summer of Expo, Claudette Lalancette promised him, no strings attached, his eyes shone with relief. This afternoon, his eyes shine with a new light, on est bien ensemble, he said that twice in the last few days, what does he mean? He gets up to make green tea, tea is discreet, doesn't scent a room like coffee. He comes back with two steaming bowls, puts one over my navel, the ceramic warms my belly, he never noticed the needle scars, discreet white dots ringing the birthspot. He reclines on his side, we look at each other, he whispers in my ear, the apartment, very quiet.

Je t'aime, Ariane Claude.

He whispers that, je t'aime. I close my eyes. End of research.

L'amour fou. I tear down the steps of le Musée, am supercharged with excitement resolve, can't wait to try out the gold purchased. Smooth purl. How will I bead? How will I do it? The expert said, goldwork is painstaking work. L'amour de Pierre. What to do with that new appetite?

With Gérard, Margot Joly eats in long-established Montréal restaurants, in new cafés, dans des petits bistros sympathiques. This summer with Ana, she recovered son appétit de jeune femme before she married Dead Man. She even risked a lamb brochette dans un restaurant grec. More than a year after the lamb incident. Reconciliations take time. Maman and the lamb are fully reconciled.

Gérard et Margot drink Dubonnet dans le grand salon, she bought a bottle for the occasion, no sweet syrupy peach brandy. Un apéritif avec glaçons et zeste de citron in her fancy cut-glass tumblers. Last December, Elizabeth began to pay maman courtesy calls, she called those visits, so Margot would know what kind of woman was taking her daughter on a world tour. On each visit, Ariane 1967 leaned on the mantelpiece. Like Christmas decorations, that Ariane was seasonal. This October, Gérard et Margot sit on the brocaded chest-her-field, their bodies turned at an angle toward each other, their knees not touching. Last December, Elizabeth and maman are having tea dans le grand salon, they sit on the brocaded chest-her-field, their bodies turned at an angle toward each other, their knees almost touching.

Margot et Gérard se font des confidences. I sit dans le boudoir to hear their words. No brass vents distortion. He tells her Elizabeth was an extraordinarily energetic woman, not passionate in the usual sense of the word, but endlessly curious about all of life. He had no right to deny her her appetite, as bound to her as the colour of her eyes. But he doesn't need that much emotional extravagance. He craves la simplicité des choses, like sleep after a long walk.

What I mean to say is, maman says to Elizabeth, it's not about not seeing, not hearing, not feeling. It's about not revealing.

I understand that, Elizabeth says. It's choosing what to say.

Not so much what to say. But to whom.

Margot tells Gérard, many years ago after her husband died, she thought she was lonely and felt obliged to begin an affair with her married boss. The briefest of encounters. Much too complicated, la dichotomie, day work and evening intimacy. She broke off cette liaison superficielle, but told her boss she had a daughter to raise alone and needed the job. If he ever fired her for no good office reason, she would tell his wife, ce qui était ridicule, because the wife knew all along. But in a way, the affair never ended, as Rita refused to believe her younger sister simply worked Saturdays to make extra money. Rita kept urging her to find a husband, but she refused to marry only for the security of a man's paycheque. D'ailleurs, Margot found her own way. She moved through the corporeal corporate ranks, from rock bottom to rarefied top. Skills, hard work, initiative. Between the lines, what she doesn't tell Gérard, I hear loud and clear. Her position, secure, as she holds her boss, the former lover, by the ballroom. No need to squeeze hard. Just run things with a firm hand. Margot, the indispensable woman.

Maman, la spécialiste de la discrétion, examines Elizabeth's suit du coin de l'œil. She recognizes something. After Elizabeth leaves, I tell her, look at it this way, ma retouche au féminin saved the black suit, moths are munching on the two other fifties suits, bientôt, yarn by yarn, the wool will be gone, like flesh that has fallen off, revealing

skeletons in her closet, of satin lining and buckram interfac-
ing, lengths of thread no longer stitching tweed sleeves and
herringbone lapels will dangle off wooden hangers like torn
spider webs. That's when she said, what's the point of being
upset? still speaking Elizabeth's English.

Gérard et Margot se font des confidences en français. The
skylight du boudoir is soaking up October evening darkness.
Je ferme les yeux pour mieux écouter.

L'amour libre? she says. Comme si l'amour esclave était
une option.

In July, drinking iced tea in the bathtub, eating
Neapolitan ice cream at midnight, maman metamorphosing.
With Elizabeth, she becomes Margot Lalancette, veuve et
femme au travail, with Ana, Margot Joly, femme émancipée
who discovers le théâtre expérimental, with Gérard
L'Heureux, Margot Joly, femme joliment heureuse with a
man craving la simplicité.

I lean on the oak doorway du grand salon. They're examining the two silver vases.

1826, I say.

Exact, Gérard says, reading the bottom. Fabriqués à
Sheffield.

He runs his finger along the dresses des bergères who
came all the way from Dresden, sure of himself, he tells us the
figurines were smuggled out before the bombing. Les
bergères escaped being burned sur le bûcher de la Deuxième
Guerre. He scrutinizes the landscape and seascape paintings
to decipher the artist's signature, a hint of fauvisme, will find
provenance.

After Christmas, Elizabeth and maman in the dining
room drink tea in cups of translucent clay and bone ash, quiz
each other between bites of fruitcake, a hint of complicity on
their breath.

You speak English very well, Margot.

And do you speak French, Elizabeth?

Je pense, as if that were the most important factor in taking the daughter on a world tour.

I understand the language perfectly, Elizabeth says. I read
with pleasure and can write without too much of a struggle,
but speak French only when necessary. It gives me migraines.

Speaking French gives you a headache?

In France, I had the most frightful headaches and, I assure
you, Margot, I'm no hypochondriac.

It was the winter mistral, I say, joking.

I've no head for speaking languages. We're learning simple words for the trip. It makes me sick to hear myself.

Je pense, does maman have an accent, do I have an
accent, is it atrocious? Our accents show provenance. No
cause for headaches.

Gérard et Margot tour the flat as museum. They view the
collection of twenty-four bronze horses, the Susie Cooper
art deco dinner set for twelve, on the sideboard the two cats,
one black one white, not plaster? non, jais et albâtre, de
Chine, environ 1890, the crystal and silverware, même les
meubles, mahogany and ebony, and, dans le boudoir, the thirties office furniture. Margot Joly showing her possessions,
unlike her to show off. Gérard l'antiquaire confirms,
Margot's things have value.

Ariane m'a apporté de belles pièces, l'hiver dernier, he
says.

Oui, mes cadeaux de mariage. Ces cadeaux et tout ça,
Margot says, sweeping the flat with her arms, toutes ces
choses héritées de la famille de mon mari.

Je pense, heirloom from the gloomy La Lancets. Heirs
looming on the loom. I had no idea.

Ce n'est pas moi, ça, Gérard, she says. Pas moi pour un
sou.

Je pense, trapped in family tapestry.

Maman and Elizabeth no longer sit stiffly dans le grand
salon on the edge of the chest-her-field, no longer sit dain-

tily in the dining room on the high-back chairs, the damask tablecloth between them. When I come home from school that day in early March, I find them in the kitchen, the ceiling light glaring, les hangars and the clotheslines casting dull shadows, they drink strong Salada tea in the one-dollar-a-dozen white mugs, a few with chipped rims, two without handles, all tea-stained. Elizabeth, as relaxed in our kitchen as in her own, blowing smoke toward our white ceiling. That was the last time she came up for a cuppa. Ariane 1967 moved back dans le hangar.

Gérard et Margot are going to dinner at Les Halles in the Mercury, this, the last night before it settles into hibernation. Because the roof doesn't close, he puts sa grandiose minoune in storage for winter and leases an ordinary box on wheels with a good heater. Tonight, Margot is going out in style.

Bonne soirée, I say, leaning over the railing of the interior staircase.

As they walk down, Gérard tells Margot he'll be fifty at the end of the month. What does it mean Gérard telling Margot that he'll turn fifty in October 1969? Like provenance announced before acquisition. Peut-être aux Halles, Gérard will say, je t'aime, Margot. Pierre just said, je t'aime, Ariane Claude. Will Margot be startled by love revealed?

Today, at the western edge of parc Lafontaine, no cop's shadow startling, no hem unravelling, but crowds of students unravel the rules à la nouvelle université erected in the park like a gypsy camp. Au collège, we played at changes too, occupied les bureaux de l'Administration, on a organisé un sit-in, sprawled on the floor, defiant, the guys looked up the secretary's miniskirt as she stepped over our legs, like fallen logs in the forest. Today, I visit le Pavillon Lafontaine, all my life across the street from home I knew the building as l'École normale Jacques-Cartier where teachers taught young people to become teachers, sûrement, these new students will absorb from the walls all the learning they need.

I'm doing research pour l'opéra rock contestation, nobody pays attention, les étudiants think I belong, they smoke in the corridors and classrooms, I sit with the noisy crowd, they say crisse like they're mon oncle Joseph, this, l'université du peuple, boys and girls, garbed in army surplus jackets, push smoke out of their mouths like they're Elizabeth, debate how the teacher should teach linguistics, la langue, c'est important, le prof stands in front of the class, les étudiants won't allow him to teach his way, they demand new ways, he knows best, they resist his knowledge, c'est ça, la contestation, I listen, any second, something will be revealed, end of class, no revelation, they leave, I follow, on rue Sherbrooke, they gather, clouds to form the storm, this, le mouvement étudiant, the rumble to clear the air, charged with electricity, difficult to decide what to change first, I know what they mean, where to begin, where to end, creativity takes practice, demands risks, j'ai une idée, run to le Café de l'horloge with my idea on the tip of my tongue.

Des Québécois fleurdelisés! Pierre and Raymond shout at the same time.

Jérôme offers a new line of teas from around the world. Pierre drinks Japanese tea, Jérôme brings me Lapsang sou-chong that tastes of woodsmoke, Raymond sips Earl Grey in defiance, Pierre tells us about the ugly tea trade les Anglais did with les Indiens et les Chinois in the nineteenth century, one day, he'll make a documentary, I speak above their voices, urge them to listen, my chorus, des gars et des filles peints de la tête aux pieds avec le drapeau fleurdelisé, no clothes, that'll be the costume for the chorus, it's un opéra, we need un chœur, non, too traditional, but but, not revolu-tionary enough, listen to me, un chœur de Québécois fleur-delisés sera un énorme succès, toute cette nudité et le drapeau fleurdelisé, Pierre shakes his head, peut-être, there's a symbol in that, Raymond strokes his new bushy handlebar mous-tache, that means he'll say yes, non, non? he sidetracks resists, insists his fisher people, students, factory workers will be clothed, sinon, the audience won't listen to the words.

They try on various prototypes. I mention mon oncle Joseph, oui, il est le prototype parfait de l'ouvrier, they can draw a character based on him. Bravo, my ideas are on the right track. I suggest la madame aux culottes d'hommes, Pierre explains la madame to Raymond, Raymond thinks she has potential.

Du potentiel! I shout.

A woman working for minimum wage in poor conditions on the clothing assembly line, that's exploitation incarnate. Jérôme comes to sit with us.

Les affaires roulent, he says.

I think he means with l'opéra rock, I tell him my chorus is gagged.

Bientôt, he says, je vais ouvrir mon deuxième café des arts.

I congratulate him on starting his chain of cafés so soon. Jérôme, a man of action, not just dreaming with his eyes open. And next thing I know, he's offering me a job.

What about the girl with no name?

Elle est partie en Gaspésie, he says. Elle est allée rejoindre la gang à la Maison du pêcheur.

Pierre, ears always tuned to the smallest vibration, leaves l'opéra rock to dive into the wave of change sweeping our Eastern coast.

Ah, I say. La révolution de la morue.

That quip draws no laugh, those people by the sea mean serious damage, nous nageons en eau trouble, for sure, they'll reject my idea, mon chœur est à l'eau, dead drowned. It may be a good idea for me to earn honest money, not get involved in pie-eyed-in-the-sky projects. D'ailleurs, a good waitress wastes no steps. I can learn that, measured steps. A good waitress listens to her customers' stories. I want to learn that, measured speak. I tell Jérôme, oui, but want to think about it a little. He squeezes my left shoulder, goes back behind his zinc-topped counter. I go look for fabric.

We have no budget, I tell le monsieur juif.

In his store on avenue du Mont-Royal, he's drinking tea with a friend, another old monsieur juif, that one has a long grey beard and shiny black eyes. The store owner pours tea for me in a tall narrow glass inserted in a metal holder with a fancy handle, Russian tea, he tells me, black and sweet, scented with spices and citrus peel.

Will you feature real people? he asks.

Non. We'll use actors who're starting out. Bien sûr, we can't pay them, but young artists expect that. D'ailleurs, it's for la Cause.

I can tell, he's disappointed. What does he expect, un opéra rock-vérité with real people doing real jobs struggling for real in real life? This is a show. Quand même, he may have a point, he's old enough to know.

Theatres are expensive to rent, his friend says, sipping.

Too straight for us, I say. I'd like to stage dans une manu-facture. You know, a factory where many women work in tight rows at industrial sewing machines making clothes pour une bouchée de pain. Crumbs.

He nods. That he knows, clothing factories and fabric, he calls that the schmattah trade. The fabric man spells the word for me, s-c-h-m-a-t-t-a-h. They think it's a good idea to stage in a schmattah factory. But Raymond wants to perform on the street, oui, mais, my chorus of naked Québécois fleur-delisés will be arrested pour outrage public à la pudeur, Pierre says, c'est du théâtre engagé. We haven't settled on anything yet.

I browse through the remnants le monsieur juif throws pêle-mêle in cardboard drums, prospect strata of bolts stacked to the tin ceiling, climb the ladder, pull a bolt here, how much is this? a bolt there, how much is that? I'll buy so many yards of that pink and orange psychedelic polyester, so many yards of that mauve nylon, so many yards of that green tulle. How much?

Sit, sit, mademoiselle, he says, pouring me another glass of tea. Let's negotiate.

I sit, we negotiate. I'm in a bazaar on avenue du Mont-Royal, drinking Russian tea in tall glasses with old men who deal in schmattah, haggling, mon monsieur juif says, haggling, I'm learning another tongue, get all that fabric for a song. Le monsieur with the grey beard gives me a peck on the cheek, tells me he dabbled in the theatre in his yoot, the fabric man gives me a pat on the ass, les deux monsieurs smile, their dark eyes sparkle.

T'en fais pas, mademoiselle, the fabric man says. Only the waning desire of old men.

I open the door, the little copper bell rings.

Au revoir, messieurs, I say, loaded like a she-ass.

Shalom, both men sing.

Spoons sing in glasses like copper bells. In Pierre's apartment, Pierre and Raymond drink Indian tea with milk and spices. Earlier, we smoked a fat joint, my throat's not burning anymore, they said, s'ils sont gelés, ils vont écrire avec leurs tripes, that's why we smoked the joint, so their guts could do the writing. I spread the fabric on the floor, try to imagine prototypes in tulle, la madame aux culottes d'hommes at her sewing machine, sainte viarge, the pirate girl in her hospital pour les incurables, whatever, Marie the teacher trapped in her classroom, in-ter-mi-na-ble, mon oncle Joseph in his machine shop, crisse, characters singing of their pain and hope and dreams and doubts, electric guitars wailing, drums pounding, Robert Charlebois sings hard on Pierre's turntable, the trick is to draw no blood, prototypes with rainbow-capped fingers, peut-être, lights shining through the coloured thread, that means they'd have to be wired, we're creating un opéra rock contestation, on fait sauter les murs. Can we do that, faire sauter les murs and draw no blood? Pierre and Raymond are arguing, les mots abstraits de la révolution contre les émotions en chair et en os de la vie. I invent free-form people in lengths of fabric. They argue, doubt their originality, we only steal from one another, declare everything a perpetual copy, they decide uniqueness doesn't exist.

Il faut mettre Elizabeth dans l'opéra, I say, twisting a length of nylon into a reclining figure.

Non non non non non, Pierre says. Cent fois non. Elizabeth, c'est pour mon film. On ne mélange pas les carottes et les oranges, ma puce.

Elizabeth n'est pas une carotte, I say.

C'est un opéra, Raymond says, pas une salade.

And he takes that opportunity to tell me to forget the chorus.

I crumple my bolts back into the bag, walk out, they don't notice, people notice nothing. That collaboration's for the birds.

And Ana invites us downstairs for a fowl supper. I know she doesn't mean a disgusting meal.

Husa, she says. Special treat.

Où ça? I repeat. That's not a problem. We can have it here, of course. We have lots of room.

No, no, she says, laughing. Not où ça. Husa.

It's like Christmas! Lenka says.

You should not have, Ariane, Ana says.

Why not? I say. Toys are made to be played with. Those have been sitting in a closet upstairs with nothing to do for years. It's my pleasure to give them to Lenka and Pavel. Except for a miniature sewing machine. Black cast iron and heavy. A pretty little thing. Didn't have a bobbin though. When I played seamstress, the thread kept bunching up underneath the small squares of fabric I tried to sew. I keep that toy as a reminder of beginnings.

Much kindness. Thank you.

Lenka and Pavel tear open the boxes, shout with each dis-covery. The five dolls, the doll house fully furnished, the con-struction set from England with hundreds of pieces and a booklet of plans to build dozens of variations on the English cottage, the xylophone, the train set, the doctor's kit, the fake fur, plastic jewellery, and plastic shoes pour jouer à la madame, the microscope, the porcelain tea set, the View Master, all in mint-green condition. They shriek and say děkuji a lot.

Margot brought wine and the bottle of Dubonnet, ma tante Rita, a jar of her famous petits cornichons maison, mon oncle, sa verve des grands soirs. The kitchen smells of cab-bage and roasting fowl.

Goose, Ana says to Rita. Taste, better than turkey.

Je suis certaine que c'est délicieux, ma tante says. Au moins, c'est pas du canard sauvage, she whispers to Margot.

The table is set for eight. Karel lifts a corner of the white tablecloth to reveal a door lengthening the everyday table, mon oncle says, crisse, convinced a miracle has happened, on aura beau dire, we live in different cultures, we think alike. Karel confesses he had a hard time removing the door han-dle, Lenka didn't know how to resolve the matter of door handles when transforming doors into tables. He reveals the tablecloth is a sheet.

À la bonne franquette, he enunciates, imitating.

Ma tante laughs and understands, mon oncle says, crisse, not sure what to think.

Children repeat everything, Ana says. Around children, secrets, better kept inside heart.

Les enfants, crisse, ont des oreilles comme des portes de grange, mon oncle says.

After Margot translates la grange for our hosts, they think we wire farm buildings to Eve's drop on people's secrets, a practice that seems perfectly normal to them. Mon oncle thinks it's a good idea to electrocute la vermine that eats crops. That jolts his memory of the epic of the kitchen faucet and his close brush with death by vicious bite. Ana smiles, Karel's eyes shine with anticipation, ma tante rolls her eyes, Margot makes a conciliatory face.

I'm on my back under the kitchen sink, Joseph says, and a rat the size of a tomcat comes out of nowhere. For a second, we lock eyes and that thing, crisse, just runs up my pants leg.

Mon oncle paces up and down, wipes his lips, like the residue of words foaming at the mouth.

I almost lost the will to live, vous comprenez, with that thing inside my pants sniffing at my manhood. But I was quicker than the rat. I gave it a good whack with my wrench. Crisse, I broke the rat's back and cracked my thigh bone too. I don't mind telling you, I didn't care if I didn't go dancing for a couple of months.

Ana and Karel find the anecdote encouragingly funny, on the heels of the rat, mon oncle offers the one about the cockroach in the bathtub, Margot lays a gentle hand on his arm.

What's the occasion, Ana? she asks.

To thank you for kindness. Ariane babysitting children. Two times. Rita and Joseph giving them meal Sunday of concert.

Mais voyons, Ana, Rita says. Ça nous a fait plaisir.

That was my fault, I say. Had to change a flat tire.

Margot pours Dubonnet, je pense, ah, debts of honour to repay, old-world ways on these new shores, nous trinquons, to new friends, nous buvons. Karel uncaps bottles of Plzeňské, not easy to find in Montréal, mon oncle reads the label, tries the pronunciation, Karel coaches him, not easy, that language, his accent, as atrocious as Elizabeth's, words, as difficult to wield as chopsticks. We move to the living room, the children to their room to play, Karel and mon oncle gesticulate in front of the mute ancestors on the corridor wall, they down beer and spill words at the same speed, they discover they both talk about everything on the same register, everything an epic, politics, cars, religion, fishing, the wiring of buildings, strikes, sports, prison for speaking the wrong words, the cost of living. Karel is now free to be a set designer to his heart's content, he is, but has lost the will, too old to start over, mon oncle's sad too, he can't be a yoot in this day and age, too late for him too, he calls les jeunes des pouilleux with their long hair, but those are camouflage words, he grows sideburns to show sa solidarité, mon oncle, born too soon, Karel laments, they came here for the children, Ana's still young, she can reconstruct, it wasn't easy, the bribes, the forms, in the end they deny you exit papers, you have to go through the bureaucratic contortions all over again, for no reason, because they're glad to get rid of orphans and old men, not that old, crisse, Joseph, Karel, of the same generation, but not from the same world, so hard to leave everything behind, learn a new language, new ways, life's an abomination, crisse.

No fighting, I say, going to the kids' room. The toys are to be shared equally.

I don't want dolls! Pavel says, puffing up his eight-year-old chest.

Don't be silly. Those dolls can be warrior queens.

He shakes his head, warrior queens exist in their legends.

They can explore galaxies, dive to the ocean floor. You're lucky. I had no brothers or sisters to play with.

What games did you play? Lenka asks.

Let's see. Maman sometimes played, not often and only when I was very small. On her knees, she washes the floor of the corridor, little Claudette jumps on her back, à cheval, maman! grand galop! maman's back arches and kicks, plus haut, maman cheval, plus haut, time to dismount, maman cheval must finish washing the floor. I invented my own games and my own playmates. I was queen and high priestess, le comte de Monte-Cristo and Radisson, I explored the seven seas. The long sea voyage along the dark passage of the corridor, we are dying of thirst on salt water, are attacked by giant sea rats, à table, Claudette, maman calls like a siren, terre! terre! we land on Kitchen Island, vegetable soup saves us from hunger from thirst, we crush four saltines in the soup, many sailors fell overboard, eaten by fish and things, we shake pepper in the soup for the drowned sailors, we chew carrot coins, les écus de la reine, swallow paper-thin celery slices, the words from secret messages, line the pasta alphabet on the spoon, invented words. The paper Christmas table-cloth, ripped, Marie-Antoinette wrapped in paper reindeer lays her neck on a chair, feels the serrated blade of the bread-knife guillotine, pushes the blade against the white skin, what are you doing? maman asks, saving Marie-Antoinette from la guillotine, nothing, just playing.

Teach us games, Ariane, Pavel says.

What were your games in Bohemia?

We had rocking horses, Lenka says. Šemík, we called them. Painted red and white with yellow manes. They burned in the fire.

Mon oncle found a kindred spirit in Karel, their words, stories of struggle, dreams thwarted, loud assault on all things absurd, I can't hear the substance of their speak, only the tone of shared tragedies while getting joyously plastered.

We have cousins in Czekoslovakia, Lenka says. We'll never see them again.

I have cousins too, I say. Rita's and Joseph's daughters. But Ginette's twelve years older and Georgette, seven years older than me. I don't remember them as cousins, only as women living in Toronto, a city nobody wants to visit. One Saturday, I tell ma tante my new friends Nicole et Diane have broth-ers and sisters, and zillions of cousins in Rivière-du-Loup, how come there's only ma tante and maman in our family? This time, she doesn't say, never mind, là. She reminds me my maternal grandparents died before I started school.

Did they die in a fire? Pavel asks.

Non. They just died. I don't remember them. That Saturday, ma tante tells me her mother tried to have more children in the ten years between ma tante's birth and maman's birth, but the babies kept dying. No fire. That happened often in those days. Ma tante stops rolling the dough, she's making blueberry pies, and she looks very surprised. Ha! The dead babies were all boys. She had never thought about that before. She resumes rolling the dough, absent-in-her-mind, puts the top crust over the bottom crust, I tell her she forgot to spoon in the filling, she looks at the pie not believing me, pulls the top crust off the plate, like peeling skin off a shoulder after a sunburn, and bursts out laughing, shrieking so hard mon oncle runs into the kitchen with his wrench. Crisse, has a rat jumped on Rita? After, for a long time, I could never eat pie without lifting a corner of the top crust to count how many dead babies were sitting in the shell.

We crowd around the table-door, tablecloth-sheet, bite into the first course, the crisp flesh of deep-fried carp, a Czech delicacy, Karel tells us, difficult to find in Montréal before December, we struggle with the bones, mon oncle, carried away par les transports de l'alcool, launches into a fish story.

I had caught le plus gros brochet de ma vie. Brochet, Margot? What's brochet in English?

She shrugs.

En tout cas. Le maudit poisson, crisse, had bitten two baits at once and the fisherman in the other rowboat was reeling it his way and I was reeling it my way and the fish in the middle, crisse, was thrashing and keeping both chaloupes from moving. I shouted, lâche mon brochet. The guy shouted, c'est mon brochet. In the end, the fish solved the problem. He bit off both lines and swam away. When we docked, the guy turned out to be un bon gars. Un brochet de perdu, bah!

there're other fish where that one came from. We had a good laugh and I invited him over pour une petite bière. Margot and the guy hit it off. And here, he says, pointing at me, is the result of that lost fish.

The fishman was Ariane's dad? Lenka asks.

That's right, ma petite. Too bad he met that bus on his way to work. Now, that, he says to Karel, that, my friend, is an absurd story if you ever heard one.

Never mind, là, Joseph, Rita says. Mange ta carpe.

Margot wipes her mouth with her napkin.

I have an announcement, she says. Je veux casser maison.

Next spring, she tells us, she'll move out. She has all winter to look for a bright, modern apartment on a quiet street with mature trees. She asked Gérard to appraise and sell the objects d'art, the cumbersome furniture, the lot. That was never her life. She looks at Ana who nods.

Ariane gave me the idea, Margot continues. First, the living room drapes, then, the wedding dress, finally, my dead husband's suit she altered for her friend Elizabeth. And, last but not least, the wedding gifts.

Seigneur de la vie, ma tante says, her hand at her throat.

Et ce n'est pas tout, Rita, Margot says.

She tells her sister the flat needs a thorough cleaning, a coat of paint, a few repairs. She and Ana talked to the landlord. They came to an agreement. Ana and her family will move upstairs. Besides, the kids are growing. They should have their own bedrooms. The way Ana and Karel nod, that's no news to them. Déjà, such complicity.

Next May, Ana says, we move. Margot explained. May first, day for moving in all Québec. Margot also told us, no need to notify police. People are free. To move in new apartment in same building or across country. It makes no difference. Police does not need to know.

Joseph commiserates, quel scandale! the way millions of people are forced to live in this day and age et tout ça à cause de la maudite politique, Rita cuts him off with more urgent matters.

Et Gérard L'Heureux? she asks her sister.

Gérard Štastný! Lenka shouts. We have that name too.

Margot teases. Non, Rita, Gérard's not moving upstairs.

Et Claudette, elle, dans tout ça? ma tante asks.

Naturellement, I'm not pushing Ariane out. Elle déménage avec moi.

Not sure, I say. Me too, I need air. Time to move out on my own.

Ana and Karel approve. They know about new air.

Crisse, Margot, mon oncle says, staring into his beer.

Oui, mais, ma tante says, Gérard L'Heureux, là?

Štastný! both kids yell, giggling.

Margot laughs. It'll take days for ma tante to absorb les grandes nouvelles. Her sister consorting avec des étrangers before telling la famille, her sister befriending neighbours, her sister giving up the flat of a lifetime and selling her precious things.

Margot and I exchange a knowing smile. That's how we become visible and occur to ourselves. I became visible in my white gypsy skirt, occurred to myself learning to speak to strangers. And now, Margot Joly is occurring to herself.

Crisse, le temps passe, mon oncle says, putting his hand on top of ma tante's hand.

We eat the husa with bread dumplings and sweet and sour red cabbage. Karel passes a bowl of orange mushrooms, we sniff the scent of butter and forest decay.

Eat, eat, he says. Safe.

He tells us mushroom picking is a national pastime in his country. The first thing they did when they arrived in Canada was to learn about local varieties. Mon oncle digs in avec emphase, Margot tries one, finds the fungus tasty, Rita takes a tiny bite, Lenka laughs behind her hand, Pavel considers his mushroom in the candlelight.

Was that the same bus that took your dad to the jungle to be eaten? he asks me.

Qu'est-ce qu'il raconte? ma tante asks.

He wasn't eaten, Lenka says, rolling her eyes. He got shot hunting. Maybe he slipped on a mushroom and his gun went off.

Qu'est-ce que c'est ces histoires à dormir debout? ma tante wants to know. Margot?

Margot shakes her head.

Non, non, mon oncle says to the kids. Ariane's dad s'est fait happer par un autobus. Happer, happer. It doesn't mean heureux. It means that, he says, striking his palms together to show impact. Mort à cause de sa claque, crisse. Au Québec, the word claque means two things. First, it's a slap in the face. And une paire de claques is a double slap, with the flat of the hand, then the back of the hand. Like that. In one motion.

Pár facek! the four Czechs shout together.

Pár facek, we repeat, delighted.

Nous dansons sur notre pont culturel. Mon oncle says, on est humain partout, but is quick to add they probably don't have a word for the second meaning of claques.

Those, he says, are a pair of rubber soles with a narrow lip men wear over their dress shoes and they keep losing at bus stops, sucked in the slush when they step on buses, you've seen those. Non? Winter's coming. When there'll be lots of mushy snow, have a look. En tout cas. That day, snow was melting, a real mess at bus stops, crisse. Léo was late for work, he ran like the devil, the bus was out of service, he didn't know that, the bus didn't stop, he bent down in front of it to get one of his claques stuck in the slush, the driver didn't see him. Paf! Joseph shouts, hitting his hands together. Crisse, he's pinned right under the wheels. The poor bugger's in shock. C'est naturel. Witnesses said he kept shouting, j'ai ma claque! j'ai ma claque! Like he got slapped by the bus. Crisse. When they got him out, he was holding sa claque to his chest like a treasure.

My mouth hangs open, Margot's face has paled, Rita fait les gros yeux, Ana and Karel bow their heads, the kids sit motionless. Something's not quite right, but Joseph, not sure what's happening, downs his beer. Pauvre mon oncle, he has no clue maman never told me. Will he get an earful! I see him and ma tante in the Buick later, ce ne sont pas des choses à dire, she'll say, et devant des étrangers, he'll wonder what the fuss is about. Either ma tante will tell him I didn't know and, to prove he didn't put his foot in his mouth, he'll shout that Margot had a duty to tell her daughter, had no reason to be ashamed or embarrassed, people don't choose their deaths, that was an accident, it happens all the time, or she'll do damage control by saying, never mind. Either way, demain, she'll phone her sister, ça, c'est certain. Either way, I'm on mon oncle's side. For him, c'est de l'histoire ancienne, and it should be for all of us. The passage of time allows him the story. Time transforms human tragedy into le théâtre de l'absurde. Et la vie continue.

So, Lenka says to me. Your daddy didn't die in a crash in his own car either, did he? Is your rat story true? she asks Joseph.

You bet your boots. C'est la pure vérité, he says, his hand on his heart.

When do we know when your stories are true or not? Pavel asks me.

When I tell you so, I say. I told you those stories were invented.

I like the one where he was eaten, he says.

Maman bursts out laughing. Not a hurt laugh. Not a release laugh. A simple, happy laugh that carries us into its ripples and breaks the spell. She looks at me, shakes her head, I nod, comme d'habitude, we fill in the blanks. Karel pours more beer, we finish eating, Margot declares everything delicious, she ate avec grand appétit, the children lick their plates like wolves, run to their room to play with their new toys, the kitchen smells of roast meat and celebration, we feel

excitement in the air, like static electricity, all at once, everyone stops talking, peut-être, we want to listen to the mood.
The sudden silence startles us.

Un ange passe, ma tante whispers.

Crisse, le temps passe, mon oncle repeats, kissing his wife.

Ana pours tea in glasses she slips into metal holders. I
wonder if she knows le monsieur juif. The kids come back
to the table, we eat apple strudel, they lift the layers of flaky
pastry with their forks to peer at the golden fruit, the way
they devour, they fancy themselves ogres in a dark forest,
gobbling up lost children. They run back to their games,
icing sugar under their noses.

Ana plays thirties tunes on a black upright piano, Rita's
sweet singing voice fills the small flat, Joseph and Karel do
harmony, Margot Joly chante avec abandon. They're back in
their yoot, Ana and Karel in Bohemia, Margot, Rita, and
Joseph in a Montréal that no longer exists. And tonight, at
the close of this decade, a time for change, they all meet on
these new shores. They sing, the children play invent secret
games, their dolls dressed in foil, ready for a long voyage far
away. Where am I going?

Not to bed, not yet. Margot sits in our kitchen, drinking
a last cup of tea. She pours me one. I stir honey and press a
wedge of lemon. The tea bleaches.

She remembers once I was sewing in my room, she heard
the box of pins fall, my growl of frustration, she was on her
way out, I bent over the railing and asked, pourquoi les gens
meurent-ils?

I tell her I remember vaguely, the pins fanning on the
floor, her on the stairs gripping the handrail to prevent a slip.

Je t'ai répondu, she says, parce que les gens sont distraits.

Ah, oui?

Ce n'est pas ce que j'ai dit?

I tell her I remember she cautioned me about all those
pins on the floor, because of my habit of walking barefoot.

We sip.

I tell her I thought Dead Man died crazy, because, once, she let words slip. Il est parti pour la gloire. At first, I thought he died in the Second World War, but people don't hide that, besides, he was too young for that war. Then, I thought, être parti pour la gloire meant être fou à lier, and he died à l'asile. That made sense, because people are usually tight-lipped about madness in the family. Donc, peut-être, I inherited sa folie. Quoi qu'il en soit, I wasn't particularly curious about him in his life, because he never had substance for me. So, I played at inventing all kinds of deaths for him. It meant nothing. I tell her the only thing that bothered me was the terrible burden she had to bear alone, whatever the secret, and I wanted us to share that weight, but she never let me.

It was no burden, Ariane, she says in English. We learn to live with our dead. You will too, in time. C'est un apprentissage, au jour le jour.

I know that now. I remind her she never allowed little Claudette in her bed, for whatever reason, thunder, devils, sirens, monsters.

Tu me disais, I say, tu ne dois pas avoir peur du noir.

Je pense, you mustn't fear your aloneness. That, I don't.

I wanted to be alone, Pierre wouldn't let me. He came walking with me sur le mont Royal.

Tu as froid? he asks, ready to give me his coat.

Non, I say, shivering.

The day is overcast, après tout, c'est déjà novembre, the cold wind sneaks under my decomposing skirt. I just told Pierre about Karel, a set designer of great experience, he'd give good advice for the show, Pierre doesn't want old guys on the project.

Oui, mais, I say, c'est un dissident.

Je pensais, cette appellation will give Karel all the credentials he needs with the young underground crowd. But Pierre dismissed that. Now, he tells me about a dizzying crosscutting technique for his film that will show Elizabeth's life spiralling toward sa fin inévitable.

Qu'est-ce que tu en penses? he asks.

I can't say. My mind's elsewhere. He hesitates, stops walking, looks me straight in the eye, takes a deep breath like he's about to dive.

Veux-tu venir vivre avec moi, Ariane? he asks, exhaling.

That is a deep dive. He may have hit his head on the bottom, he looks that stunned.

Pierre's and Raymond's project together. Viens avec nous, they invited. What am I to them? A muse or an equal? I'll end up playing la muse. Ariane, le trait d'union entre Pierre et Raymond. Ariane, la fille dans le milieu. La muse qui amuse. Raymond said something like that the first time we met. Do I want to be un trait d'union? Do I want to be une conjonction?

Réfléchis, he says, holding me by the shoulder. Prends tout le temps qu'il te faut.

D'abord, l'amour de Pierre. And now, this. Living together. What do I do with that?

Passage

Elizabeth, allô, c'est moi. A little out of breath. You're hard to find, Woman. Couldn't remember your postdeath address.

Came to speak to you, one last time. Déjà, December dusk. Gates close early. Winter hours. Shiver. Your hands, blocks of ice, you swore you weren't cold. Are you still immune, down there? Will breathe the air for you, look at the bare trees for you. Snow hasn't fallen. Pas encore. Last spring in your garden. Snow melting. Le lilas embaumait l'air, you're embalmed now. What's the smell in your underground city? Garden earth after snowmelt? after a summer shower? Your body staining your white satin. What's your secret scent now?

This skirt. Coming apart. Le tissu est mûr. Can you hear? Silk taffeta rips in frigid air. RIP, Elizabeth. Your body so damaged. Impossible à réparer. Another strip falling off. Bientôt, no more gypsy skirt. Wore it non-stop, for you. That too must end.

Bringing news.

How often do the living bother showing the dead their final day? This, Elizabeth, your day.

Gérard, l'amour fou. Gérard, fou de peine. His body suffering comme un écorché vif. His heart haemorrhaging in two languages. Sa colère at your death. His fury at the

damage done to your body. His outrage at your pain, too
much to bear. He's beyond normal feelings. Son outrage, like
we say, outre-mer, outre-tombe. We, Elizabeth, should be
outre-mer. You're outre-tombe since June. Apologies.

 The day of your burial, Gérard, feverish but sharp. Tiré à
quatre épingles in a tailored black suit, a fresh white shirt and
a red silk tie. His black shoes so polished they shine in the sun
like jet. Later, we meet where your life ended, his skin flushed,
he hasn't washed, hasn't changed since les funérailles. But the
day of your burial, he reminds me of a man in a painting from
la Renaissance. His black hair streaked with silver combed
back, as if wearing an ancient helmet. His pale bony face
accented by the deep lines carving the skin between nose and
mouth. His beauty heightened by his loss. Ah, Elizabeth,
you're loved by such a man. Apologies to both of you.

 Waiting for the ceremony. No one talks. You, no longer
on the ground to link us.

 Nancy and Mike read the oldest headstones. The names
and dates nearly worn out. Those dead, invisible now. The
living who knew them, no longer alive, no longer responsible for them. And so, rain and wind and frost erase their
names from the stones.

 Pauline and Moffat examine the trees. His beard floats
fluffy-clean in the breeze. He tells Pauline cemeteries have
the healthiest trees. Il a raison. The roots seek the mineral-
rich juices of the dead. Like tongues, lick lap the nutrients.
Two rows of trees shade the alley below your grave. In June,
the branches formed a green canopy. The sap of the dead had
the long summer to rise out of the ground into the leaves.
To see the light. To feel the warmth. Was it too soon for your
sap to rise? Now the leaves are on the ground, the dead back
in their underground city. L'été prochain, Elizabeth, you who
loved light, will see the light again.

 Pierre and Raymond sit at the base of a huge tree with
boughs that invite climbing. Your private tree to shelter you,

for you to climb as often as you wish. A basswood, Moffat said. In winter storms, your bass will play for you. Comme une contrebasse plays soft jazz. Des notes graves dans la neige. But in June, Pierre and Raymond rest against the basswood. See them? Feet planted firmly in the grass, legs wide apart, knees bent against chest, elbows resting on knees, chin in hands. Pensive, your two young lovers. Déjà, even before you've been lowered into the ground, can they feel your vibrations?

In December, Pierre talks about making un film cinéma-vérité based on you. It won't be your truth. More cinéma than vérité. Your character will marry Gérard's character. Pierre says, ironie. Your character will rise from the dead. Love conquers all. And Raymond no longer looks like un intellectuel français. He shaved off his collier de barbe, now has a handlebar moustache. His hair, half-way down his back. Still smokes a pipe, but has gone rock. Your lovers, collaborating on art projects.

In June. Virginia's face. Marble mask. Her body restless. She needs to sit to smoke a cigarette, no seats provided in cemeteries, except the ground. Some people have installed stone benches on their family plots. She'll not trespass. Trépasser, as you know, means to die. With her one tongue, she can't make that connection. She paces up and down the shady alley, not wanting to step on anyone's grave, unaware that the dead up in the leaves, enjoying the June light, are watching her.

Maman Margot stands quietly by my side. And so do Nicole et Diane. Their husbands, Robert and Roger, sent apologies. They dread cemeteries. Marie couldn't leave her classroom. En pleine période de révisions pour les examens. You understand, n'est-ce pas? Did she walk to your studio at noon? What did she tell you?

Waiting to lower the late Elizabeth. Can you hear the rumours? They're whispering about the accident. Peut-être, they don't want you to hear. But it concerns you. Listen.

Caked with her blood, they say, staring at my gypsy skirt. On this day, as white as Gérard's shirt.

Men in white, they say, kneeled in front of the grille of the silver Chrysler with tweezers. To extract bits of your flesh and fragments of your bones.

Someone says, morbide. Someone says, macabre.

Gérard saw you. At the morgue. They had washed your body, but could not make your terrible injuries disappear. Gérard had to identify you.

A woman in black, a dark wave sucking in the June light, comes over to ask me what happened. She speaks slowly, forming her questions, lining up her words in pretty sentences. Une sentence de mort. What happened?

For six months, evading. Not wanting to sew lies with half-truths, not wanting to be wrapped up dans un tissu de mensonges, honestly, Elizabeth, for once, no desire to talk at all.

Wasn't wearing my cat's eyes. Leave me alone.

Stepped away from the woman, walked away from all questioners. Reckless driving. Reckless speaking. Causing death.

Verbal exhaustion, Elizabeth. Pure and simple.

Your site. Do you want to see how it looks from above? Since June, the dirt has settled. Hardened. Grass has grown over your mound. Now, dormant.

Your headstone. Oh, yes, you have one. Black granite. Elegant. Simple. Your name and lifeyears. Elizabeth Gold. 1926–1969. No day no month of beginning or ending. But your name! Huge provenance. Le monsieur juif at the fabric store on avenue du Mont-Royal said Elizabeth is a Hebrew name that means God has sworn. It's all true. Peut-être, you knew that. You knew much.

This thing that thwarts the thoughts thrusts through thrilled throngs. Used to practice that tongue twister in the mirror. Elizabeth. Your difficult ending. Elizabeth. That is your name.

Something else on the stone. Your last words to Gérard. You argued that day. He said you said, see you later. He had that carved on your tombstone. Under your last words to him, he had added, farewell. Only, the stone carver, un francophone, a fait une faute d'orthographe. He spelled farewell faire well. You do appreciate that meaning translated, n'est-ce pas? Savoir-faire. The well of eternity. Fare, the high cost of passage. So many meanings. A single context.

Carved in stone 'til erased by time. See you later. Your last words to Gérard. But not your true last words. This very instant. They've just come back to mind. Clear clean crisp.

And now, you'll laugh. Someone brought you carnations. Couldn't be any of your friends. We all knew how much you hated cut flowers. Peut-être, Newspaper George heard of your death, planned to come to your funeral, couldn't make it, sent those in December. Oh, the flowers of death! How lovely, Ariane dear. Should have known better. The day of the minestrone soup, you had told me they meant broken promises. How easily the mind forgets.

Let me get rid of them, Elizabeth-style.

That day, forgot my gloves on your kitchen table. Walked to the back. In fading winter light, saw you through the wall of windows. Breaking the stems, crushing the heads à pleines mains. Your hands, stained, wrapping the mess into newspaper. And, soudainement, you're outside, not three feet away, lifting the metal lid, throwing the package into the garbage can. An interesting choice. Why not burn the flowers in the fireplace in the front room? You used to burn garbage in it. Ou simplement, why not burn them in the wood stove? It was going full blast. You closed the lid with a clank, took a deep breath of icy air.

Today, you can breathe easy too. Don't worry. See? The stems, broken, the petals, crushed. My hands, also stained red. Let's throw ce bouquet as far from you as possible.

Your close friends came, sauf Marie, all tied up. Your grave site also surrounded par une mer d'inconnus who knew of you et par des gens célèbres we didn't know knew you. No flowers, please. Didn't read your obituary.

No priest, bien sûr. Gérard spoke. Can't tell you what he said. Étais dans un état second.

They lower you. Tears rising, nostrils tightening. Don't want to cry, même si, cemeteries are made for crying. Bite tongue. Hold breath. Lungs bursting. Heart pumping, frantic.

Didn't have the right to cry for you, Elizabeth.

In June, maman's hand squeezing my hand. In December, we're letting go. She too is feeling the change. Margot moving forward, getting rid of everything. Like you. This, her once-in-a-lifetime closet-cleaning cure. Margot et Gérard se font des confidences. You don't mind, do you? Do you think Margot the living has a chance against Elizabeth the dead?

Pulling clumps of your grass. Staining what's left of the skirt. Weeds, as in mourning, weeds, as in mauvaises herbes. That skirt, soon to be discarded.

Oh, Elizabeth, under black granite, alone in your grave. Gérard wants you all to himself. Non, ce n'est pas ça. He knows you best. How much you love your solitude. In Saint-Pol, the dead in the village churchyard. Too crowded for you. Les anciens Québécois vivaient avec leurs morts. They also feared them. You never wanted to be the bogeywoman on the hill. That brings us to your house.

You often said, a cadaver is nothing. When you bought it, you said the house was a cadaver. The first night you slept in it, it felt abandoned. You brought it back to life. How do you do bouche-à-bouche to resuscitate a house? You said, by living in it day by day.

In September, your studio, empty. The house, still standing, but missing you. In July, found a book in Gérard's apartment. You know the one. He'll have your house demolished.

He said you said, a fine tradition. You could say, ultimate closet-cleaning.

Rumour has it, Elizabeth, your friends will build une bibliothèque on the site. Plenty of shelves for all your books to stretch out on. Words for everyone to share. In your honour.

This too, in your honour, Elizabeth. This summer this autumn, our seasons of travel, did mouth-to-mouth to keep you alive. Exhausting work. Bientôt, must let you go. You do understand? This, for you to keep. Gold Rush 1969.

Recognize the shape? C'est ça. The caftan. Opening night. You gave me Ariane 1967. Gold Rush belongs to you. Your spirit in each cut-out. Each held to the others with fishing line, nearly invisible, floating apart together, like birds flying in formation. Recognize those strips of cloth? Non? Your travel clothes. Flapping in the wind. Prayer flags, you said, hang on rocks and buildings and in trees. Gold Rush, a ten-foot prayer flag. For you, Elizabeth. For you.

Should do a little grave digging in this cold afternoon. But don't want to touch your wood. How to give this to you? Tell you what. Ce collage ce montage was meant to float free. What better place than in your basswood.

D'abord, brought something special to show you. Gold thread. Used in goldwork. Very ancient needlework technique. Thought of adding a length. But this gold doesn't belong in this composition. You see, the cut-outs and strips of cloth are from your photos and your clothes, those red strips, from my visiting-you shirt. Alors que, this gilt thread, a discovery after you were gone. Aftermath. For a different work. Now, let's install this one.

Was never much of a tree climber. Will be careful. Can you feel the rough bark through bare feet, bare hands? See the gash down its middle? An old lightning scar. It survived.

There. Done. Look up. Even in the dull December light, the brass eyelets shine bright. On a sunny day, you'll catch a glint of gold. Like a wink. In the spring, you and all the dead

are invited to the opening. You'll climb into the new leaves
to view each of the one thousand seven hundred and seventy-
six photo fragments. That many, oui. Your basswood, better
than any art gallery ramp. Hundreds of branches, big and
small, for full viewing, from top to bottom, recto verso. In
secret, you, deep in the ground, and Gold Rush, high up in
the tangle of branches, going through transformation in a
parallel course. You and your life's work.

C'est fini, Elizabeth. Your friends are leaving, you're staying. They're walking to their cars, doors shutting you out,
engines starting, tires crushing gravel, motors fading away.
Above, swinging in the leaves, the dead will again enjoy their
peace and quiet.

You squat on your mound, smoking a last cigarette.
December doesn't bother you, n'est-ce pas? Immune to the
last. Ah, Gérard did bury you in the black suit. Fitting. It fitted you so well. Still does. That's it, blow smoke toward the
sky. See Gold Rush hanging? Well camouflaged, n'est-ce pas?
In summer, in the full foliage, not one living soul will spot it.

We're losing the light. Bientôt, they'll lock the gates. This,
our last visit. This, our last talk together. Can we be secure in
silence?

Lips to your ear. Listen. One last bit of news. They said,
Elizabeth got distracted. Non. Ariane distracted Elizabeth. Ce
n'est pas la même chose. They asked, what happened? Mais
la vérité n'est pas toujours bonne à dire. What to say, what
not to say, to whom and when. That must be learned in
silence. Oui? The silences between the words. The intertidal
zone between our two tongues. Stories are good. So are
secrets. Silence is speak's shadow. Alors, if you want to keep a
secret, keep it. Don't burden anyone with it. D'ailleurs, people don't always mean to, but they speak and then, where's
your secret? Étalé sur la place publique.

Non. Not seeking your absolution, non. Time to practise
silence. To learn the right cadence. Pure and simple.

Your shadow's getting thinner. You have no choice, but to seep back underground. Wait. One more second.

People say the smell of death. Unbearable. L'odeur d'outre-tombe. Untranslatable. Peut-être, the composite smell of all things overwhelms le nerf olfactif, as white, all colours spun together, burns le nerf optique. You said, corpses are nothing. The skin rolled back to reveal the mysteries. What are your mysteries? You taught me not to fear body or speak. Oh, Elizabeth. This mouth shouted, le temps n'attend pas. You weren't even late. We had all the time in the world. And you looked up. So happy. Words can. Words have. Stopped. Time dead.

Lips. Alive. Will wear your silence for a while. To feel its physicality. Beading. Smooth purl. Cracking the gold. Always a risk. Those words, learned only in your language. This gold thread. Your last kiss. Non non. No burden. Don't let anybody push you into anything you don't want to do. You remember saying that? Nobody's pushing me. Not even you. I choose this.

You're disappearing. Is this you, whispering?

Do it, Ariane dear. Get me out of your system.

You always understood à demi-mot. Your voice, still in my ear. Clear clean crisp. Je me souviens.

Relax, it'll be great.

There. Your last words then. Your last words now. Relax, it'll be great.

You breathe six feet underground. Faire well. Cross out the eye. Fare well in your crossing, Elizabeth, chère.

Shiver. Skirt, rags. Dark. Fence, padlocked. Winter hours. Silence, deep. Wind scatters silk strips. What remains, seventeen pearl buttons, one oyster-shell-shaped clasp.

Must go. Une dernière danse. Feet stepping lightly on your grassy knoll. Slow release. Dance dance. Climb fence.

Will practise Ariane Claude sans toi. Start from scratch.

New Flight Plan

B egin at western front of flat. Move through to southern
edge. Back up north, progressing along east flank of corridor. End at eastern front. Le grand ménage du printemps in
December.

Work through le grand salon, bare of mahogany. Le petit
salon. The guest room. The dining room, bare of ebony. The
kitchen. Cross the corridor. My bedroom. Margot's bedroom, bare of casuarina art deco suite. The bathroom. Le
boudoir, bare of thirties oak office furniture. The television
room. The front entrance, free of its ponderous hall stand.

Wash walls, ceilings, floors. Polish windows, clear and
stained glass, mirrors and French doors. Oil oak wainscots,
doors, and wood frames. Scrub with a small brush plaster
baseboards with wave crests and plaster mouldings with
grapevines, as intricate as the human ear. Rub with un cha-
mois crystal doorknobs and brass heat grates. Unscrew, wash,
and screw back switch and plug plates. Dust all light fixtures,
the hanging pendants and les plafonniers, the wall fittings
and les lustres, the floor and table lamps. Clean bathroom
ceramic tiles. Wax kitchen linoleum and oak floors. Travailler
en silence. Comme une méditation.

Dans le boudoir, the body takes a break, stretches on the
floor, legs relaxed. The eyes catch the skylight. How can light
push through strata of Montréal soot? How to get on the

roof and wash the black away? House cleaning. An addiction.
In the spring, an army of house painters will invade the flat.
Un ramoneur will clean the fireplace chimney, so our
Bohemian friends can enjoy a fire and the kids learn to undo
their fear. Faire d'une pierre deux coups. Ask le ramoneur to
wash the skylight.

Pendant tout l'automne, Gérard carries away Margot's
many things. The silver vases, the landscape and seascape
paintings, les bergères de Dresden. The twenty-four bronze
horses, Margot's silver-plated dresser set, the Wedgwood
candy boxes. The Susie Cooper dinner set with its matching
platters, gravy boat, and serving bowls. The dining room
crystal bowl and all the doilies. Surprise! Des guipures de
Flandre. From the sideboard, the jet cat and the alabaster cat.
How many more lives will those Chinese felines live?

Prends tout, Margot insists.

Shelves, sideboard, display cabinet, walls. Bare. Gérard
passes through like a cyclone. Pendant tout l'automne.

Gérard organise une vente aux enchères pour nous,
Margot says.

Why not donate or sell cheap some of our furniture to
Ana and Karel?

Non, Ariane. L'honneur des immigrants. Tu comprends?
Et puis, j'admire leur courage.

Ce n'est pas du courage, ça, Margot. It's pigheadedness.

C'est la même chose, she says.

The first Saturday in December, Gérard arranged for his
moving van to collect mahogany, casuarina, ebony, oak.

The van backs up dans la ruelle, an event at this time of
year. A good-looking guy with black curly hair and a lumberjack jacket directs the driver, bake up, bake up, he yells, 'til the
truck blocks the way. The blond driver turns off the ignition
and jumps out of the cab. Gérard supervises. Le trio talks
about the iron hook jutting from under the roof des hangars.
They'll rig a block and tackle to lower the heavier furniture.

They discuss the logistics of not scratching the furniture on its voyage down. The two partners have worked pour l'anti-quaire many times. They know the ropes.

We switch on the light. Margot unlocks the door to la ruelle. We say, bonjour bonjour. The blond mover climbs the steps two at a time, carrying the rope and pulleys. Won't the rusty hook pull out of the masonry?

Non non, he says. Tout est beau.

The blond ponytailed mover removes his Irish sweater. Climbs on the lip of the opening. Braces himself, one hip against the frame, plants his feet shod in work boots with lime green laces well apart. Il a de belles fesses rondes in his tight jeans. Stretches. Armpit hair sticks out of his tee-shirt sleeves. Gérard comes up from la ruelle to help the younger man set up the rope.

Lenka and Pavel join me dans la ruelle to watch. And so does tout le quartier. Eyes squinting, fingers pointing. Down come the ebony sideboard and dining room table and display cabinet, the mahogany couch, the casuarina bedroom suite, the solid oak office furniture, including the rolltop desk. C'est surréel to watch the highly polished ebony hall stand hanging in mid-air, its mirror catching glimpses of its descent.

The movers slip on work gloves and sling the lighter pieces with leather straps to bring them down by hand. They also carry end tables, twelve dining room chairs with soft leather seats and many items in cardboard boxes. Gérard carries the Underwood himself.

Now empty, le grand salon echoes comme une gare. Margot asks me to vacuum the Persian rug. Gérard tells us it can be restored. Is it worth the trouble? It'll be expensive. What's the point?

Donc, qu'est-ce que tu décides? I ask her.

Margot suggests to roll it up and bring it dans la ruelle. In no time, someone will take off with it. Gérard calls in the blond mover who shoulders the rug and runs downstairs.

Gérard shakes hands with his men. They know where to go what to do. The ponytailed one waves to me.

Salut, he says. Hé! Es-tu libre, ce soir? On pourrait aller au cinéma.

Why not go out with a mover? He moves me. We're on the move. We arrange the logistics of first date.

Now, mid-December. The Great Cast Off.

After work, Margot empties closets. Sitting on the floor of her empty bedroom, she sorts out Dead Man's belongings. Shirts and sweaters, socks and underwear, scarves and ties and leather gloves. To give to l'Armée du Salut. His footwear too. Stored for years in shoeboxes. Black loafers, laced brown shoes, green tartan slippers. So clean. The inside, no traces of smelly feet. Even the soles have been scrubbed. No archeological traces of what he once stepped on. Total erasure. The photos, the one in the copper frame, the ones in the double silver frame. Disappeared. Margot la discrète dealing with her past in her private way.

We discard together. No consultation needed. We clear away the chiffonier in the guest bedroom. We'll give away my baby clothes preserved in tissue paper. High quality crocheted tiny things. A poor woman's joy. We throw away my schoolgirl's drawings and compositions. C'est de l'histoire ancienne. Margot fills the empty drawers with her clothes. She's taking over the guest bedroom, like mental preparation for the real move in May.

She goes shopping with ma tante, Rita delighting in the spree. New sheets, sunny dishes. A modern kitchen set. A simple light-weight bedroom suite. Forme et fonction. Margot will keep on using the fifties beechwood furniture from le petit salon. And she kept her leather rocking chair and ottoman. Not changing everything at once.

Tu es chanceuse à ton âge, Margot, d'avoir mis la main sur un homme aussi raffiné que Gérard, ma tante says over a cup of tea.

Ce n'est pas comme ça, Rita.

Ma tante ne veut rien entendre, sauf wedding bells. Margot fait les gros yeux. We understand each other. No words. Margot et Gérard. Sans doute comme Pierre et moi. Des amis. Peut-être, also fuck buddies. Margot doesn't say.

And that's the problem with Pierre. His idea of moving in together. When we're old, fifty, like Gérard, would we still be friends? Moving in with him would change things. He won't believe that. But it would.

Feel like a change in my old bedroom, 'til moving out on my own. Store boxspring dans le hangar. Put mattre.s directly on floor, cover it with sleeping bag, as bedspread. Pierre had also set his mattress on the floor. One day, a pipe broke. His wet bedding reminded him that he peed in bed jusqu'à sa confirmation. Now, his mattress rests on milk crates.

Empty dresser. Keep socks and underwear in boxes in closet. Empty desk. Throw away mes travaux de cégep. Not so ancient history, but moving forward. Keep desk chair to throw clothes on at night. Hang chair on wall pour un effet surréaliste. Drag dresser, drag desk into guest bedroom for Margot's use. Must not scratch floors. We lift the furniture an inch off the floor, walk à petits pas, we laugh. Pierre uses bricks and boards as book and record shelves. Get old crates and boards dans le hangar. Cover them with lengths of fabric bought for a song. Change light bulbs from sixty to forty watts pour l'effet beatnik. But keep good reading lamp intact. Set lamp on floor beside mattress. Bring candles from dining room. Will burn incense for no reason.

Bring les chansonniers québécois from le petit salon to keep on new shelves with candles and incense. Display cast iron toy sewing machine. Throw the seventeen pearl buttons and oyster-shell-shaped clasp in glass bell-shaped jar with earrings. Rearrange books on old wall shelves. Gustave Flaubert et Réjean Ducharme, Jean Cocteau et Albert Camus, Anne Hébert et Marie-Claire Blais. Those and all the other books, not in alphabetical order, not by categories. Behind the French English dictionary, une découverte. Wise Blood. Hiding. An early borrowing from the labyrinth of books in Saint-Pol. Forgot to return it. Flannery O'Connor won't sit dans la nouvelle bibliothèque du village. Wise Blood, dog-eared, the spine broken, a bookmark at an early page. Un défi de lecture. Put novel on floor beside reading lamp. Will crack its meaning during days of silence.

Empty closet. Launder handmade clothes. Except gypsy skirt. Discarded. Except maroon velvet coat. Sold. Fold into backpack tablecloth djellaba, gold bedspread party pyjamas, black velveteen jumpsuit, rust-coloured winter coat tailored from Rita's fifties giveaway, pants transformed into long skirts, shorts into navel-grazing tops. Ariane's alterations. Liquidation. The pack. Heavy.

What to do with Ariane 1967? Alone dans le hangar. Under her old-sheet shroud. We look at her again. Like we did back in 1968 when Gérard drove her into town. We didn't want her over the mantelpiece, like rich people, hanging portraits of themselves. Margot's boss has a painting of himself in his office. The painted boss watching the flesh-and-blood boss.

Si j'étais lui, Margot said then, je n'aimerais pas ça.

Do you want to hang it over the mantelpiece? she asks now as she asked then.

I don't want to stare at myself all the time, I say again.

So, you won't want to put it in your bedroom, will you?

Pourquoi est-ce qu'on se parle en anglais? I ask.

We laugh. She picks a length of white thread off my black sweater, rolls it into a tiny ball between thumb and index finger.

C'est à toi de décider, she says.

She suggested then to store the portrait with her wedding gifts 'til we decide where to hang it. For now, let's put her back dans le hangar. But soon, must make up my mind about her.

Wearing jeans, clogs, the Afghan coat. Grab ma valise de fin de semaine. Out the door.

À la caisse populaire, la valise on the counter. Fill out withdrawal slip. Three thousand four hundred and fifty dollars and ninety-two cents. The total amount in that account. Inform la caissière, will take the money cash. Snap open clasps.

Je veux fermer ce compte-là.

She judges in silence. Crazy girl, she thinks. She's not difficult to read.

En argent liquide? her voice quivers, her eyes staring at la valise ouverte.

D'accord. C'est peut-être un peu trop.

New instructions. Still close that account. Count thirty one-hundred dollar bills. Transfer the change into my regular account. The one with my own money. Earned working.

She calls in her supervisor, they whisper, enter monsieur le directeur's glassed-in office. The three of them glance at me, examine the slip as if it said, c'est un holdup. What's the holdup? This summer, cashed in my traveller's cheques, redeposited the money into the account, and now. More cash withdrawn than needed for groceries. That, to bank people, smells of illicit activity. La caissière comes back with crisp one-hundred dollar notes, telling me they had to open the vault. She counts the money.

Merci.

Slip the notes in three bundles into the back pocket of la valise. What's that? She looks, as if to provide the answer. The camping snapshots. Slip them into the Afghan coat pocket. Snap the lid shut. Leave. Feel eyes glued to the back of the sheepskin. Is it their duty to report? Will a detective follow trail of wedding-gift money?

Margot refuses to take the money.

Garde l'argent, Ariane. Pour l'université, pour ton loyer. Pour commencer du bon pied.

Margot sending her daughter into the world. Her daughter won't start life near the poverty line. L'indépendance au féminin, Margot taught without ever opening her mouth on the subject, commence par l'indépendance financière. This, truly my inheritance.

Merci. Tu es très généreuse.

She doesn't reply, but eyes ma valise. Her daughter walking the streets with a suitcase full of cash.

So, retrace my steps. Deposit most of it into my remaining account. Ignore comments.

Give sa valise back to Margot. Weekend trips may be in her near future. We're conjugating our verbs, with their many voices and moods, tenses and numbers and persons. Margot resuming ses verbes au futur. My steps bringing me closer to mine.

The Army Surplus store on boulevard Saint-Laurent. Door unlocking for business. Inside, darkness. Floorboards creaking sagging.

Going through the racks. Rack after rack. Khaki and its attendant earthy tones. Grey, brownish, yellowish, olive drab.

Est-ce que je peux vous aider? asks a tall skinny man with pointy ears. Le kaki, he says, sipping his morning coffee. C'est facile d'entretien.

Checking cuts, seams, features. Feeling twilled cotton, twilled wool.

Des vêtements durables, he says.

Smelling textile. The scent informs my nose a few washes will be necessary before the size leaches out and the fibres shape themselves to the relief of the body. Clothes to walk in, clothes to run in en toute liberté.

Tu sais ce que ça veut dire kaki? he asks. Ça vient d'un mot hindi ou urdu. Tout dépend qui tu crois. Du mot khâk qui veut dire poussière.

My face shows appreciation. The mind surmises. That explains why khaki's so facile d'entretien. No dirt can dirty dust. Khâk to khâk. He helps me take off the Afghan coat, we let it drop to the floor on top of the pack. He holds an ankle-length grey Air Force coat for me to try on. Looking good in mirror installed between rows of leather marching boots and camouflage rubber waders. Feeling cozy warm. My head nods with satisfaction. Le monsieur puts the coat on the counter.

Marching to the rear into a foxhole of a fitting room. Try on pants with six pockets. Buy two pairs. A jacket with four pockets, two sweaters, one shirt, one belt. Back at the front, select a jute shoulder bag. Try on several pairs of walking boots 'til one pair fails to torture the feet just walking up and down the sagging floor. Pair off that footwear with wool socks that fit without squeezing the toes.

Look at les boussoles under the glass-topped counter. On a whim, buy an inexpensive one. Le monsieur tells me it will always point the way.

Tu pars en voyage? he asks, helping to stuff the new clothes into the pack.

My face my hands make the sign of, on ne sait jamais.

We push hard to jam in the long coat. He helps me slip on the Afghan coat. Holds the door for me.

Merci, monsieur.

Tu n'es pas volubile, toi, hein? he says, bending at the waist, his ears reddening to the tip of the tips.

Chez Messier, the gum-chewing girl at the counter takes my cash without batting an eyelid. Never breaking the rhythm of her jaw, she deftly folds. Four camisoles and a half-dozen panties, all white cotton, for easy dyeing later, a sage green colour, grey cotton socks, yellow wool gloves, a multi-colour scarf, as long as a boa. Let her place my purchases into an outside pocket of the pack. She blows a pink bubble that pops surprisingly loud. Just short of a rifle shot.

How short?

Walk-ins on Fridays. Risky at any time of the year. Down-right foolish with the Christmas rush around the corner.

The receptionist cranes her neck to survey the floor, makes sucking noises while tapping her pencil against her lip. Ten-thirty Friday morning. Not yet tearing their hair out they aren't that busy. Throw the pack on the floor, the Afghan coat on top. The body sinks in the posh plush purple settee.

No rush, I say.

This, a snotty hairplace not far from Pierre's rue de la Montagne apartment. The nose itches from spray and perm fumes. Giant b&w photos of models with extravagant hair-dos cover burnt-orange walls. The eyes fix on a big-lipped model, her hair done in small tresses sculpted airily on top of her head like prehistoric spiders. Flick through a stylists' magazine. Page after page of hair creations by masters from New York London Paris Tokyo. Montréal, not featured.

It's her, the receptionist says.

A young woman in a black leather miniskirt, black knee-high boots, and a tight-fitting black lace blouse stands in front of me, waving a black comb and pointy scissors.

I'm Dora, she says, running her fingers through my hair. Beautiful. Come this way.

Sit in Dora's swivel chair. Face self in walls of mirrors. A fuzzy pale mask surrounded by chocolate hair cascading below the waist. Dora's co-workers coo.

Quelle belle chevelure! one says.

We rarely see that, another says, mounting a client's hair into rollers.

Tu les laisses pousser depuis combien de temps? the same French girl asks.

My answer, a shrug of the shoulder, not meant as cold shoulder. Simply don't know.

You have split ends, Dora says, as if diagnosing the terminal stage of syphilis. I could snip off a good five inches. Up to your waist. It'll be easier to care for and it'll look a whole lot healthier.

Non. Shorter.

How much shorter?

Short.

I have to make sure we speak the same language, she says, lifting strands. There's short in the client's language and short in the stylist's. I don't want you to walk out of here unhappy or angry. I don't want to be blamed.

To avoid catastrophic misunderstanding, my thumb and forefinger open slightly apart in front of the mirrors. For all to see.

You want me to trim off only an inch?

Non non. All this has to come off. A sharp stylish short cut. Something striking.

The French-speaking girl flicks through a hairstyles magazine. My finger points at a model looking like Jeanne d'Arc au bûcher.

Tu es pas sérieuse, la coiffeuse francophone whispers, mourning la chute des cheveux magnifiques.

Are you crazy! Dora exhales, more to the point.

Even the busy stylists abandon clients in hair disarray to opine.

Pretty radical.

That cut's not for everybody.

What'll your friends think?

Penses-y. C'est un gros changement.

So, it'll be radical, I say. My friends'll be shocked. They'll get used to it. Et puis, ce n'est pas permanent.

She's right, Dora says. Hair grows back. If you're sure.

She pulls my hair back to make it look like it's already short, checks in the mirror. The others keep an eye on her mute assessment. Her verdict, a go. My face will survive such exposure. Someone else washes my hair. C'est toute une affaire, in so small a sink. Back in the chair. Hair dripping. Dora holds the scissors in front of her face, a knight pledging with her sword.

Ready?

I nod.

Sure?

Cut!

The others. In a trance. Combs and dryers idle. Dora takes a deep breath. The first cut. She presses her lips together, as if about to burst into tears. The blades cut crunch through the first strand. The sound, not quite a Nile crocodile tearing flesh. More like a barracuda brushing against seaweed.

Done.

A brown mass lies on the polished floor. Sculpted wisps of hair on top of my head. Uneven spikes on forehead. With a hand-held mirror, Dora shows me the back of my head. Can't see a thing despite heavy squinting.

What do you think? she asks, terror-stricken.

My head nods approval.

It's striking all right, she says, relieved.

Sensing the mood of the room, can't be sure we have consensus. No matter.

In any case, this cut's a first in this city, Dora says, ripping the bib off in a wide arc, a matador at a corrida, the bull down. You may have started a trend, she adds, straightening une mèche rebelle with her comb.

La rebelle de Montréal. Feeling light as a bubble. Glancing at self in store windows. Men women pivot on their heels to stare. My head catches every air vibration. Will need a sailor's wool cap.

Just in time to catch airport bus in front of le Reine Elizabeth. This, le 19 décembre. Midday flight landing. Time to meet me returning home.

At Dorval. Harsh light in airport washroom. Self, exposed in mirror. Cropped hair. Lips. Des lèvres ostentatoires. Rip off false lashes. Throw away in waste bin. Nose to mirror, kohling eyes. Mascara not needed on natural lashes. Long and dark. No lipstick. Bien sûr que non. A little blush. Finishing touch. Done.

Cut tags off new clothes. Turn up hem of one pair of olive
drab pants. Will do other pair at home, cross-legged on mattress on floor while camisoles and panties soak up sage dye.
Sitting on bench, sewing, fast and calm. Long stitches to save
time. Soon, plane from London landing. In a cubicle, strip.
Clogs and jeans, keep. Brown sweater, old socks, nylon panties,
discard. Slip on cotton panties and camisole. Cotton then wool
socks. Pants and sweater. Marching boots. Will need a lot of
walking to break those in. Put on Air Force coat. Coil rainbow
scarf. What to do with Afghan coat? Stuff it into pack. Last
glance in mirror. Go meet plane in full army regalia.

People arriving departing, greeting waiting. Women on
loudspeakers. Important announcements. Impossible to
decode. Thoughts of Ana working at this airport. As if not
quite landed in the new land. Airports. Les limbes de l'immi-
grant. Perpetual arrival. Passengers sipping a last drink, reading a book a newspaper, speaking on the phone, snoozing on
a bench. On attend les départs.

Squinting at schedules. Arrival, departure. Flights on
time, cancelled, delayed. London flight. International terminal. This, domestic terminal. Zigzag through masses of people blocking doors and escalators. Pardon, excusez-moi. The
crowd resists. Walk fast. Plane landing.

Passengers from London stream out of the gate, Ariane
Claude caught in the flow. Coming home.

Jump into a taxi. Where to? Downtown. Via Saint-
Polycarpe. Pardon? Dans les Laurentides. Return trip, how
much? No meter. Flat rate. How much? Playing the seasoned
traveller. Versed in the art of haggling. We strike a deal. Done.
He wants me to sit in front. Non. Need to think. Will ride in
the back. Drive.

Ariane Claude, the tripper. Been through rough country.
The driver wants to talk. Where have you been? What have
you seen? How does it feel to be back? This, day trip, not
sightseeing. This, silent trip, not power trip. Drive.

Parler, ça passe le temps, he says.

He doesn't like tight-lipped fares. Surtout, on long distance trips. He puts on loud music.

The mind trips sur une pensée fulgurante. Hands search the Afghan coat, the pack. Nothing. The camping snapshots must have slipped out of the pocket. Where? On the street? At the airport? Everything coming to an end. Laugh out loud. The driver's eyes dans le rétroviseur. This fare's on a bad trip. No matter. Sit back and enjoy the ride.

Sitting up.

Stop! C'est ici, monsieur.

Ici, où? he wonders.

The road deserted, trees everywhere, except for an empty lot, no house on which to hang an address.

Attendez, je reviens, I say, rushing out of the car.

The lot. Cleared. Quelques débris. Like the way animals scatter dry bones. A sign planted in the earth where the kitchen was. The sign announces le site de la future bibliothèque de Saint-Polycarpe. La bibliothèque Gold L'Heureux.

Je n'ai plus rien à faire ici, I say, not looking back. Rentrons à Montréal. Tout est bien qui finit bien, I add, as le chauffeur stupéfait seems in need of enlightenment.

The December light fades. On the wind, snow.

Snowing. Ariane 1967. Dealing with her, now. Heavy awkward to carry in cutting wind. White storm gathering. Soon raging. Caressing hard. Rough lovers, Montréal and her storms. Today, everything in focus. Sharp. La nouvelle Ariane. Close-cropped, khakied. On a roll. Too hot to freeze.

The silver bell rings.

Laying Ariane 1967 sur la méridienne, unwrapping her from her old-sheet shroud.

Prends-la, Gérard. S'il te plaît, prends-la.

The master of provenance agrees silently, looks at me with searching eyes, as my hands unfold the Afghan coat out of the pack.

Pour ta collection de costumes, I say, stroking the sheep-skin.

My lips indulge themselves, pressing hard, pressing fully on his clean-shaven cheek.

The silver bell rings. Back walking the storm, scarf sailing.

Evening au Café de l'horloge. Jazz québécois playing, people stamping their feet, snow falling out of their hair. Pierre straddling a chair, smoking sa rouleuse, talking. Bursts of laughter. Jérôme grating nutmeg over grogs. Raymond with a new girl, kissing the inside of her wrist, that tender spot the razor slices when love's gone bad.

Unpacking handmade clothes on table by grandfather clock. Announcing vente de table.

Tout doit être vendu, I say. Les prix sont négociables.

Pierre staring at me, frowning, cutting through the crowd, like swimming across the sea.

Ma puce? Ma puce!

Raymond looks up from the kissable wrist. Les habitués recognize don't recognize me. Girls flock to the table. Des fripes à vendre. Beau, bon, pas cher. You may haggle.

Forme et fonction, I say to Pierre, staring at my fatigues.

Est-ce que tu déménages? he asks, excited at the sight of my bulging backpack, nibbling my exposed neck.

No time to give him my true answer, right away, he tells me he'll gladly empty a few drawers for my things. Girls ask questions all at once. How much? What kind of material? Pierre goes back to his crowd. Lost sa rouleuse in transit, must roll another. In no time, sold everything.

Sit with stockinged feet on heat vent at base of brick wall, boots under table. Feeling mighty fine. Sipping grog with cardamom seeds. Tomorrow, will start drinking with straw, eating with des baguettes chinoises. No shovelling forkfuls for a while. Dainty eating. A morsel at a time on the tips of bamboo.

Hé! Ariane! one of the regulars says, leaning his chair in my direction. Qu'est-ce que tu as de bon à raconter?

Thumb up. Much said in the lifting of one finger. He reenters his friends' wordline without tripping, like a good rope skipper.

Pierre with his evening crowd. Les soirs de parole au Café de l'horloge. Ease. Les matins de l'écriture. La résistance des mots. His writing face. Melancholy, anger, intensity. His speaking face. Joy, fun, release.

Crush cardamom between teeth. Tang of pepper. Pierre would expect me to wash his bathrobe, make his expresso. He's not revolutionary enough for equal partnership in arena domestica. In novels about les intellectuels de la gauche française, the women are still fixtures. Les femmes, les luminaires de la révolution des hommes. Pierre was my first. Doesn't mean we owe each other anything. Will not enter arena domestica. Je suis Ariane, pas Hestia. Will always give him plenty of thread to help him escape his minotaurs. That, the special friendship. But won't tend his hearth. His heart on fire.

Raymond comes to sit with me. Talks fast, eyes shifting from my face to the brick wall, back and forth. He met that girl, she works at Radio-Canada in the costume department, costumes aren't the same as clothes, you need special training, study textiles, learn different sewing techniques, and much more, on stage, people move differently than on the street, perform complicated movements, costumes can't fall apart during a performance, seams can't split during rehearsal, actors, singers, dancers can't be constricted.

Put my finger across his lips. Stop that unstoppable flow. Raymond, in the stage of excitement. Act one. Lust love. Dynamite detonator.

Donc, I say, ta blonde fera les costumes pour ton opéra rock. C'est ça?

He nods. My eyes tell him, no matter, not a problem with me if that's what makes him happy. Will she steal my idea for the chorus of Québécois fleurdelisés?

Non, Ariane. Il n'y aura pas de chœur.

He kisses my cheeks, pretends to slip, kisses my mouth. A long exploratory kiss. He goes back to his new girlfriend. His body, pure relief in motion. Raymond est parti pour la gloire. Bonne chance, chum.

Will drape my bedroom walls with the fabric. Will stage mon propre opéra.

Alors? Jérôme says, sitting down, stretching his arms across the table, clasping his hands. As-tu réfléchi à l'emploi que je te propose?

He considers the haircut, the olive drab clothes. Is he changing his mind? He tells me, not just waitressing. Also, managing, organizing. Being in charge.

Oui, Jérôme. J'accepte.

He asks me to come back tomorrow morning, after the breakfast rush. Pour parler affaires. Les détails, le salaire. Tout. He wants me to start immediately.

Non, I say. Pas avant le 7 janvier.

Pourquoi le 7 janvier? he asks, trying to guess the answer by scrutinizing my new look. Tu me diras ça demain, he says, getting up, squeezing my shoulder.

Clients are lining up at the counter.

A sudden motion in the room gives me the chance to slip out of sight.

Waiting for closing time. In Jérôme's basement. Dry since October flood. The furnace pumps heat upstairs. Above, word flood. Exclamations. Interrogations. Affirmations. Arguments. D'accord, pas d'accord. Everything recto verso.

Later, when everybody's gone, will get to work. Doesn't seem so necessary anymore. Aha, c'est la peur qui parle. Now that the moment has arrived, will you weasel out? Non. Won't evade. Aller au bout de ce qui est nécessaire.

Later, when everything's quiet. In washroom upstairs. Ariane's private alteration room. Will decide how to proceed. This, not mutilation. Not gagging. Will need to breathe through mouth if body catches a cold. Must eat, must drink. Brush teeth. Sustain, not deny, life.

Upstairs, Pierre announces that sa puce is moving in with him. Someone asks, quand? He says, ce soir, demain. Bientôt. He tells our friends, Pierre and Ariane will look for a bigger place together. Someone says, c'est le grand amour, hein? He laughs. Happy.

Ariane Claude waiting. For closing time.

Cracking the Gold

Time to pick up after the dead. Seule. But not alone.
Drag table next to sink. Lock door. Cover table with
white cloth.

The tools. A hand towel. A soup bowl with ice cubes. A
pot of boiling water. In another bowl, drop four sharps, the
thimble, tweezers, small scissors, threader. Cotton wool in
saucer. Rubbing alcohol. Peroxide. Vaseline. Measuring tape,
silk thread, gilt thread, small gold pearl for finishing touch.

Put on cat's eyes. Look in mirror. Le point zéro. Seule.
But not alone.

Relax lips. Measure mouth from corner to corner. Two
inches. Open mouth. Measure one inch vertically at centre of
mouth. Sous le sillon naso-labial. After work is done, must be
able to open. One inch. For mouth maintenance. Sustenance.

The design. Five stitches joining upper and lower lips in
a zigzag pattern. Starting at upper right corner of mouth and
ending with silk thread dangling down left corner of mouth.
A one-half-inch space between each stitch.

The needlework. Sharp to enter edge of lip horizontally,
as shallow as possible and to exit one-eighth of an inch past
point of entry. Total, ten pricks of the needle, points of entry,
points of exit.

In this goldwork, the gilt thread will not pierce the skin.
Only organic thread will perforate living tissue. Will work

with a double silk thread for a more solid construction. Will bead four short lengths of gilt thread across lips. After the job's done, so silk thread doesn't seal itself in healing skin, will need to move it around. Same as with hoops in newly pierced ears.

Déjà, only at planning stage, experiencing muscle contraction, tingling sensation along nerve paths, light sweat, more rapid heartbeat.

Pee. Wash and dry hands. Pour alcohol on hands over sink, rub, let evaporate.

Cut a silk thread, eight inches long. Thread with threader, double up, make a knot. Drop sharp and thread in hot water.

Measure and cut four lengths of gold thread, each three-eighths of an inch. Plus one piece one-inch long.

What's this? Un point au cœur. Not now! Don't panic. Don't move. It'll pass. Breathe. Deeper. Deeper.

Open wide. Your last chance. Yawn. Give it all you've got. Your great lioness yawn exposing the back of the mouth all the way down to la luette, that fleshy bit. Burst of laughter. Droplets of saliva spatter mirror. Laugh hard. Let it rip. Speak out loud. Exaggerate enunciation.

Relax! It will be great!

Now, get to work. Wipe mirror clean.

Pinch, stretch lips. Slight burning sensation.

Ice lips numb.

Drop ice cubes back into bowl. Soak cotton wool with rubbing alcohol. Dab lips.

Use tweezers to retrieve threaded sharp from hot water. Soak in alcohol.

Deep breath. Pulse, normal. Vision, clear. Hand, steady. Begin.

Touch point of sharp to upper right corner of mouth. Push. Eyelids close. Stop. Open eyes. Hold breath. Push. Not too deep. Frowning. Catch thinnest layer of fleshy part inside lip to hide knot. The deepest intrusion. Reflexes. Facial muscles contract, shivers run through body in short shock waves. Skin, tight with la chair de poule. Push sharp with thimble. La résistance de la peau. Surprising. Point of sharp exiting one-eighth of an inch past point of entry. Push. With tweezers in left hand, pull on sharp. Tickling sensation of stainless steel and silk boring through small catch of inner lip. Needle out. Exhale. Pull length of silk thread through, with knot secured against fleshy part of inner lip. Tout de suite, the tongue goes for the knot. Bead first length of gold through needle. Deep breath.

How does it feel? Exciting fear and spasmodic reflex. How deep does it go? The whole body rooting for the one single part. That, body-zoning. The entire cache of sensations sent to the lips.

Stitch two. Deep breath. Hold. Half an inch from corner, pierce lower lip, catching the thinnest layer of skin, steady, keep needle horizontal, push, exit one-eighth of an inch further. Clean stitchery. No tearing. Exhale. Nose tingles, mucus forms. Tweezers pull sharp, silk traversing skin, tightening across mouth. Dab with alcohol. Blow nose, wipe tears. Deep breath. Heartbeat, rapid, navel, throbbing, feet, swollen. Bead second length of gold. Take a break.

Intense awareness of body's strata, layer by layer, from light to acute. Nerves, overstimulated. Like a mute scream. Ah! Comme le corps crie jusque dans ses entrailles! Skin contracts from top of scalp to tip of toes. The tongue plays with silk knot.

Pause-couture. Finger strokes the philtrum. Le sillon naso-labial. That depression between nose and mouth. Where beads of sweat pool in moments of delight in moments of distress. Zone érogène between smell and taste. Between life and death. Seule. But not alone. Continue.

Hesitation. Pinch lip at base of philtrum with fingernails. Pinch hard. The passage of sharp will make nose sneeze. No sneezing permitted. Inhale exhale. The third stitch, the crux under the philtrum. Le point de non-retour. Take your time. Can't rush goldwork. Goldwork, painstaking. Labour of love.

Ice again.

Brace yourself. Legs apart, feet firmly planted. Hold breath. Sharp enters. Résistance. Push with thimble, not deep. Steady. Stay in stratum corneum of epidermis. Control. Deep frowning. Sous le sillon naso-labial, the sharp, most keenly felt. Highest coloratura note. Exhale. The entire body screams on the point of that needle. No sound in my ears. And yet.

Concentrate. Will sneeze. Can't sneeze, pinch nose between thumb and forefinger of left hand. Steady. Heart rate, elevated, hands, sweaty, involuntary muscle spasms contract philtrum. Beginning of nausea.

Deep breath. Hold. Push again with thimble. Needle exiting. Red bead on point of steel. Exhale. Dab with alcohol. Pull needle out with tweezers. Lower back, tense from leaning position close to mirror, navel, sans sensation against cold porcelain sink. Sharp not so bad now, more like love bites. Sharp out. Breathe easy. Silk moving through skin. The brush of a kiss. Sweat pooling. Philtrum pulsating. Bead third length of gold. Stop. Goldwork, exhausting.

Light-headed. Legs like water. Mouth, dry, ears, ringing, pupils, dilated. That stitch, anticipated the hardest, because at most sensitive area of lips. Entering the great unknown. Cet objet de la peur. Now, behind me. Have acquired knowledge. Fear level drops. Breathe. Will be easier. Heart rate, decreasing. Slow flow. Pure motion. Sharp skin gold silk. La géométrie organique. Elation can't be hurried. Each stitch, elation.

Lips, burning. Dab with alcohol. Evaporation, cold fire. Deep body heat. Fever pitch. Illumination from within. Supreme focus.

Fourth stitch. Adrenaline, surging. Control. Deep breath. Steady hand. Begin again.

Push sharp in lower lip. Trickier working on left side of mouth. Not ambidextrous enough to dare a sleight of hand.

Needle digs too deep. Frowning. Shock waves race through body. Reflex moaning. This, not delight. Muscle contractions, severe. Stop.

Body shaking. Blood beads at site of penetration. Dab with alcohol. Ice again to dull touch of needle into dermis. Swallowing, difficult. Mouth, parched.

Push needle horizontally with thimble. Sewing fingers, numb. Remain just below surface. Push with thimble. Pull with tweezers, silk becomes taut, bead fourth length of gold, it lies softly across lips.

Mouth test. Open a little. La résistance du fil. Careful. No jerky movement. Measure one-inch opening at centre. Good. The four lengths of gold stretch nicely, just enough to allow silk thread to slide freely through needle holes. Déjà, pulling sensation. That, the physicality of silence.

The last stitch. Home stretch. Ne t'assois pas sur tes lauriers. Pas encore. Concentrate. Deep breath. Hold. Push sharp through upper left corner of mouth. Exit one-eighth of an inch past point of entry. Pull, let silk slide all the way. Exhale. Done. Needed only one sharp to complete job. Wasn't sure whether skin would dull point of needle. Despite its resistance, more resilient than expected.

Finishing touch. Bead the one-inch length of gold through dangling silk. Don't push all the way against lip. Leave three-eighths of an inch of exposed silk at left corner of mouth for extra stretch. Insert small gold pearl at end of gold thread. Knot silk firmly. Cut unused thread, free needle.

Dab cotton wool soaked in peroxide all over mouth. White bubbles fizz at needle points of entry and exit. Burning sensation, throbbing. Evaporation cools skin a little. Smear mouth with Vaseline. Lips, swollen. Expected, après la chirurgie labiale.

Elation, exhausted. Sense of loss. Tristesse. Can't believe it's over. Anticipation. Appréhension. Focaliser. Fini. Legs, weak, arms, heavy. This gold fragile. Will crease in no time. Cracking the gold. Comme la vie. Dizziness. Vision, blurred. Light-headed. Body sweating shivering. Le thermostat interne, hay-wire. Major intrusion. Like death penetrating life. Adrenaline withdrawal. Arythmie cardiaque. Eyes fill with tears.

Wash hands. Sterilize used sharp. Store all the needles back in case. Coil leftover gilt thread in its box. Cap rubbing alcohol and peroxide bottles. Flush used cotton wool down toilet. Throw melting ice cubes in sink. Wash and dry vessels. Shake and fold white tablecloth and linen towel. Not a single drop of red on whiteness. Wipe tears.

In the days ahead, must open and close mouth often, in silence and with care. To prevent silk and gold from getting sealed in healing skin. To prevent tearing. That new awareness of mouth pulling. Hesitating. The mere opening of seduction.

Wonder how long the body will take to absorb dissolve silk. Then, the gold, cracked, scales of silence, will fall off.

Store instruments in pack. Unlock door. Drag table into café. Le tic-tac of the grandfather clock in empty dark room. Loud. Go back to wash hands. Look up. What do you think?

Pretty radical. Gold lipstick avec un pendant de lèvre. Not quite like hanging earrings. Not for everybody. Pollen-plated lips. They'll be shocked. Tongue explores silk knot. Like the tongue, they'll get used to it.

Le grand œuvre labial. Had to be done. This Ariane needed to know your special agony. Not equal sharing, bien sûr. But your suffering that day and my fear. Linked. And fused to our joy.

Open café door. Snowing. Feels good, returning home after a long trip. Montréal. The same, but different. Let's go walking. These boots need serious breaking in.

Lock door. Street sounds, muffled.

Touch goldlips.

Maintenant, je sais. Flesh is not silent. It sings, but with notes inaudible to the human ear.

Acknowledgements

In Calgary, my warmest thanks for their support and insight go out to friends and colleagues from the writing community, particularly, but not exclusively, to Anne Sorbie, Jacqueline Honnet, Athene Evans, Adrian Kelly, and Marika Deliyannides. And special thanks to Aritha van Herk, the mentor par excellence.

In Montréal, I thank friends and family members whose memories of my hometown in the sixties are sharper than mine and who helped clarify many muddy questions. They are Christiane Gendron, Lucie Dion, Sol Levinson, Madeleine Deschênes, Claire Villeneuve, and Monique Villeneuve.

I am especially grateful to my editor-publishers, André Vanasse in Montréal and Rhonda Bailey on the West Coast, who accepted this novel with enthusiasm and deftly navigated alongside me through the shoals of two languages.

I also wish to express my love to my spouse, Tom Back, the constant companion whose encouragement, clear-minded critique, and keen sense of humour never fail to keep life and its mercurial double, the writing life, in perspective.

An excerpt from an early draft of the novel was published in *Dandelion*, Volume 27, Number 2, 2001.